FEUD

"Lenny"

"Vanity Publishing"

DEREK BIRKS

This is a work of fiction.
Names, characters, places and incidents
are either the product of the author's imagination
or are used fictitiously, and any resemblance to any
persons living or dead is entirely coincidental.

Derek Birks asserts the moral right to be identified as
the author of this book

Published by Derek Birks

ISBN- 978-1-910944-00-4

To my parents who thought books were important and
encouraged me to read from an early age.

ACKNOWLEDGMENTS

Thanks to Rob for his editing, to Katie for her work on the
cover design and to Janet for putting up with me.

CONTENTS

1   Part One: The Old Feud   1

2   Part Two: Hunted   127

3   Part Three: War   249

4   Part Four: The Bloody Meadow   411

5   Historical Note   545

DEREK BIRKS

PART ONE: THE OLD FEUD

DEREK BIRKS

1

Yoredale Forest, Yorkshire, September 1459

Ned...

In the ancient forest Ned Elder sat motionless in the saddle. His father and brother were long overdue and his ride along the Yore valley had become a daily, empty ritual. He had found nothing out of the ordinary - until now.

The sound was faint, but unmistakable: the ring of steel upon steel. It was not the sound he wanted to hear but he urged his mount forward to pursue it, picking his way through the densely packed hazel and birch. His friend Will followed close behind on a track that was barely discernible.

Soon Ned pulled up and listened again but the sounds of struggle were fading. He walked his horse on through a labyrinth of green shadows and hazy shafts of light. Birch gave way to beech and the pair emerged into a broad sunlit glade.

Dazzled by the September sunshine Ned stopped and shaded his eyes. He thought he saw movement on the far side of the clearing and squinted into the sun. A horse wandered towards him, its rider slumped forward over its neck.

"Is it him?" asked Will, drawing alongside.

Ned looked long and hard at the lone horseman: he could see the man was harnessed for battle but wore no helm. He nodded and rode into the clearing.

"Tom!" he shouted. The rider's head jerked up; his bearded face was cut and bruised and his mail and breastplate spattered with blood. When he saw Ned he smiled wearily and came to a halt alongside his younger brother.

Ned scarcely recognised the gaunt face but took his outstretched arm with relief.

"We've expected you for weeks," he said, a question in his tone.

"I'm glad to be here at all!" replied Tom, nodding a greeting to Will.

From somewhere in the wall of trees behind Tom came a shout of triumph. He glanced back. "We'll have to lose them in the forest."

"Them?" asked Ned.

"The Radcliffes fell upon us ... the others are lost…"

"But …" Ned broke off open mouthed as an arrow sped across his chest and flew on into the trees.

"Come on!" ordered Tom sharply but Ned wasn't keen to run and didn't move.

"Ned! Come! You two aren't even harnessed for fighting! This isn't one of your noble causes, Ned - you can't win here!"

Ned was about to argue when the next arrow struck Tom's horse in the rump and the tired mare reared up in outrage, throwing him to the ground. Through the mottled curtain of leaves behind them thundered a mounted knight, encased in black burnished steel and tracked on foot by two men at arms, breathing heavily as they struggled to keep up.

Tom, dazed by the fall, staggered to his feet and drew his sword. Another arrow shot past him.

"For Christ's sake, Ned, go!" he shouted. "You don't understand: the old feud's begun again! Father's executed, we're all attainted … lost! Now, ride!"

The oncoming knight rode at Tom and raised his sword. Ned glanced at Will who nodded: they were not about to leave Tom having just found him again.

"Go to Lord Salisbury - trust no-one else!" Tom cried and turned to face the rider who was already upon him and hacking down at his unprotected head. The blow caught him on the neck, cutting him deeply. He cast a despairing look at Ned and fell to his knees, dropping his sword. The knight's momentum took him back into the trees but the men at arms hurried forward to finish Tom off.

"Look to Tom!" said Will and turned his horse to meet the two men head on, drawing out the pair of fine blades given him by Ned's father. He was a week past nineteen years old and had never drawn his swords to spill blood. The men at arms hesitated but, hearing the knight returning, they stood their ground. Will rode at them hard, great shanks of red hair flying behind him. He drove between them slashing down with both swords and left the pair clutching at their bleeding faces. They stumbled away into the bracken and Will turned to meet the oncoming knight, closing on him fast. He met the jarring force of the knight's sword with one blade as he lashed out with the other, striking his opponent's helmet and driving him off into the trees.

Will almost lost his balance but managed to wrestle his horse to a standstill. He was trembling in the saddle, his hands shaking so much he had to sheath his swords to avoid dropping them. He was about to follow the knight but then, remembering the arrows, he dismounted and walked cautiously into the trees. The early fallen leaves whispered softly under his feet as he crept between the tall grey shafts of beech. A few yards in front of him some drooping stems of bracken wavered and there was movement in the undergrowth to his right. He took a deep breath and slid the narrow steel blades silently from their scabbards.

Ned gripped Tom's hand as if faith alone might revive him. Tom tried to speak.

"Get your sisters, Ned ... and run," he said, his voice no more than a rustle of dead leaves.

Ned pressed his hand to the neck wound, but his brother's life trickled away through his fingers. Another horseman rode into the clearing, armour glinting in the sun. Ned shook his head, laid Tom gently onto the ground and got to his feet, snatching up the fallen sword. He was a year younger than Will and equally untried, but he lifted the blood stained weapon high and held it steady in front of him, as he had done a thousand times in practice. He willed himself to focus on the steel clad rider pounding towards him with a poleaxe in his hand.

"Shit, but he's well harnessed," he muttered to himself, "Lord, if I die, pray make it swift."

Then his assailant was there, swinging the poleaxe down at him. Ned kept his bare head low, scything his sword up under the axe and striking his opponent's elbow. The armour cracked, the bone joint snapped and the knight cried out. The axe slipped from his hand and thudded into the long grass at the forest edge as his frightened mount bore him back into the trees.

Ned rammed the point of the sword into the ground and stood motionless, then his shoulders drooped and he laid his hand on the sword hilt once more for someone else was coming. When he looked up he saw with relief that it was Will, emerging white faced from the trees, wiping the blood from his swords.

Ned knelt down once more to Tom and his brother's eyes fluttered open briefly.

"What do they want, Tom?"

"All we have," breathed Tom.

§§§

Emma...

There was a powerful hammering on the tall oak gate at Elder Hall. Emma watched Lynton, the elderly estate steward, trudge up to the top of the small stone gatehouse to see who was making such a clattering.

"It's your ... neighbour, Lord Radcliffe, my lady," he announced apologetically, "with some men at arms…"

"What does he want?" Emma asked. The interruption was an irritation but also intriguing for she knew well enough her father's opinion of Lord Radcliffe and it was far from favourable.

"What's your business, my lord?" Lynton called out brusquely from the wall.

"My business is with your mistress, you old turd, so fetch her here!" shouted Lord Radcliffe.

"Better wait then," said the steward.

Emma couldn't suppress a smile as the taciturn retainer took his time making his way back down the narrow steps to the courtyard. She had been cutting the last of the lavender in her small herb garden – one of the indulgences her father allowed his seventeen year old as a reward for her management of his household. The blue flowers of borage and lavender were past their best now, she thought as she got up and went to the gate, still clutching the bundle of lavender stalks.

"God give you good day, my Lord," she called through the gate, "how may I be of service?"

"Lady, I'd gladly bid you good day but please open the gate. My news is grave."

Emma looked at Lynton and he shook his head. "With your father and brothers not here, my lady – it's not safe."

Emma hesitated but she had no reason to fear Lord Radcliffe.

"Oh, let him in, Lynton, there'll be no peace until we do. I'll see what he wants but the rest can wait outside."

The old man muttered to himself as he struggled to unbar the gate. Emma brushed some broken stems from her robe and pushed a stray lock of black hair under her wimple whilst Lynton slowly dragged one of the gates open. Before he had done so, however, it was given a hefty shove from outside as Robert Radcliffe rode through, his horse knocking Lynton to one side. The old man tumbled back onto the cobbles and rolled on to his knees, cursing.

"My Lord!" protested Emma.

Lord Robert dismounted. She had not seen him for several years: he was a powerfully built man in his late forties: his dark shock of black hair was beginning to reveal flecks of grey and she observed that time had not been generous to his once handsome face.

"Your dear father is dead," he stated bluntly, "tried and executed for treason."

This terse announcement delivered, he carried on whilst she was struggling to grasp what he had just said. "Your brothers are also dead ... killed by outlaws in the forest."

Emma let fall the lavender stalks. She had not seen Tom for weeks but Ned had ridden out only a few hours earlier.

"Surely Ned is on the estate still?" she said.

Lord Robert took her arm but it did not reassure her.

"Lady, we've no time for delay. I'll take you to Yoredale Castle – you'll be safe there."

"But I'm safe here, my Lord," she replied, shrugging off his hand. Abruptly the veneer of sympathetic cordiality fell away. He seized her by the throat and pinned her to the dusty gatehouse wall.

"Hold your tongue, girl! Your shit of a father married into what little nobility he had and you're but the dregs of his traitorous loins!"

Without hesitation, he lifted her bodily and threw her onto a horse.

"Still, now he's dead, I'm sure I'll find a use for you."

"No!" Emma screamed and Lynton made to seize the horse's rein but stumbled as he did so and Lord Robert cuffed him down with his gauntlet. Then, mounting his horse, he took her reins and dragged her out of the gate and along the road to Yoredale Castle, whilst his retainers dismounted to begin the plundering of Elder Hall.

§§§

Eleanor...

Eleanor and Becky ran as if death pursued them, abandoning the open grassland near the falls and hurtling into the forest. As they fled through the trees the falling leaves swirled a trail of ochre and red in their wake, marking their passage for the men at arms who followed them. The girls were younger and fitter than their pursuers and they knew the forest as well as anyone. The longer they evaded capture, the safer they felt. Finally they went to ground and listened breathlessly for the sound of the chasing pack but their pursuers now seemed further away.

"Who are they?" whispered Becky.

Eleanor shook her head.

"Well, we can guess what they want," Becky went on, "it might be easier if we just let them have it!"

Eleanor frowned, not sure at first whether her servant was serious or not, but Becky's grin told her.

"We should split up," said Eleanor, "then at least they won't have us both!"

"You should've covered your hair – we could've passed for lads."

"I'm not covering my hair for any man. Wait here. I'll draw them off and meet you back at the Hall."

"Your hair marks you out," persisted Becky.

"Yes, it does!" She smiled and hugged Becky to her, "now lie low for a while."

She set off at speed into a thinner part of the forest which stretched from the riverbank almost to the walls of Elder Hall. She flitted between the trees, confident she could elude her pursuers then she noticed a line of men ahead threading their way methodically down the hillside of oak and hazel towards her. Surely, she thought, these men had not just chanced upon them thinking they might try their luck.

She darted away from the advancing line, trying to keep to a route which would take her back to the Hall, but all too quickly she realised that she was being driven towards the River Yore. Her initial confidence began to waver in the face of the sheer number of men tracking her and for the first time she considered she might be in real danger. She changed course and began running parallel to the river, crossing the many small becks that trickled into it, scrambling over sharp rocks and careless tree roots. She weighed up the likelihood of success higher up the slope but realised with a jolt of anger that they were trapping her against the river once more.

Now she had no choice: she made for the riverbank. If she was lucky she might surprise them by crossing at the ford ahead of them but when she reached the bank she saw at once that she would be caught. There were already men at the ford and the rest were steadily closing in behind her. She stopped at the river's edge and turned to face the encircling line.

They slowed to a halt several yards from her, distracted by her stunning beauty so at odds with her leather breeches and jerkin. She was accustomed to that but if they intended to steal what little virtue she had left she would make sure they paid a heavy price for it. She stretched her arms out slowly behind her, reaching over her shoulder for the long knife she carried in a scabbard strapped to the small of her back. The soldiers watched mesmerised as she arched her back and the leather stretched tight across her breasts.

"We'll help you with that!" called one and reached out to her. She drew the knife and lashed out. He jumped back, yelping as the blade sliced across his palm. She smiled and held the weapon out in front of her, swinging it from side to side as the others began to close in more warily.

"Well, what do you want to do?" she shouted at them. "Kill me or just run your grubby little fingers all over me?"

As she expected they were stunned by her speech and manner but she didn't wait for them to consider for long. She seized upon their doubts, running at them, twisting this way and that and turning her blade on any man who got too close. Several tried to disarm her but clutched handfuls of air as she moved rapidly around them, stabbing at them and using her swift, lithe movement to wrong foot them. Cornered once more on the edge of the riverbank, she thrust out towards an unprotected neck and was rewarded by a spurt of blood splashing onto her face. She smiled grimly as her victim fell to the ground, blood pouring from his wound as his comrades tried to wrest her lethal blade away. She broke from their grasp once more, her confidence growing.

"Enough!"

The single commanding voice paralysed them all and the overbearing tone left her in no doubt as to who was in command of the pursuit. Brandishing the knife in front of her, she remained still, whilst the owner of the voice surveyed the scene. Then he barked at his men: "I told you to take her quietly. Look at her! She looks as if she's been scourged!" They stared back at him sullenly.

"What do you want with me?" demanded Eleanor. For if they were not seeking her body then she could not imagine what else they wanted from her.

She felt his eyes upon her, taking in her beauty as all men did: her long tresses of blood red hair, the green eyes that Will found so bewitching and her smooth skin no doubt still glowing from the chase. Yet she could tell from his expression that she was not to his taste.

"I'm your neighbour, Richard Radcliffe, my lady and you're in no danger from us," he replied smoothly, "but there are men in the forest... outlaws who respect no law but their own. You'll come with us for your own safety."

Eleanor laughed. "If these 'men of the forest' are as dangerous as yours... Dick, then I've little to fear! You can leave me to defend myself."

"No," he replied, "I fear not."

She was already on the move before he'd finished speaking, darting between the two nearest men and slashing at an exposed face. One man caught her arm and she raked her knife across his chest. They were chasing shadows but there were so many of them she couldn't get clear. An outstretched foot tripped her to her knees but she rolled and hacked at the forest of legs that surrounded her. She raised the knife to strike again but a boot kicked it from her hand. At once she sprang to her feet and threw herself at Richard Radcliffe, clawing at his face until he punched her hard in the chest and stomach. Only then did she drop to the ground but she leapt up again and snarled at her adversaries like a wounded she-wolf, blazing eyes frantically seeking an escape route.

She looked desperately towards the river but the blows rained upon her from all sides and, with a final, bitter scream, she succumbed.

2

Elder Hall, Yoredale

"Attainted?" said Will.

"That's what Tom said," replied Ned, glancing down at his brother's body slung over the horse beside him.

The walls of Elder Hall came into view through the trees and the anxious pair slowed to a canter.

Will glanced behind them. "Do you think they're following us?"

"It hardly matters - they know where we're going."

Will was about to ask another question when Ned checked his horse to walking pace and then pulled up. The stone ramparts ahead were deserted and the gates hung wide open. Ned hesitated for only a moment and then rode cautiously forward through the narrow gatehouse. The courtyard, usually so busy, was still and deserted but just inside the gate he saw the steward. At once they dismounted and, whilst Will tethered the horses, Ned knelt down by the old man. He winced, for Lynton's chest was laid open to the waist.

"Butchered!" said Ned fiercely. "He was a bloody minded old sod but he didn't deserve this." Angrily he scattered the flies crawling around the blood encrusted wound.

"What's happening here?" asked Will.

"An old feud, Tom said…"

"Feud? What feud? How do we not know about it?"

Ned shrugged. "When did they ever tell me anything?"

"And it's the Radcliffes?"

"So it seems." He looked down at Lynton and beside his body on the blood-stained cobbles he noticed some broken lavender stalks, ground into the stones by the gateway: Emma, he thought.

"Come on," he said, "remember why we're here; we need to find the girls!"

They hurried to the broad oak doorway that opened into the Hall but on the threshold they came to an abrupt halt. Ned looked around in disbelief for the cavernous room had been stripped bare from its stone-flagged floor to the lofty timber framed roof. Only the scattered rushes and a few overturned oak benches remained of the world in which the Elder household had lived, laughed and wept since Ned was old enough to recall. Its desecration hit him hard.

"Even the large tapestries have gone – the ones father brought home from Burgundy. They must've been stripping the place for hours."

He walked to the dais at the far end of the hall and bent down to pick up a pale blue strip of cloth from the floor. They had torn to shreds the banner that identified his father, John Elder, and this was all that was left.

"Ellie and Emma?" reminded Will.

"Yes, I know," said Ned crossly and wrapped the length of cloth around his waist. Then he hurried across to the wooden staircase that led up to the private chambers.

"Emma! Ellie!" Their voices echoed along the bare stone walls but the girls were not in their chamber. Will stared long and hard at Eleanor's empty bower; only a trace of her familiar scent lingered. In his own chamber Ned reached under the thin wooden bed frame for the ancient arming sword and Turkish dagger his father had given him in his fifteenth year. He was relieved to find them still there and pulled them out. He'd barely touched them in the past year and saw with regret how dull the neglected blades had become.

They quickly searched through the upper floor chambers but all they discovered was a hastily set fire in the north tower. Ned irritably kicked out the smouldering embers and they returned once more to the Hall. The painted wooden panels that screened the doorway to the servants' rooms had been splintered beyond repair. Pulling the remains aside, they passed through the kitchens to the brew house and storerooms but all had been cleared or smashed and there was no sign of Eleanor or Emma.

"The cellars?" suggested Will but a quick investigation revealed neither the sisters nor any of those who had looted the Manor.

On their way back up Ned paused on the steps to the kitchen.

"Did you hear that?" he said.

Will nodded. "Horses!"

They raced up through the Hall and out into the courtyard with swords drawn. They were half blinded when they emerged into the sunlight but the yard was empty and only a haze of dust hung in the air by the gateway.

"Shit!" said Ned.

"So," said Will, "Ellie, Emma, and now the last of the thieves – all gone."

"And so have our horses," said Ned, staring at Tom's body, which now lay on the cobbles where it had been dumped.

"Come on," he said and headed for the far end of the courtyard, where a small stable lay against the curtain wall. There they found no horses but in the stalls sat two of the estate workers.

"Holton?" said Ned, recognizing the apprentice smith, "and you are?" He addressed Holton's tall, lean companion.

"Birches. I'm one of your father's foresters - Radcliffe men are all over the estate."

"But not in here," said Ned with a wry grin.

"Yet," added Will, "look!"

But he could already hear them and he stalked out of the stable to see a dozen or so mounted men ride into the castle yard, greeting the pair with shouts of derision.

"Oh Lord Christ!" said Will, "There's too many this time, Ned!"

"Aye, and as poor Tom said, we're not harnessed for this."

Nevertheless, they drew their swords and prepared to meet the riders by the stable doorway. Suddenly, another horseman rode out of the sun right through the group, setting about them with ferocious blows of his sword.

"Who in God's name's that?" asked Ned.

"No idea but at least he seems to be for us!"

"But he's on his own!" Ned watched mesmerised as the rider passed amongst his surprised adversaries, striking with brutal efficiency.

"That's what I should be doing!" said Ned.

The unknown rider drove the intruders back so that many sheered away and he then pursued them out of the gate. The remainder, however, dismounted and made for the stable.

"Well, now's your chance," said Will.

Ned glanced around the stable: it was a poor wooden structure that leant against the stonework of the wall for support and its builder had surely not constructed it to house a quarrel. There was hardly enough head room to raise a sword let alone wield one in anger. Their assailants came at them so hard that Ned and Will were driven back into the stalls. They stumbled backwards into the straw and horseshit, barely able to parry the blows, but a scream of pain punctuated the attack.

Holton had decided to lend a hand and Ned saw that, in his very ample hand, he held a heavy, iron hammer. The burly youth swung it with no skill but frightening power into the knot of men crowding in on Ned and Will. One was struck squarely in the chest and collapsed to the floor like a rotten tree in a winter storm. The attackers fell back as Holton bludgeoned down another and when he wrestled a third to the ground, Birches joined in. He skewered a man clad in a worn leather jerkin, pinning him to the wooden shuttering with a stable fork. The wounded man looked up at Birches in shock as blood poured from several holes in his chest.

A young, well harnessed knight made straight for Ned, sword in hand, and pounded him with blows whilst Will, Holton and Birches made short work of the rest.

"Will! Get their horses!" Ned called out, as he parried a wild swing. His opponent was pressing him hard, forcing him back against the stable wall. Even after what he had witnessed in the forest, the young man's relentless hostility shocked him.

"Why do you strive so hard to kill me?" he demanded, breathing hard.

"I'm Ralph Radcliffe!" his opponent declared, as if it explained all.

"I've no quarrel with you!" Ned shouted, struggling to push him back.

"You're Ned Elder, aren't you? That's quarrel enough!"

No, thought Ned, it's not enough but he began to understand what his brother had meant by "the old feud."

"Come on, Ned, leave it," called Will from the doorway, "we've got the horses!"

Ned tried to clear his head: his opponent was far better equipped for a fight than he was but if he ran from this he'd have lost far more than just his lands and titles.

"Leave it, Ned!" Will pleaded from the threshold.

"Not this time, Will!"

Ralph and Ned both drew their daggers, circling each other warily.

"Seen your sisters today?" taunted Ralph.

"What do you know of them?" Ned snapped.

"I know one's a whore!"

He knew Ralph was provoking him, eager to force a fatal mistake but he put the words from his mind, knowing he must finish the contest before Ralph's comrades returned. They lunged at each other, parrying sword against sword, dagger against dagger; cut for cut, blow upon blow. All the while Ralph baited him with crude insults.

"They'll be on their backs by now!" he cried, thrusting his armoured shoulder piece into Ned's chest. For an instant their sweat-traced faces almost touched but Ned pushed him away.

Both were starting to tire, moving more raggedly to avoid each other's blades and not always succeeding: there was a cut to Ned's arm, a slash to Ralph's thigh, just as he almost opened up Ned's face with an expansive sweep of his sword. Ned bloodied Ralph's neck with a flash of his curved dagger. Both slammed their blades against the low roof beams, each disappointed not to have struck a telling blow. Ned watched him closely, noticing his uneasy glances towards the stable door; he's rattled, he thought but the noise outside distracted him too.

"Riders coming, in a hurry - Ned!" shouted Will. "And our friend's coming back. Who is that Birches?"

"Oh, shit!" said Birches, staring at the stocky, grey bearded horseman, "that's Bagot! I thought he was dead - now we're really in trouble! Bagot's as hard as flint."

But Ned shut out their voices; whoever Bagot was he didn't care for he had to focus only upon killing his opponent or he wouldn't make it out of the stable at all. They were still trading blows but Ralph was weakening with every exchange. Ned knocked the tired sword from his hand but lost his footing and the latter's dagger slid along his ribs– Christ, that hurt! Ralph leant forward for a second thrust and Ned, down on one knee, reached up and plunged his sword hard up to its hilt under the breastplate, through Ralph's groin and into his midriff. Ralph grunted and for a brief instant they were trapped in a grisly embrace. Then Ned felt at once the sting of his own cut and the weight of Ralph's body on his sword – so heavy he couldn't free himself and he toppled backwards with the dying youth on top of him. His grey eyes were fixed on Ralph's terrified face and he thought he would never shake the image from his mind.

He heaved the body off him onto the stable floor, where the blood began to darken the straw and flagstones. He took a deep breath and regretted it: the wound in his side wouldn't kill him but he still felt it keenly. Ralph's blood was all over him; he got up and stumbled towards the doorway but he was light headed and his legs failed him.

Bagot caught him as he fell, dragging him outside the stable and launching him roughly onto a horse. They rode out through the gate but further trouble was on its way in the shape of a score or more horsemen in the red and gold livery of the Radcliffes. Bagot set off up the steepest side of the forested valley and the rest followed. Ned knew that once Ralph's corpse was discovered, Lord Radcliffe would scour the valley for them.

They hurried through the trees to the east then spent the next hours hiding in the thick forest, scrambling up and down the wooded slopes until, as the evening light faded, they sought some shelter, some respite for the night.

It was Holton who found the small low roofed cottage and forced the flimsy door open. Ned stood in the doorway with Bagot. It was long abandoned: a cold, stinking shell, with a meagre supply of filthy, half rotten rushes on the damp ground inside but it would serve them for the night.

Once inside, no-one said a word. Ned glanced at Will, slumped beside him; he wondered whether he looked as utterly spent as his friend. In the space of a few hours he had lost all that he loved – and, for the first time in his life, he had killed a man. He touched his side where the blood had already dried to form a thin ugly crust. He felt the sting of the wound, though the bleeding had stopped hours before and Bagot had dismissed it as 'hardly a scratch.'

No-one slept; instead they lay despondently in the dark, listening to the cracked timbers groaning above their heads. Occasionally some small animal or bird scratched its way across the thatch; then there was a different sound and they held their breath as the door creaked open.

3

Yoredale Castle

Emma lay stiff and cold in her new bedchamber at Yoredale Castle. Her hair, normally so neatly tied back, hung in black tangles on her shoulders; her deep brown eyes were red rimmed and her cheeks streaked with tears. She had lain awake for hour upon hour, sifting through the chaos of the day. Lord Radcliffe had certainly been clever, capitalising on the absence of her father and brothers. How naïve and trusting she had been: she should never have opened the gates and now she must face the consequences of that careless moment.

She took a deep breath and rose to make her way through the anteroom and down the wide spiral stair to the Great Hall. Nervously, she entered the lavishly decorated Hall.

Lord Robert greeted her with exaggerated cordiality: "My dear lady; you are calmer now, I trust?"

Emma merely nodded as she awaited her fate.

"As you know, I've been most concerned for your safety, which is why His Majesty has granted my petition that you become my ward."

Emma forced a grim smile: he must have been planning this for months.

"I assume you have a very favourable marriage arranged for me, my lord?"

"Ah, I see that we understand each other, lady; yes, I've arranged an advantageous marriage. I must admit if I was a little younger I might have married you myself but I've chosen a fine alternative: my eldest son, Richard; thus our two families, and their estates, will be united."

Emma was unsurprised by his decision and, since she would have regarded marriage as unwelcome but inevitable, her present situation was hardly any worse than she expected.

"I am, of course, yours to dispose of as you wish, my lord," she conceded. Keeping her voice even and controlled, she continued: "I'm concerned though for my sister. Do you... do you have her?"

"Oh yes, for she too is now my ward," confirmed Lord Robert.

Emma struggled to conceal her relief but he continued: "Such a ... spirited girl; she'd be ill at ease in my stiff old household, so I've found a place for her where her ... independence will be better accommodated."

"Where would that be, my Lord?" she asked, unable to keep a slight tremor from her voice.

"I have a connection... at a nunnery in the west," he said vaguely.

"A nunnery! For Ellie? May I see her before she goes?"

"Well, as for that, I fear she's already left."

Her self-control wavered for a moment and she closed her eyes, lest they reveal her crushing disappointment. Then she recovered her composure, not wanting her new guardian to have the satisfaction of witnessing her distress.

"Well, it's done then. I would return to my chamber, my Lord, if you please?"

Dismissed by his curt nod, she swept out of the Hall and hurried back up the staircase to her chamber in the north west tower. She half stumbled at the top of the steps and almost fell into the room, tears already stinging her cheeks as she threw herself on to the ornate and finely covered feather bed and sobbed.

§§§

She must have lain there for hours, only dimly aware of the light changing as longer shadows infiltrated her room. For all her tears, she knew there was nothing to be done: she would submit to her guardian, she would marry Richard Radcliffe, she would play the dutiful wife, she would pray for God's help and she would bide her time.

She did not notice the young man in the doorway until he knocked slowly and deliberately on the door frame. She thought at first that she was imagining him, for he appeared to be the most beautiful man she had ever seen.

"You must be ... the spoils of victory," he said, smiling.

"You must be Lord Radcliffe's son?" she observed, thinking how very different he looked from the gawky young boy she had met once many years before.

"Indeed, I am. You look dull – dull and miserable. Are you? Or is there some fire somewhere in that breast? Perhaps we should find out."

She frowned; it was not the greeting she had hoped for from her intended spouse. He moved swiftly from the doorway to sit on the bed where she remained nervously and without further conversation, he drew her to him. Briefly she hesitated but then she thought: what's the point? Soon he'd be her lawful husband – and this would be a commonplace. It might have been worse: he could have been ugly.

She looked hard at his face, seeking the soul in his eyes but finding only an icy blue stare.

"I'm told Eleanor is more beautiful," he said with a sudden grin as he gathered her breasts in his hands, squeezing them hard. Emma gasped, unsure whether it was the pain or the cruel comparison with her sister that wrung some tears from her eyes. He kissed her roughly on the mouth; his hair smelt of sweat and something else she could not place. He gripped her tightly for a moment and she began to regret her easy acquiescence. He pulled her linen tunic down to the waist and manhandled her onto her back, kissing her on the mouth and biting her lip in the process, making it bleed.

"My Lord! Have you no respect for me?"

23

"No!" he laughed, "none at all!" He slapped her face to emphasise the point and now she lay tight with fear: both appalled and fascinated. What he did to her next hurt her more than she'd hoped and as he lay on top of her she identified in a bizarre moment of insight the smell that mingled with his sweat: blood, the thick scent of blood. She felt nauseous and, when he had finished, she pulled away from him and gathered her torn clothes tightly around her.

"Is this how our marriage is to be?" she asked in a small voice.

"Marriage? I don't think so. I'm sure it's my dear brother Richard you're promised to, not me!"

Emma stared at him, speechless.

He laughed: "I'm Edmund, and let's say I see myself as a sampler of my brother's fare. We'll not be married we two but don't despair for I will always be here - and you may find that Richard has very little to offer you."

Abruptly he got up from the bed. She listened to him descending the spiral stair and slowly drew the bedcover up over her naked body then she lay down quietly on her side to allow the raw pain between her thighs to subside.

§§§

Below her in his richly decorated Hall, Robert Radcliffe reflected moodily upon the events of the past week. He had coveted the Elder lands for so long and they perfectly complemented his own. Yet he had never expected to get them. Then John Elder had thrown in his hand with York and the Nevilles - a rash gamble, leaving him utterly exposed. So Robert had struck hard and fast. The Queen had swiftly sent him a royal writ granting him the estates of the traitor, John Elder and the ambush had removed the only dangerous man, his son, Thomas. Now he had the two sisters, his new wards, isolated and he had revealed to the Lady Emma her future. He had little doubt that his sister Edwina would soon bully into submission the peevish and arrogant little bitch, Eleanor.

All had been progressing so promisingly and his outrageous political gamble had come very close to complete success, but the failure to kill or capture Ned Elder was a cruel piece of luck. As a result he was mourning the loss of his youngest son and the remaining offspring of John Elder still eluded him. Those who had failed would pay dearly, though the loss of one of his sons would always have been an acceptable price to garner such a valuable prize. And at last, after all these years, John Elder had been punished.

His crushing of the Elder brood was all but complete and he had despatched Edmund to hunt down the youth and avenge the death of his brother Ralph. Edmund would not be so easily thwarted. So, all in all, things had gone well enough.

4

The Elder Estates

Ned was nearest the door and turned towards it. A low, husky voice from the open doorway broke the silence. "I know who you are."

There was a pause; no-one dared move.

"I followed you here," the voice continued. No-one dared reply.

Ned crouched, poised to spring at the intruder.

"I would stay here - if you'll let me".

He unsheathed his dagger. "Come in then," he breathed, "slowly."

The door creaked shut.

"Come over here," he said, holding the blade ready.

A short, scruffy figure ghosted up to him.

"You won't mind my sharing this place with you," the girl said. It was more of a statement than a question.

"If she found us, others can," warned Bagot.

"Who are you?" asked Ned.

"My ma named me Margaret, but if I'm called anything now it's Mags." Her voice was deep and earthy.

"So, why are you here?"

"I've been working up at the Castle."

"That's all we need: she's from Radcliffe's own household," groaned Bagot.

"Well, she's here now," said Ned, "and she doesn't seem very dangerous - Holton, see if she's armed."

Holton reached for the girl but she punched him hard below the waist and the big man doubled up in agony.

"Touch me again and you'll not be pissing straight for a week!" she shouted.

In the darkness Bagot chuckled quietly whilst the others crowded around her.

"What's in the bag?" demanded Ned, referring to the shabby brown leather pouch she wore slung over her shoulder.

"If you want to look then you'll pay with blood! I carry only what's left to me and I don't see why I need show it you."

"Leave it!" ordered Bagot. "If she's an assassin, then by St Michael she's a bloody noisy one!"

Mags sat apart from the rest but there was anxious muttering all around. However, one by one, they succumbed to sleep - all save Will and Ned; the latter was still haunted by images of his dead brother and Ralph Radcliffe, but Will's thoughts clearly lay elsewhere.

"What about Ellie?" he whispered, "- and Emma, of course. We can't just leave them!"

Ned knew why Will would be more than worried about Eleanor, though his friend had never actually told him.

"We'll find them, Will; we'll find them." But he feared it wouldn't be soon.

"I know where the lady Emma is," interrupted Mags, "I'll tell you - if you let me stay."

"What do you know?" demanded Ned. "I'll surely turn you out if you don't tell me!"

Everyone was wide awake again. Mags seemed to hesitate.

"Are you telling me or not?" said Ned.

"Alright, but I'm trusting your word. She was at the castle - I saw Lord Robert bring her in."

"Are you sure?"

"Lady Emma was very kind to my pa… I think I'd know her well enough."

"Radcliffe won't harm her, she's more use to him alive than we are," advised Bagot. "Mind you, it won't help matters that you've killed his son."

"Well, I wish I hadn't," said Ned shortly, "but it's done now and I can't undo it."

"Aye, they'll hunt us down for that, sure enough - still, rather him than you."

Ned crouched down by Bagot and whispered: "You seem to have much experience and I have little, but I'd rather you didn't fling orders at me – it makes me look a fool."

"Hah! Only you can do that!" retorted Bagot, "now get some sleep - all of you!"

And they all meekly obeyed, including Ned.

§§§

The following morning began badly.

"I'm going to Lord Salisbury at Middleham," Ned announced.

"Do you know what sort of a welcome you'll get from his Lordship?" enquired Bagot. "Surely we should wait for your father: he'll know what to do next."

Ned's face clouded. "My father's dead – executed, Tom said."

He looked at Bagot, who was studying his boots; he saw that the news had caught the older man off guard. Bagot leant against the wall but seemed to recover himself and, in a gruff voice, dismissed Ned's concern. No-one else had noticed but Bagot acknowledged it with Ned.

"Your father made me - saved me a few times, by St Stephen; I'd like to think I saved him once or twice too." He paused awkwardly. Ned was surprised by the old soldier's reaction and, before he knew it, there were tears welling in his own eyes.

"I'm sorry for his death but let's gossip no more about it," said Bagot, "with your brother Tom killed, the lordship falls to you - unless you want the Radcliffes to have it…"

Ned's reproving look told Bagot what he thought of that notion.

"But this idea of yours is risky; you don't even know for certain that Salisbury's at Middleham! For all you know, he's hundreds of miles away!"

"No-one is bound to come with me; I release you from any obligation; you're all free to go!"

"I could no more abandon you than cut off my right hand!" Bagot declared and the rest seemed minded to follow Bagot's lead.

Thus they all made their way the ten miles east to Middleham Castle, the Earl of Salisbury's great stronghold in the north.

"Whatever your father intended it went badly wrong," said Bagot as he rode beside Ned.

Ned hardly needed telling so. "We're attainted – so we're talking about treason."

"Doesn't sound like him - in all the years I fought with him, Sir John was as loyal as any knight could be. But Salisbury – he's a different matter; whatever he means to do, I wouldn't be surprised if it was treason. Do you know the Earl?"

"I've heard of him of course but I couldn't say I knew him."

Bagot expelled a prodigious sigh.

"The Earl's the head of the Neville family and he's a dangerous man to know. You think you've got trouble with the Radcliffes but they're just weasels; now, the Nevilles – they don't kill their enemies, they rip them apart like wolves. The Nevilles already have blood enough on their hands."

"You've come across them before?"

"A long time ago," said Bagot, but he was clearly not going to elaborate.

Well before they reached the village of Middleham, they saw the great Neville fortress rising above the surrounding fields. A forest of black and red banners flew from the battlements which towered above the old motte nearby. As they approached they came across a few small armed encampments and it soon became clear that these bands formed only the outer fringe of a sprawling army centred on Middleham.

"There are few banners in the fields," Bagot observed bleakly, "a sure sign most of these men don't know what they're about."

"Well, they're certainly not gathering under the King's colours," said Ned.

They could smell the small village of Middleham before they reached it, for it was hopelessly overcrowded with soldiers who occupied every squalid lane and outhouse cluttering the castle perimeter. Ned's small group set up camp beyond the outer courtyard and like many others they displayed no badges or livery to reveal their identity to prying eyes.

Ned told Birches to settle their horses, whilst Mags and Bagot attempted to light a fire; to see the unlikely pair trying to work together was amusing to the rest but no one dared comment for fear of a severe tongue lashing from one, or more likely, both of them. They had eaten nothing but a few crumbs of dry oatcake all day, so Mags and Holton were then despatched to find ingredients for an evening pottage.

"They'll find nothing, those two!" predicted Bagot confidently.

But in the late afternoon the pair returned to the fire with a modest haul of autumn roots.

Bagot shook his head disparagingly. "Small, rotten or half chewed," he said.

"True," replied Holton, "apart from these," and he held up a brace of large onions.

"Where in God's name did you steal those beauties?" laughed Bagot, "someone's going to be bloody angry!"

Holton shrugged. "Don't blame me; I just carried them back…"

Once they had established themselves, Ned decided it was time to seek an audience with the Earl but before he could do so, a tall, elegant knight walked into their camp.

"I'm Sir Roger of Wakefield, captain to Lord Salisbury; you display no pennants or badges and no lord seems to know who you are, so tell me in whose name you've come here?"

"We're not alone in the absence of badges, Sir Roger," Ned replied, "but if you're indeed in the service of the Earl then we're glad to see you, for it's him we've come to see."

"This is not a camp to wander into carelessly." Sir Roger's voice carried a threatening tone.

"My father, Sir John Elder, and my brother, Tom, have been killed and I've come here to seek the Earl's protection."

Sir Roger visibly relaxed and his voice softened a little. "I knew your father, and I knew of his death, but I'd not heard about poor Tom."

"More than that: my estate is under attack and my family abducted or killed by Lord Robert Radcliffe!"

The older knight frowned. "You should learn to keep your own counsel. I'm a shire man and I know of Radcliffe; for all you know I might be his closest ally; luckily for you, I'm not! You'd better come with me, just to keep you out of trouble!"

Ned set off to pay his respects to the Earl, taking only Will with him. He ignored Bagot's protests and happily abandoned, for a while at least, the overpowering smell and cacophony of the soldiers' camps. Their guide was tall and strongly built, with a face that was weathered, though not scarred, by warfare. He was not a man for expansive explanations, saying little as he strode along with an air of calm authority.

As they neared the castle they were assaulted by the powerful stench of the vast warren of pigsties and hovels which occupied the castle hinterland. Sir Roger led them on through the majestic stone gatehouse, into the inner courtyard and up the steep flight of steps that gave access to the first floor of the mighty keep. They passed through the Great Hall, bustling with the clerks, store men and soldiers employed to meet the needs of a growing army. Their guide stopped outside a heavy door and ordered them to wait whilst he himself knocked and entered the chamber immediately.

Ned and Will paced the floor nervously; as two young lads with no experience of either politics or war, they felt completely out of their depth. Around them the palatial splendour of the building impressed upon them that they had entered a very different world to their own. Every wall bore rich tapestries or banners of red and black; however, they had little time to ponder their inadequacies further as Sir Roger reappeared to usher them into the Earl of Salisbury's Great Chamber.

They stood then almost transfixed before the aged but powerful figure of Richard Neville, Earl of Salisbury. They understood at once that in his own domain this man was king and – as Bagot had said - a dangerous man to know. All the same, he greeted the son of his late ally, Sir John Elder, warmly and listened sympathetically as Ned related the events of recent days. But his response was measured and cautious.

"I knew your father, Ned, but I can do little to help you. Your family's struggle with the Radcliffes is but one of many: law breaking is rife and the rule of law must now be supported by force. It matters not that you have right on your side, if you don't have power. I count Radcliffe amongst my many enemies – but you, Ned, don't have the power to oppose him and, regrettably, I can't spare any of my men to help you."

"He can just ignore the law, then?"

Salisbury half suppressed a smile before he replied: "The King is weak, so men like Robert Radcliffe vie for the patronage of the Queen. You'll have seen from the force gathering outside these walls that I'm not ... well disposed towards Queen Margaret - nor was your father; like me, he chose to support her rival, Duke Richard of York, and for that he was executed."

Ned was now beginning to grasp the train of events a little better: because Radcliffe was a client of the Queen, his father had been forced to submit to his power or become a client of the Duke of York. There was more than one feud at work here: Sir John's execution and attainder had left the way clear for Radcliffe to destroy the Elders in Yoredale.

"Ned, you've stumbled into a civil war and it's going to get a great deal bloodier. There are small armies everywhere - both for the King and for his Grace, the Duke. All is in the balance; so I fear there's little time to dwell on private matters."

"I must abandon my lands and my sisters then into the hands of Lord Radcliffe?"

"It seems he already has them – so, for now, there's nothing to be done; the best I can do for you is take you to the Duke in Ludlow, though I can't promise you'll be much safer there."

§§§

It was early evening when Ned and Will made their way out of the Great Hall and descended the steps into the castle bailey. They found the courtyard even more crammed with soldiers than before, many having just arrived in full battle harness and bristling with weaponry. They forced a path through the noisy throng and out of the gate where they saw stretching out before them in the outer courtyards to the east and north a turbulent sea of men, wagons and horses. Ned wondered at the large numbers of men that the Earl had been able to attract to his cause and he began to realise for the first time the scale of the enterprise in which they had become embroiled.

They returned much chastened and spent the evening brooding around their camp fire, with a hundred such fires flickering around them wherever they looked. Ned could scarcely believe that only the day before he had ridden across the Elder estates without care or caution and with no inkling of feuds or civil war.

Bagot emerged from the darkness beyond the fire and sat down to join them.

"So, what will the noble Earl do?" he asked.

"Nothing!" replied Ned.

"Ah." Bagot disguised his lack of surprise poorly. "What will you do then?"

"Well, I can't make my peace with the Radcliffes!"

"No; if it wasn't a blood feud before, it surely is now."

"So, I must throw in my lot with Salisbury and York – perhaps, in the end, I can get back what's been taken."

"If you ride with Salisbury, there'll be no turning back, however it goes."

"I'm going with Salisbury but you don't need to come."

"I served your father a long time and I swore an oath to him."

"You're not bound to me by any oath to my father."

"No, I'm not – but I'm obliged to your father, so I'll ride along with you for a while – if you'll have me, of course."

"As you please," said Ned, staring into the dying heart of the fire, watching the white logs slowly turn to ash.

5

Blore Heath near Market Drayton, late September 1459

They had travelled for two days under a sky of unbroken grey and now the drizzle was turning into steady, driving rain. Their column churned up the land as it passed, horses and men trudging southwards. Ned's companions, wet and miserable, seemed to view the journey as a penance he had exacted for some unknown transgression.

"Tell me again why we're going all this way?" asked Mags.

"If you don't like it you should've stayed at Middleham!" grumbled Bagot. "In fact you should've stayed in Yoredale – you came to us, remember!"

But Ned too was already beginning to doubt the wisdom of his decision to join Salisbury.

They advanced through a sweep of forest and dismounted to walk their horses slowly forward under dripping elm and beech. On the far edge of the trees they halted and were ordered to dig in. Their few supply wagons were drawn around them and they battled against the mud and tree roots to prepare a substantial ditch to their rear.

The mood in the camp was subdued: the soldiers quiet, weapons more carefully honed and last minute plate repairs speedily carried out. Though Ned had never seen a battle, the sight of the men preparing convinced him that he was too poorly equipped to survive one. He had no long sword, helm, plate armour or even a mail coat. The arming sword he had picked up at Elder Hall was too short for battle and for all his natural strength it simply wouldn't be enough. Bagot, despite his professions of loyalty, seemed to have little sympathy.

"Well *lord*, when you've killed your first man you can take his sword, and if you don't kill him, then it won't matter will it? I suppose I'd better see to the horses. Holton, Birches! Get some dry kindling for the fire - you're not here for a rest!"

"Dry kindling; some hope!" Birches mumbled, as he set off into the trees.

Ned was stung by the blunt reproof, but within a few minutes Bagot returned and handed him a heavy package wrapped in a thick, greasy piece of cloth.

"God's blood, lord! If you're shortly to die, then you may as well die with this in your hand."

He winked darkly at his young protégé. Ned removed the cloth and stared in awe at the long, tapering blade he held in his hands. It was a sword he had never seen before: a simple, but well-wrought weapon. It had the popular two handed grip at its hilt with a plain iron cross-piece; the blade was at least four feet long and double edged, though not especially sharp.

"It's your father's old war sword," said Bagot, with a rare smile.

Ned held it in his right hand, feeling its weight and balance. He transferred his grip to wield the weapon two handed, lowering the point in front of him in the guard favoured by the Italian sword master who had taught him so well. He practised four or five guards, familiarising himself with the new blade.

"How did you come by it?" he asked.

"When we returned from France the last time, your father told me to take it, that he would never need it again and I was to do whatever I liked with it."

"But you kept it?"

"I kept it, just in case… but he won't need it now."

"I'm grateful, Bagot."

Bagot looked Ned over: "You've no mail or armour – not even a leather jerkin, or sallet! I'll see if I can find something for you."

Ned was learning quickly that Bagot had a great facility for 'finding' what was required.

"It doesn't look very hopeful, does it," he said.

Bagot nodded: "One of the scouts told me we're trapped: to the west is the river, to the east thick woods, ahead of us on the road to Ludlow is a large royal host and most likely there's now one behind us as well. It's war, that's all: mud, blood and misery."

His gloomy words hung in the damp air around them. He looked at the two youths and shook his head. "You look like a pair of startled field mice!"

"We're both handy with a sword!" asserted Ned.

"Well, don't worry too much about waving your sword; you're more likely to get crushed to death anyway!" He chuckled as Will and Ned stared at each other in confusion.

"You'll learn quick enough – or it won't matter! You'd better find somewhere dry to sleep for a while, there'll be blows enough struck tomorrow."

§§§

It was dark. Dawn was still several hours away, but Ned and Will were wide awake, sitting beside the failing glow of their fire, when Sir Roger came across them.

"Nervous?" he asked.

"Terrified," said Ned.

"Well, that's honest I suppose; perhaps I can distract you for a while. I've a small task to carry out - you can come with me, if you like."

Ned looked at Bagot, snoring comfortably; they could certainly do with some diversion.

"Should we go armed?" he asked.

"I don't expect trouble but, this close to the royal lines you'd better bring a weapon."

"Where are we going?" enquired Ned.

"No questions – or you don't come. Is that clear?"

The two youths nodded.

"And go quietly!" whispered Sir Roger, as he led them through the dripping trees.

They did not seem to follow any recognisable track and, since the rain that had dogged their every step had been replaced overnight by a damp clinging mist, Ned did not have the least idea where he was. Eventually they walked up a steep incline and arrived outside a church.

"Where are we?" asked Ned.

"Quiet!" hissed Sir Roger, "this is St Mary's Church, Mucklestone. Now, wait out here!"

Ned could only make out the outline of the church, but it seemed quite large with a tower some four storeys high; the whole building was cloaked in darkness and apparently deserted.

They waited dutifully at the top of the stone steps that led to the door, whilst Sir Roger slipped inside. While they waited, the light drizzle began again.

"Why did we come?" asked Will, huddling his damp cloak around him for warmth, though it provided little.

Ned paced impatiently. "To take our minds off being slaughtered."

"I suppose it's worked then – till now."

The rain persisted and large puddles formed at their feet; the wooden roof that covered the small porch was in need of repair and their cloaks were soon soaked through. It seemed to Ned that they had waited long enough.

"Come on, let's go inside," he said.

Will needed no further invitation and they shuffled into the church. It was almost as gloomy inside as out, but at least it was dry. The only light came from a large candle at the far end of the nave and in its wavering light they saw a woman standing motionless beside Sir Roger in front of the decorated rood screen. Her exquisite beauty took their breath away.

"You're still safe at least," said Sir Roger, pulling her gently to him.

"But you are not!" Her voice was heavily accented; Ned thought French, but he wasn't sure.

"I suppose there is no point in asking you to leave with me," she said.

"No, war will begin in earnest now: if we fail, I'll die a traitor's death and if I survive, it'll be too dangerous for us to meet while you're in the Queen's household; you must leave her, make your way to Ludlow and wait for me there."

The woman smiled; it was a smile in a thousand, thought Ned.

"You think you'll get to Ludlow? I am not so sure, my love. But, you are right: my mistress already begins to suspect me…" She hesitated, then continued: "There is something else: when I leave, she will assume I've betrayed her; so I will take with me something of hers that might help us … if things go wrong. I will stay with her to know the outcome here first, then at Ludlow perhaps, I can slip away to you."

She flashed him another wicked smile, kissed him quickly and then she was gone through the side door of the church and away into the night.

Sir Roger sighed wearily after she left; then he frowned as he became aware that Ned and Will were sitting inside the church porch.

"You were to wait outside - do you young people not do anything you're told?" he rebuked them.

"We're very sorry," said Ned, showing little sign of contrition. "It was cold and wet. We didn't realise that we'd be intruding on such a … private meeting; and well, by the time we did, it was easier to stay than go."

"You'll have heard far more than you should; see you hold your tongues – the fellow fighting at your shoulder today may be on the other side in a month's time – mark that well!"

"She's beautiful," said Ned.

"Yes, she is; and she's no concern of yours!"

"Who is she?" asked Will.

Sir Roger fixed him with a disapproving stare: "did I not say: no questions? The less you know, the safer she is! Now, we must leave before the priest gets here."

Only briefly chastened, his two young companions trooped after him as he began a hasty return to their lines. It was not yet dawn; the rain had eased but settled upon them again as mist. The route back downhill was not easy to follow and after an hour of scrambling through thickets and trudging across a seemingly interminable swathe of bracken, Sir Roger had to admit that he had spectacularly lost his way.

"If we're not careful we'll return to the enemy's lines and not our own!" he muttered.

The weather and the darkness had put doubts in Ned's mind too: where he had expected to see the dull glow of the Yorkist campfires, they were obscured by the mist and the woods. As night drew slowly to an end, he knew they must be perilously close to the rear of the royal army. They moved with increasing care, as every step seemed to crackle noisily in the early morning air. Ned hardly dared breathe, expecting at any moment to be challenged by a picket. But as the light improved, Sir Roger began to get his bearings.

"Listen, there's not too far to go, but we'll be close to their flank. If the mist lifts and the light gets any better, we'll likely be seen; we might have to make a run for it – but by the time they work out there's only three of us, we'll probably have reached our own lines."

"'Probably', you say," whispered Ned with a grin, "but go on, I can't move this quietly for much longer!"

But at that moment they walked straight into a pair of sentries sheltering amongst the trees. Sir Roger reacted swiftly, his heavy sword clubbing one in the throat, as Will and Ned hastily overpowered the other. They all stood still for a moment. The misty shroud was wearing desperately thin and other shadowy figures were closing in upon them as soldiers nearby were drawn to the commotion. Ned swung wildly in the mist and Roger struck down another man at arms. They headed off again towards what they hoped were the Yorkist lines, but ran into a high thick hedge.

Sir Roger cursed loudly. "We're right in their front line!" he hissed. It sounded as if the whole Lancastrian camp was now on the move around them, but the three fugitives remained indistinguishable from their enemies.

"This confusion won't last forever," said Sir Roger.

They worked their way along the hedge until at last a gap presented itself and then leapt through it onto a sloping stretch of meadow land that lay between the two lines. Even so, they still had three hundred yards of open ground to cross with the mist steadily clearing.

"There should be a brook at the bottom! Make for that!" urged Sir Roger.

There were shouts from the Lancastrian forward ranks who, seeing them, assumed a royal attack was being launched against the Yorkist positions and hurried to join in. When Ned dared glance around he was horrified to see hundreds following them, but by then they had reached the mill brook that ran parallel to their own front line.

"Roger of Wakefield!" they shouted, as they waded across, climbed the steep bank beyond and then hurried towards the tree line. Behind them, a score of armoured horsemen charged into the narrow mill brook and were met by a ragged flight of arrows from a handful of Salisbury's archers. Some Lancastrian riders were cut down or turned about, their wounded horses frenzied and bloodied; others found deeper water and struggled out of the stream.

Ned and Will ran to their comrades and hastily prepared for battle. Ned took up the long strip of pale blue banner and wrapped it around his midriff.

"Where in God's name have you been?" demanded Bagot; then, suddenly aware that he had publicly berated his liege lord, he lowered his voice: "Don't ever do that again… lord!"

Ned was annoyed by Bagot's outburst, but there was no time for any riposte – nor could he think of one. Holton and

Birches fussed around the pair of them, helping to strap on breastplates that Bagot had somehow acquired, but it was little enough protection. Bagot handed Ned a helmet and clapped him on the back. Ned thought wistfully of his father's fine plate armour that had once seen service in France and now no doubt adorned Robert Radcliffe's Great Hall.

"Stay near me!" ordered Bagot, "and watch your arms and legs, you've nothing but leather there."

"Alright," said Ned.

"And don't turn your back!"

"Perhaps I should ask my opponents to strike me only on the breast!" retorted Ned.

He turned to Will and the two friends looked each other up and down for a moment, then grinned sheepishly; they knew they were in a place somewhere between exhilaration and terror. They took their places with Bagot and other men at arms on foot in the ranks behind Sir Roger, as Salisbury's army made ready to repel the royal attack.

Ned watched a broad wedge of men at arms cross the brook below and climb the slope to launch a furious assault on the narrow Yorkist front line. He was relieved to be in the third rank whilst more experienced men fought ahead of him, but he flinched as the two lines met in a mist of blood.

"Sweet Jesus," he breathed, for even with his head encased in a dented steel basinet, he was stunned by the monstrous noise: the cries of the soldiers, the shrieks of wounded horses in the brook and the relentless clang of metal on metal. He felt wretched: his legs shook and his stomach churned.

Then, quite abruptly, a man fell and the line parted in front of him; it caught him completely unawares and he hesitated to step forward and close the gap. A fully armoured and explosively powerful opponent charged at him like an angry bull, battering his great sword at Ned's head and body. Ned had to give ground but he parried every stroke, feeling the shock of each one as it jarred the blade in his hands.

Yet miraculously he survived the first onslaught and found that he was holding his own. Breathlessly, he hung on and slowly became more confident as it became clear that his opponent was tiring. Then the man beside him took a succession of terrible blows to the head: the first knocked his helmet clean off and the second smashed through his bare head showering Ned with a thick spray of blood, flesh and bone. Suddenly Ned was blind, his visor obscured by the bloody debris; he had to step back and raise the visor. But by then his adversary had reached forward and delivered a ringing blow to his helmet. His head felt as if it had been split in two and there was a thunder of pain in his ears; off balance and falling backwards, he knew he wouldn't defend the next strike. Shit! Is that it? I didn't last long, he thought.

Time seemed to slow as he watched the sword arc down towards him. He stared numbly at death and muttered a prayer, but a falchion blade swung lazily across his body to deflect the blow. Ned blinked in disbelief and then, as his head cleared, he saw Bagot beside him. Then he threw his weight forward, finding the strength to lift his sword again and stab it up under the knight's armpit. It seemed to barely penetrate the joint in the armour, but it was enough. He sucked in a lungful of cool, damp air and drove the injured man back with blow after blow. Bagot was still alongside him, the brutal falchion chillingly effective in the hands of the veteran. He bludgeoned his opponents ruthlessly, cracking bone and tearing flesh. Together they muscled their stretch of the line forward so that their enemies were fighting at the very brink of the steep bank they had climbed, where the ground was slippery with blood and mud.

As Ned stepped forward he felt a bone crack beneath his feet and realised with a sick feeling that he was crushing the fallen underfoot – friend and foe alike. How far removed this was from his boyhood training: here in the sweated press of battle, brute strength counted, not finesse.

He stood visor to visor with a new adversary and they wrestled each other back and forth. A dribble ran down his leg and he hoped it was sweat. Abruptly the knight drew back, switched his grip on his sword blade to drive the point hard at Ned's open visor. He swayed and the sword scraped against the side of his helmet; instinctively he responded in like manner, and was shocked as his own sword passed clean through his opponent's visor and into an eye socket behind it. The man cried out; Ned hesitated and then stabbed the sword point through into his skull. The man dropped stone dead and his lifeless body slid down the bank, colliding with several others on their way up.

The fighting had been fierce all along the line, but the royal troops were being thrown back and their front ranks broke, retreating back across the mill stream under sporadic Yorkist archer fire. Ned dropped to his knees and then scanned the field for Will; his friend was close by, sitting on the bloodied ground head in hands.

Bagot dragged Will to his feet. "Go back and get Birches to look at that wound," he ordered.

"Thank God, it's over!" said Ned.

"Hah! It's not done yet," retorted Bagot, "they're not beaten men; they'll be back!"

6

St. Mary's Church, Mucklestone

Edmund Radcliffe stared sullenly at St. Mary's church. He was already tired and saddle-sore when he received the Queen's summons. Why she had to meet him here he couldn't imagine, but he could hardly refuse. He opened the church door and stepped inside. The interior was dark, for it was a miserable day. He could hear her pacing restlessly in the tower and trudged up the steps, wondering what she wanted - still, as long as there was honey in it for him, he didn't really care.

She was standing at an arrow loop, looking across to the battlefield, but turned as he reached the wooden landing. He bowed low, casting an admiring glance down her body as he did so: no-one would call her a beauty, but she had an attraction – of that there was no doubt. Perhaps it was simply the scent of power, for she certainly had plenty of that; and there was surely a hint of lust in the way she looked at him.

"What service can I perform for your Majesty?" he asked with a knowing smile.

"I have a tiresome but important task for you, Edmund," replied the Queen, briskly adopting a formal manner. "There is a troublesome servant who needs to be punished – mortally."

So, he thought, it was to be a simple execution; it seemed to him that she viewed the world as a landscape of black and white; she could discern no shades of grey. Thus she knew only one response to those who betrayed her trust: swift retribution; and he was to be the agent of that retribution. Well, it wouldn't be the first time.

"Who is it?" he asked.

"You don't need to know, but she must be punished for her disloyalty and ... for the knowledge she holds."

"A woman?" he murmured with rekindled interest.

"Possibly two, if her maid is with her. Drooling does not improve you, Edmund; just do what is needed and don't get distracted. I want them both dead."

"You want me to kill the servant too? Does she know too much as well?"

"What is it to you? Is it beneath you to kill servants?"

"It's nothing to me, your majesty," he conceded.

"I have arranged for them to be here later this evening. When it is done, come to me at Ludlow, where I shall be impaling Salisbury's head upon a stake. You'll be well rewarded – as always."

An idea had occurred to him earlier. "I'll waive my customary rewards," he said, "if you'll grant a special petition for me."

"Intriguing," replied Margaret, briefly interested, "what is it then? I am in haste!"

"A warrant for the murderer of my brother, Ralph."

"Touching. Have it drawn up; it'll be sealed at Ludlow – provided you carry out your task satisfactorily of course."

She swept past him down the steps; had she brushed her hand against his thigh as she passed him? He grinned with satisfaction: like most women, she struggled to withstand his charms. It had been a feature of their very productive relationship, but he knew he was playing a dangerous game in flirting with her. He watched her depart and then settled down to await his prey. He looked out onto the struggle at Blore Heath; the Queen, he knew, was short sighted, so he wondered how much she had actually made out. By contrast his keen eyes enabled him to judge that her men at arms were not doing very well. I should be there, he thought, not wasting my time up here slaughtering women; however 'troublesome' they may be, they are not worthy of my sword.

It was still daylight, so he would have to wait several hours – but it would do no harm to be prepared. He went downstairs and lit a torch, placing it in the entrance at the base of the tower; then he took a single candle up the narrow staircase to the top floor of the tower.

He had only arrived at Mucklestone in the last few hours, having ridden for the best part of two days, tracking down Ned Elder whom he now believed to be with Salisbury's army. He was far more tired than he wanted to admit and, as he sat waiting and watching from the tower, daylight faded and he drifted into an unwanted sleep.

§§§

Blore Heath

Ned stared bleakly across the brook. Bagot had been right: a fresh, even fiercer royal onslaught was on its way. Again the attackers had to struggle across the stream, weighed down by their heavy armour and weapons; yet they came in wave after wave, men at arms breathing heavily and mounted knights cajoling their horses once more up the increasingly treacherous slope. A few riders made it and charged into the waiting Yorkist ranks, but most were forced to dismount and continue the attack on foot.

The two lines shuddered together and Ned found himself in the thick of the battle again, thrusting and hacking with all his strength. Knocked this way and that, at times he struggled to keep to his feet in the confusion. But you learn fast, he thought, for now he was often holding his sword with one gloved hand firmly gripping the upper blade, as he had seen others do, driving the point of the weapon into the most unprotected parts of his adversaries. It was sickeningly brutal and Ned's heart was screaming at him to stop, but he shut it out and drove his sword hard into an opponent's groin. He was already beyond exhaustion, every sinew in his arms bursting and his legs buckling from fatigue. But every time he seemed likely to be swallowed up in the midst of the fighting, Bagot appeared at his shoulder. Yet he could see no end to it: the battle ebbed and flowed with neither side able to break the resolve of the other.

Then a triumphant shout came from the left flank and he glimpsed Sir Roger striking down a Lancastrian knight. The men nearest the fallen knight dragged him back and a ripple of hesitation flowed along their battle line.

"Sir Roger's done for their commander!" shouted Bagot.

At once the Yorkist front ranks harried them back down into the brook, where scores were butchered and the retreat suddenly became a rout. But Ned was too weary to take part in the chase that followed, as the Yorkist veterans scattered what remained of the royal army. Instead he fell once more to his knees. As the sounds of the pursuit receded, he tried to remember what had happened, but found that he couldn't recall a single detail; he had never felt so utterly spent.

"So many dead," he murmured, as he lay with Will on the bank surveying the carnage that was laid out before them down to the narrow, bloody brook.

Bagot sat nearby wiping the blade of his sword. "Hmm," he grunted, "you'll both need to beef up, or you won't see the end of another battle."

"Why in the name of God would I want to fight like that again?" said Ned.

"Perhaps there won't be any more," said Will.

Bagot merely shrugged and smiled.

Ned took him by the hand. "It could've been me down there in pieces; but you got me through it, Bagot."

"Bah, you got yourself through it – I just helped a bit."

§§§

St. Mary's Church

Edmund suddenly sat bolt upright. He listened, cursed silently and wondered how long he had slept; voices outside had mercifully awoken him. His untended candle had gone out and the tower was in utter darkness for there was little moonlight. The voices stopped and then almost immediately he heard footsteps: his prey was obligingly climbing the tower steps and coming to him. But as Margaret had predicted, the victim was not alone: he would have to manage this carefully.

He could hear the two women slowly climbing the steps up to the tower, one carrying the torch he had left downstairs. Drawing his dagger, he allowed the first woman to pass him at the top of the steps and then moving swiftly, he stabbed at the second woman who carried the torch. At the moment he struck she turned and saw him at the top of the steps. She cried out and dropped to the floor, losing her grip on the torch which rolled back down the steps plunging them all into darkness. Edmund stepped back against the wall as the other woman called out in alarm.

"Amelie?"

He remained against the wall, as still and cold as the stone itself, studying her shadowy form as she peered around, her eyes, like his, beginning to adjust to the sudden absence of light. She was backing away from the steps to the far side of the tower.

"Who is there?" she demanded.

Even in the poor light, he recognized her; he had seen her at court often and remembered her incomparable beauty. How far she had fallen from grace, he thought - perhaps the Queen had tired of such a radiant presence so close by. Well, so be it; her life would buy him Ned Elder's death.

He watched her edge forward and stumble over the prostrate body, falling to her knees and gasping as her hand discovered blood. Edmund moved silently to stand behind her, sorely tempted to stroke her dark glossy hair. Sensing his presence, she started to lift her head towards him and instinctively he seized her hair, pulled back her head and, before she could cry out, slit her throat with a single cut of his blade.

"What a waste," he said, as he released her lifeless body on to the floor.

He carefully wiped his dagger on her cloak and descended without haste to the base of the tower, where the torch had landed on the stone floor and was barely alight at all. Leaving it to gutter or flare as it pleased, he pulled open the heavy church door and closed it quietly behind him.

7

Blore Heath

It was not yet dawn and the Yorkist campfires were still illuminating the forest, but the army was preparing to break camp for Salisbury was clearly keen to reach Ludlow without sustaining any further losses.

"There's a mystery in the camp this morn," announced Bagot gruffly.

Ned was barely awake and his limbs ached as if he'd been on the rack.

"Is it a mystery I'll care about, Bagot?" he asked, trying to get up and work his legs.

"Well you might, since you're so thick with Sir Roger."

"What about him?"

"No-one's seen him since last night."

Ned was interested at once. "Is anyone looking for him?"

"I can't see Salisbury losing much sleep over it – nor should you."

But the sudden disappearance of Sir Roger troubled Ned; he couldn't forget what he'd witnessed at the church. Thus he went to Lord Salisbury and offered to search for the missing knight.

The Earl looked doubtful. "He's a good man, but he is only one man. Yet I suppose he may have been injured in the rout…Very well, do so; but take care – and join us at Ludlow."

"I will, my lord."

Ned's willingness for the task was not matched by his companions, who felt he had put them all at risk for no good reason; Bagot in particular made no secret of his irritation. However, Ned was adamant; he found it hard to believe that Sir Roger had been wounded in the pursuit - in fact he thought it far more likely that the knight had run off to meet his beautiful lady - but he had to be sure. Only Will, who understood Ned's concern, made no complaint.

So, when the main army moved off to the south, Ned made for St. Mary's, for it seemed as good a place as any to start his search. Bagot and the others followed reluctantly, expecting a royal army to appear from behind every clump of trees. As they approached the church, Bagot pointed without speaking to where a saddled, but riderless, horse sauntered into view, casually munching on some long grass by the nave wall.

"It's his," said Ned.

"Wait ..." began Bagot, but Ned had already dismounted and was on his way in. Bagot hesitated for only a few seconds and then, cursing, followed his master inside. Will and the others looked at each other and then shambled in after them. They searched the ground floor of the building quickly and found nothing and no sign that Sir Roger had even been there. Yet when Ned came to mount the steps to the tower he saw the abandoned torch and began to feel distinctly uneasy.

At the top, he found Sir Roger, sitting on the dusty wooden floor with the body of a woman in his arms: the woman they had seen the night before. Against the wall by the top of the steps, lay another corpse. Will, Holton and the others followed Ned up the steps and stood, appalled, on the landing.

Sir Roger nodded wearily to them.

"I thought I recognised you fellows down there – you made so much noise." They were all silent enough now.

"I've known Marie Sainte a long time," he continued softly. "I expected to die here myself with so many of the Queen's men in the area, but now you young fools have blundered in I suppose I shan't be dying alone."

"We'll not be here that long!" said Bagot sharply.

Ned cursorily examined the other body, a young girl; he started in surprise when he found she was still warm and groaned at his touch. He was shocked by the pallor of her face; she must have lost some blood, but the wound could not have been great or she would have been long dead by now. He studied her more closely, drawn in by the simple beauty of her face; her eyes flickered open, looked up at him and in that moment he was hers. When the brown eyes gently closed again, he knew he wouldn't leave her behind.

"Lord?" enquired Bagot, "what are we doing? This is no place to dwell!"

Ned dragged his attention from the girl; for a moment he made no answer, then he made up his mind.

"Mags, Bagot: take a look at her. Birches, Holton: keep a watch outside."

Holton went below and Birches moved to one of the narrow arrow loops in the tower wall.

"She's been stabbed," said Mags, "she's stopped bleeding I think, but we should bind up her wound."

Sir Roger looked across at her in surprise. "Curse me; I thought the maid was dead…" He hung his head.

"My lord, I can see some riders bearing a white swan pennant," announced Holton from the base of the steps.

"Royal troops," confirmed Bagot.

"How many?" Ned called down.

"I can only see about half a dozen."

"Ned, get out now – while you still can!" said Sir Roger.

"It's too late," said Bagot and looked at Ned. "What now, lord?"

"This church has two doors. We bar the side door, get them in here and trap them. Birches, you've been carrying that bow with you ever since we set out and I've yet to see you use it. Can you hit anything?"

"I can hit a deer," Birches murmured.

"Now would be a good time to start hitting something else with it. Stand at the north wall and take out any man that tries to escape through the door - but don't waste your arrows, it could be a long day. Will, let's go down."

He turned to the strong, young smith: "Holton, be ready to join us if need be, otherwise stay upstairs and help Mags get the girl ready to move – she'll die anyway if we don't get her away."

"You're not going to fight them in the church, are you?" asked Holton.

"What passed here in the night has already stained this place with blood – shedding a bit more isn't going to make much difference."

"What am I supposed to bind the wound with?" shouted Mags.

"Are you asking me or the men outside?" hissed Ned. "Find something! Just do it; get the girl ready and hold your tongue for a while – if you can!"

"Lord, she'll die soon enough," said Bagot quietly, "we could just go now and leave her with Sir Roger. What's she to us?"

"No!"

Bagot seized his arm. "Are you going to rescue every well favoured wench you find?"

Ned shook off Bagot's hand and faced him. "I'm not going to leave this wounded girl behind – well favoured or not!"

The constant questions were wearing him down and he turned to Sir Roger for support but the desolate knight had returned to cradling his lover.

"You shouldn't have come here, Ned. Get out while you still can."

Bagot was right, it was already too late to leave, for Ned could see from the tower that a band of soldiers in royal livery was approaching the church. They looked half-hearted and casual – until they saw the horses and at once they were alert.

"Will, go down and bar the north door," he said.

The men outside were moving towards the main door. Ned drew his sword and went down the steps; Will joined him and they concealed themselves in the shadows by the entrance. Even on a bright day, the church interior was dimly lit and the men coming in had to accustom themselves to the gloom.

As the six men funnelled into the nave, Ned and Will attacked them ferociously. Ned wielded his sword with a savagery he would not have believed possible a few days before and in the narrow aisles Will's arcing blades sliced down the men at arms like shafts of wheat. Two survived the first onslaught and ran to the north door. They managed to unbar and open it, but only one escaped as Ned felled the second with a single crushing blow to the neck. The last man fled out of the door, stumbled down the steps and around the tower to gather others to the fight.

"Birches!" growled Ned, "I hope you're paying attention!" But before he had finished speaking the fleeing man was hurled forwards into the churchyard wall where he lay still, Birches' arrow barely protruding from his back. Inside the church, two of the wounded were bleeding to death and crying out for mercy. Ned and Will stared aghast at the carnage they had wrought: they had made a bloody battlefield of the nave.

"Holton was right," murmured Will, "all this blood ... so much split in here; we'll be lost to God!"
Bagot shrugged and went to each of the dying men, despatching them swiftly.

"You can't always help where you fight, Will," he said, "but if you're going to kill a man at least make it quick!"

Ned turned and ran up the tower steps. "Let's move!" he urged.

Holton and Mags brought the young maid down to the ground floor; Birches followed with an arrow nocked in his bow ready to let loose at a second's notice. Ned glanced at the unconscious girl; perhaps Bagot was right, for she looked deathly pale.

"Head down into the valley," he instructed, "and get into the mist."

"Stay in a tight group," added Bagot, "if you separate, you'll die; we must make as much speed as we can – and as little noise." He glowered at Mags and she glared back.

"Go on! I'll catch you up," said Ned.

Bagot looked uncertain. "Lord?"

"Go on, take them out, Bagot! I'll be right behind you!" Without waiting for Bagot to argue, he returned once more to the top of the tower.

"Will you not come with us, Sir Roger?" he said.

"I lost three young sons in war - all dead in the service of kings. I care nothing for kings now; I was fighting only to be with this lady and now there's nothing I want to fight for."

He reached into his boot and took out a tiny bejewelled dagger, no more than six inches in length. "Here, take this," he said and passed it to Ned. "Put it safely in your boot. It's not just a knife – Marie gave it to me - but it'll likely be more use to you than me. Now get moving, before it's too late. I'll do enough to gain you some time."

Ned hurried down the steps, snatching up his sword on the run and following the others out. He scrambled awkwardly onto his horse and rode down the slope past the bushy yew trees that lay close to the church. Beyond the trees he could see his comrades tracing a slow route down towards the mist that covered the valley floor. But he could also hear more royal soldiers approaching from the north side of the church – and they were only moments away.

8

Ludlow, October, 1459

"What are we going to do with her now, lord?" asked Holton.

Ned was exhausted and he knew his companions were too; they had just ridden into Ludlow and passed through the bar on the north road into the town. Salisbury, Ned imagined, would have arrived several days earlier, for their own journey had been slow. They had managed to lose their pursuers in the mist and make their way south. Birches and Holton had rigged a makeshift litter to carry the girl between their horses but, despite all their care, her hold on life was tenuous.

"We'll have to find somewhere to leave her," replied Ned.

"We could've left her somewhere..." muttered Bagot.

"Somewhere she can be cared for! There'll be an abbey, or such like..."

"Know about abbeys – and such like - do you?"

"Just keep your eyes open!"

However, even with their eyes shut they would have struggled to miss the large religious house they passed as they rode up towards the town gate.

"There you are!" said Ned.

"It's huge!" said Will, for the building covered the whole frontage of the street almost up to the gate.

"It'll not be short of alms then," remarked Bagot.

"Well, let's see," said Ned.

It turned out to be a Friary of the Carmelite Order and initially the Friars were most solicitous about the young maid, until they discovered the nature of her injury.

"I beg you to take her in," Ned implored the Prior, "the wound is hardly her fault."

"– nor ours!" added Bagot quickly.

"She's innocent of any wrongdoing," continued Ned, darting a sharp glance at Bagot, "if she stays with you, she may yet live."

The Prior clearly had his doubts, but finally agreed to take her in on condition that all the others left. Reluctantly, Ned acquiesced and they left her there; then they crossed the bustling heart of the town to leave by a broad gate which led them across a fine stone bridge over the river to the south of the town.

Beyond the river, the Duke of York had dug in his front lines behind a large ditch, next to which he sited his cannons protected by a screen of wagons and stakes. Ned thought it looked a formidable defensive line but from the moment they arrived Bagot made it clear that he didn't like what he saw.

"If this is the Duke's full strength, it's what I feared," he confided to Ned, "there aren't enough men here."

Soon Ned could see for himself that the camp of York and Salisbury was not a happy one. The persistently wet autumn weather had done little to raise morale in a squalid camp, where the stores were so damp as to be unusable and the much trodden ground had already turned into a stinking, clutching mud. The small, well ordered camp at Blore Heath had not prepared Ned for the squalor he found at Ludford Bridge. For some of those with him this was also unfamiliar territory: Holton had never set foot outside the Elder estates, let alone visited a town; only Bagot and Mags seemed completely at home.

"We've nothing to eat," observed Birches. Ned had noticed that for such a thin man, Birches was often the first to mention food. Nevertheless, he was right and there was little to be found in the camp.

"Holton, Mags – take a look in the town and see if you can find some vittles," he said.

"Find?" asked Mags.

"Just go and see what you can …find," he ordered.

"Are you telling us to steal?" asked Mags, "town folk'll take that bad!"

"No!" said Ned, "well, not really…"

"Well, are you giving us some coin, then?"

"No! But… just be careful…"

Mags tossed her bedraggled hair to one side and stalked off, taking Holton's arm with her.

As they meandered through the Ludlow streets, Holton absorbed the urban atmosphere. He was wide eyed like a child, colliding clumsily with passers-by when his attention was anywhere but where he was walking. In the narrow streets overshadowed by the walls of Ludlow Castle, merchants were peddling a bewildering array of goods – anxious to take advantage of the crowds whilst their good fortune lasted. Holton and Mags were in no position to purchase, but by the time they had passed all the stalls, Mags seemed to have acquired a tidy collection of foodstuffs.

"We've done well – we work well together, you and me," she said.

Holton felt awkward. "You mean, while the stallholders' eyes were on me in case I knocked their whole stall over, they didn't notice you?"

"Just picking up little fallen things, John - just little ones," she patted her bulging bag and smiled up at him. He was surprised how comfortable he was in her company and chuckled to himself: who would have thought that this girl with the rough tongue and leather hide could be so engaging. The others would scarcely have recognised her.

"Let's go to the Friary!" she said, "see how that poor girl is?"

"I don't think we should," said Holton, recalling the Prior's misgivings.

Mags smiled again, mischievously. "Don't you think our 'Ned' would want to know?"

"Do you think so?" Holton was dubious.

"Well, I think our lord would be very happy to know she's alright…"

She took his arm and dragged him off to the Friary, where the Prior was less than pleased to see them.

"This is not some hostelry, for folk of all sorts to come and go as they please!" he protested.

Holton could tell by the flush in Mags' cheeks that she was going to enquire further what he meant by 'folk of all sorts', but the prior grudgingly allowed them to make a brief visit and the sight of the girl's death-like pallor made them forget all else.

"Is she still alive?" Holton asked.

The friar tending her replied: "yes and she's lost no more blood and for that we should all thank the Lord."

Mags shook her head. "She looks as if she could just … slip away."

"This isn't the best place for her," said the friar, "but the nearest house of women is many miles hence; so let us hope that prayer can save her, for there we can surely play our part."

They left her to the care of the friars, and wandered back through the town; they took their time, for Holton was keen to see every lane and alley and besides, they knew that when they returned to the grim camp in the evening their cheerful mood would all too quickly evaporate.

§§§

On Bagot's advice, Ned had camped a little upstream from the bridge opposite one of the fulling mills that hugged the town bank of the river; the smell was appalling, but the ground was much drier. Around the campfires outside Ludlow there were mutterings of discontent as the prospect of imminent annihilation loomed.

"They say the King's here himself," said Will, "it seems different somehow, fighting against him if he's actually here."

"And have you seen all the noble banners flying for the King?" remarked Bagot, "There's precious few in our ranks – only the Nevilles. You can smell the fear."

"I can't smell anything but the fulling mill," said Ned.

"There's a rumour we can have a pardon if we give up the Duke," said Will.

"Keep those thoughts to yourself!" snapped Bagot.

"Why? What's the point of dying here in Ludlow, when Ned's sisters are somewhere else? This isn't our fight."

Ned shook his head. "It's easy to think so Will, but this war, the feud with the Radcliffes, father's execution and all the rest – it's all one. He was dragged into it and so are we. We'll not end our own strife till this matter is ended."

§§§

They talked on into the night, while the others huddled together in the encircling darkness. Mags drew her rough blanket closer around her as she sat watching them, silhouetted against the flickering fire. The dancing flames played upon Ned's profile, teasing her so that she could scarcely drag her eyes from him; but at length she did, for he was not for her. Holton, on the other hand, lay close by snoring noisily. She had found herself drawn by his gentleness; she could do much worse than John Holton. Wistfully she turned her gaze once more upon Ned, who had started pacing restlessly in and out of the firelight. He stopped when he noticed that Mags could not sleep either and he came over to squat down beside her.

"You didn't happen to go to the Friary, did you?" he asked. She smiled inwardly, as she had already guessed the reason for his sudden interest in her.

"Yes, lord, we did."

"Well?"

"The friars are relying on prayer now."

"I should have left her where she was; all I've done is make her suffer more. We don't even know her name." He nodded his thanks to her and returned to the fire.

By the chill small hours of another murky morning, most of the soldiers' fires had smouldered into the mist as the first weak glimmer of light appeared in the eastern sky. By then Ned had succumbed to a fitful sleep, but Bagot shook him roughly awake.

"Trollope's gone across to the King!" he announced.

"Who's Trollope?" asked Ned.

"Spare me, good St Stephen!" grunted Bagot, "he's our captain, our guide, our rock! Without him we're lost – and he's taken all his veterans with him."

As Ned struggled to grasp the enormity of the defection, Bagot went on.

"There's worse: our noble Duke has buggered off too and left us in the shit!

"What about Salisbury?"

"Oh, the Nevilles have gone too! I never bloody trusted them …"

"Gone?" Ned got up and stared at the centre of their lines. "But, their banners still fly! Look!"

"The fucking banners are all that's left of them; go and see for yourself!" He spat the words out in disgust.

News of York's capitulation scorched through the camp, galvanising not only the remnants of his army, but also the population of Ludlow. Soon everyone was on the move and the town's streets were heaving with the armed bands of York's fragmented army streaming out of the north and east gates in the wake of their leaders. For the townsfolk of Ludlow their gravest fears were about to come to pass: nothing and no-one would be safe. As the rump of York's army retreated across Ludford Bridge into the town, the King's army seized the opportunity and easily overran their front line.

Ned had only seconds to decide what to do. They were camped more than fifty yards from the bridge and when they reached it they would have to join the crush of men fleeing across it.

"We'll never get across the bridge; we'll have to ford the river," he said.

"Holton, get the horses!" ordered Bagot.

"There's no time," said Ned, "leave them!"

"We won't get far without them!" retorted Bagot.

"We won't get anywhere with them – the King's men are almost upon us!"

"What then?" asked Bagot. But Ned was already on the move leading them under the stone arch of the bridge and downstream along the banks of the river, hoping to find a good place to cross.

"Wait!" shouted Bagot struggling to make himself heard above the clamour of the men converging on the bridge. "The river's too high and it's flowing too fast and ... there are rapids along there! It's too risky to cross!"

Ned glanced back at the carnage on the bridge.

"Risky? It looks risky enough back there!"

Bagot looked at the bridge and turned pale, conceding for once that Ned was right.

"You alright, Bagot?" enquired Ned, "Only you're the same colour as the water!"

"Yes, lord! I can ford a river as well as any man!" retorted Bagot.

Ned picked out a street which ended at the far bank of the river and he guessed that in drier weather there must be a ford there but Bagot had a point: the autumn rains had swollen the river so that it was now rushing powerfully along its course towards a large weir. Yet he could see that a terrible slaughter was being carried out on the approaches to the bridge and the right wing of the King's army was sweeping around to scour along the river bank; they could not escape that way.

"We'll have to risk it," said Ned. He slithered down the bank and into the muddy brown water, followed with varying degrees of reluctance by the others.

"Wait, lord!" called Holton. "I'm a miller's son - I'm used to rivers, so let me go first."

Ned didn't argue, for he knew little enough about rivers.

"Lock your arms together and keep on your feet," instructed Holton, "we mustn't get too close to that weir!"

They linked arms tightly and Holton powered them across to the centre of the stream with Bagot bringing up the rear; even so, the current was too strong and it soon buffeted several of them off their feet.

"Have faith! Hold on to each other!" shouted Holton.

As the water dashed them to and fro, they clung together and stumbled beyond the middle of the river; the Lancastrians, now on the riverbank, poured scorn upon their attempt to cross.

"We're nearly there!" Holton cried, though Ned knew they weren't.

The river pounded them mercilessly, tipping them over and cracking their bones on the hidden rocks. Each time one fell heavily someone else just managed to gain a hold on them before they were swept away, but it was only Holton's strength that anchored them to the river bed. Ned looked to the back of the line, where Bagot seemed to have his eyes half-shut, but was still using his powerful legs to help Holton keep the line steady.

The water was numbingly cold and Ned could feel the strength draining from his body when Will slipped and fell, dragging Mags down with him. She let go of Birches' arm and screamed as she went under; Holton spun around at once. The watching Lancastrians jeered the fall enthusiastically.

Ned stopped to see if Bagot was still standing; he was, but he was straining every muscle to hold onto Will and Mags as the current did its best to drag them away.

"Keep on going, lord!" Holton ordered and waded past him back to the middle of the river.

He plunged a large arm into the murky water and scooped up Mags who instantly wrapped her arms tightly around his neck, her soaking body trembling against his chest.

"Holton!" Bagot shouted desperately; he was still gripping Will's arm but could not raise him up. Holton quickly hoisted Mags over his shoulder, then bent lower into the torrent and with a grunt of effort pulled Will up by his jerkin.

"Christ! He's turned blue!" said Bagot.

"Hold him upright!" cried Holton, for Will looked dizzy and there was blood on his temple.

Holton, still carrying Mags, towed Will and Bagot towards the others and they linked arms once more.

"Keep on, lord!" urged Holton, and Ned moved off again, leading them towards the bank.

Soon it was only a few yards away and Ned realised with relief that they were actually going to get there. So too did the enemy, a few of whom began to let fly wildly with their bows while some others less wisely jumped into the river to follow the fugitives, but were swept away in the torrent and disappeared over the weir, where their cries were abruptly cut short.

Ned stumbled up onto the bank with Holton helping him to drag the line of sodden bodies in and they all staggered, chilled and battered, towards the town.

"Well done, John!" declared Ned thumping him on the back; the young blacksmith smiled with modest pride. An arrow thudded into the muddy bank behind them and they scrambled to take refuge beside a corner town house out of sight of the enemy archers. Will was bleeding from the temple and Mags had bruised her ankle, but the rest were simply soaked through and shivering.

"We can't go far like this," said Bagot, breathing hard.

"Can't we just join the crowd?" said Ned, "who'll know us?"

"Our enemies are already on the bridge - do you want to take the risk?"

"We'll have to hole up somewhere in the town," said Ned.

"If we're caught in the town it'll go badly for all of us," argued Bagot, looking at Mags. "Once the king's men are off the leash they'll not be reined in."

"We're not in France, Bagot! This is an English army in an English town," said Ned.

"Hah! They're just men and no-one will stop them, not even the king!"

"Even so, we need to rest up for a while; then we can slip away when they've all drunk themselves stupid."

"But where, lord, where?" demanded Bagot.

"One of the inns?" suggested Mags.

Bagot favoured her with a withering glance. "Where would you go first Mags, if you were a thirsty little soldier?"

She glared at him. "Alright then: a church? The Carmelites?"

"I can't see the Prior wanting us back just now!" said Ned.

"One of the small chapels?" ventured Holton.

"At last, a sound idea; but where are they?" asked Bagot.

"We don't know the town at all," said Ned.

"I've an idea of it," Holton said, "there's a small chapel called St Thomas's, but it's on the west side – if we can get up to the High Street before most of them, we can slip across to it. Most'll be heading in the other direction."

Bagot squinted around the edge of the house wall.

"Wherever we're going, it'd better be now! The King's men have crossed the bridge!"

"Holton, lead the way, we're in your hands," said Ned.

"God help us," muttered Bagot.

Holton moved quickly up the street and then cut left along a narrow lane, running past the large Talbot Inn where a host of men were already engaged in dismantling its doorway. One made a half-hearted grab at Bagot and was cuffed round the head with a mailed fist for his trouble. Holton, half-carrying Mags, then darted nimbly up another lane to the right.

"Do you have any idea where you're going?" yelled Bagot, but Holton ignored him. They emerged out of the lane into the High Street and ran towards the castle, where a large crowd was gathering.

"Holton!" Bagot shouted again, "we surely shouldn't be going this way!"

"Peace, Bagot! He knows this town better than you do!" chided Mags.

Holton led them alongside the castle ditch and back in the direction of the river. There were far fewer soldiers there, as most were heading into the market square. Ned and Birches, uncomplaining so far, were supporting Will between them.

"Is it far now?" asked Ned.

"It's here!" replied Holton triumphantly as he reached the chapel. At once, they hammered on the tall doors, but there was no response from within: if there was anyone left in the chapel they were certainly not going to invite the enemy host in to sing a mass.

The doors, though large, were not particularly strong, nor in very good repair; so Holton managed to lever one open and they piled inside, shutting and barring it behind them.

In the small chapel a torch was still burning. "Someone left in a hurry," observed Bagot.

"This'll do for now," said Ned.

"Aye," agreed Bagot, "let them scatter themselves all over Ludlow and then their captains will move them off. The only thing we've to worry about is some little thief who thinks there might be something in here worth taking."

"We're going to be very hungry," observed Birches.

"Better than lying in some doorway with your belly split open," said Bagot.

Ned looked at an inscription on the wall: "St Thomas the Martyr," he read aloud.

"Let's hope we'll not be joining him," said Bagot.

9

Broad Street, Ludlow

Felix of Bordeaux was in deep trouble.

He ran through the crowded street with his quarter staff in his hands ready, if required, to defend himself against the soldiers streaming into the town from the south. He scanned the houses on both sides of the street for the one he sought, the description given at the tavern still fresh in his mind.

Ahead of him a jostling mob was forcing its way towards him but at last he identified the house he wanted. He reached the doorway safely only to be swept aside by the surging mob and thrown against the door, which being slightly ajar, allowed him to fall clumsily inside. He sprang to his feet, pushed the door shut and waited, alert for any sound in the house and surveying the contents of the room in which he stood.

He heard nothing, so he made a quick search of the ground floor and cellars: it was certainly a vintner's house, as the pipes and hogsheads of wine he discovered in the cellars proved. The house had seen better days though – not surprising since the owner owed him a very large sum. Glad of an opportunity to get his breath back, he helped himself to a generous measure of dry sack and sat on a bench by the large hearth.

Felix was used to misfortune, for the Lord tested him with adversity on an almost daily basis. He had been found by a monk on a rocky shore in southern France - a child as black as death, the monk had said. He had forgiven the monk's dark humour in naming him Felix, but he had never forgiven him the years of abuse and beatings. Yet, from the same monk he had learned to read and write and without that he would not be the man he now was.

If he was inclined to blame God for some of his earlier misfortunes, this particular one was entirely his own fault: he should have stayed in Bristol; instead he had arrived in Ludlow in the midst of a battle. He could have turned about on the Hereford road when he saw others fleeing in the opposite direction. He, on his fine black mare with three pack mules in train, was clearly ripe for the picking and it was not very long before he was attacked. He managed to free his staff and delivered some hefty blows at his assailants, but was soon knocked from his horse and it, along with his mules, was taken. Only when his opponents realised how deadly he was with his quarter staff did they leave him alone and move on. His weapon of choice was a seven foot length of oak, three fingers thick, hardened and stained dark by heavy usage and capped at each end with a piece of iron – in normal times it was a formidable deterrent but barely enough now.

He had completed the remaining few miles of his journey on foot – and mercifully he had now arrived, but where was the errant vintner? There was a noise on the stairs behind him and he turned to see a woman's face peering around the corner of the first floor landing.

At that moment there was a thunderous crash against the house door.

"Get upstairs and keep quiet!" he ordered and she duly vanished.

He waited, staff poised; perhaps the soldiers would pass on by. His thin hopes disintegrated along with the central planks of the door; though the oak was strong, the carpentry let it down.

Several men burst through the opening, bearing a heavy timber as a battering ram. Seeing Felix in front of them holding a quarterstaff, they hesitated. He took a pace towards them and they dropped the beam to fumble out their weapons. He punched his staff expertly at the nearest man, knocking him off his feet, and the others retreated out of the door. He followed them out, cracking a few more heads with thrusts of the iron shod weapon. There were others outside amongst the crowd but they backed away, dragging their injured with them.

Felix stepped inside once more and waited; this was not how he had envisaged his first morning in Ludlow.

§§§

On Broad Street

Edmund Radcliffe's men were under strict instructions to pick out only the finest looking houses, where they were to seize the most valuable goods and capture wealthy merchants, who could later buy their freedom. At the outset they had captured several large houses towards the market square but the onslaught was brutal as the Lancastrian army ran riot. Stronger forces simply wrestled control from the men of Yoredale and thus they returned to their master to report the disappointing news.

"Are you telling me you have taken nothing?" Edmund cajoled his men in disbelief.

"We're pressing for one merchant's house, sire, but its owner is putting up a bit of a fight," said one.

Edmund accompanied his troops to the house in question and passed through the open door where a tall black skinned man sat supping wine. When he saw Edmund, he leapt to his feet.

"Is that all?" said Edmund, drawing his sword. Emboldened, his men followed him but were abruptly halted when the defender feinted to swing his staff and instead drove it into Edmund's chest, dumping him out of the house onto the muddy cobbles. His shocked followers stood back, waiting for their lord to get to his feet. He did so gingerly, blood trickling down the side of his head, which he had cracked on the stones; he shook it like a wet dog shaking off droplets of water.

"Come on!" he yelled. "What are you standing about for?"

He launched himself back into the house and the rest followed. Felix was obliged to concede ground and was forced back towards the staircase, where he was unable to wield his staff freely; nevertheless, he struck Edmund on the head, eliciting an angry shout from the knight as he fell to the floor. However, very soon force of numbers pressed Felix into a corner and he was cut several times before being disarmed. The soldiers closed in for the kill, but Edmund bellowed from the floor: "Leave him!"

He got unsteadily to his feet and staggered over to where the troublesome Felix was being pinned to the floor. He kicked him on the side of the head.

"Who are you?"

"I am Felix," he replied simply, revealing his thick French accent.

"I'll take great pleasure in stripping this house of your best wares."

Felix coughed up some blood. "Very well; it is not my house."

"Then why have you been fighting for it?" demanded Edmund, his head still aching from the blows he had taken.

"I was fighting for myself, not the house!"

Edmund was in no mood to argue: "beat the French shit out of him and then pin him to the wall – I'll have some sport with him later."

He gently felt his head where two large lumps had already appeared. Some of his retainers carried out his command with alacrity, keen to impress with a victim who now offered no resistance. The Frenchman was clubbed to the floor and repeatedly kicked in the head and torso. When he stopped crawling around on all fours and lay still, he was picked up and leant against the beamed wall. Thick chunks of cob wall were hacked out around the beam with an axe and his arms were bound tightly to the horizontal timber. Edmund nodded with grim satisfaction.

"You'll wish you hadn't crossed me!"

He turned to his men; they were an unlikely mix, few of whom he trusted: some from the Elder estates had been pressed into reluctant service by his father's threats against their families, whilst others were only willing to fight if they were paid good coin for doing so. He sent half his men onto the streets again to bring back whatever plunder they could find, whilst the rest remained ready to defend the house from rival bands.

"Now, search this place - and make sure our 'comrades' don't take it from you!"

But the search of the house had hardly begun before there was a great shout of jubilation as the wine cellars were discovered; this was then followed by a long scream from the floor above and several minutes of noise and commotion as the soldiers found the lady of the house. Felix briefly opened his eyes under swollen lids, but he was powerless to help her.

Two hours passed before Edmund realised that none of those he had sent out were coming back any time soon and those who remained were desperate to get out - it seemed that even his iron will could not hold them. To stop desertions he finally let his mercenaries go too, warning them to return by dawn or they would not be paid at all. Only one man remained with him: Mordeur.

Mordeur was a veteran from Normandy and he answered only to Lord Radcliffe. The latter had sent Mordeur with his son ostensibly to 'advise' him; however, all three parties knew that Mordeur was there to keep Edmund alive.

"Well," said Edmund, "let's see what this house has to offer; it looks bare but we may find a few worthwhile items. When we get tired of that, we'll entertain ourselves with the woman and then we'll get to this man – unless of course you don't want to harm your fellow Frenchman."

Mordeur smiled. "He's from the south…"

10

St. Thomas's Chapel, Ludlow

It was cold and damp in the chapel, but at least it allowed for Mags' ankle to be expertly bound up by Bagot and gave Will's cracked head a little time to heal. They remained there all day and through the night, but they were all restless – Ned most of all. At first light the following morning he decided that he would visit the Carmelite Friary.

"It's too soon, Ned, wait another day," advised Will.

Mags smiled knowingly. "I don't think you'll persuade him," she said quietly.

"They'll all be sleeping it off," said Ned, hoping that they would be early enough to find few stirring.

"Very well, I'll go with you," said Bagot.

"I thought you didn't care if she lived or died."

"I don't; but I do want to keep you alive – if you'll let me! Anyway, we should see what state the town's in."

What they saw horrified them: everywhere there were bodies - the corpses sometimes indistinguishable from the large number of drunken soldiers adorning the streets. Ned was shocked, despite Bagot's earlier warnings, but even Bagot looked unnerved by what they found in the market place: the streets had been drenched with wine and ale so that the gutters were still wet and a ripe stench hung in the damp air.

"I didn't know there was this much wine in all England, let alone Ludlow!" said Ned.

Bagot was distraught. "The fools! They must have smashed every hogshead and pipe of wine in the town!"

If King Henry had made any attempt to control his armies as they rampaged on their drunken progress through the town's fine houses, inns and shops, Ned could see little evidence of it. All he saw were houses with doors broken in and stalls ransacked and stripped bare.

Bagot shook his head in disbelief. "These folk'll be poor forever."

The Carmelite Friary, however, seemed to have survived unscathed, for its gates were guarded by soldiers. For a while they merely watched from a safe distance.

"They're wearing the King's livery!" hissed Bagot.

"Are you sure?"

"Of course I'm sure! It was the same king when I was in France and the livery's not changed much."

Curious, Ned thought, that one religious house should enjoy such royal protection and perhaps too much of a coincidence that it should be the one place they wanted to visit.

"What do you think?" Ned asked.

"I don't like it, lord; I think we should go back to the chapel with all haste … but I don't suppose we will."

"Let's see how keen they are," said Ned and he strode confidently up to the two men lounging by the Friary entrance.

"We've come to see my sister, who's in the care of the friars," he informed them.

They were cold and dispirited so, to his surprise, they allowed Ned and Bagot through the gate without any argument. They were greeted rather more warmly than before by Prior Thomas, who took them through to see the girl in the infirmary.

Ned was pleased to see that she was awake and looked a good deal stronger, fortified no doubt by some of the friars' thick potage. She seemed to have no recollection of either Ned or Bagot and at first she looked alarmed to see them beside her bed and sought reassurance from Prior Thomas.

"They brought you in here, my child, so if they meant you any harm they surely could have saved themselves the trouble of carrying you all the way here."

Ned observed the trace of colour in her cheeks.

"I'm Ned... We found you in the church at Mucklestone," he said.

"Ah, the church," she murmured in lightly accented English, "I was with ... a lady - did you see her?"

"We won't tire you; perhaps for now, just tell us your name at least."

"I am Amelie." The soft musical tones of her voice enchanted him and he found himself looking into her dark, frightened eyes. For a fleeting moment she returned his gaze, until Bagot touched Ned's arm to urge him away.

"We'll come back," he said and they went out with the Prior.

"You've the king's men guarding your doors, I see," he said.

"The Queen's in fact," the cleric explained proudly. "Indeed, it's a strange matter: here's the town being pillaged all around us and who should pay us a visit but the Queen herself! But, apparently, she lodged here with His majesty a few years ago – turned down an offer of hospitality from the Duke at the Castle," he confided. "She said she remembered as she rode past and stopped to see that we were safe – a most pious lady."

"Indeed," agreed Ned, intrigued, "she just came in and then left?"

"Well, something else very odd occurred: her majesty spied the girl and asked who she was. Of course she was still sleeping then and we didn't know who she was - but this is the most curious part," he continued enthusiastically, "when the Queen looked at her she turned quite pale - just as if she had seen a spirit! She rushed straight out of the house and posted those guards you see at the gate. They've been there all night and I don't think they're very pleased! But even so, to have the protection of the Queen is quite remarkable, don't you think?"

"Aye, it is indeed most remarkable," Ned agreed.

Could the Queen really have chanced to go there? She must have recognised Amelie but been unsure how the girl came to be in Ludlow; perhaps the guards were a precaution whilst the Queen considered what to do next.

"And did anyone else come later?" he enquired.

"No," replied Prior Thomas, who seemed crestfallen there was nothing more to relate.

Bagot shuffled impatiently in the small vaulted anteroom, indicating with his usual lack of subtlety that they should remain no longer. Ned bade farewell to the Prior, promising to return the following day.

The streets were now much more crowded as they returned to the town through the small portcullis at the Corve Street gate.

"There's too many idle men about; we should make haste," advised Bagot.

They began to hurry a little more but when they rounded the corner beyond the gate they ran into a small knot of men moving just as fast in the opposite direction. They were jostled out of the way by the others and Bagot was sent sprawling, ending up on his backside in the gutter. Ned drew his sword and Bagot leapt to his feet, unsheathing his falchion. Then he took a step back as he studied the battered features of the man facing him.

"Jack?"

The other man peered suspiciously at him. "Bagot?"

"Jack Standlake! It's a long time since Normandy," said Bagot with a grin.

"You're still alive then?"

"It seems," replied Bagot, "and you survived marrying that wild girl Alice!"

Jack laughed and put up his sword; he took Bagot's hand and they embraced like long lost brothers, whilst everyone else looked on uncomprehendingly.

"Bagot," Jack turned to his companions, "you remember my brothers, Tom and Walter, and these are my two sons: Hal and James and their cousins, Robert and ...." His voice tailed off as he recognised Ned.

"What?" asked Bagot.

"It's not safe for you here," Jack said to Ned, "not safe for folk talking to you either."

"Who brings the men of the Elder estates to Ludlow," asked Ned coldly.

Jack shifted uncomfortably. "Edmund Radcliffe - we're men of the Radcliffe estates now ..."

Ned felt a shiver cut through him; he knew he shouldn't be surprised, but still he took it hard.

"Can you give me any news of the Lady Eleanor, or Lady Emma?"

"Well, the Lady Emma is to wed the Radcliffe heir: Richard."

Ned cursed silently. "And Eleanor?" he asked.

"She's not been seen in the village," said Jack.

"Surely, someone must have seen her!"

"Even my Becky's heard nothing," said Tom Standlake, "and if anyone would know, she would."

"Why would any of you fight for such as Edmund Radcliffe? He's not worth your piss!" said Bagot.

"Brave words, Master Bagot," retorted Tom, "but, unlike you, we've families on the manor."

"If we must serve such as him to keep our own folk safe, then so be it," added Walter.

"There'll be no treachery from this quarter – you can rely on that," Jack reassured them swiftly, "but you should get as far away from here as you can."

"We're holed up at St Thomas' chapel for now," said Bagot.

"Then leave, for the man you should fear most is here in Ludlow. God be with you ... lord. Take care, Bagot."

Jack walked away without a backward glance, leading his kinsmen off along the High Street.

"Can he be trusted?" Ned asked, as they continued more thoughtfully to the chapel.

"I've trusted him often enough with my life; if the likes of Jack Standlake are against us, we'll surely fail."

§§§

In the house which Edmund had commandeered, Jack and his brothers had laid claim to the back cellar. The hogsheads had been manhandled to the hall many hours before and were now drained dry. Somewhere on the floor above the woman was weeping and when the brothers returned from the town they were in subdued mood. They had looked away as they passed the unfortunate tied to the wall.

Tom glanced at his elder brother. "I know what you're thinking, but he's no concern of ours, Jack!"

Jack shook his head, but said nothing. He had been unsettled by his chance meeting with Ned and Bagot, but to desert to Ned Elder now would offer the Standlakes nothing but certain death.

They remained in the cellar for the rest of the day and the night that followed, whilst many of their comrades were still groggily adjusting to sobriety. But in the early hours of the morning, Jack arose and climbed the short flight of steps to the ground floor, stepping over several slumbering men along the way. He paused in front of the prisoner, who had clearly been beaten further during the evening; abruptly the man lifted up his head and looked right at him. He did not move his lips, but he did not have to. Jack stared at the haggard, blood-stained face with its eyes still bright under half closed lids. He looked at the door, where the guard Mordeur had posted lay asleep. Then he turned and retraced his steps back down to the cellar where Tom and Walter had already stirred, noticing his absence.

"I'm going back to the manor," he said, "and then I'm going to take the family away from Yoredale. It's not so hard these days to settle somewhere else. You two must decide for yourselves, but it'll surely go hard with you if I go and you stay: this lord is not a forgiving one."

Tom and Walter exchanged a fleeting glance: they knew their course was already plotted.

"One more thing: I'm going to release that wretch upstairs as I go. I'll not be party to that, not even in the King's name. I saw enough of that in France."

"We could slip away more easily if we leave that fellow where he is," said Tom, "we didn't cut him or put him there. Besides, he's an alien - what's he to us?"

"Alien or not, he did nothing more than any of us would if we were set upon by so many and I'll not leave him to die. We'll take him from the house and then he's on his own."

They woke their sons and, a while later, crept up the steps as quietly as their fighting harness permitted; then they carefully freed the battered captive so that even those lying in the same room slept on without noticing. They bore the barely conscious man out of the house and Jack retrieved his formidable quarterstaff so that he was able to support himself. Then they guided him into a side alley, leant him against the wall and gave him some ale.

"You're in no state to run; do you have friends in the town?" Jack asked.

Felix slowly shook his head.

"Jack, if they follow us, he'll never last," said Tom.

But Felix seemed to understand their predicament. "You've done enough," he murmured, "I thank you. Go."

Still Jack was reluctant to leave him helpless.

"St Thomas's chapel, down towards the river," he said, "seek out Bagot – he may be able to help you."

Felix nodded and Jack led the others on to the stable nearby which housed their horses, expecting a hue and cry to break out at any moment, but the town slept on and they collected their mounts without incident. They would need all the time they could get if they were to return to Yoredale, pack up their families and leave the manor before Edmund Radcliffe returned.

§§§

Felix watched them go, then with the aid of his staff he made his way in the direction they had suggested. He thought briefly of the young woman he had seen so fleetingly at the house, but knew he could do nothing for her. His head and torso burned from the ill-treatment he had suffered and he only hoped that his sturdy legs would have strength enough to bear him as far as the chapel.

11

Ludlow Castle

Edmund was barely in control of himself as he rode to Ludlow castle, for he had just discovered the desertion of the Standlakes when the Queen's summons reached him. The castle walls were swathed in a low early morning mist rising up from the nearby river Teme. He dismounted at the gate and was led around the curtain wall to the north, where he found Queen Margaret pacing along the foot of the wall. He delivered a curt nod rather than the respectful bow she probably expected, but the look on her face almost froze his blood and her first words thrust all other thoughts from his mind.

"You did not carry out your task!" she said. "I warned you about the girl and still you let her live! And it cost me a dozen men just to find out she was still alive!"

He was shocked but said nothing whilst he rapidly replayed the events through in his mind: his strike at the girl had been swift; he had thought the blow was sure, but had she twisted when he stabbed her? He knew at once that he should have checked, but afterwards both women lay so still and silent that he had not investigated any further.

"Have you no answer?" she said. He could feel the cold anger from her eyes, but he thought then, not for the first time, how sensuous she looked and sounded, her heavy Anjou tones accentuating her sexuality.

"If I have failed you, your majesty, I beg your indulgence. I'll make amends: I will find the girl and kill her." He dropped down on his knees before her - it was a well-judged gesture.

"Get up," she told him, "I've already found her but now you must finish it. She is here in the town at the Friary of the Carmelites ... but Edmund, this cannot be a single death; there will need to be other ... casualties - it must seem just a tragic moment in the sack of the town."

Edmund nodded his understanding. "I need no instruction on the subject of killing, your majesty; it shall be done properly this time. You may safely assume she'll be dead by the end of the day."

"I have learned, Edmund, that there is nothing in all Christendom I can safely assume."

There's something else here besides her anger, he thought; she's actually worried about this.

"There is one more matter," she said. Her voice was softer now and he risked a smile.

"She may have something, an item belonging to me; search her carefully and bring me anything she has – anything, you understand?"

"Very well, as you please, your majesty," Edmund replied, intrigued; for she was certainly worried – but about what?

§§§

St. Thomas's Chapel

Ned and Bagot were awake early discussing what he should do now that the cause of York and the Nevilles had failed. Once the town returned to some semblance of normality, their safe haven would have to be abandoned and, if the Lancastrians remained in the town for long, escape would be all the more difficult.

"We're agreed then," Ned concluded, "we return north with all haste, try to free Emma and hope to trace Ellie. We raise the men of the estate against the Radcliffes, retake Elder Hall and try to hold onto it. Sounds simple enough, doesn't it?"

"It's all you can do now, lord; if you don't take the fight to Yoredale, you may as well give up all hope. In any case you're no safer here than there!"

A sharp banging on the chapel door seemed to give immediate substance to Bagot's words. The others awoke in alarm instinctively snatching up their weapons and moving away from the door.

"Steady," cautioned Bagot, edging to the side of the doorway, sword in hand.

"Holton, open it - slowly," said Ned.

Holton dragged open the heavy oak door, flooding the chapel with early morning sunlight. A tall shadow stood against the light, leaning on a quarterstaff.

"Who are you, and want do you want?" demanded Bagot.

The shadow's only response was to fall silently through the doorway as if some invisible prop had been removed. It was the nimble footed Holton who darted forward to catch his head and shoulders before he slammed into the stone flags. Bagot quickly kicked the prostrate stranger's legs out of the way and banged the door shut.

"He's black," said Will, staring at the man's face.

"I suppose you've never seen a black man," said Bagot, "he looks like a Moor."

"Probably some pilgrim trying to visit the Chapel; he looks well-travelled," said Ned.

"Travelled? By St Stephen, I don't think so," said Bagot, "well trampled, more like! He's been beaten out of his senses by the look of him."

They lifted the stranger up and sat him down on the stone floor, leaning his back against the wall.

"Dear God, but he's taken some blows!" exclaimed Will, studying him more closely. "His face is one great bruise."

"By the look of his staff, he's more than capable of giving a few blows himself," replied Bagot, tapping an iron cap.

"He doesn't look as if he's from Ludlow," observed Will.

"How would you know? You've only been here a few days!" scoffed Bagot.

"He's coming round," said Mags.

"Who in God's name are you?" demanded Bagot.

The stranger looked up at them. "I am Felix of Bordeaux," he said, his voice husky.

"And who in St Michael's name is Felix of Bordeaux?" retorted Bagot.

"I'm sorry; I was told you might help by... a friend."

Bagot nodded. "Ah, Jack…"

"We've a common foe, I think."

"Jack shouldn't have told you where we were," said Ned, "but, for all that, you're welcome to share our simple refuge – though it's not exactly ours, of course. It belongs to St Thomas the Martyr but, by the look of you, it should suit you very well!"

"Let him get some rest," chided Mags, "he surely needs it!"

Bagot drew Ned to one side. "It's time we got moving," he said quietly.

"Yes, but I'm going to the Friary first; you see if you can find some horses and I'll meet you at the north gate."

"Don't forget, lord: Edmund Radcliffe is close by and still looking for you. Be careful, and don't … get distracted."

Ned smiled almost apologetically. "I feel responsible for her Bagot, that's all. I'm just going to make sure she's safe."

"Ha! You'd better make all speed then for you can't talk of her without a grin splitting your face in two!"

"Ox shit, Bagot, you talk nothing but ox shit. Will and Mags will be with me, you just try to find some horses!"

"Try? I'll find some horses – don't you worry about that!"

The short walk to the Friary provided ample evidence that the town was slowly recovering: in the market square a few traders were once again displaying a few wares for sale; elsewhere some shops with a solar above had started to remove their shutters and welcome in the local populace. By the time they arrived at the Friary, Ned was feeling much more optimistic, but his hopes were swiftly deflated when they reached the main gate. The royal guards were no longer outside and instead a noisy crowd was busily engaged in pillaging the Friary.

"Get Bagot and the others!" Ned shouted to Mags and pushed his way into the midst of the throng, shoving aside enough men to gain entry through the main door. Once inside he hastened to the infirmary, but there was no sign of Amelie. He seized a passing looter by the shoulder and threw him unceremoniously against the infirmary doorpost.

"What's happened to the inmates here?"

"I don't answer to you," the man replied, his head bloodied from the blow.

Will swiftly drew his swords and laid them across his throat. "You won't answer to anyone ever again if you don't speak with some respect now," he said softly.

"What's happening here?" demanded Ned.

Their captive smiled, showing no fear. "In truth sir, I know not; but I'm going to profit from it. Rumour was: there were things we could just …take – that no-one would try and stop us."

"Nonsense, the inmates have done nothing to warrant it; they even had the King's protection yesterday!"

"Well they don't have it today. It's said they've been helping traitors. Now, either kill me or let me go – the others'll soon have cleared the place out."

Ned nodded to Will, who carefully removed the blades from his neck; their captive grinned and made to move off, at which point Ned struck him hard on the side of his head with his gloved fist.

Will glanced at his friend in surprise.

"I didn't like him much," Ned muttered by way of explanation.

"You must be keen to find her," laughed Will.

Ned refrained from comment, but drew his sword and stepped out of the infirmary and into the open hall where he found Prior Thomas pacing ineffectually as the other friars tried half-heartedly to discourage the intruders from helping themselves. Ned beat away several looters with the flat of his sword and the rest scattered.

"I don't understand," the Prior said, "where are the King's guards? The Queen herself promised us her protection. We'll be ruined!"

He looked to Ned for an explanation, but Ned's mind was elsewhere. "Amelie, where is she?"

"Amelie?"

"Where is she?" repeated Ned.

"Fear not, sir; she's just walking in the cloister – she's much recovered."

Ned sheathed his sword and went into the cloister, which backed onto the south side of the hall. Amelie sat on a narrow stone seat set into the exterior wall; he paused and turned sheepishly to Will.

"Alright, I'll help out the friars," said his friend with a grin, "but don't be too long."

Ned sat down beside the slight girl, whose thin white gown was almost translucent in the morning light. She still looked pale, but seemed somehow stronger, more confident.

"You must be cold," he said, for the October air was cool.

"Yes," she replied brightly, "I am very cold, but I am alive – and it is so good to feel alive."

She had only to speak a word and her soft French tones enchanted him; once more he was lost in her deep brown eyes, but he forced himself to turn away and break the spell.

"How did you find me?" she asked.

"Do you remember the church?"

A single tear traced a glistening path down her cheek.

"Is my mistress dead?" she asked.

Ned nodded and her shoulders slumped.

"I thought she must be."

"Did you see her killer – the one who attacked you?"

She shook her head, brushing away more stinging tears. "Everyone loved her – even the Queen."

Ned frowned. "But someone didn't love her and they tried to kill you too."

"Am I safe now?"

"I'm not sure; do you think you're well enough to travel?"

"I would stay here with the friars as long as they'll have me. They are very kind to me; I think I would be safe here." Ned rose and left her side. "I'm not so sure," he said and took his leave.

He found Will losing an argument with two brawny young men armed with heavy pots and utensils they had stolen from the friars' kitchen. Ned weighed in, seizing a large iron ladle from one of the pots and cracking both men about the head with it.

"Get out!" he said.

They dropped their weighty acquisitions and ran off in search of easier pickings. Slowly and methodically, Will and Ned walked from cell to cell and evicted the remainder of the thieves. Finally they stood outside the main Friary gateway, in what they hoped was a suitably intimidating pose.

"Those fellows were stealing cooking pots," said Will.

"Mm. A cook pot is worth a lot to some; more interesting though is: why now? Why not days ago when the whole town was in uproar and ransacking the friary would have passed unnoticed?"

"Well clearly because the royal guards are no longer here?"

"Yes, but why, Will? Why aren't they here?"

"I see what you mean."

Ned's attention was drawn to a dozen or so men at arms riding down the street towards them. The small knot of heavily armed men came to a halt almost opposite the Friary entrance and stared briefly in their direction before continuing on a few more yards to the Lower Bar, which marked the northern edge of the town. They dismounted outside a row of rough built cottages with small square shuttered openings along their frontages. Some paced nervously in the street, whilst others leaned awkwardly against the cottage walls.

"They don't seem to be doing anything," observed Will.

"They are doing something: they're waiting and watching us; and before you ask, no, I don't know why."

"You don't think one of them might be Radcliffe?"

"He could be there; I haven't seen him since we were boys, so I've no idea what he looks like – dark, I think."

"But what if he's here?" persisted Will.

Ned studied the group again; they seemed to be led by a tall knight with long black hair and an unkempt beard; he was well harnessed, but could he be Edmund? He shook his head.

"None of them bear themselves as he would, a nobleman; I doubt he's there."

"Well, that's a relief," said Will.

§§§

Mordeur stared at the pair of youths across the street at the Friary door. They looked green, but first appearances were not always accurate; would they put up a fight – if it came to it? Nearby, his own men were fretful and uncertain – he recognised the signs and didn't like it. He cared little for the motley collection of misfits that accompanied him, but he cared a great deal for himself and nervous soldiers made mistakes. Edmund was treading a reckless path on this private errand of his – whatever it was.

Eventually, he was relieved to see Edmund appear at the upper gate at the top end of the street; but he also saw that he was being shadowed by several other horsemen and there was something irritatingly familiar about one of them. When Edmund stopped and dismounted to speak to him, the other rider also dismounted to converse with the two youths at the Friary gate.

"Lord, I was concerned: where have you been?" Mordeur asked.

"Don't question me, Mordeur; I'll do as I please and if you don't like it you can go back to my father and tell him so - but he won't thank you for it!"

Mordeur smiled tightly and inclined his head in deference.

Edmund looked towards the Friary. "Who are they?" He demanded.

"I've no idea, lord; perhaps if I knew what we were doing here, I could be of more help."

"Well, my Norman friend, I want to walk into that Friary, I want to kill a few of its inmates and then I want to walk out again; and I don't want those fellows there when I do it."

"Then we should wait for them to leave: waiting is easier than fighting," said Mordeur.

"Wait? I'm not waiting! Just make sure you're ready to back me," he said and strode towards the Friary gate.

12

The Friary of the Carmelites, Ludlow

"So, what you're saying," said Bagot, "is that you don't know who these men are or what they want, but you don't want to let them have it without a fight?"

"It doesn't sound quite so reasonable put that way," admitted Ned.

"Well, that's because there's no reason to it at all! Did you notice the tall knight who rode before us?"

"No, should I?"

"You should, because it's Edmund Radcliffe! Now he's standing across the street and you're in a lot more trouble than you thought!"

"He killed Tom ..."

"Now isn't the time for that!" snapped Bagot.

"Do you think he knows me? I haven't seen him in years - we didn't spend much time with the Radcliffes..."

"Probably just as well," said Bagot.

"If he doesn't know who I am, then what's he doing here? He must surely have recognised me; otherwise why's he at the Friary?"

"Well I doubt he's come to pray! But if he knew who you were, we'd be trading blows by now; he must have another reason for being here."

Ned looked at the others. "So, what then? What does this Friary have that it didn't have before we came?"

No-one replied, though they all knew the answer.

He sighed. "Amelie," he breathed softly.

Bagot shook his head. "Hold hard - we're making foolish leaps here; how can he know of her?"

"Oh, shit!" said Will, who had glanced down the street; Edmund Radcliffe was walking briskly towards them.

"Be on your mettle!" growled Bagot.

Ned moved swiftly to block Edmund's path to the Friary gate.

"Be careful Ned," murmured Bagot.

"God give you good day, sir," said Edmund, "I'd be obliged if you'd let me pass, I have business at the Friary."

Ned stood his ground. "Good day to you, sir. I would know your business at the Friary."

On the other side of the street the men at arms, one by one, edged a few yards closer. Bagot saw the movement and placed a firm hand upon his sword hilt.

"Surely you would not ask me to discuss my privy business here in the street?" Edmund replied smoothly, "my affairs are for the ears of the Prior alone."

Ned gestured for Mags and Birches to step inside the Friary door and Holton edged across to block the entrance with his considerable bulk. Bagot drew Ned to one side, leaving Holton filling the door way.

"This is putting all at risk, lord; let him see the Prior, you can go with him and make sure nothing is amiss. If he stands here much longer, he's sure to work out who you are and, believe me, we'll be up to our balls in blood."

Ned reluctantly waved Holton to one side. Perhaps, it was for the best, he thought, at least for now; but there would be a reckoning with Edmund before long.

"I regret that we've delayed you, sir," he said tightly, "but this morning we found the Friary being looted and were concerned for the inmates."

"Your concern does you credit, sir, but I intend no harm to the inmates."

"Then I'll take you to Prior Thomas myself."

"I'm sure it need not take up your time; I simply wish to ask him about a young girl."

Ned stopped mid stride and turned slowly towards Edmund. "What girl?" he asked quietly.

Birches stood beside Holton and set an arrow in his bow.

Ned was rooted to the threshold. "What girl?" he repeated.

For the first time, Edmund seemed to hesitate. "She's ... a ward of my father," he declared.

"She's of gentle birth then?"

"Yes, of course."

"Then you have no business here, for there's no such lady in the Friary. Good day to you, sir."

Ned could almost taste the tension as they stared each other down. Then Edmund looked to each of the others in turn, surprise registering on his face as he noticed Felix for the first time. Then he nodded and Ned knew that Edmund had put some of the pieces together.

"Ned Elder ..." Edmund seemed almost to choke on the words. "I need to speak to that girl and you'll bring her out to me or I'll rip her out of there myself and finish you at the same time!" He turned his back and crossed the street to join his waiting men at arms.

"You may as well leave now then!" Ned shouted after him.

"That'll help," said Will.

"Lord, I beg you be careful; there's all at stake here!" said Bagot.

Ned surveyed the gatehouse: it was stone built, but its gates did not look too sturdy. The oak panels were surprisingly thin – if they had to defend the Friary, it would not be easy.

"Holton, take the horses to the court at the rear," he ordered and then he waved the rest of them inside, slamming the gates shut behind them.

He turned to Bagot. "I'm not discussing it. This is Edmund Radcliffe! He killed Tom! I wouldn't hand my worst dog over to him!"

"But now we are trapped in here!" said Bagot.

At that moment, there was an almighty blow to the gate.

"Someone's found an axe," said Will.

"Keep the horses saddled, Holton," called Bagot.

Ned was in no mood for compromise. "Will, at my signal throw open the door; Birches, if there's an armed man in front of it, shoot him down; Bagot, be ready to take the fight to them – Felix, are you up to standing with us?"

"No, but I am ready to try," declared the Frenchman, changing his grip on the staff he was leaning on. There was another blow on the door and a shard of timber spun across the cobbles towards them; they drew their swords in readiness.

Ned nodded to Will, who pulled open the door to reveal a burly man in mid strike with his axe. Before Birches could release an arrow at him, the momentum of his swing carried him through the open doorway and across the threshold, where his axe embedded itself in the opened gate. The quick thinking Bagot knocked him down with a sharp tap on the back of the neck with his sword hilt.

The rest of Edmund's men sprang back from the gateway and retreated back down the street, seeing Birches with a flight notched to his bowstring.

"Birches, get up the steps and keep a close watch!" said Bagot. He wrenched the axe from the gate and shut it once more.

Amelie and Prior Thomas appeared in the doorway to the Hall; Thomas looked distastefully at his splintered gate. "I shall lead the friars in prayer," he said, "we've already had quite enough violence in God's house today."

Ned stalked into the Hall with Bagot. "What are our chances?" he asked the older man.

Bagot shook his head. "Whatever we do we're in the shit: if we run with the girl, they'll catch us, kill us and take her; if we stand and fight here, they'll kill us and take her; and, even if we give them the damned girl ... well, he knows who you are now and he'll not have forgotten his brother, so he'll kill us anyway."

"I've not forgotten my brother either!" said Ned.

"What about the girl?"

"I told you: I won't leave her."

"That's all well, but she can't ride far - the journey will kill her!"

"We've come this far with her, Bagot."

"Well let's hope then that her prayers will carry some weight with Our Lord."

There was a shout from Birches on the parapet above the gate. "They're moving! Oh, shit!"

"What?" asked Bagot.

"They've got a crossbow! And another axe!"

"Holton, watch the gate. There must be another way out of here," said Ned, "those gates won't last long."

"There's a postern gate…" It was one of the novices, Friar Michael, who spoke quietly.

"Go on," encouraged Ned.

"Well, it leads out on to Linney."

"Linney?"

"The wet meadows - you could go down through the wet meadows to the river Corve."

Bagot's interest was immediately aroused. "Is there a boat down there?"

"A small one – it'd only hold a couple of you."

"Surely, Radcliffe will have the rear gate watched," said Ned.

"I'm not so sure; he probably expected less trouble," said Bagot.

"With a boat, we could get Amelie away."

"Where to?" asked Bagot. "Where would she go in this boat?"

Ned bowed his head disconsolately. "You're right."

"No, wait Ned, perhaps I'm not. I'd forgotten but, as I recollect, some of your father's estates were here in the Marches; Corve Manor, I think, is just about within our reach - with God's help."

"I've never heard of it."

Bagot shrugged his shoulders. "It's a small manor - I only

went there twice myself, and many years ago it was. For all I know it's in ruins, but it's a lot closer than Yoredale!"

"They're breaking through!" Holton shouted.

Ned smiled at Bagot. "I'm obliged to you once more; we'll make for this lost manor then – and hope it's well defended."

"My lord," said Michael softly, "I'd willingly row Lady Amelie up the river."

"She's not a lady," said Bagot.

"The task would be dangerous, Michael," said Ned, "you don't need to do it."

The young novice beamed at them. "I was born in the Corve valley, so the Lord has already marked me out for this task. I'm content to do it."

"Don't argue long about it," growled Bagot.

"Very well, Michael, I'll take her to the boat for you. Mags can go with her. Bagot, get the rest mounted and ready to go."

But Amelie was a less than willing passenger. Her fists were clenched and her slight frame was as tight as a bowstring.

"I am not going out in a boat! Who are you to send me off like this? Why must I go? I'll be safer with the friars."

When she's angry she's even more beautiful, thought Ned. "Listen to me, please," he said, taking her hand; it was cold and thin, but she didn't pull it away. "Someone outside these walls wants you – and by God he's no friend to you or me; soon he'll be in here… and in here I can't protect you from him. I know this journey will be hard for you – you're still not strong, but it's your best hope. I can't leave you here; I won't leave you here."

She didn't say another word, but nodded.

"Come on then," he said and lifted her into his arms.

The path down to the river through Linney, as the local folk called it, was slippery and the soft mud of the wetlands clutched at their boots as they squelched their way to a flimsy landing stage by the river. The Corve was not a deep river, but the heavy autumn rains had swollen it more than usual so that Michael declared that it was easily navigable. It was a cold day and though Amelie was wrapped in a thick woollen cloak provided by the friars, the chill air struck her like a poleaxe and she wheezed and choked in Ned's arms. He set her down alongside Mags on the jetty and she looked at him miserably.

"Off you go now," he said with a reassuring grin, "we'll see you both soon. Mags, you know what to do; stay out of sight along the river until you're sure you see us. God will keep you safe!"

Mags darted him a murderous look. "I've had more than enough of shitty rivers!" she said, but she clambered into the boat and helped Michael guide Amelie in. The small craft drifted slowly into the middle of the stream and Mags gave a dismissive wave of her hand as young Michael began with short, shallow strokes to take them upstream. Ned watched until they turned a bend in the river and hoped he was right.

When he returned to the Friary, all was in readiness at the gate.

"Birches, let's make a move!" he said.

The first of Birches' arrows lifted a man at arms clean off his feet and threw him back across the street. In reply the crossbowman released a bolt which ricocheted against the parapet and fell harmlessly into the courtyard beyond. Ned knew that Birches could fire several arrows whilst the crossbow was being reloaded.

"Make it count!" he said. The second arrow took the crossbowman in the shoulder.

"That'll do!" Ned said, "let's go!" Birches leapt down onto his horse, Holton pulled open the shattered gates and Ned rode through, his horse thrusting aside the owner of the axe. Bagot and the rest followed, launching themselves at Edmund's men at arms who scattered before the horsemen. Ned led them down the street towards the Lower Bar, where all the Radcliffe horses were tethered. Edmund's men could only watch whilst Ned and his comrades stole their mounts away and then wheeled past the Lower Bar and onto the north road out of the town.

All of them were gone save one, for Felix remained. Wielding his heavy staff with alacrity and venom, he cantered back up the street, pounding man after man to the ground with a succession of swift blows. Edmund was seething, but could not get close to Felix so instead he slipped through the Friary gate with the remainder of his men. In his haste to get inside, Edmund abandoned his injured men.

Outside, Felix led his horse, a fine bay mare, down the street to tether her once more at the Lower Bar. Then he sank down on a low stone wall nearby, suddenly overcome by weariness; he pulled his cloak around him and settled down to wait. He had enjoyed himself for a moment and, with a little respite, he might yet win his new friends some more time.

§§§

Michael continued to work the small craft steadily upstream, though he found it hard labour. He toiled without a break until he reached the point where the river narrowed to a gentler stream. All the while the two young women remained huddled together on the rough oak board in the stern of the boat, in a vain effort to keep out the cold.

"Won't be long now," he said breathlessly, "for I can't get you much further upstream."

"You've risked enough to help us," said Mags.

Michael grinned sheepishly. "Truth is, I needed to escape for a while; I love Prior Thomas as a father, but he can be a little too much sometimes. This snap of cold air is doing me a lot of good."

"How much longer will you be a novice?"

"Three more days!" he replied with a wide grin, for his heart sang at the thought of formally joining his brother friars in their work.

Mags smiled with him, but the moment was brief for the keel of the boat scraped alarmingly on the river bed and he began searching for a place to set them ashore. The bow juddered as it grounded on the stony bottom and they came to an abrupt halt. Michael steadied the boat for Mags to step out into the shallow river bed.

"Let me help you," he offered, making to get out of the boat.

"No!" said Mags. "Your boots'll make great holes! We can manage - but thank you."

She helped Amelie out of the boat and put her arm around her as they walked to the bank.

Michael hesitated. "You'll be alright?" he enquired, sure that they wouldn't.

"You'd better go," said Mags with a smile, "they'll be searching for us."

Still he was loath to leave the pair, seeing them standing on the bank; they seemed so vulnerable.

"Go on," Mags urged, "or you'll not get back before dark – go, Michael!"

Reluctantly, he pushed off the gravel bed with one of the oars and swung the boat slowly around to face downstream.

"God be with you both!" he called as he set off. He would be relieved to get back, but he thanked God for his blessings, for he expected to remember this daring escapade on the Corve for many years to come.

§§§

For no reason she could quite fathom, Michael's departure made Mags weep for the first time since she had watched her father die in France. She felt very alone, set down in the barren and wintry river course. She tried to recall Bagot's final instructions: he had been most specific that they should leave no trace when they disembarked – no careless footprint in the muddy margins of the stream. But the bitter cold had turned Amelie into a shivering mess and Mags strained with the effort of helping her out of the water. She surveyed the bank where they had trodden; she had been careful to step up onto the grass, but there was an imprint of Amelie's boot in the sandy mud. She rubbed it over with her freezing palm; that would have to do.

She gave Amelie a gentle shake. "Come on, we must make haste and get out of sight!"

It would be dreadful waiting near the river. "Fuck you, Ned Elder," she said aloud.

She stumbled with Amelie towards the meagre shelter of a stand of young alders; not a leaf remained on their slim dark branches, yet they might just hide them from view. To add to their discomfort, the weather was deteriorating: the dry cold of the past few days giving way to a debilitating drizzle of icy sleet.

She examined Amelie's wound: it had opened up a little and blood was seeping through the bloodwort poultice so carefully applied by the friars. Her face was grey with cold and pain; she sat at the foot of the trees and drifted into sleep. This is no good, thought Mags, for sleep is not our friend.

"Amelie?" she said softly. Her companion stirred without opening her eyes. Mags talked gently to her trying to keep her conscious but to little avail; indeed, within only a few minutes she was having trouble keeping her own eyes open. She wrapped her cloak tightly around the pair of them, binding them together; then she sank back wearily against the tree trunk, as the sleet covered them with a soft wet blanket of ice.

"Well, live or die sister, this is where we wait."

§§§

The Carmelite Friary

Edmund all but tore the Friary apart before he accepted that the friars had told him the truth: the girl was no longer there. Nevertheless, he stalked about angrily venting his frustration on any of the inmates who ventured near him. Mordeur drew him out into the cloisters away from the others.

"What?!" said Edmund, exasperated by the further delay.

Mordeur stood close. "Tell me what is so important about this girl, that we must waste our time looking for her, lord?"

Edmund, temper barely under control, seized Mordeur by the shoulder and spat out a response:

"The queen has charged me with finding and killing this girl and if I, and thus you, want to continue to enjoy the fruits of the Queen's favour, then I suggest that we find and kill the girl with all possible speed!"

He relaxed his grip on the Frenchman, who took a half pace backwards.

"Well, now that you've explained it to me so ... clearly, I will search more thoroughly."

He strode across to Prior Thomas who was kneeling in prayer before the altar rail; he grabbed the old man roughly by the neck, lifting him off his feet. The other friars cried out in alarm.

"Tell us where the maid has gone or I shall rip out your miserable little heart!" he bellowed.

Gripping the cleric in one hand he drew out his dagger with the other. Prior Thomas began to entreat his captor: "God will punish you for your cowardly actions here -"

Mordeur did not hesitate for a second: "I'll worry about God when I meet him," he replied and in one savage movement he carved his dagger up through the Friar's stomach and chest and dropped the twitching body onto the altar rail spattering the flag stones with his blood and entrails. Even Edmund was momentarily taken aback; but impressed that he had provided Mordeur with a sufficiently persuasive motive.

"Who then will follow his holy brother to meet God?" Mordeur asked the remaining friars, "for we will know the answer today, or all of you will leave your blood on these steps!"

They looked at each other in shock and despair, and almost as one they cried: "the river!" and proceeded to pour out any other knowledge they possessed.

Edmund nodded in satisfaction. "Come, we can easily overtake them," he said.

"Aren't you forgetting something?" asked Mordeur.

"What!" Edmund said.

"Horses?" suggested Mordeur.

Edmund shook his head in frustration, but he led Mordeur and the others out of the Friary gates at a run, only to come to an immediate dead stop as he saw that the two wounded men at arms he had abandoned outside were sitting slumped against the gatepost. He started to walk down towards the Lower Bar, where he saw several of their horses wandering past the cottages; but then a dark cloaked figure rode deliberately out into the middle of the street.

At once Edmund understood. "Tiresome, tiresome; come on then!" he shouted, urging his men to arms, "remove that oaf from the road! And find my horses – or any horses! There's some haste needed here!"

§§§

Felix was ready for them and worked his heavy staff enthusiastically as Mordeur and several others came at him warily. He feinted to swing at Mordeur's head but instead, as the latter stepped back, with a rapid change of grip punched the iron tip of his staff at one of the other approaching men at arms. The staff crunched into his cheekbone, fracturing it and producing a screech of pain. Mordeur moved to close on Felix, but was compelled to retreat as the staff whirled within an inch of his head and thereafter he maintained a more respectful distance. Nevertheless, whilst Felix could hold several at bay, he could not prevent others slipping by to find their mounts. This they eventually did and he was forced to give ground. As soon as Edmund and some of his men found mounts, Felix admitted defeat and rode back into the town; Edmund was already thundering along the north road.

Well, Ned, thought Felix, I have gained you a few minutes more; pray God you make good use of them. He rode under the portcullis of the Corve Gate with a further onset of exhaustion; he had nowhere to lodge and the town was eerily quiet behind shuttered or boarded up windows. He knew there would be little welcome for strangers from folk who were only now licking their wounds from the pounding they had suffered at the hands of the King's army. His only option was to try the house on Broad Street which Edmund had just vacated and which he hoped would still be empty.

He paused at the house and dismounted as sleet swirled around him; a few well-cloaked locals hurried down the street away from him. The door was still in pieces so he stepped across the threshold and surveyed the carnage, staring for a moment at the wall where he had been bound. With a darkening sky the interior of the house was dim, so he thought it prudent this time to carry out a more thorough search. The house had three floors and a cellar, so it took him a while but he found no-one; then, when he passed back through the doorway to the ground floor, he was met by a young woman.

There were several striking things about her. Her clothes were in tatters and loosely drawn around her body, revealing more than a glimpse of her ample breasts. Her face was bruised, her mouth badly cut but by far the most interesting feature was the blade that she thrust out at his neck. For a moment each studied the other anxiously, assessing the risk they posed.

Then Felix smiled. "Lady," he said softly, "you have a very powerful scream; forgive me for not coming to your aid earlier."

The knife remained motionless at his throat.

13

The Corve Valley, near Ludlow

Edmund's men had trailed miserably through the freezing rain, following the river Corve into the low hills where it became shallower. They had found no trace of the fugitives and they were cold, wet and mutinous; even Edmund, fuelled by anger and frustration, was close to abandoning the search when Friar Michael's boat drifted into sight through the gusting sleet.

"At last! Come on - get him to the bank!" shouted Edmund.

At once one of his knights ploughed his horse into the stream to intercept the oncoming boat and hold the friar at the point of his lance. But as he lunged towards the cleric, the boat, carried by the downstream current, suddenly swung towards him and the sharp iron point of his lance buried itself into the friar's midriff. There was a brief look of astonishment from the friar as he was lifted clean off the boat. He fell into the water, but managed to work the lance free and claw his way to the bank. There he tried to stand but dropped to the ground, blood colouring his wet habit.

Edmund looked on in disbelief as several of his men at arms retrieved the friar. In his right hand he gripped his bloody scapular tightly, choking on blood as he tried to pray aloud. Edmund ripped the piece of brown cloth from him and tossed it into the stream.

"Where did you land her?" he snarled, punching the friar's wound, which bled even more profusely. Michael tried to speak, but only blood came from his lips as he watched the torn scapular float away. Edmund dropped him on the edge of the river bed where he took a few more minutes to die, his blood and his dreams washed away with the current.

Edmund turned darkly upon the knight whose lance had killed him.

"What's the point of capturing him if he's dead? He was our best hope!"

"I'm sorry, lord; I sought only to bring him to the bank," said the knight, "A clumsy mistake – I shall ask God's forgiveness for taking the friar's life."

"You should be more concerned about my forgiveness! You want God's? Well, ask Him now then!"

In his fury he pulled out his dagger, plunged it into the man's throat and just as swiftly withdrew the blade to wipe it on the knight's body as it fell into the stream.

All except Mordeur stood open mouthed in shock, for several had known the dead man well, but they held their tongues when they saw the murderous look on Edmund's face.

"Ride on!" he ordered. "They can't be far - watch for where they've left the river; find that place and then we can hunt them down!"

They obeyed, but Edmund knew it was only through fear; they stared at the river banks, but they saw nothing. He was pinning all his hopes on Mordeur and the Frenchman did not disappoint him, spotting the tiny arc left by a small boot heel in the gravel.

"Here! Here, lord, is the start of our chase," he shouted in triumph, picking up tracks beyond the river bank and increasing his pace.

For a time Edmund began to hope, but it was late in the day and heavier clouds were rolling in from the north east. Before they could overtake their quarry, darkness fell upon them like a thick black cloak.

Mordeur pulled up. "My lord, we cannot track them further in this light but tomorrow, we will find them."

Edmund thought about arguing, but conceded that Mordeur was right.

"I need this girl, Mordeur; she's got the Queen worried and I want to know why."

"You want her more than Ned Elder?"

"I want them both."

"Well, tomorrow you shall have them!"

§§§

Further up the Corve Valley

Ned saw them first, huddled together under the trees; when he knelt beside them, he thought they were dead, for Amelie looked as pale as she had at Mucklestone. He touched the back of his hand against her cheek: it was like ice. He glanced at Mags: she looked exhausted. He shook her gently, but she only groaned in response.

"Come on lass, wake up!" said Bagot, prodding her shoulder.

"Be careful!" said Holton, elbowing Bagot aside and gently prising Mags' protective arm from around Amelie. He massaged her shoulders to warm her while Ned tried to revive Amelie.

Mags shuddered awake to find herself in Holton's arms; she smiled up at him, drinking in the warmth of his embrace.

"We mustn't tarry, lord!" insisted Bagot.

Ned ignored him, folding Amelie's hands in his own to warm them. Will helped him to lift her up.

"Her wound's come open," Mags said, her voice hoarse and tired, "she's not fit to ride!"

"God's blood!" nagged Bagot, "come on! They'll not be far behind."

They set off into the shallow water with Ned cradling Amelie on his lap as he rode at barely walking pace, though Bagot was straining at the leash. As they toiled up the narrowing stream in the fading light, sleet laden winds drove relentlessly into their faces. When they left the stony river bed behind them, Holton and Birches scanned their route meticulously on foot, carefully replacing any stones dislodged by hooves. But with every step the sky darkened further and the temperature dropped. At length Bagot stopped and Ned drew alongside.

"It's getting heavier, Bagot – how far now?"

"We must be very close, lord."

"Must be? Are you lost?"

"God's blood, of course I'm not lost! But it was a long time ago; I hoped there might be a light, a torch giving some helpful glow from the ramparts."

"We can't sit around in this weather – if not Corve, then somewhere!"

"Have faith, Ned." Bagot put an arm on his shoulder and then he nudged his horse forward again, brushing aside the sleet which had settled thickly on his head and chest.

It was all but dark when they reached Corve Manor, a mere shadow against the sky. If they hadn't found the track that led to the gate, they would have missed the building altogether. There was a small stone gatehouse over a narrow moat; the short drawbridge was down, but there were two tall gates barring their passage. At once Bagot hailed the gatehouse, where a glimmer of light showed, but he was greeted only by silence.

"God's Cross!" he railed, "is there none at the gate? Is the house abandoned?!"

But the swirling wind dragged away his words, so he dismounted and strode across the broad beams of the bridge to hammer on the gate with the hilt of his sword.

"Have you all hanged yourselves?" he called out.

Ned was still awkwardly cradling Amelie and waited impatiently with the sleet settling upon them fast. Bagot stopped his pounding for a moment and listened for signs of life. The others were glancing anxiously around them for signs of pursuit, but saw none. After what seemed an age, a tall thin shadow of a man appeared on the gloomy rampart above the gatehouse. He raised up a torch and looked down upon them suspiciously – he seemed ill at ease, nervously switching his gaze from one to another of them.

"What do you want here?" he demanded.

"This is your new liege lord, Edward Elder," said Bagot, indicating Ned. "Make haste and get this bloody gate open before we all freeze to death!"

The custodian of the manor seemed unimpressed by this revelation. Bagot stared hard at the figure illuminated in the flickering torchlight, then he relaxed his stance.

"Stephen Betwill!" he announced with satisfaction.

"Do I know you?" the steward enquired.

"Well, I knew your sister rather better than I knew you!" said Bagot grinning.

Betwill peered again at the unkempt figure below.

"Bagot?" he breathed, "but surely you died ... in France."

Bagot's new bonhomie faded a little: "It seems not!" he retorted.

"Hurry up, man!" said Ned, "we're freezing out here!"

A few minutes later the gates were swung slowly open and the fugitives rode gratefully into the small courtyard within. As soon as they were safely inside, Bagot ensured that the gates were shut tight and barred and the drawbridge was raised. He began barking orders across the courtyard and Betwill descended to greet his unexpected visitors.

"This is your new lord, Edward Elder," said Bagot.

Betwill looked wide-eyed at Ned, who was still carrying Amelie; he gave a formal, if curt, nod of deference. Ned took an instant dislike to him: if the estate had been left in this man's hands he feared the worst.

"First, we've a girl who must be cared for," he ordered, as he transferred Amelie gently to the security of Holton's strong arms. Mags stepped forward and took Holton's arm. "Come on, we'll settle her in."

"Who's she to decide?" Betwill enquired crossly.

"Where can we put her?" asked Ned.

"Well, who is she? Is she your lady?"

"Where can we put her?" repeated Ned.

"You can put her in the lord's chamber in the north tower," said the steward, "since no-one sleeps there ... at present."

"When did Sir John last come here?" asked Ned.

"A long time ago... my lord, we've heard rumours about your father; but, if you are now lord, what has become of Sir Thomas? He came here just after harvest and took away most of our garrison. He swore to me he would return within two weeks, but he hasn't. As you'll see, we have few men left here."

"My brother Thomas and my father are ... in the same place," replied Ned, with little show of emotion. "It's a new order we find ourselves in, Master Betwill, and we must make what we can of it. I need to know that I can rely upon your loyalty."

Betwill shrugged his thin shoulders. "My loyalty alone won't suffice. This house is solid enough: we have high, strong walls, a useful moat and gatehouse, and a safe water supply; but we have so few to defend it that a few strong men with ladders could overwhelm us in no time."

"Surely, you overstate it," said Ned.

"Well lord, there are three men capable of bearing arms and one of those has seen too many years' service; that's all!"

Ned saw Bagot give the steward a warning look, but he knew that Betwill was probably all too accurate in his assessment and he also knew that Edmund wouldn't give up easily.

Nevertheless, he left them to their dark mutterings and went in search of Amelie. He found her installed in the north tower on a simple mattress of straw, lying as still and grey as a stone effigy. Mags sat slumped on the wooden floor with her head resting against the wall near the fireplace, which glowed with a little welcome warmth. The floorboards creaked noisily as Ned crept towards the bed. Mags stirred and sat up.

"How is she?" he asked.

Mags shook her head: "I think you can see well enough,

lord."

"I'll sit with her for a while," he murmured.

Mags padded out of the room to curl up alongside Holton in the small anteroom outside and Ned sat down on the edge of the bed, studying the girl's ashen face. It was a chill reminder of how she had looked the first time he had seen her in the half light of the church; surely, he thought, she would not last the night. The floorboards creaked once more and Will came to his side and placed a hand lightly on his shoulder.

"How fares she?"

"Slowly leaving us, Will. I should've left her in that church and she would've been spared all this – and so would I. I've lost two sisters, dearer to me than anyone and here I am watching over a complete stranger - and much good it's doing either of us!"

"Well, I suppose as things are you can't do much for Ellie or Emma."

"No, but I've made up my mind. Tomorrow I'm leaving for the north. I'll stay here tonight and say my prayers for Amelie, but tomorrow I'm going."

"And I'll be riding with you," said Will, clapping him on the back. He left soon after and Ned knelt beside the low mattress, stroking Amelie's black hair, so coarse and matted after the journey. He stayed with her and kept the fire burning deep into the night, until Mags awoke and came in.

"Despite the fire, she still feels cold," he said.

Mags said nothing, but lay down beside Amelie and rested her head gently against hers, covering them both with her dirty woollen cloak. Ned put another log on the fire and left them.

§§§

When he awoke, it was almost dawn and it felt much colder; he should have stayed in the chamber with the fire, he thought ruefully. Leaving Will asleep on the ground, he descended the steps to the Hall where it was rather warmer, for there was a well stoked fire in the hearth despite the early hour. The floor of the hall was carpeted with sleeping bodies and he thought idly that there seemed to be more than there had been the previous night.

He felt more at ease, having taken the decision to return to Elder Hall. He walked to the great oak door, pulled it open and stood stone still in disbelief: for outside there was a wall of white that reached halfway up the door frame and light flurries of snow drifted carelessly into the Hall. He remained in the doorway, oblivious to the snow settling upon him. His disappointment was almost tangible: he would not be travelling north for many days now. A small log interrupted his thoughts as it hurtled past his head and bounced off the half open door outside onto the snow. The object was accompanied by several shouts, some less polite than others. He slammed it shut and pressed his forehead against the unforgiving timber.

"Sometimes you just can't do what your heart wills you to," said Bagot, sitting unobtrusively on a small bench beside the door. Ned turned and leaned his back against the door without showing any sign of having heard him, but the older man continued quietly. "It wouldn't have been a good idea to go. It's too soon."

Ned saw that many of the estate workers had begun to stir: they were almost all women and children forced in from the outlying cottages by the weather. Their men had not yet returned from service with his brother Tom and he knew they never would.

"Come lord, there are too many ears here," said Bagot.

They went into a small chamber off the Hall on the ground floor of the north tower.

"You should be pleased to see the snow, lord; the weather has been your friend again. Our tracks will be well covered and Radcliffe won't be worrying about us, but about saving his own wretched hide. So, you have some time to plan; to consider."

"And what of my sisters?"

"God's blood! You've a duty to others as well as your sisters. They'll be safe enough – why would Radcliffe harm them? And a wealthy marriage won't hurt them!"

He paused for a moment and then continued: "Even so, this business with the girl has a strange smell to it."

"Well, it's beyond me: I killed his brother, he's hunting me down and yet when he had me at his mercy, he was more concerned to find Amelie?"

"Indeed, Ned. Why does a servant hold such interest for him?"

"Well there must be some connection with the Queen! Lady Sainte was close to the Queen and she was meeting with Sir Roger, who was York's man - perhaps the Queen knew about it."

"But even if the murder was somehow the Queen's doing - and that is surely hard to believe – why would she, or anyone else, pursue the serving girl?"

"Prior Thomas told me that when the Queen saw Amelie, it was as if she knew her and she looked shocked to see her. Then she posted royal guards at the gate and a day later they're no longer there."

Bagot shook his head. "Even if we believe all that, I can't see how Radcliffe could even know the girl would be in Ludlow – never mind exactly where."

"But still we come back to it: what is she to him?" asked Ned.

"We need to find out what the connection is – unless of course … she dies."

§§§

When evening arrived, it brought with it a driving northerly wind and fresh, heavy falls of snow. Ned listened to the whine of the wind as he sat in the north tower chamber watching over his frail charge. His father had probably slept in the room more than once and the heavy wall coverings reminded him of those at Elder Hall – the thought gave him some small comfort, some distant connection with his father.

Mags had reheated some thin potage concocted by Betwill's ancient mother and she was dribbling a little of the warm, flavourless liquid into Amelie's mouth. Ned left her to it, but at first light the following morning he returned and found Mags again coaxing Amelie to take more potage.

"Have you been doing that all night?" he said with a grin.

Mags shook her head and gave him a rare smile. "She's still weak, but she's better than she was – I think she's going to be alright."

"Good, that's good," he said.

He visited her each day and saw a rapid recovery as she regained her strength. He knew he should talk to her about Edmund, but kept putting it off. Then after a few more days, he decided she was well enough to talk and he could wait no longer.

"Mags," he said, "give us a few minutes on our own." Mags gave a disapproving look, and stumped out.

Amelie sat bolt upright on the mattress, not sure what Ned intended.

"We should speak of what happened at the church," he began.

Amelie looked surprised, but nodded solemnly. "If you think we must…"

"There's a mystery here and for your safety, I must know what lies behind it."

"Very well; ask me and I'll try to answer." Her voice was trembling and he could see at once that she was nervous and that was before he'd asked her anything at all. It did not bode well.

"How did you come to be at the church?" he asked.

"My mistress, Lady Sainte went there," she replied simply.

"And do you know why she went there?"

"I think my Lady went there to meet a friend." Her top lip quivered, as she said the words.

Ned glimpsed the tear before she brushed it away; he wanted to reach out and take her hand but he didn't.

"Her lover?" he prompted.

"Why do you say that?" she asked, tiny flames sparking in her pale cheeks.

"Because I know Sir Roger of Wakefield was her lover."

She sat silent, tight lipped; he had touched a nerve somehow and he knew it. He knew he was probing into matters she didn't want to discuss with him, but he tried again.

"You went up to the top of the tower?" he asked.

"Yes, my lady went up the tower steps and I carried the torch for her."

"The man that killed her, and so nearly killed you, made a mistake: he let you live. I think that man might be the one who pursued us at the friary: Edmund Radcliffe; but you're the only one who can tell me. Did you see him?"

Amelie lay back on the mattress and wept. "It was dark! I remember being hurt, dropping the torch, and then falling; and the next thing I see is the old Friar standing over me. That is all I know; I saw no-one."

He took a different tack, hoping to calm her a little.

"You lived at court; how well does the Queen know you?"

"I was not often in her chambers. I am – was – Lady Sainte's servant, not her majesty's."

"If she saw you, would she know you?"

"I don't know…"

He was getting nowhere: either she knew nothing or she was saying nothing.

"Why do you question me so?" she demanded suddenly, "all that matters to me is that she was killed! The rest I don't care about at all. If I die, I die. Why should you mourn? You don't know me!"

"No, I don't," he said, shocked by her anger.

She turned away from him and he left without another word.

14

North Wales, September 1459

The nunnery's bleak, grey profile, barely discernible against the slate sky, did nothing to lift Eleanor's spirits. The journey from Yoredale had been wretched enough, but when she rode through the gates and the two great slabs of oak, blackened by relentless rain, closed behind her, she felt entombed. The drear impression created by the exterior was more than matched by the austerity of the regime that prevailed within. A thin, sour faced woman introduced herself as Sister Margaret and then led her silently through a deserted courtyard to a small, bare cell. Against one wall there was a narrow straw bed and the only other item in the room was a wooden bowl of watery broth in the middle of the stone flagged floor.

"The Prioress has generously allowed you to have your first meal here in your cell," announced sour face. "The potage is cold … you're late."

Sister Margaret went out and Eleanor heard a bar drop on the other side of the door. She sat down cross legged on the cold floor next to the bowl, dropping her head wearily into her hands. She needed her sister – strange, she couldn't remember ever wishing for that before. But just now she needed to hear that soft voice, with its deep reassuring tones telling her she was safe.

She was so hungry she poured the cold pottage down her throat, almost choking on it. Exhaustion should then have allowed her to fall into a deep and all-embracing sleep, but instead she lay miserably awake on the straw bed. By the time the grey shafts of dawn intruded into her cell, she had dozed only for brief periods and dark rims had appeared under her pale green eyes. She ran her hands through her hair; it was tangled and dirty from the long ride. In this fragile state, Eleanor was taken before the Prioress, Edwina, in the Chapter House.

Edwina presided over a Cistercian house where hope and charity found few friends. Whatever lofty motives the founding sisters had, the present regime had long since abandoned them. Over the past twenty years Edwina had surrounded herself with an ill-featured and bitter collection of women who were the product of despair in their own lives but who had found a brutal sense of community in the remote Welsh valley. Thus in her own small domain, Edwina Radcliffe was a very powerful woman indeed.

Eleanor knew that she was being closely scrutinised, so she stood still and said nothing. She had never been in a Chapter house before; the room was very grand with its ceiling arching above her, decorated with gold, reds and greens; yet for all that, it felt cold and severe.

"You've fallen foul of my brother, it seems, and must spend your days here with us," said the Prioress suddenly, "and no wonder: look at you – hair uncovered, jerkin and breeches – are you man or maid?"

Eleanor remained silent, choosing instead to give the Prioress a similarly thorough examination with her eyes. Edwina's face might once have been a work of beauty, but now lines of age were chiselled across her brow, down from her mouth and most of all under her steely blue eyes. It was a stern countenance. Then Edwina smiled disarmingly and her face came alive.

"I knew your mother very well; we were the young 'princesses' of Yoredale – the pair of us against all the young – and sometimes not so young - suitors our fathers encouraged us to accept. We were close ... like sisters. You're so like her: the hair … the eyes."

Eleanor was used to comparisons being made with her mother, but somehow this felt different.

"I don't remember her; she died when I was very young."

"Your mother was the dearest friend I ever had in my youth."

"Then, Mother Prioress, for my mother's sake, I beg you to let me leave."

"Before begging too much, you should know that, despite our love for each other, at the end we shared more bitterness than friendship." The stony face had returned.

"For how long must I stay?"

"For as few or as many days as God grants you to live."

Eleanor fell silent again, slowly absorbing the life sentence the prioress had pronounced.

"You're thinking perhaps that you have loved ones who'll take you away from here; but they'll never come. We've had proud young heiresses before – far more high born than you - and they all died here, unmourned."

"No, I wasn't thinking that," said Eleanor, meeting Edwina's eyes with her own fiery gaze. "I was thinking that if I'm here for life, then you are in for a very hard time."

Edwina smiled again. "Yes, you come to us with a … reputation, of sorts. I want you to be clear about this: I won't tolerate any disobedience or insolence by the inmates, however new they may be. Do you understand, child?"

"I understand," said Eleanor, in a manner that hinted understanding did not ensure compliance.

"Very well; now we must introduce you to your new life: take off your clothes and put that on," she instructed as Sister Margaret held out a rough habit.

"I'll wear my own clothes," said Eleanor.

"No… you won't."

Eleanor stared her down.

"Our order requires it…" said the Prioress.

"Oh, very well," said Eleanor and without further argument she began to disrobe, removing her leather outer garments and belt, leaving only her sleeveless linen shift and half hose on.

"All your clothes," said the Prioress.

Again Eleanor considered resisting, but thought there would be other, more important, battles to win soon enough, so she acquiesced and donned the habit. It was even more coarse and uncomfortable than she had expected.

"It itches, but I suppose there are worse fates... satisfied?"

"Good... now, your hair..."

"What about it?"

"We have a simple faith here, and we believe that all that tumble of hair is unseemly. I'm afraid you'll have to lose all that."

"Lose it?" She almost laughed, but the prioress' expression did not change.

"No!" Eleanor shouted. "You will not cut my hair!" Her hair defined her; as Becky said: it marked her and she wouldn't cut it for anyone.

Edwina showed little reaction, but insisted: "it will bring you closer to our Lord."

"The only thing I want to be closer to is your gate!" said Eleanor.

Abruptly the prioress stepped forward and slapped Eleanor hard on the side of the face with the palm of her hand. She was off balance and fell to the floor, shocked and gasping for breath; she raised herself onto her knees, touched her cheek and found a smear of blood there.

"You will not cut my hair," she said again as she lifted herself unsteadily to her feet.

Edwina shook her head and struck another blow even harder than the first. Eleanor cried out and sprawled onto the floor again. She cursed herself for being stupid enough to be struck twice - she could hardly remember an occasion when she'd allowed herself to be hit once. She leant on the cold stone, feeling the lines of Latin carved into it beneath her; Emma would have been able to read it, she thought absently.

Edwina was speaking again: "You'd better stay there, unless

you can control yourself better; you have anger in your eyes and anger makes you do the wrong thing, my dear. So only get up if you're able to stifle that anger."

Eleanor remained on the floor a little longer, but when she got up she came up fast and threw herself at Edwina.

"Anger? You haven't seen me angry yet!" she screamed and swung her fist at Edwina's jaw; her aim was perfect but the punch never reached its target, for the back of her head exploded in pain and she dropped to the floor once more.

When she came round, she was still on the floor and the Prioress was standing over her. She felt a little dizzy and all around her on the stone flags were pools of blood; but when she reached out to touch one, all she found was a long tress of red hair. She tried to gather them to her, but almost passed out from the throbbing pain in her head; beside her were fragments of pottery, clearly Sister Margaret's weapon of choice in such situations.

She was so livid she bit her lip. Her head was still spinning and she knew it was too late now and nothing would be served by further futile outbursts. Shakily she got up onto her knees and then warily to her feet, head bowed for she could not trust herself to look at the Prioress.

"Better," acknowledged Edwina. "I'll speak to you again, when you've ... adjusted to our ways. Sister Margaret will show you where to go and what to do. Just make sure you do it."

She swept out of the Chapter House with triumph in her eyes and Eleanor watched as the hem of her habit dragged some of her curls towards the arched doorway.

Sister Margaret collected up the discarded clothes and the remainder of her hair; then she led Eleanor back to her cell. She threw a white wimple onto the bed.

"Cover your head with this – from now on you'll show only your face."

When she had gone, Eleanor sat hunched on the bed; her head ached and the tears came all too easily. She could not bear to think how she must look; she ran her fingers gingerly over her scalp, wincing when she touched the bruised area – she would not quickly forget Sister Margaret's intervention. As for her beautiful hair, once admired across the shire, only ragged stubble remained.

She could scarcely comprehend how swiftly she had fallen. When Lord Radcliffe had told her that she was to be sent to a nunnery, she had been horrified, assuming it would mean solitude, prayer and meditation – none of which appealed to her in the slightest; never in her worst nightmares had she expected to be an actual prisoner, in the hands of a gaoler such as Edwina. If Lord Robert was to be believed, then her father and brothers were dead, but what of Will? She smiled at the thought of him: she could see his sweet face, smell his scent, almost touch his hair. Their illicit love was the only secret she had ever kept from her sister. What would Emma do? Emma would tell her to make the best of it – Emma would tell her to bide her time and endure, endure all; but … she was not Emma.

PART TWO: HUNTED

15

Elder Hall, Yoredale, March 1460

Ned and Bagot crouched in the snow leaning against the crusty bark of an old oak. They had been watching Elder Hall since midday; at first it had seemed deserted, but then they had seen the children by the gate.

"Squatters!" said Bagot, "we could've done without them."

"Better than Radcliffe's men at arms," said Ned.

"No, not better, not better at all. Men at arms are easy to handle – but families, children … it can get messy."

"Do you think these folk will be loyal?" Ned asked.

"Squatters aren't known for it," Bagot said glumly.

"Well, there's only one way to know: I'll go and ask them."

Bagot shook his head. "No lord, we can't risk that. I'll go." Before Ned could reply, he moved swiftly off across the silent snow towards the curtain wall. Ned watched him disappear from sight as he rounded the familiar gatehouse; he looked for some reaction from the upper tower windows or ramparts, but there was no sign of life.

Time crawled slowly by as he waited uncomfortably in the cold; even through his heavy cloak he was feeling numb. Perhaps he should have stayed at Corve, but what would he have done there? Everything he wanted was here in Yoredale and when, by Candlemas, the snow in the Corve Valley had begun to thaw, he had seized the moment. The journey to Yorkshire had taken them four slow day's riding, on the last of which they had crossed above the snowline again. The snowdrifts had been rough going and the low temperatures had done little for the group's fragile morale.

How long had Bagot been gone? How long should he wait? He was on the verge of moving when Bagot suddenly reappeared striding confidently towards him, a broad grin on his face.

"I take it the squatters are friendly," said Ned.

"It's Jack Standlake and his brood!" Bagot announced with a chuckle, "he's squatting with his brothers and all their families – brats all over the place! When they got back from Ludlow they were snowed in like us. They found Elder Hall empty and thought they'd put its large roof over their heads. They were scared witless when I walked in – they thought I was Robert Radcliffe!"

"You don't look much like him! But they are with us, then?"

"I didn't say that exactly; the Standlakes are honest enough folk - they've farmed your father's land for years. But they weren't expecting to see us, and they weren't that pleased to either. They're pretty damned nervous."

"So they don't want to help me, but they've little choice."

"Well, they can't afford to make an enemy of you as well as the Radcliffes!"

"We'd better get moving then, before they change their minds!"

They rejoined the others on the higher ground above the Hall. All had made the journey, including a reluctant Amelie, for Ned dared not leave her behind. It was mid-afternoon but the leaden sky threatened another snowfall; pushing through the deep drifts was heavy work for their horses, but they made their way safely down to Elder Hall. Their entrance, however, offered Ned little encouragement.

"Forgive me, my lord," ventured Walter Standlake, seeing Ned's tiny retinue, "but you hardly come here in great force. How will you take back your lands?"

"You're right, Master Standlake, for you can see well enough that I don't have the power to take back my lands. I've come to free my sister, Lady Emma, and for that task I would ask your support. I don't demand it, but I ask for it. Soon I will regain my lands and, when I do, you may be sure that I'll restore you to your tenancies."

"I've chewed it over with my brothers," said Jack, "we're a family, not an army. We'll help if we can, but we have youngsters to look out for. We can't just stand and fight."

"We didn't all agree to help," said Jack's wife, Alice.

"Alice, you always were a bitter little shrew," grumbled Bagot.

"Now Bagot, there's no need for that," returned Jack, "she's got reason enough to worry."

"We've all got children," persisted Alice.

"I was with my father on the battlefields of Normandy before I was six years old," said Mags in a surly tone, "you'd be surprised what shit young girls can put up with."

"Aye, and look what it made you: a soldiers' whore," replied Alice sharply.

"Who are you calling a whore, you fucking bitch!" shouted Mags, launching herself at Alice, but Holton quickly intercepted her and carried her, protesting loudly, outside.

There was an uncomfortable silence in the Hall.

Ned quickly changed tack: "Does anyone know you're here yet?"

"A few," replied Jack, "but until Sir Edmund returns, or the snow thaws, we're safe enough. By then, we'll have the gates back up."

"But you can't hope to defend this place?"

"Maybe not, but we'll be a damn sight safer in here than out there."

Alice looked Ned coldly in the eye. "We know you mean us less harm than the Radcliffes, Edward Elder, but you'll still get us all killed, just the same."

§§§

Before dawn the following day Ned was mounted in the courtyard with Will, Bagot, Mags and the three Standlake brothers in attendance.

"I don't see why we need her," said Walter, pointing to Mags.

"She knows the castle better than anyone," said Ned.

"So she says," muttered Bagot.

"She'll just get in the way!" said Walter.

"I can stand up for myself," said Mags and without warning she punched Walter Standlake so hard that he fell from his horse, provoking a chorus of laughter from the others.

Even Bagot grinned. "She's makes a good point," he admitted grudgingly. Walter picked himself up and shot her a black look, but he raised no further objections and they set off.

Even in the half-light it was clear that the snow was melting: the persistent drip slap of wet snow falling from the branches accompanied them through the forest. Their mounts slipped in the sludge and ice as they picked their way up the slope towards Yoredale Castle.

When the first rays of sunlight emerged over the trees on the rim of the valley, they were still several miles from the castle. The horses slithered awkwardly as they tried to climb a steep bank, and the riders were compelled to dismount and lead the nervous animals up onto the snow covered higher ground. Then they were in amongst the trees again, only stopping when they reached the edge of the large expanse of open ground around the castle's intimidating walls.

There Jack and his brothers left them and the others waited anxiously in the shelter of the trees.

"We're taking a lot on trust here and you've always told me to trust no-one," Ned said to Bagot as they tethered their horses in the icy glade.

"Aye, but this is different: Jack's worth your trust, believe me."

Despite the thaw by the river, it was a perishing cold wait under the dripping trees and Ned was relieved when the brothers returned having acquired a wagon pulled by oxen and laden with wood.

"Don't ask us where we got this lot," warned Walter, before

anyone could open their mouth to do so.

Jack jumped down from the wagon and turned to Ned. "Lord, are you sure we can do this? We're so few and it's such a big place."

"Jack, we're all desperate men now," replied Ned, "but I swear if you can get me into Yoredale Castle, I'll surely fight my way out of it."

Jack nodded.

Mags, Ned and Bagot climbed onto the wagon, leaving their mounts secured in the forest, whilst Will and the three brothers rode in escort.

Everything now hinged on two factors: that the Standlakes were recognised at the gate as friends and that the others were not recognised at all. To this end Ned had covered his head and instructed Will to do the same, for he suspected that every girl in the dale would recognise his friend's red locks.

The wagon trundled along the slush covered track that led up to the massive gatehouse. Ned was in awe of the castle, for it was a substantial fortress which no doubt boasted a large household and, in such troubled times, a significant garrison of men at arms. It was not the sort of place one entered without some trepidation and the guards on the gate provided their first test.

"Where do you think you're going with all that?" one asked, moving in front of the wagon.

Under his cloak, Ned drew out his dagger.

"Kitchen and brew house," replied Jack airily.

"No, you're not," replied the guard.

"We're not? Why's that?" asked Jack. Ned felt the sweat on the back of his neck.

"Too many in there already – you'll have to wait or the yard'll get blocked up!"

Bagot obediently pulled the wagon over to leave room for others to go out, though none were in sight.

One of the guards noted the number of riders.

"Guarding wood are we now?" he asked, resting his hand

on the side of the wagon.

"Hard winter… not much wood cut," Bagot improvised unconvincingly.

"Keep calm," he whispered to Ned; then he turned to Mags and spoke in a low voice.

"Make yourself useful – go and take their minds off asking us awkward questions."

She favoured him with a bitter look of disdain and Ned thought that perhaps it wasn't just Alice that thought her a whore. Reluctantly she jumped down from the wagon and sauntered over to the two men at arms. It seemed an age before an empty wagon appeared in the gateway, but finally one did; by then Ned's nerves were threadbare.

Bagot moved the wagon on at once, shouting to Mags: "Come on girl, get up here; we've work to do!"

Ned feared she might strike him, but she restrained herself and forced a smile at the guards as she walked alongside the wagon.

They passed under a weighty portcullis, through an archway and a second portcullis into a damp central courtyard, where an assortment of wagons and oxen were jammed into the cramped space - the guard had not exaggerated, thought Ned.

"We mustn't get trapped in here," warned Bagot, "we'd be dead meat. Keep to the chambers – they're built into the walls – so there's many more ways in and out."

Ned could see for himself that the courtyard was a killing ground, with each of the four entrances to the living quarters protected by a small portcullis to trap unwanted visitors in the courtyard.

"Lead on, Mags," he said, and she took Will and Ned, well cloaked to conceal their weapons, to one of the courtyard gates. Bagot paused briefly to speak to Tom Standlake and then, after a few minutes, he, Jack and Walter followed, leaving Tom on his own to unload, as slowly as possible, the stack of wood they had brought in.

They hurried unchallenged past the brewing room and bake house to mount the steps to the first floor.

"There's a lot of floors," said Mags breathlessly, as they climbed a wide circular stairway to the first floor. "She'll most likely be in this tower – there are guest chambers up here."

"Depends whether she's being treated as a 'guest' or not," said Bagot, "but if we disturb someone else we'd better be ready to take them out before they start shouting their heads off!"

Ned and Will paused at the top of the next spiral of steps, listening for sounds of movement. The others crowded in behind them, filling the narrow passage.

"Come on," urged Bagot, "now we're here just choose a door!"

Ned eased open the first door and stood on the threshold: no shriek of horror greeted him. He leaned into the room, but it was not a bedchamber; it looked like a solar and was unoccupied. They passed on through the door and into the chamber beyond; Ned glanced at the others, moving swiftly to another spiral staircase which they ascended quickly in single file. He entered the first room on the next landing: again unoccupied. They had cleared one complete range of rooms but it was taking far too long.

"More haste!" hissed Bagot. Ned took them at a run into the adjoining living quarters within the west wall of the castle and hurried along until they reached the final chamber on the top floor at the far end of the western wall.

"If she's not in here I'm going," said Mags.

"What lies beyond?" asked Bagot.

"The Hall - and she won't be sleeping in there!"

"Peace, girl!" he snapped.

Ned's heart was pounding as he lifted the latch and stole into the chamber; he sighed with relief at the sight of Emma, asleep in her bed. Bagot and Will followed him in and the rest waited outside. He shook Emma gently by the shoulder; she tensed and struggled briefly until she recognised her young brother and immediately hugged him to her.

"Ned! They told me you were dead! I think I started to believe it…"

"I imagined the worst about you," said Ned.

She smiled and sat up, studying him carefully for a moment.

"You look older, brother; yes, older," she said with a tinge of sadness. She turned to his companion. "And Will, it's good to see your handsome face again!"

"What news of Ellie, lady?" asked Will.

"They've taken her, but I don't know where."

Jack put his head around the door: "Lord, we should go!"

"You can discuss the past months later!" said Bagot.

"Yes, come Emma."

But she drew away from him. "Ned, why would I leave? I live here."

"Yes, I know, but you were forced to!"

"Ned, I'm married! I never looked forward to it as some do but, if I had to marry - it may as well be Richard Radcliffe."

Ned was stunned. "But the Radcliffes killed our brother Tom; they're hunting me down now - and you're sharing Richard Radcliffe's bed?"

"What was I to do, Ned? Should I have fought? Should I have taken my own life? Should I have waited for you to rescue me?"

"Yes! Yes!" he shouted.

"And how long should I have waited for you, Ned? I thought you were dead with all the others! This marriage holds no more fears for me than any other! My husband treats me a good deal better than many. Besides, I thought it would put an end once and forever to the bad blood between our two families."

"Bad blood! It's rather more than that! And your marriage changes nothing." retorted Ned.

He would have remonstrated further, but their voices were already carrying beyond the chamber and others in the household were taking an interest.

"Come on, Ned," said Bagot, "if she won't come, you must either leave her or pick her up and carry her!"

"Emma, come with me," he pleaded.

"No, Richard's a good man."

"He killed your brother!" said Will savagely.

"Not him! Others – Edmund certainly - but not Richard! He has a gentle nature - you'll see."

Jack burst into the chamber. "If you wait any longer, we'll never get out! I'll meet you down by the solar in the south wall."

"Go, Ned," said Emma, "go with my love, but go without me."

"I'm not going without you," said Ned and he seized her by the arm and lifted her struggling onto his shoulder.

"No, Ned; please!" she screamed.

Bagot stood in the doorway. "Ned – leave her, or you'll kill us all!"

Ned threw her down onto the bed. "I'll come back for you and you'd better pray I don't have your husband at my mercy when I do."

Emma said nothing, for this was a Ned she had never seen before.

They ran from the chamber, but as they started back down the steps there was a warning shout from Jack on the floor below.

"We can't get out the way we came in!" declared Bagot.

"Down the stairs by the Great Hall!" suggested Mags, running along the first floor passage.

"Aye, why not? It can't get any worse," said Bagot.

"Just push on through the Hall - we don't want a full scale melee in there," ordered Ned.

"Go on, Ned, we're behind you," said Will.

They rushed through into the Hall, overturning tables and knocking aside anyone in their path. Ned ignored the torrent of crude abuse and ran on but there was no way out to the courtyard and instead he crashed through the door at the far end of the Hall towards the castle kitchens, scattering servants and pots in all directions. Dodging a battery of culinary objects hurled at them, they raced out into the courtyard to join the chaos of men, beasts and wagons.

Some men at arms near the inner gate were drawn to the

noise. Ned paused by the kitchen tower and the others quickly formed into a ragged line behind him. The soldiers stood uncertainly, allowing Ned time to improvise.

"I regret all the noise," he said, walking forward with an engaging grin. "It's my fault – a jest with Sir Richard got out of hand. Just ignore us; no harm done."

The guards were visibly relieved and they relaxed, laughing with him and allowing him to pass by with the others to make their way across the courtyard towards their horses.

All was well until a door at the other end of the courtyard was flung violently open and a half dressed Richard Radcliffe stood upon the threshold: "Hold those men!" he bellowed.

Ned reacted faster than anyone else and swiftly turned his sword onto the nearest man, clubbing him to the ground. "Make for the gate!" he shouted, but within seconds they were caught up in a struggle he knew they could not win.

"This is no place to be caught," said Jack, fending off the attention of two men at arms.

"Where's the wagon?" asked Will, working hard with both swords drawn.

"Sweet Jesus!" exclaimed Walter as he took a cut on the leg, "I don't care which way we go, but let's get out!"

Their route to the main gate was already blocked and what Bagot had feared most was happening: they were trapped in the inner courtyard. Ned looked for another way out and then headed not for the gate, but straight for Richard Radcliffe. Ill prepared to fight, he was quickly disarmed and Ned then planted his own knife at Richard's throat.

"Lay down your arms!" he shouted. "I've killed one Radcliffe and I'll willingly kill another today!"

His opponents were thrown into confusion, but Richard nodded and reluctantly they submitted. Will and the others gathered in a tight knot around Ned and his prisoner. Together they shuffled their way through the hostile crowd towards the gate, where all save Bagot were surprised to find their wagon stationary under the main portcullis. He had left instructions with Tom concerning what should be done if there was trouble and the youngest of the Standlake brothers had carried out his task perfectly. There were archers and crossbowmen on the ramparts but they dare not open fire for fear of what would befall their master.

As they passed under the portcullis, Emma appeared in the courtyard and Ned shouted a reminder to the watching garrison: "Let every man be clear: if we're pursued, I will kill Sir Richard – heaven knows, I've reason enough to do so!" Then, looking across to his sister, he added: "If there's no pursuit, I give you my word that I'll release this knight before sunset unharmed."

He dragged Richard to the wagon and threw him in – there Tom crouched with a drawn sword across the captive's unprotected throat. Those with horses mounted quickly and the rest dived into the wagon as it passed through the gates. They half expected a flurry of crossbow bolts as they cleared the gateway, yet no bolts came from the battlements or anywhere else as they scurried away from the castle. Only when they reached the forest glade where they had left the remaining horses did they pause to look for signs of pursuit. Seeing none, they abandoned the wagon and set off on a path through the woods to the south east.

They rode for an hour or more until they had left the castle far behind them and then they stopped to rest their horses. When they dismounted, Richard Radcliffe confronted Ned.

"Is this where I'm to be butchered like my poor brother Ralph?"

"Did you play any part in the murder of my brother Tom?" asked Ned.

"I have sworn to your sister that I took no part in his death, but if my word is not enough for you, then do what you will. I don't fear you, Ned Elder."

Ned felt nothing but hatred for the man facing him, but he could not countenance killing him out of hand. He still regretted Ralph's death and he now knew where his sister stood. If he had not already lost her, he certainly did not want to risk doing so by summarily despatching her husband.

"If I release you, will you swear not to pursue us?"

"Yes," answered Richard stiffly, "but only for your sister's sake - and I don't speak for either my father or my brother, for I know that both will hunt you down for this."

"They were doing that anyway," laughed Ned dismissively, "and they've not been too successful so far. Yet I thank you for your honest answer."

"For Emma's sake, I would warn you that my brother Edmund is not to be taken so lightly; you'd be a fool to do so."

"Yes, I've met your brother. There's one other condition: I must know where my sister, the Lady Eleanor, is being held."

Richard shrugged. "I don't know where she's held; I'd tell you if I did. All I know is that she was taken to a nunnery beyond the Welsh March. Whatever you may think of me, I swear to you that Lady Emma is safe in my charge."

Ned looked him in the eye. "If she isn't, I'll take your head!"

"If you let him go," said Will, "they'll still come for us – he's said it himself!"

He drew out a sword. "Tell him Bagot!"

"Peace Will! It's your lord's decision, not yours."

"Go!" Ned told Richard, "while you can."

Bagot put a large arm around Will's shoulder. "Leave it lad; your lord's given his word and if it's not worth spit, then I for one will be leaving his service today. There'll be enough bloodletting before we're done."

Will shook off the older man's arm, but sheathed his sword and simmered in silence, as Richard trudged off on foot back to Yoredale Castle.

"All that," he said, "and we're no nearer finding Eleanor - 'Beyond the Welsh March' is a world away."

They made their way despondently back through the melting snows to Elder Hall.

16

Elder Hall

There was little to cheer them at Elder Hall: though the snow still lay on the upper slopes of Yoredale, down by the river it was very different for the deep drifts that had shielded Elder Hall for months had all but disappeared. Ned knew that as soon as the Radcliffes returned to the vale, an assault would come and few in the household believed they would survive it. When he had returned to Yoredale, he had not considered the presence of so many children. To abandon the loyal Standlakes and their families to a bloody fate was unthinkable, but to effect an escape with all the young children seemed equally impossible. With every day that passed, spring drew inexorably nearer and they began to prepare the Hall for a siege.

Ned could see no way out until the resourceful Jack Standlake came to see him with Bagot.

"Jack's got an idea, lord," announced Bagot.

"What sort of idea?" asked Ned.

"The sort that might get us out of here alive," said Jack.

"Go on."

"Well, there's a village ... Penholme – it's a couple of valleys to the south west."

"I've ridden all over the fells and dales there – and I've never heard of Penholme," said Ned.

"That's because it was deserted long ago," explained Bagot.

"Hear me out, lord," said Jack, "Penholme's where my kin lived, but they left when the village began to waste away."

"The black fever?" said Ned. A sad smile appeared on Jack's face.

"No, the fever came and went, but the Lord brought them to a slower end, for after the fever passed came another plague – a terrible murrain amongst the sheep. The Penholme flocks were all but wiped out, though for a score or more years the herdsmen struggled on; but in the end most left to find work in the other dales - that's when the Standlakes came to Yoredale. "

"So, how does Penholme help us, Jack?" asked Ned wearily.

"Well, it's far enough away, but not too far to get to; there's good water and some tree cover. It's out of the way there."

"I can see that, if we covered our tracks well enough, we might get there," said Bagot, "but is there aught there?"

"I was up there four or five years back; a few squatters lived there for a while and if they could, so could we."

But Bagot shook his head. "Jack, it's surely a likely place to aim for, but still we have the same rub: Radcliffe will be watching: he'll simply follow you and hunt you down."

Ned scanned the faces around the Hall; half were children.

"We must get the young ones and womenfolk away," he said, "send them up to Penholme, as soon as we can. If we do that, we can hold this place."

But Tom's wife, Lizzie, spoke up for the women.

"Either we all go, or we all stay! I'm not leaving my man here." Tom was surprised by his wife's interruption, but in the silence that followed he looked upon her with quiet pride.

"You could always give yourself up, lord…" said Alice.

"You do me shame, woman," said Jack quietly.

Another uneasy silence followed, for they had resolved nothing.

"I'll carry on shoring up the gates then," Bagot said and stalked out.

§§§

Becky Standlake waited until her cousins were all asleep; then she got up from her straw bed, wrapped her blanket around her and went downstairs to the Hall, patches of moonlight guiding her bare feet as they skipped down over the cold steps. Harry was waiting for her in the Hall doorway and he folded her into his arms at once, gently kissing her lips.

"Wait!" she whispered and took his hand to lead him into the pantry. He stopped her suddenly in a pool of moonlight, studying her face.

"You're almost glowing," he said, "it wouldn't be anything to do with your Ellie would it?"

"Lady Eleanor to you," she said, "but yes, just to know she may still be alive – I've lived the last six months thinking she was dead."

"You've been a right misery!"

"How would you know? You were down south with your Pa for two months! Besides, when she disappeared it was a big shock to me; I'd spent almost every hour of every day with her since I was about six!"

"Well, since I got back we've not been … together once," he said.

"In this place, with all our bloody nosy cousins under foot? It's hardly been easy!"

"Aye, and if your Pa catches us, he'll kill me."

"Listen, I've found somewhere for us, down in the cellars…" she said, putting her hands on his shoulders and moving them lightly down over his chest.

"Down in the cellars? It'll be freezing!" he hissed.

"Sshh! It's the only place no-one goes; I've taken some straw and bedding down there – it'll be fine, you'll see and … we'll be warming it up a bit anyway." She moved one hand onto his thigh. "Of course, if you don't want to…"

"No, no, I do! Let's go down there now before someone stirs up here." He seized her hand and they hurried down through the old brew house to the cellars.

"It's the one at the far end," she said breathlessly, "you have to climb past some fallen stones."

"I thought we'd never have a moment to ourselves!" he said, as they clambered down into the smallest cellar. They sat on the straw and he pulled her towards him. Wickedly, she backed away, beckoning him to her. "Come on then," she said, shamelessly lifting her shift up to reveal her bare thighs and giggling as she arched back against the cellar wall.

"Come on, Harry; I know it's been a long time – have you forgotten what to do?"

He pushed against her, exploring the warmth of her breasts under the thin linen. She squealed. "Oh, your hands are like ice!"

"Peace! You'll bring everyone down here!"

She leant back against the wall drawing him with her and they relaxed finally into each other's arms.

She sighed contentedly, "Oh, this is definitely the place, Harry!" she said.

There was a muffled crack and with appalling suddenness the wall at Becky's back disintegrated. Becky shrieked as they were plummeted into a chill, black void beyond the wall. They fell a short distance and then rolled a lot further until they came to rest in a painful tangle on a cold, wet slab of rock. They were lying in a shallow icy pool of water and at once tried to scramble up out of it. Harry cracked his forehead, for there was a low, rocky ceiling; he dropped, stunned, to his knees.

"Harry! Harry?"

He groaned and tried to get up, only to bang his head again.

"Hold still!" she said, as she tried in vain to examine his head in the dark. For a moment she wrapped her arms round his shivering body and he clung to her.

"Harry, where are we? It's so cold; we have to get out of here."

He mumbled an answer and she realised that if they were to going to get out, it would be up to her.

"Harry, I'm going to get help," she said; then she began to crawl, feeling her way around the shape of the black hole into which they had somehow fallen. A dim glow marked their point of entry; it had to be the torch burning in the brew house, but she could not see how to get back up to it. She felt the cold sapping her energy and struggled to concentrate, but some chill drops of water falling from the rock above brought her awake.

Leaving Harry huddled on the damp floor, she started to climb towards the faint flicker of light. It was hard going, scrambling up an unstable heap of rock and for every few feet she went up, she slithered back almost as far. Yet she persevered, inching higher towards the gap through which they had fallen. In the cold air, she could hardly breathe and her straining muscles ached beyond any pain she had ever felt. She was nearly at the top when she started to slip again; her sore fingers clawed in vain at the rock. She closed her eyes and held on but it was no good; she knew she would not make it. She tried to call out but her throat was dry and her teeth rattled against each other in the cold.

Then, abruptly, her arms were seized from above and she was hoisted up into the cellar. Relief overwhelmed her and she sobbed into the arms of Jack Standlake. In the half-light she saw Bagot too crouched low peering into the hole.

She tried to tell them about Harry but she was so chilled she couldn't speak clearly. Jack had already guessed that his son would not be far away. He and Bagot exchanged brief glances. Ned joined them in the cramped space.

"I'll go down," said Bagot quickly, seizing one of the flaming torches they had brought with them.

By the time Harry was passed up to Ned, Becky was beginning to recover and the entire Standlake family were attempting to squeeze into the tiny cellar.

With the aid of torches, Bagot and Will explored the hole into which Becky and Harry had tumbled.

"It's a passageway!" said Will.

"No, it's a natural cleft in the rock. I've heard stories about it, but I thought they were just tall tales."

As they edged their way forward, the roof dropped lower

and the ground underfoot grew wet and slippery. Soon the air became thicker, almost foetid and they were ankle deep in water.

"Christ, the lower garderobes must drain into here; what a bloody awful stench," said Bagot.

Soon, however, they were relieved to detect fresher air, although the gap became more difficult to squeeze through. After another thirty paces or so, and almost without warning, the rock ahead of them seemed to disappear. Bagot hesitated and turned to Will.

"Wait here, we don't know where this comes out," he whispered and moved forward cautiously.

"God's blood!" he exclaimed and pulled his hand back sharply.

"Thorns!" he explained and drew his long knife to hack into the wall of thorns. He cut a hole so narrow that he was obliged to wriggle through the gap on his knees. When his head and shoulders emerged he remained motionless, listening intently. He could hear the sound of rushing water nearby and realised that he had come out at the upper end of the millstream by the river where it was almost engulfed by Yoredale forest. They had found an underground watercourse that fed into the mill stream. He looked around him anxiously in case any of Radcliffe's watchers might be nearby, but there was no-one; nor was there a reason for anyone to pass by so close behind the mill. Having satisfied himself that the thorny entrance was still obscured, he returned carefully and the pair climbed back to the cellar, assisted by a rope now firmly installed there by Holton.

Ned was waiting for them with Jack. "Well?" he asked.

Bagot quickly explained what they had found. "We may have the answer to our problem – another way out, but it won't be easy."

"Nothing's going to be easy, Bagot. Birches has just come from the castle: Edmund's back and he's brought at least three score men with him!"

"Then we've no hope of defending this place."

"So we have to go; it's just a question of where. Can we get to Penholme, do you think?"

"Where else can we go?" said Bagot. "No-one in Yoredale will welcome us. Even so, with all this lot it'll take the best part of two days to get to Penholme."

"Very well. We'll leave tomorrow night and take only what we can carry. We must clear the Radcliffe estates by the following morning."

Ned could see that Bagot was still concerned.

"What is it?" he asked.

"The horses – we can't take them down there…"

They all knew that with no mounts, they could be overtaken; and if they did make it to Penholme, Ned could not ride south to Corve.

"We must have them!" declared Ned, "You and Birches must take all our mounts tonight to a safe place within reach of Penholme and return on two of them – those two we'll leave behind."

"It'll take hours!" protested Bagot.

"You've got hours – now come on, let's run through it with the others," he said.

He called them all into the Hall and outlined Jack's plan

"What about food?" enquired Alice Standlake when he had finished.

Ned eyed her apprehensively, but she had a point: their supplies were almost exhausted and lines of hunger were etched on every child's face.

"That's true enough, there'll be nothing at the village," said Jack.

"We'll have to forage then," said Ned.

"Don't worry, lord," said Alice, "we women have our uses; some of us'll go out tonight and … forage."

Her resentment on his arrival had cut him deeply and she was still cool towards him, but he was reassured by her suggestion.

"I don't do it for you, lord, but to feed my children; I'll do anything to keep them safe."

"Something else, lord," said Bagot, "when we go, this place will be deserted and it'll look and sound deserted; we know we're being watched – surely they'll come looking for us before we've gone a mile?"

"I know, Bagot, but we can't leave anyone behind!"

"Someone should stay – make a bit of noise; keep a fire burning, so they think we're still here. Then after a day or so, that man follows on. It could make all the difference."

"Only you could do that, Bagot, but we need you with us!"

"Birches could do it; he's a handy fellow."

"Very well; ask him."

Bagot shook his head. "I'll tell him as we ride – for we'd best take the horses now."

He drew Ned to one side. "Make no mistake," he said quietly, "if we're caught tomorrow, it'll be bloody."

"It's the children," replied Ned, "it's them I'm worried about."

The sunset, red and angry, seemed to last forever.

§§§

They all sat waiting. Bagot, who would take the lead, had ridden through the night and returned only at first light; he had not rested for many hours and looked exhausted even before they set off. Ned stared impassively at the western sky until the sun receded to a glowing crimson line; then he judged it was time to move.

The children, roused from an enforced afternoon sleep, were edgy and anxious now that the journey was about to begin. Ned watched as, one by one, they were lowered down into the dark, dripping rock passage. The thorn bushes concealing the entrance had been cut back further by Birches and Bagot led them out past the mill and along the riverbank where the heavily forested ground afforded them good cover. They were to cross the river at the ford but the water level was rising daily with the melted snow and the crossing was deeper than Ned had hoped. Bagot paused at the bank, staring at the fast flowing current; they could hear the river racing carelessly over the rapids and falls further downstream.

"Bagot, we can't stop here!" whispered Jack.

"I know! Why don't you lead the women across and I'll help the others."

Jack gave a shrug and pushed past him whilst Bagot waited for some of the younger children to arrive.

Ned envied the boys, who thought it all a great adventure, and would have run across the ford if he hadn't stopped them. He knew Bagot was nervous, but the gruff veteran took a deep breath and linked arms to cross with two of the older boys. Holton and Will carried several of the girls across, whilst Ned in his turn took the youngest boy, John, on his shoulders. They continued on the muddy, slippery track on the other side of the water until they reached the first village. They gave a wide berth to the dark cluster of buildings there and turned southwest to pick up one of the becks that fed into the river Yore. They would follow the beck now almost to its source in the hills above Penholme.

Ned walked at the back, always keeping Amelie near him. He noticed that the youngest children were becoming spread out through the entire party, dropping further and further back, some desperately clutching a mother's hand. After the river crossing young John attached himself to Ned, much to the surprise of his companions, but Ned remembered how he had often trotted after his own older brother.

"Come on then," he said and lifted the bright-eyed lad up onto his shoulders again. "Keep quiet, mind!"

John stared in awe at the large battle sword Ned carried on his back.

"Do you kill folk with that?" he asked in a whisper.

Ned smiled. "I try not to."

"But ... isn't that ... what it's for?"

"Enough questions," said Ned firmly. Amelie, walking alongside him, smiled to herself.

They walked on for several more hours but the melting snow and churned up mud was taking its toll, even of the adults. For the first time that night the moon stole through the broken cloud giving the forest a silver sheen. Ned slowed and looked back.

"We're leaving tracks they could follow with their eyes shut," he said.

Alice Standlake had caught them up. "The children can't go on at this pace, lord," she said, "can we not rest awhile?"

"I'll think about it," he said.

"Think well, lord," she replied and dropped back again.

She was right: the youngsters were flagging and most were now being carried; if they pushed on too hard they might never get to Penholme.

"Are we going to stop?" asked Amelie.

He studied the soft outlines of her face in the moonlight, but couldn't read her expression. He nodded and shepherded the group towards a nearby stand of oaks where they would find some respite from the cold and damp. They had covered less distance than he would have liked and when Bagot joined them he was not slow to voice his disapproval.

"Why have you stopped?" he demanded.

"The children are tired."

"Tired is better than dead! I don't like it, lord; we should move on. It's not safe."

"I don't like it much either, so let's just hope that our Lord is watching over us tonight. We can't press any further – and I don't want to hear any more about it."

Bagot shrugged. "We'd best keep a lively watch then."

§§§

Jack found Harry among the gloomy trees and undergrowth; he was seated on a fallen tree with Becky. Some of the younger children were slumped at their feet.

"Where's your mother?" Jack demanded. Harry looked up in surprise at his father's tone.

"She's here - or at least she was. She said she was going to find you, just now ... she was fretting a bit."

Jack wandered thoughtfully to the edge of the trees where

they were making their camp and scanned the forest beyond. What was she doing? The other wives were with their children.

"Watch the others," he ordered curtly and set off through a clearing of browned bracken stems towards the wall of bare oak and ash.

Becky took Harry's hand and hugged him to her.

§§§

Edmund Radcliffe interrupted his pacing. "Are you sure about this?" he demanded of his father.

Lord Robert was used to his son's surly impatience and ignored it. "They'll be travelling slowly, so you may have to wait a deal longer yet."

"I've waited long enough," said Edmund, "it would have been easier to track them."

"No need, when you know the way they'll take. In any case, better to let them come deep into the forest, to a place of our choosing – a place like this … far enough from Yoredale."

Around thirty of Robert Radcliffe's retained men at arms and a score of archers were deployed in a long cordon on the outer edge of the clearing. He knew that, like Edmund, they were not enjoying their miserable night sojourn in the forest, for there was plenty of muttering and grumbling in the ranks.

"I don't have your confidence in informers," said Edmund, "you can't trust them."

"That depends on what they want; they'll come. You know what to do?"

His son nodded with disdain.

"You'd better spare the women and children; these men may be traitors but His Majesty dislikes tales of excessive bloodletting." Edmund laughed ironically. "His Majesty wouldn't know if it's Tuesday or Friday! And … your favour with him is assured by my favour with the Queen," he added pointedly.

Lord Robert's pride would not allow him to bow easily to his son's bullying, but he was all too aware that his entire dynastic strategy relied heavily upon his son's ability to retain the Queen's support. "Well, who can say what can happen in the dark and confusion? I'll leave it in your capable hands, Edmund."

He mounted and set off to return with his personal retinue to Yoredale Castle.

Edmund was glad to see him go and started pacing again, but then he stopped: he could hear them coming. He waited impassively. He could see no-one, but he knew they were not far distant and when he saw them they were making camp exactly where he had expected. A slight figure ghosted through the trees to his left and walked towards him.

"About time," he snorted crossly, "are they all here?"

"Yes, Sir Edmund, but you'll let me take my family out first," said Alice Standlake.

"Yes, yes, of course," replied Edmund, unable to disguise his distaste.

"And there'll be no harm to the women and little ones?"

"No! Now go, while you still may!" he said through gritted teeth.

Alice stumbled away to find Jack and her children.

Edmund gestured impatiently to Mordeur, who waited beside him.

"Take the men at arms to the far side of those trees and finish off those who avoid an arrow. Then get in there and bring that maid to me. As for the rest, I don't want to go back to Yoredale with a host of whining brats falling under my horse...."

Mordeur nodded and disappeared at once into the shadows.

As Alice hurried back Jack broke through the trees in front of her. He stared at her; then twenty paces away he glimpsed Edmund and finally he focused wide eyed on the archers waiting along the dark tree line.

"What've you done, Alice? What've you done?" But he already knew the answer.

She grabbed his arm and pulled him with her. "Come, we must get the children away!"

But he shook off her grasp. "Are you mad, woman? I've got two brothers in those trees – do you think I'm just going to leave them?"

"This was never our fight, Jack! And I'm not losing my children for the sake of Ned Elder!"

But Jack was looking across to where Edmund had stood a moment before. The knight had vanished, but there was a ripple of movement as each archer in the line put an arrow to his bow.

Jack turned to shout a warning to those camped among the trees, but before he could do so Edmund swiftly punched a sword through his chest. Alice stood transfixed for a moment and then she began to scream as Edmund clubbed her down with the hilt of his sword. At once he raised the weapon again to signal his archers and the arrows flew.

17

Elder Hall

He'd got a good fire burning and had set two large lighted candles in the upstairs solar; all in all, Birches considered he was doing an excellent job – then he heard a crashing at the rear of the building that told him the postern gate was being battered in.

"Oh, shit!" He raced down the stairway and on down into the cellars, pausing only to scoop up his bow and quiver before he descended into the rock passage and then, after two faltering steps, he stopped dead. It should have been as black as night, but it wasn't: ahead of him was a glow of light. Was it his comrades returning for some reason, or was it the Radcliffes? But if the Radcliffes knew of the passage, then the whole escape was buggered.

Instinct took over as he drew an arrow and set himself with great care. He would have to let them get close – too close, but he certainly didn't want to be explaining to Bagot why he had shot Ned. The flickering torches they were carrying gave him an edge, but his survival would depend on how many stood between him and the exit by the mill. Three figures appeared as the torchlight illuminated the cavern and in the same instant he released the arrow, for these were not his friends. The first flew true to its target and he loosed another that also skewered its intended victim. Even as the third sped through the void the torch was falling to the ground and darkness fell with a scream of mortal pain.

He knew the last arrow would not hit, so he drove forward running low towards the spot where he had last glimpsed the third man. His bow was thrust across his back, he gripped an arrow in his left hand and a sharp knife in his right. He was relying on impact to get through, spurred on by the sound of more voices from the cellar above. He crashed into the surviving man and lashed out with both hands; there was a grunt as his knife punched into his opponent's body and lodged there. He abandoned it and pushed the man aside, hoping there was no-one else ahead of him. He hurried towards the entrance, forgetting the place where the rock overhead dipped, and rapped his head on it. He was stunned for a second and felt blood on his temple, but the sounds of pursuit pushed him on. He scrambled the final section to the thorn bush, breathing hard, a throbbing pain in his head. Seeing no one, he took his chances and lurched out towards the shelter of the mill, scrambling down the bank and hoping that the rushing millrace would disguise any noise he made. In the cool air he felt light headed and simply fell down the rest of the bank into the stream, where he lay dazed until the near freezing water shocked him into life. He dragged himself into the nearby trees and hid shivering under some old bracken fronds.

§§§

Ned stared intently towards the open ground on his right; he had heard something: a small shard of sound and while he was still wondering what it was, there was a rush of air as a volley of arrows sped past him. Several feet away Harry took two shafts in the back and Becky screamed. Ned watched the pair drop to their knees and Becky fell back, her breast covered in blood - the arrow tips must have nicked her.

All around him was chaos. Others had been hit, children were wailing and crying; most had taken refuge behind the larger trees or thrown themselves down onto the forest floor. He shouted in vain for calm, but panic had already set in as the hail of arrows showed no sign of abating. He winced as a goose feather flight brushed his cheek. Bagot darted in to crouch alongside him.

"We've only one chance, lord!"

"Well?" asked Ned, trying to shut out the pandemonium all around him.

"They're going to come in after us. Here, with the families, we can't fight – we must take them in trees as they come in."

"Leave the women and children?" said Ned, in disbelief.

"Aye, leave them with the Standlake lads and Holton; they're good men with a bow so they can stop anyone crossing the open ground."

"But we can't leave them!" Ned protested.

"As soon as they rush us, we're buggered - we have to move first!"

"Just the two of us?"

Bagot looked him in the eye: "Aye, the two of us – and Will, he's handy enough."

"Very well then," he conceded, "go tell the brothers."

He glanced across at Becky, now hunched over the young Standlakes, then down to Amelie who lay under the bracken beside him; his face softened as he looked at her with a fondness he had often been obliged to hide since their unhappy words at Corve.

Mags crawled on her knees towards Becky and they gathered the children closer together. Ned handed Amelie the blade Sir Roger had given him. She took it without a word and scrambled over to join Mags. He drew his sword and rushed into the trees after Bagot and Will.

"Keep close!" shouted Bagot as he ran, "we must draw them to us; make as much noise as we can so they'll think they're following most of the group. They'll try to block us in, so we fight as a tight group; we strike hard and fast, we break them up, kill them; but we always keep together. Clear?"

"Not really!" said Will.

"Well, you'll learn fast enough!"

"Then what?" asked Ned.

"We keep doing it until they - or we - are all dead!"

The time for talk had run out: a dozen or so well-armed men charged at them out of the black forest. Ned followed Bagot's lead and they fought as a wedge, driving at the men at arms, attacking without quarter, denying their opponents a moment's respite. Never one for extravagant sword strokes, he was in his element: chopping to the neck, thrusting under the ribs and hacking down his foes with a freedom he'd never felt before. The three of them were a killing engine: his power, Will's speed and Bagot's sheer bloody will. Then the merciless butchering stopped.

Ned sucked in a draught of air, his sword blade held in mid-air, his hands dripping blood and his two comrades still standing. The sudden stillness was unnerving; he looked around him. A head lifted up from the ground by his foot and he rammed his blade into the neck. All was in shadow, but he could hear more men coming.

"We must do it again," he said softly, wrenching his sword free.

"Aye," said Bagot.

Men at arms burst upon them and the fickle moon lit up the stark carnage they had already wrought. Radcliffe's soldiers, seeing the shattered bodies of their comrades, stopped in their tracks and then scattered back into the trees.

"Don't let them fall back!" urged Bagot, "Spare no-one - if we let them go, they can still harm the others!"

"I know," said Ned, "I know! What else do you think could drive me to this godless slaughter!"

One by one they hunted them down until they cornered the last two men in a small clearing. The pair put up a brave resistance and one of them shouted: "Mordeur - he told us you'd be strong, did Mordeur – said you'd work us a bit."

"Who did you say?" growled Bagot, battering him to the ground.

"Mordeur!" It was his last word.

"Who's Mordeur?" Ned asked.

"He was at the Priory, with Radcliffe. I should've recognised him then."

"So, who is he?"

"I knew him in France."

"Fought against him?"

"Christ no, he was on our side! But if he's here, we're in trouble."

"It seems he was expecting us to do what we did – what does that mean?" asked Ned.

"How should I know, but I doubt he expected to lose so many."

"We should go back to the others," said Ned.

"Aye," Bagot agreed and they set off once more at a run.

A scream pierced the still night air like an axe splitting a young oak. Ned kept running, hurtling through the forest towards the source of the scream, tripping and stumbling as the wilful moon came and went. In his mind's eye he saw them all, being ripped and torn by sword and arrow – and, most of all, he saw Amelie.

§§§

Birches lay on the bank alongside the millstream. He had no idea how long he had lain there, but his legs were partly in the water and the creeping cold had turned them to ice. His head felt like it was being hammered out of shape, but the cold water seemed at least to have staunched the bleeding. He stared up at the night sky, trying to estimate how much time he had lost. Gingerly he tried to get to his feet but immediately dropped to the ground for there was no feeling in his legs. He rubbed them vigorously and then tried again, peering anxiously in every direction as he rose. He could barely feel his feet, but he stamped them one in front of the other for several yards and, as the stiffness began to wear off, he broke into an ungainly trot.

He stumbled along, willing himself to go faster, though he knew it was hopeless - he would not overhaul the others. He knew the forest as well as any man alive and took frequent short cuts along tracks which few would even have noticed.

His path crossed and re-crossed the route they had taken: broken stems and sliding footmarks telling him a story of tiring children and ever more frequent rests along the way. Then he suddenly stopped dead, for he found another set of tracks made by heavily armed men earlier in the day. He set off again and, though his legs ached and his head throbbed, he ran as hard as he could, for now he feared the worst.

He was making good ground until he fell over Jack Standlake; at first he couldn't quite believe it, poor Jack. But the fall had probably saved his life for when he got up onto his knees he spotted a line of bowmen ahead of him. He crouched down to get his breath back and then crept carefully between the trees, skirting a wide loop around the Radcliffe archers. For a time the moon bathed the forest in light and he glimpsed figures on the far side of the clearing.

§§§

Amelie watched Ned disappear into the forest with Bagot and for the first time she felt the loss: a dull emptiness in the pit of her stomach, for he was their leader, their warrior – how could they survive there without him? Then, like the others, she steeled herself to face an attack; the children were manhandled, shivering and terrified, along the ground into the centre of a protecting ring of adults. Those who had bows waited with them at the ready; among them, young Jim Standlake, barely fifteen years of age, nervously picking at the flight of an arrow. If they raised their heads above bracken height an arrow was loosed in response from the other side of the clearing – as Walter found when a shaft grazed his leather cap.

Amelie crawled alongside Becky, rummaging under her skirts to free the dagger from the velvet garter on her thigh. She took it from its soft hiding place and thrust it firmly into the earth close at hand. She felt much better to see its fine jewelled hilt protruding from the ground, but it made no difference at all when a mail clad figure flew out of the shadows and seized seven year-old Annie. He thrust her

160

mother aside and stood in the open before them with his dagger at the girl's throat. Annie let out a piercing scream.

"Give it up or I'll cut her throat!" he shouted and as he did so Mordeur and several more men at arms emerged from the cover of the trees. Amelie knew what would happen next: Walter Standlake looked sorrowfully at his daughter and tossed his sword to the ground and the others lowered their weapons. Annie's captor smiled, but slowly the smile froze and he dropped to his knees, letting his dagger fall harmlessly to the ground and releasing the girl as he clutched briefly at the long shaft protruding from his bleeding neck.

Walter snatched his daughter up and drew her to him, but Mordeur furiously hurled his own dagger to bury itself in the small girl's back. Walter stared at his daughter in disbelief as she crumpled in his arms.

Ned burst out of the trees with Will and Bagot a few paces behind him. He sliced his sword across the back of one of Mordeur's men at arms and a confused melee broke out. Mordeur headed straight for Amelie, who was still lying on the ground. She picked up her knife and scrambled to her feet. Holton took a pace towards Mordeur and swung his staff; the latter batted it away easily with his sword, but it gave Amelie time to get behind Holton. Stubbornly the smith held Mordeur at the end of his staff until Bagot reached him.

"Mordeur!" he bellowed, forcing the Frenchman to turn and defend himself.

"Ha! Bagot! You should've been dead long ago!" he shouted, lunging at Bagot's chest. "Have you even lifted that rusty old sword since you fled from France?" he taunted, delivering a hammer blow that Bagot barely managed to counter.

Amelie backed away from the two veterans as they matched each other blow for blow; she gasped when Ned appeared at her side covered in blood. He took her hand in his bloodied gauntlet.

"Are you alright?" he demanded. She nodded; it was all she could do.

"Good!" he said, "stay low!" She nodded once more, mesmerised by the blood he had left on her hand. Two men came after her together: Ned rolled around the first to stab him in the throat with his dagger and then took a full blooded swing at the other, carving him open from chest to navel. She watched horrified as blood and guts began to spill out and Ned clubbed the dying man to the ground. He left her with Holton and bludgeoned his way through man after man: her saviour, her brutal and pitiless warrior.

§§§

Mordeur remained sparring with Bagot until an arrow from the far side of the clearing pierced Bagot's thigh and curtailed the contest. He stumbled sideways and Mordeur shaped to cut him down, but Ned stepped forward and thrust his sword out at full stretch to divert the stroke. Mordeur swept his eyes around as the moon shone out once more; then he was gone, back into the safety of the trees.

All was quiet for a few moments in the forest and then the silence was fractured by Edmund's angry voice: "Ned Elder! I'll raise every man I have! I'll hunt you down! And mark me: I'll spare no-one next time!"

His words echoed around the forest and their impact was written on the despondent faces of the Standlakes.

"Will, follow them a way," ordered Ned, "make sure they're really leaving."

Will disappeared obediently into the darkness, whilst the others began to take stock of what had happened. Bagot leant back against a tree whilst Lizzie Standlake tended to the leg wound, which was slowly dribbling blood. He gave Ned a long, slightly bemused look. "I trust most of that blood you're wearing isn't yours – still, you did well tonight."

"Well? Aye, as well as a butcher's apprentice. Take care of that leg; you're going to need it."

"You know he won't give up," the older man said.

"They must have tracked us…"

"Perhaps not," said Bagot seeing Birches bring in Jack's body, followed by Alice Standlake, her eyes wild with grief.

"I found her wandering in the trees," said Birches.

Alice cried out when she saw Harry's body. "He said you'd be spared," she said, almost to herself. Then she looked up and saw young Annie in Walter's arms.

"He said the children would be safe, Walter ..."

Her brother in law stared at her in disbelief, struggling to grasp what she meant, then he gently laid down his daughter and walked towards her.

"It should have been alright," she pleaded.

"You murdering bitch! How could you do this to your own kin?" he growled and seized her around the throat. He spat into her eyes as he squeezed the life from her; Will and Birches dragged him off her, but he struck her head with his fist, knocking her on the forest floor. There she lay, weeping and moaning in the mud for none went to help her.

Walter took Birches arm. "Only you could've made that shot and, but for that other bastard, you'd have saved my girl." He turned away to gather up his daughter's body once more.

A desolate silence followed.

"So..." said Ned eventually.

"Aye," agreed Bagot.

Will returned. "They've gone; not many of them left as far as I could tell. If he's coming after us he'll need to raise more men."

Ned nodded; it was scant comfort though, given their own losses.

The next hour was one of the worst he could remember: they carved out shallow graves in a glade nearby for Annie, Jack and Harry. It was desperate work, with little light and no proper tools and there was the knowledge that even with a few stones piled on top, the graves would most likely be disturbed by wild boar or forest scavengers. Whilst the families grieved, Ned reluctantly turned his mind to what they should do next.

"How far do you think we are from Penholme?" he asked Bagot.

Bagot gave him a bleak look. "Too far; we won't make it with the … 'baggage' we're carrying. He'll catch us."

"You heard what he said; we can't put the children at risk again…"

"Then we must split up: the Standlakes take one road with the children, we take another – Radcliffe will follow us. If we can reach our mounts we can outrun him."

"What if he tracks the women and children instead?"

"Why would he? It's you he wants."

"At the priory he had me, but he wanted Amelie more - and tonight Mordeur made a grab for her too. If it's her he wants then splitting up is more of a risk."

"Whatever we do is a risk, Ned – and sitting here much longer makes the risk greater. Just do what seems best and put your trust in God."

Ned shook his head, for his confidence in the Lord was less sure than Bagot's.

"Alright, so we go for the horses and the rest go on up the valley to Penholme. That's the plan – talk to Walter and Tom."

"One other thing," said Bagot and he walked across to where Alice still sat alone.

"Did you tell him where we were heading?" he demanded.

She shook her head.

"Are you sure?" he rasped at her, "for the little ones' lives will depend upon it!"

"I didn't tell him!" she insisted.

The Standlake brothers needed little persuasion for they could see the sense of the proposal.

"We'll be safe enough if we can get to Penholme," said Walter, "it'll probably be deserted - but Jack said …" He swallowed hard. "Jack said the squatters had kept some of the cottages alright."

"Good. We'll pick up the horses and meet you there," said Bagot, "God willing, we should get there around the same time as you - before nightfall tomorrow."

"Take care through the forest," said Ned, "we'll leave the clearest tracks we can to draw Radcliffe after us, but stay on your guard."

"Are you alright?" he asked Amelie, but she didn't reply, staring instead at his blood-soaked mail coat.

"Are you alright?" he repeated.

"Yes, lord," she said flatly.

"You should be safer with the Standlakes and Lizzie will be glad of your help with the children."

He tried to show a confidence he didn't feel.

"Yes … the children give us hope." She gave him a curt nod of farewell – it was not the parting he had hoped for. He joined the others and they set off at a trot into the dark of the forest.

§§§

Almost at once they were gone. Amelie stared after them for a long time until she felt Mags eyes upon her, then she hurried to help Lizzie gather up the children. She admired Tom's wife, Lizzie; she has not asked for this burden, she thought, but she has borne it better than anyone.

Now they were in Tom's hands, for he had reluctantly taking up the mantle of his dead brother. He trudged grim-faced at the head of his family as they set off to walk through the remaining hours of darkness, leaving the more obvious track alongside the beck to follow a shallow overgrown ditch through the trees. Using the gully would make them less conspicuous, but it meant they were constantly hemmed in by a tunnel of branches overhead and Amelie hated seeing the thin fingers of the trees reaching out to each other above her head.

She found the long trek exhausting and even when they stopped at dawn, thoroughly drained, they were still deep in the forest. The weary children embraced sleep willingly, but for the rest there were more than enough fears to keep them awake. Mags found a hollow filled with decaying leaves and bracken fronds, but it was dry enough to sleep in. "Here, share this with me," she said taking Amelie by the hand, "it's not the first time we've been on the run together, is it!"

But they were unlikely bedfellows, Amelie thought, as she lay down in the undergrowth beside Mags. Despite her tiredness, Amelie could not sleep and when she sat up and turned to Mags she discovered that she too was still awake.

"You look terrible, sister," whispered Mags.

"Why do you always call me sister? Are we not very different, you and I?"

"Oh, I don't know. Let's see: where were you born?"

"Me? In Angers and I was not supposed to be born at all, so I grew up in a nunnery."

Mags pulled a face.

"It wasn't so bad," said Amelie, grinning, "How about you?"

"Birth wasn't my best moment..."

"You asked…"

"My pa was in France in the wars; he used to try and patch up the wounded. I was born in the camp: born to a whore, delivered by a whore – a great start…"

Amelie smiled. "Not so different then: whorehouse and nunnery; we could well be sisters!"

They laughed and talked on in low voices, until eventually sleep claimed them.

At dawn the sun's fibrous rays barely penetrated into the darkest recesses of the forest. Amelie, like many of the others, slept long into the morning. When they set off again, they maintained their course for several hours along the rugged ditch until it petered out where the ash and hazel began to thin. At long last they were nearing the fringes of the vast Yoredale forest. Amelie walked with the smaller children, for whom the journey had long ceased to be an adventure. Their nervous chatter of the day before had been replaced by a resentful silence, born of fear and exhaustion.

Yet, despite all her fears, the final hours of the journey were surprisingly uneventful as they struck out south and re-joined the beck - now a wider stream that meandered up the gentle slope of the valley. They entered some woods and then, as evening closed in upon them, they emerged into a flatter, open space beside the stream where they found the ramshackle huddle of deserted cottages that had once been the thriving village of Penholme.

"Thank God!" she said, "I thought we'd never get here."

18

The Yorkshire Dales, south of Penholme

This is all we need, thought Ned as he approached the shallow ford ahead. Opposite them at the stream's edge half a dozen or more riders were spread out across the width of the ford. Their bearing and equipment revealed only that they were men of war, for they wore no identifying badges.

"Mercenaries," muttered Bagot leaning forward onto his horse's neck to speak unobtrusively to Ned, "Flemish, by the sound of it."

"We can't afford any more wasted time," said Ned, "it's taken us a whole day to pick up the horses – the others are depending on us!"

He did not stop when he reached the ford but rode straight in, trying to force the riders to give way or pass by him in single file. Bagot and Will followed close behind him.

As he reached the leading horseman Ned smiled and called out: "God give you good morning, friend. It seems that there are many of us harnessed men on the road today."

The rider did not, however, seem willing to concede passage to Ned and instead he manoeuvred his grey mare to stand across Ned's path through the ford.

"We are not yet sure whether you are a friend or no," the stranger declared evenly.

"Flemish, my lord," Bagot confirmed quietly.

Ned sighed audibly. The last thing he wanted was a needless, and almost certainly costly, confrontation with a band of foreign mercenaries.

"I've no quarrel with you." Even as he was speaking he realised that if these men were already under some indenture they would have ignored him and ridden on. "Are you seeking employment?" he enquired, adding pointedly, "Since you clearly have nothing particularly pressing to do."

"Tell us who you are and what you have to offer," replied the rider, playing idly with the hilt of his sword. "You have some spare horses, I see."

Out of the corner of his eye, Ned spotted Birches carefully making his way down from where he had crossed unseen further upstream.

"My name is Ned Elder and I'm in great haste; I need the horses and I've no quarrel with you so please move aside unless you'd like me to move you." He gestured towards Birches who now appeared in full view thirty yards upstream, an arrow already notched in his bow. Several of the Flemish soldiers began to unsheathe their swords, but their leader just grinned and turned his mare to cross the stream and allow Ned to ride past him.

"Ned Elder," he acknowledged, "I give you passage – for today. You're right: we have no quarrel, but who knows where our work may take us tomorrow? Antoine de Noges looks forward to meeting you again – when you are in less haste."

He laughed lightly and led his men on past Bagot and Will.

Ned spurred his horse on and swiftly mounted the bank, with the others close behind him and Birches joining them.

The four men rode hard through the gently undulating terrain to the north west, crossing wooded valley after wooded valley, avoiding settlements to attract as little attention as possible. Once they had collected their mounts, they had covered their tracks as well as they could, but it had taken time and now they would have to ride through the night if they were to reach Penholme by morning.

§§§

As soon as the Standlakes arrived at Penholme they began the task of making the crumbling clutch of cottages fit to house them. It seemed to Amelie that several of the long cottages could be made habitable enough and within a few hours of their arrival she had ensconced herself, Mags and Becky in one of them with all the children, whilst the remainder of the family set about reopening the village well, reusing old thatch for roof repairs and scouring the land for anything that might be eaten. Jim Standlake, Harry's younger brother, was posted to keep watch on the track out of the woods north to Yoredale.

When they settled down for the night Amelie couldn't ever recall being so weary, but she drifted in and out of a restless sleep with little John curled up on the straw under her right arm. In a hazy waking moment her thoughts strayed unbidden towards Ned and the words they had exchanged at Corve. John stirred irritably in his sleep, but the others slumbered on uninterrupted and Mags snored noisily on the other side of the room. The boy turned over but Amelie could not get back to sleep; she examined her hand, there was still dried blood under her nails. She felt chilled; her soft breath was a swirl of white in the cool air of the cottage and she was stiff from lying cramped in the cold.

Carefully she extricated herself from John's trusting embrace and stepped lightly over the other children to slip silently from the cottage, wrapping her woollen shawl around her. The sky was lightening in the east, but a low lying mist had the village in its grip.

She wandered over the dew sodden ground, passing several derelict cottages and a row of fallen posts that she imagined must once have been sheep pens. Some houses had simply collapsed in a heap of rotten wood and straw, yet the final cottage in the row looked in better condition than the rest, so she wondered why Tom had not used it. She pushed at the door; it was stiff at first but then swung open. She stepped tentatively across the threshold into the dark, musty interior and stopped. There was a rectangular patch of thin straw in the centre of the floor, where she would have expected the stones of a hearth. After a moment or two of squinting in the gloom, she was able to make out two skeletal forms on the straw - perhaps the very last inhabitants of the dying village. She shivered at the sight of them, long since decayed and lying side by side. Despite the macabre nature of the scene, she felt the sadness of it. Were these two lovers stricken by plague, or an ageing couple seeing out their last days together in the village of their birth? What would it be like to be so devoted to someone that you would want to embrace death with them?

Suddenly a cold hand was clamped around her mouth and she was seized firmly from behind; for an instant, she froze in terror.

§§§

From his vantage point in the tree tops, Birches looked away to the northeast and swore under his breath. Penholme was ringed by woodland except to the south and southwest where hillside pasture was scarred by rocky outcrops and fast flowing becks. Birches had chosen a position affording him an excellent view of the cottages and also the woodland to the northeast. If Radcliffe was going to come, that was the way it would be. Even so he was surprised to see him so soon, coming up the track with some thirty or forty men. He must have scoured the estates to raise such a force so swiftly. They were arriving at pace and Edmund was drawing up his men at arms in a tight arc around the village.

He selected an arrow from his bag, put it to his bow and took careful aim.

§§§

"Be calm," breathed Ned softly.

Amelie relaxed a little and he released her, but for a brief moment she lingered close to him, surprised at how relieved she was that he had returned. Then she turned to face him: his thin beard was matted with sweat and dirt; he looked

172

gaunt and worried.

He took her hand. "You weren't with the others," he said.

"I needed to walk... Ned," She hesitated then, but didn't pull her hand away. "Why not let me stay here? I wasn't born to a life at court; I could be content with these people, with a simple life."

He didn't answer for a while, but kept her hand in his; then he seemed to make up his mind.

"If Edmund is hunting you, as you've seen, anyone who gets in his way will suffer and the Standlakes have many children..."

She knew he was right. "Yes, they have suffered enough," she said, but the prospect of being forever dragged around the country from one lonely castle or manor to another filled her with sadness.

Bagot appeared in the doorway and she let Ned's hand fall.

"Lord, we should be ready," said Bagot curtly. It seemed like a command, she thought.

"You'd best get back to the others," Ned told her and he followed her to the door of the cottage, where she joined Mags again to watch over some of the children.

Ned stood outside where he was joined by Will and Bagot - the latter, despite his many protestations, still impeded by his leg wound.

"Well, at least we all got here safely," said Will. An arrow thudded into the open door and several of the children cried out in alarm. Will dived into the cottage as his friend calmly reached across to retrieve the arrow.

"It's a warning – from Birches," Bagot explained, unable to hide a grin at Will's expense, but even he took cover when a second arrow hit the door and all of the children cried out. Amelie huddled them to the floor.

"What the hell does that mean?" Ned asked Bagot.

"If I know Birches, it means we've a crock of trouble heading our way!" said Bagot.

"Radcliffe?" asked Will, rising from the floor.

"I told you: it's her he's following – not me!" said Ned

bitterly.

"We can hold them, lord," asserted Bagot, but his voice betrayed his words.

Ned grimaced. "Hold them? We don't even know how many there are! And you can hardly move, man!"

"Will, talk to Tom and Walter; we must be ready. Oh no!"

He was staring at the track leading into the village from the south, where Antoine de Noges was leading in his band of Flemish mercenaries.

"What in God's name are you doing here?" shouted Ned angrily, "there's nothing for you here!"

De Noges grinned across at him, but his good humour did not last long for two of his men were instantly plucked from their saddles and more arrows burrowed into the crumbling walls around them. The rest dismounted and scrambled behind the ruins, accompanied by a fierce bout of cursing and recrimination.

"What's Birches doing?" said Ned.

Bagot stared in the direction the arrows had come from. "That wasn't Birches," he said slowly.

"Stay there!" Ned yelled across to De Noges, but the arrows were just a foretaste and, whilst he was still considering what to do next, men flooded into the village from the north – men wearing the red badge of the Radcliffes. He darted a final look at Amelie, who met his glance with anxious eyes.

"Stay here, Bagot; keep them safe - I'm better off on the move."

Bagot gritted his teeth, but nodded and drew out his falchion.

"And Bagot, don't let her out of your sight. Will! Come on, let's show them our steel!"

He filled his lungs, lifted his sword high and launched himself out of the cottage, with Will close behind. He met the men at arms head on, punching and chopping his heavy blade into man after man without breaking stride; somehow Will managed to protect his back. But despite the belligerence of their assault, Ned could see they were hopelessly outnumbered.

"Birches!" he bellowed, expecting to see arrows rain down upon his assailants, but none came. He hacked his way across to the other cottage where Walter, Tom and their young sons were fighting for their lives. Everywhere he turned an opponent faced him; he thrust forward and then clubbed aside a grey haired knight with a sharp blow from his sword hilt. Out of the corner of his eye he glimpsed Tom falling to the ground, his younger brother by his side.

"Will! Look to Tom," he said, then he turned swiftly to avoid a cut at his shoulder; angrily he swung his sword with such force that he all but removed his assailant's head.

"But you'll be on your own!" protested Will.

"Just hold here!" Ned shouted and took a step forward once more. They stood off him now and he took up his customary stance: head still, balance perfect and sword held vertically beside his head. He took another deep breath, surveying the open ground before him and the bloody scenes being played out all across the village. Tom was badly wounded, Bagot was still standing – only God knew how - and the Flemish... the Flemish, in self-defence he assumed, were occupying much of Edmund's force but if they caved in, he knew they were all doomed. What in God's name was Birches doing?

For a few more moments he held the men at arms facing him with his eyes, but they were edging closer. He swung his weapon slowly around in a sweeping arc in front of him.

"Come on then," he roared, "and this blade will eat you alive!" and with a suddenness that rocked them back, he ran at them, striking to left and right, cutting down two in quick succession. He did not pause but drove on, parting their ragged line with blow after quivering blow. Where he advanced, they fell back, but still their fellows closed in behind him. With no one at his back, he was obliged to twist and turn simply to stay alive – and with his father's heavy battle sword, he knew he couldn't keep it up for long.

§§§

Jim Standlake was perched uncomfortably in the splintered crown of a storm damaged oak. Cramp gripped his legs, so that when he tried to shift his position he found he could barely move. He had watched in dismay as the attack on the village had unfolded, but he dared not intervene for Bagot had told him not to fire unless Birches did. But Jim could not see Birches and the terrible thought crept into his head that Birches might already be dead.

He gripped his bow ever more tightly and continued to watch nervously, but when his uncle, Tom, was struck down and Ned's cry to Birches brought no response, the fifteen year old knew he must act. Jim had never killed a man; in fact he had never shot at anything larger than a hare: this was different altogether. He reached for an arrow, but could barely fit the nock to the bowstring as his fingers were greasy with sweat. When he did successfully take aim, his entire body shook uncontrollably and the arrow was unleashed so wildly that it passed over the cottages altogether, unnoticed by any of the combatants.

He gripped a branch to steady himself; then he tried again, raising his bow more carefully and taking a sight on the small knot of soldiers who were pushing the limping Bagot back through the cottage door. Despite the chill in the air, sweat ran down his forehead and stung his eyes as he tried to hold the bowstring taut. Upon its release the shaft flew truly and struck one of the men at arms with such force that he was knocked off his feet. The effect on the attackers was dramatic, and when he released a second arrow, others began to take notice and unease spread among Edmund's men. Jim began to relax his upper body and, blocking out all thought of those whose lives he was harvesting, he settled into a deadly rhythm of fire.

§§§

Edmund could see the struggle was turning against them.

"Where are all my archers?" he demanded of Mordeur.

"You ordered most of them into the village with the men at

arms," replied Mordeur, "we have only these three with us."

"Find that goddamned archer!" Edmund told them. "He must be in the trees somewhere."

"Shall we go in?" asked Mordeur as the archers set off.

Edmund ignored his question. "Have you seen the girl yet?" he said.

The Frenchman shook his head.

"When we do go in, make sure you find the girl first. Are you certain the men know not to harm her?"

"Every man knows that if he kills the wrong girl, I'll cut his balls off."

"Good. Do you remember that village near Calais – the plague village?" murmured Edmund.

Mordeur nodded. "We put a torch to it – several, if I remember correctly."

"Well, you know, I think there might be a touch of plague in this village too."

He waited until no more arrows came and then drew his sword. "I think their archer is done with; come on, let's finish it."

But Mordeur laid a restraining gauntlet on his arm. "Better to wait a little more," he said, pointing to their own archers who had just reached the far side of the village.

"Light a fire," ordered Edmund.

§§§

The fresh volley of arrows caught Ned unawares and forced him to scramble for shelter behind the stub of an overgrown wall. He crouched in the long grass, looking across at his unlikely allies, the Flemish, who were also pinned down amongst the ruins. Two more had been wounded and De Noges was being harangued by his seething comrades. Whatever gamble he'd intended at the start, it had surely backfired badly. He'll pull out, thought Ned, he must do – or lose everything. He watched in a daze as De Noges carefully sheathed his sword, took out a short length of white cloth from under his breastplate and waved it in the air.

Ned's head dropped, but when he looked up again something odd had happened: De Noges was on his knees, choking and the white banner lay on the ground beside him. An arrow had somehow found a gap between bevor and helm and had lodged in his neck. The soldier beside him, a vast brute of a man, let out a great roar and dragged De Noges behind a section of broken wall. There was a rumble of dismay from the tight knit band of mercenaries, for even Ned could tell that De Noges' wound was mortal.

He knew he must rally them before they surrendered, so he charged into the open; at once Edmund's men at arms came at him. He raised his blood smeared sword and hacked into them, scattering them like frightened sparrows as he ran towards the mercenaries. He was almost there when an arrow brushed the edge of his breastplate and punched across his ribs; it knocked him onto all fours and he crawled the last few yards. He'd never felt such pain, so he quickly examined the wound: it was shallow, but the arrowhead was firmly embedded. He snapped off the shaft and struggled to his feet. The tall mercenary loomed over him, a bull of a man harnessed in heavy, well-worn armour and bearing a massive axe. Ned watched in astonishment as he swatted an arrow away with his gauntlet.

"Will you fight?" demanded Ned, waving his sword to reinforce his words.

The rest were arguing angrily amongst themselves, but the giant soldier seemed to grasp Ned's meaning and barked at his comrades in a harsh guttural voice – at once they were silent. But Ned could see more men at arms emerging from the trees and among them he recognised Edmund himself.

§§§

Birches had not moved since he loosed his second warning arrow; he had cramp in both legs and his arms felt as stiff as the oak branch to which they clung. Edmund and several archers stood directly beneath him, thus he could do nothing without at once attracting their attention – it would have been suicide. So he had been lying motionless in the tree, whilst the carnage had unfolded in the village. He had just decided he must intervene, when the archers moved off. First he tried to take a shot at Edmund, but there were too many thick branches in the way. Then suddenly there was no-one under the tree and he realised that Edmund was heading into the village.

§§§

"We must push them back now or we're finished!" Ned shouted.

He doubted the Flemish mercenary understood, but he wasn't going to stand still waiting for another stray arrow to strike him down, so he did what he always did and it was the mercenaries' turn to be surprised. He charged Edmund's advancing line, though every step caused the protruding arrow to catch on his armour and tear the wound a little more. He felt the warm blood inside his gambeson, but put it from his mind.

It seemed to him that he had accounted for dozens of them, but there were still too many and Edmund was heading directly for him. Suddenly an arrow flew past Edmund and struck the man to his right in the shoulder. Edmund and the others hesitated and the attack faltered; Ned held back too, unsure whether the arrow was fired in error. Then he smiled as Edmund took an arrow in the thigh and fell, cursing angrily and glaring at Ned. The nearest man at arms helped him up and, still swearing loudly, he hobbled back into the trees. With the Radcliffes retreating into the trees, Ned cast his gaze around the arc of cottages and what he saw made him sink to his knees.

Bagot was staggering out of the doorway he had defended so resolutely, dragging his useless leg; Tom was leaning white-faced against the cottage wall, chest red with blood from the fearsome neck wound he had sustained almost from the first blow; de Noges and half the mercenaries lay dead and the remainder looked angry and dispirited; and finally, most telling of all, the women and children who peered out of the cottages looked terrified and without hope.

He closed his eyes to shut out the misery.

19

Penholme, March 1460

"Now's the time for a clear head, lad," said a gruff, familiar voice – somehow, Bagot had worked his way across to him.

"It's not over with, Bagot!"

"I know, but let's have a look at that wound first."

A flaming arrow seared over their heads to land on one of the thatched roofs; another soon followed.

"No! It's too late! We've got to get them out!" said Ned.

"We can take our chances in the forest," suggested Bagot.

"Can we outrun them?" Ned asked.

Bagot's look told all.

"No, I thought not... so, we may as well die here!"

Bagot shrugged. "We can get the children away and some of us might make it - we're in God's hands now."

"I want Amelie out of here," Ned said, "whether God wills it or not!"

"Of course, if some were to stay, then those that go have a better chance," said Bagot.

"We could give our Lord a helping hand," Ned said.

Bagot met his eyes. "Are you sure about this?" he asked.

"Let's just do it!"

The large mercenary with the axe took Ned's arm and spoke urgently to him.

"Bagot, do you know what the hell he's talking about?" asked Ned

"About one word in five."

"Well, that's one word more than me! Tell him what we're doing and see if they'll help us."

He left them and walked unsteadily over to Tom and Walter.

"You can do no more; take your families west into the hills for a day or so; we'll try to hold Radcliffe here – you may be sure I'll not forget what you've done. God be with you both."

The brothers nodded wearily and Ned could tell from their faces that they didn't expect to be seeing him again.

When he found Amelie he began to explain to her, but she stopped him with a gesture.

"I know; it's in your face: we must go."

Even as they stood together in the cottage doorway, several more burning arrows buried themselves into the thatched roofs and cottage walls. Ned dropped to the floor, pulling her with him, forgetting his wound for a moment. The fire had already taken hold in several places and flames were leaping from one cottage to another. More arrows followed, setting every hut and storehouse in Penholme ablaze.

Will and Holton ran to the well to raise some water.

"Leave it," ordered Bagot, "it's too late." Then he raised his voice: "Birches! Jim! Come in!"

Becky and Lizzie Standlake hurried the children out of the burning buildings.

Walter called to them: "take them to the west end! We'll follow on!"

Bagot limped off with Holton and Will to bring up the nervous horses. Ned took Amelie's cold hand to lift her up. Mags was soon beside them.

"You can stay with the Standlakes, if you want to," Ned told her.

"What are you doing?" Mags asked Amelie.

Her voice was flat, her face grim. "I'm going with Ned."

"Then, I'll go too, sister." She took Amelie's arm in hers and they went to the horses together.

Birches came into the village at the run, bearing Jim's young body on his shoulder.

"I'm sorry, lord; they were all over me, I could barely get a shaft away." He gently laid Jim down. "I couldn't leave him out there."

"First the father, now the son," said Ned. Becky fell upon her cousin's body and sobbed.

Alice stumbled out of a cottage and screamed, seeing another son dead. "You brought this on us!" she railed at Ned, throwing herself at him, scratching at his face.

Walter picked her up and threw her angrily against the cottage wall: "No! Don't you ever forget, you bitch; it was you who brought this on us all! I'd kill you myself, but you've still got others to look to – now see you do!"

He shepherded the rest of his family out of the village leaving Ned still standing there, drained; but Bagot had all the mounts ready.

"The Flemish will stand with us," he said, "and the big one's called 'Bear'- at least I think that's what he's called…" He ducked as another arrow passed over.

"Tom and Walter have got their families away," said Ned.

"Aye, they're all heading west; everyone else is mounted up and ready to go. Come on!" urged Bagot.

The village was burning and no more arrows came; it would not be long before Edmund attacked. Perhaps they should all go; but no, they would be reeled in, squirming and screaming perhaps, but reeled in nevertheless. So, there was no choice: if she was to get away, he must stand; he must stand and he must kill Edmund. He unclasped his great sword and scabbard.

"What's wrong?" asked Will, but he knew Ned all too well; he started to dismount.

"No Will," said Ned, "I'm relying on you, my friend, to get Amelie and the others out. I'll meet you at Corve in a couple of days."

"I'm not leaving you, Ned, not now!"

"Do this for me, Will. Quickly, give me one of your fine blades and look after this for me." He handed over his heavy battle sword for he knew he could not fight with it mounted

– and in any case he was no longer in any fit state to wield it.

"Ride on!" he shouted to the others and slapped Amelie's mare on the rump. She looked back at him, bewildered, and then Will hauled on her bridle and took her away to race off through the trees with Mags, Holton and Birches.

"It's supposed to be the other way round," said Bagot, "the servants are supposed to get themselves killed letting you escape!"

Ned frowned without reply and mounted his horse. He brandished Will's sword to try its weight; it was much lighter than his own, a weapon made for speed and skill.

He looked at the others: there were only six of them: he and Bagot mounted, whilst the heavily armoured mercenaries formed up in a line between them.

Without warning Edmund's horsemen came out of the trees and made for the mercenaries who stood like four tall stones before them. They rode hard and shouted loudly, but when Bear buried his axe into the chest of the leading horse and its terrified shrieks sliced through the air, their nerve failed. With his second blow, Bear despatched the falling rider. Bagot charged into their flank, timing his attack exquisitely as the riders tried to sheer away. He burst through the pack, striking to right and left, whilst Ned tried to reach Edmund in the second wave of riders.

Again and again, he and Bagot hacked into the chaotic melee, bleeding their enemies beyond forbearance, destroying their will to fight; but all too soon the older man was exhausted, his falchion feeling like a great anvil in his hands. Reluctantly he slid from his horse, braced his back against a wall and determined to make a stand alongside Bear. The latter was busily chopping at Mordeur, who had just cut down one of his comrades; Bear struck his horse so hard that Mordeur was thrown roughly to the ground and lost his helmet. Before he could get up, Bagot staggered forward to club him down. To his surprise Bagot found Ned's horse alongside him and the young knight leant down and bellowed above the din, "no matter what it costs, Edmund must not escape - or we may as well die here!"

"We are fucking dying here!" retorted Bagot. Ned could see that the bloodied veteran was already a spent force; so, tight-lipped, he persuaded his reluctant stallion back once more into the fight. In the seething tangle of wounded men and screaming horses, he wrought death wherever he went.

§§§

Edmund looked aghast across the bloody scene, astonished at how utterly his force had been dismembered. Then through the haze of smoke he fixed on Ned: it seemed that now there were just the two of them, for all the rest were wounded or had fled. Suddenly, after so much wretched clamour, only the moans of the dying men and animals could be heard and nothing else moved. He stared across at Ned, weighing up his chances. His opponent sat awkwardly in the saddle: he looked bloody and badly mauled. Somewhere Edmund had lost his sword; he couldn't remember how, but he drew out his long dagger and walked his mount slowly and deliberately towards Ned; he too urged his horse forward, but both beasts were so exhausted that they converged at barely a trot. The two horses nudged each other irritably as their riders clashed and they passed side by side. The exchange of blows was brief but deadly: Ned sliced his narrow blade precisely under Edmund's breastplate below his ribs. Even as he felt the steel cut him deeply, Edmund plunged the dagger he held into Ned's unprotected side.

Neither was unhorsed but, after a few yards, both stopped. Edmund struggled to remain in the saddle and, seeing Bagot limping towards him, he walked his mount back into the trees where dizziness began to engulf him. Blood was flowing freely from his wound and he wanted to clamp his mailed fist over it. He looked at his arm, but it would not move and then he surrendered to unconsciousness.

§§§

Bagot had watched the clash but at first he couldn't tell whether Ned was hurt or not, and then, as if in slow motion, the youth simply slid forward and rolled from his saddle. Bagot, carrying his own rich assortment of wounds, could only hobble over to him. He bent down to examine Ned, who was conscious but bleeding badly from his wounds. He called to Bear, who was leaning exhausted against a door frame; the mercenary stirred himself enough to limp over and join them.

Bagot surveyed the body strewn ground around him: there was no-one else still standing. At the back of his mind, as he examined Ned's wounds more closely, there was a nagging doubt: he remembered striking Mordeur down, yet his body was nowhere to be seen.

Ned tried to sit up and failed.

"Steady lad, I think we've broken them."

"Bagot, we're all broken; is Radcliffe dead?"

"Don't know; first let's see to your wound or you'll be falling off your horse again!"

"Be swift then, for he might still be alive!"

"I'll take as long as I take," muttered Bagot.

Ned allowed himself to be helped to a sitting position so that Bagot and Bear could bind up his wounds with torn strips of cloth to staunch the bleeding. Having taken care of Ned, Bagot then took a few minutes to tend to his own wounds. Bear went to retrieve their horses and when he returned Ned was on his feet, waiting impatiently.

"We've tarried too long," he said.

"You've done what you needed to do," said Bagot, "Radcliffe will be running home by now; if he still lives - believe me, he looked done for."

"Yes, but where is he?"

§§§

Mordeur walked groggily through the trees away from Penholme, blood seeping from his head wound and dribbling down the left side of his face to congeal in his beard. When

186

he found a stray horse he made a clumsy attempt to mount it, but swayed in the stirrup and so instead he leant upon the animal's back for a moment and then pushed it through the trees until he happened upon his master. Edmund had fallen from his horse and was muttering profanely, his hand pressed to the wound in his midriff. Mordeur cursorily examined the wound: the damage looked lethal, but he did his best to staunch the flow. He tried to raise Edmund onto his newly acquired horse, but his head was swimming and Edmund fell awkwardly across the saddle.

"You trying to kill me too, you clumsy bastard?" grumbled Edmund, seizing the horse's mane to support himself. He saw that several of his men had joined them.

"Where are the rest?" he demanded.

"Dead, gone, run off? Who knows?"

Mordeur suspected that by the time they arrived back at Yoredale Castle, Edmund would be dead too, but he took him anyway – explaining his death to Lord Radcliffe would be difficult enough without leaving the corpse behind to rot in the forest.

"Did you see the girl?" asked Edmund.

"No. She must have gone with some of the others."

"Gone? Gone where?" Edmund felt as if the blood had drained out of him; he was starting to shiver and Mordeur wrapped a cloak around him. He looked at his remaining men at arms accusingly.

"Where are the women and children?" he demanded.

"They left the village before we went in, Sir Edmund," replied one.

"Then we'll skirt the village and track them!"

"Leave it!" advised Mordeur.

Edmund stared him down.

"Very well, track them," conceded Mordeur, "but it'll probably kill you!"

§§§

"We could make a run for it," said Bagot quietly, "follow Will and the others."

"First I want to know Edmund's dead," said Ned and he rode off slowly into the trees.

They explored the forest cautiously, following several blood trails all of which petered out or circled back onto each other.

"He's got to be here," insisted Ned.

"I told you: if he lives, then he'll have gone back to Yoredale," said Bagot, but then he studied the track ahead of him carefully. "This is a different trail," he said thoughtfully, "and it's fresh…" Bear held up six fingers and Bagot nodded.

After half a mile or so, they stopped.

"Ned…" began Bagot.

"I know," Ned said, his voice trembling. "They're heading back to the village."

By common consent, they quickened their pace.

"Be watchful," advised Bagot softly, as they rode back into the burnt out village where only a few stubborn timbers still smouldered on. At first they saw nothing out of the ordinary. Bagot dismounted to study the tracks more closely; he led them on foot through the village and paused where Will had turned south with Amelie and the others.

"Well, that's something: they haven't followed Will," he said.

"Thank God!" said Ned. "Where then?"

"West, by the look of it."

"Oh shit, he's following the Standlakes!" Not waiting for Bagot to remount, Ned urged his horse forward. "I knew we should've moved quicker!"

"Wait!" shouted Bagot, but Ned ignored him and rode on, following the two sets of tracks which climbed beyond the cottages onto the high pasture land alongside the beck. The beck narrowed, flowing faster, and other smaller tributaries joined it. The pasture became rock strewn scrubland where the becks twisted and turned as they forged their paths down the slope. After another mile, they found Tom in a shallow gully; his neck wound had not killed him, but several sword thrusts to the body had.

"Help me down, Bagot," said Ned.

"Stay where you are, Ned; you can see well enough from there."

"Help me down damn you, or I'll throw myself down!" snapped Ned, "we'll do this on foot."

Reluctantly Bagot acquiesced and Ned stumbled on up the rocky gully, scanning the slopes on either side of the beck. A few yards further on, he stopped. The boy was lying face down in the water; he was such a slight lad, John, so the arrow in his back must have lifted him off his feet and thrown him into the beck.

Bagot stared at the small body in disbelief. Ned worked his way further along the gully; in a moment Bear gripped his arm and turned to where the beck swung sharply round to the right and was joined by another small stream. Bear pointed to the reddish brown water that trickled over the rocks below the beck. Ned moved more quickly, wincing with pain more than once as he negotiated the uneven terrain. Then he passed a larger group of rocks and there it was, all laid out before them like a terrible scene plucked from a mystery play and frozen for all time. For a while he could not, dared not, move; thinking perhaps that if he didn't look upon it, it would not be there; but it did not go away.

"Why would he do that?" asked Bagot, his voice breaking.

Scattered along the gully and in the beck were the rest of the Standlake family.

Ned started forward again, biting his lip as the tears dropped unbidden from his cheeks.

Bagot and Bear followed him and together they went from one to another in the vain hope of life; they found none. Walter had defended his family to the end and beside him lay his young sons and nephews, all with swords in their hands. Their blood was still seeping into the beck.

Beyond them lay the women. Lizzie and Alice lay together.

"Lizzie...you were always a fighter..." Bagot knelt beside her blood covered body, shaking his head.

Her hand still held the knife which she had plunged into Alice's throat at the end.

"They must have been terrified," said Ned, "but surely… I hurt him badly, Bagot; surely Edmund was too far gone to do all this!"

"Others would do it gladly if it brought them enough reward," said Bagot.

For a time afterwards the three of them just sat in the bloody place; they all knew what had to be done, but none could summon the will to do it. In the end Bagot got up stiffly and stood beside Ned; he dropped his hand gently onto the young man's shoulder. It was a rare show of emotion from the old warrior, but though he had seen his full share of death in all its grisly guises, even he seemed overwhelmed.

"Come, Ned," he said and helped him up. They began the task of moving the bodies up to a piece of high ground where they could bury them. The ground was still hard: it would be stern, unremitting work.

When they had recovered them all, Ned looked puzzled.

"Some of the children aren't here."

At once Bagot and Bear scoured the area around the gully and then further up towards the head of the valley, but they found no-one else.

"I should've seen at once: the girls are missing: Becky and the three younger ones," said Bagot.

"Shit! Do you think they escaped?" said Ned.

"No … they couldn't have got that far; we'd have found them. I'm afraid he's taken them."

"I should never have brought them from the Hall…"

"Ned, this isn't your doing; sometimes in war, men become little more than animals; things that shouldn't happen do."

"War isn't the word for this, Bagot."

20

The Nunnery in North Wales, November 1460

A small bead of perspiration dropped from her forehead and splashed onto the stone floor. In the darkness Eleanor couldn't see it but she knew the growing damp patch would be there. She flexed her arms, forcing her body up and then lowering it again; raising, lowering, raising again, relentlessly working her body as more sweat accumulated beneath her. Soon she could smell it, just as she could feel the sinews stretch and bend, for in the hours of the night she could indulge her senses: she could feel and she could dream.

During the day she conformed, she hated it, but she conformed; she attended the procession of daily services and she carried out her work, which was usually spinning and always tedious. The first months had depressed her: there was so much silence – she thought she might drown in the silence. If it wasn't silence then it was listening to some turgid reading; well, she didn't exactly listen.

In those early, angry days Edwina had kept her apart from the other inmates and put her in a tiny cell on her own. Yet it was not quite the penance the prioress had intended, for in time Eleanor filled her nights alone with everything the church condemned most. It started on a warm autumn night when she removed her woollen habit and wimple and in the darkness explored her naked body; she was distressed to discover that in only a month or so it had become soft and flaccid. So at once she lay down on the cold stone by her bed and began to exercise her limbs; that night she carried on until she could no longer push herself up from the floor.

Now, on this cool November night almost a year later, her body was trimmed to lean muscle: her jaw was tight, honing a hard edge to her face and her legs were as strong and supple as willow. She ceased her exertions and reached in the pitch black for the bowl of water; she cupped the water into her hands and poured it over her hair, so that it trickled down cold onto her warm back and breasts. Then she wiped off the water and sweat with a linen cloth and lay down on her bed pulling a single blanket over her. Her body was still tingling and she ached for Will. She had learned much from the Yoredale midwife about being with a man, but it turned out that the most useful thing the old woman had confided in her was how to do without a man: 'my dear young lady, you'd be surprised what you can do with oil - a little oil can go a very long way.' Indeed it could and when she went to the chapel for Matins in the small hours of the morning she was still glowing.

She was late so she took a shorter route through the infirmary – not for the first time. She dashed out of the infirmary door and down the short flight of steps onto the dark cloister; there she almost collided with another figure walking briskly towards the dormitory. Both stopped and stared at each other for what seemed a long time, though it was only an instant.

"Ned?" The moment she posed the question, she knew it wasn't her brother; the stranger said nothing and merely continued on his way. She stood for a moment, collecting herself – the face had seemed so familiar that she had offered Ned's name, yet in the poor light it could have been anyone.

"Fuck!" she said, realising she would be late and hurried on to the chapel, arriving breathless and drawing the attention of all, not least a frowning prioress.

Throughout the service her mind wandered far from the scriptures and her responses were halting and tardy. She could think of nothing but the young man she had seen -

what was he doing inside the priory at the dead of night? Was he a servant? Perhaps one of the sisters had a lover? Was he Edwina's lover? The delicious thought caused her lips to stumble over the phrases and she avoided the suspicious glances of the sisters nearby. Then her shoulders dropped and soon she returned to the rhythm of the responses, for a more likely explanation had occurred to her and the mystery was solved: the young man was simply a visiting pilgrim.

Later, returning to her cell, she berated herself for her fanciful imaginings; the priory did not have many visitors, but there were some, and that was an end to it - except the thought of him still lingered. Of course, if she went to the guest hall she could make absolutely certain; but it was still dark and the guest hall was far from her cell. If she was discovered there she would be punished severely, yet it was the only way she could think of to rid her mind of him.

After Matins most of the inmates took the night stair to the dormitory, but her cell was further away. She stopped, weighing up the risks, then she retraced her steps along the cloister, trying to walk as softly as possible. She cut through the refectory, knowing no-one would be there and went on into the kitchen, unlatching the small door at the rear that led out into the courtyard behind. She swiftly crossed the yard to the guest hall and when she reached it she flattened herself against the wall, surprised to find that her breathing had become short and fast. She sank against the stone at her back and tried to calm herself; any sign of her own weakness irritated her. Footsteps sounded on the other side of the courtyard; she held her breath as the steps continued along the far wall: slow rapping steps. She breathed more easily when she recognised Sister Ursula's clogs.

She waited until the footsteps had faded, then she went to the door of the hall; if there were any visitors in the priory that night they would be sleeping there. She opened the door, which creaked noisily on its old hinges and she froze in the door way. She paused, listening; but there were no sounds of breathing, no snoring, no restless snuffling in sleep. She hesitated in the doorway then went in leaving the door open, lest its noise disturbed any occupants. There was no light, not even a rush light, so she cautiously crossed the floor of the hall, and began to examine each of the sleeping bays. She groped her way from one straw mattress to another; this is madness, she thought, for if anyone were here they would surely cry out if she laid her hand on them. Nevertheless, she carried on around the hall, checking each of the six bays, but all were unoccupied. She smiled; if the youth was a visitor, then he was sleeping somewhere else.

The following day there was no sign of him, but days later she still could not stop thinking about him. He was just one young man, but she convinced herself that he was part of a secret − a secret that might help her gain her freedom. She knew it was unlikely, she knew she was risking all in a baseless gamble, yet she had been compliant long enough: it was time to challenge Edwina once again.

Slipping out of her cell after Vespers, she arrived unbidden at the private quarters of the Prioress. She knocked boldly on the door, knowing that Edwina would not be pleased to see her, and she was not disappointed.

"Go back to your cell," ordered the Prioress before Eleanor had even uttered a word.

"Mother Prioress, I beg you to forgive this intrusion; but for many months I have been most obedient. I beg you to ask Lord Radcliffe to allow me to return home."

Edwina grimaced. "Obedience is just the beginning… and you're not being very obedient now."

"I'm certain he'd listen to you," she implored.

"Yes, he would; but I shan't ask him, you foolish girl, because it was I who asked him for you; otherwise he would long ago have married you off to some well-connected knight."

"You? But why? What do you want with me?"

"I want nothing of you at the moment except that you return to your cell before Compline."

Eleanor knew that she stood on a precipice: if she was going to go through with it, this was the moment.

"I saw a young man," she said, "three nights ago." She studied Edwina's face for any reaction, but the Prioress did not even blink.

"A young man, in the cloister at night," persisted Eleanor.

Edwina waved a hand dismissively. "A pilgrim visitor; now go!"

"There were no visitors that night," said Eleanor softly.

Now there was a trace of doubt in Edwina's face; she opened her door a little wider and stood back, but the eyes that ushered Eleanor in were cold and calculating.

"You make up this young man," said Edwina, "but it won't get you anywhere."

"I want to know about this man," she insisted.

Edwina gave her an indulgent smile. "There is no man; go back to your cell."

"The youth - just tell me!"

"No. You came here knowing nothing and you'll leave knowing nothing. Now go."

"Not until I know all!" declared Eleanor.

Edwina faced her in silence for a moment; finally she said: "You'd do well to remember what happened last time you defied me."

"You're alone this time."

"I don't need Sister Margaret."

Eleanor braced herself for the expected blow, but instead Edwina put her hand affectionately on her shoulder.

"You don't know me well enough, child," she said with a smile, and as she said the words she slid a fine, narrow blade through Eleanor's habit and into her ribs – not deep enough to kill, but enough to inflict pain. Eleanor recoiled, clutching at the wound, but then she flew at the prioress, seizing hold of her scapula and hurling her to the floor. Edwina was stunned and let the blade fall; swiftly Eleanor struck her on the side of the head with her fist and retrieved the weapon. She dropped on top of her and pinned her to the floor with her knees. She put the knife point to her throat and the blade pricked the skin, drawing a speck of blood. She considered driving the point home; her face was so close to Edwina's she could feel her breath on her cheek.

"Do it then," said Edwina softly, "do it – you can leave if you do; so do it."

Eleanor was angry and confused; her wound was sore and it nagged at her.

She cleared her head. "Tell me about the youth," she said again.

"If your mother was holding that knife, I'd be dead by now. She'd have punched it through my neck without a thought - but not your father... because he loved me."

"Will you stop about my mother and father!" warned Eleanor, pressing the point down harder. She could see the sweat on Edwina's brow and chin; she felt her tremble under the blade.

"But they are the answer to your question, for the youth you saw is your half-brother."

"I don't want to hear lies!"

The Prioress said nothing, so Eleanor pricked the skin of her neck, making her gasp.

"I can't tell you about him without speaking of your mother and father."

"Very well, but leave nothing out: how is he my half-brother?"

"If I leave nothing out, you'll know everything and you'll wish you didn't, I can promise you that!" said Edwina.

"Everything!" Eleanor spat at her.

"Let's start with your mother, Kate - you're the image of her, you are just ... Kate. You're certainly as fair as she was; and then there's the spirit ... I thought for a while you'd lost it, but obviously not."

The knife point pressed down again, but Edwina stared up at Eleanor and she withdrew the blade a little.

"Kate and I were rivals once - for your father – and I lost. She married him, had a son and then he went off to war in France. He was away a long time and while he was away,

Kate became …restless; you're her daughter, so you'll know about that."

Eleanor felt nauseous, for Edwina's words struck home hard: she knew all about 'restlessness'.

"She got very, very restless," continued the prioress, "so that when your father returned he found her with child - my brother Robert's child."

"I told you, no lies!"

"You know this is no lie, girl; you're cast from the same metal as she. Your father left her and for a while he came to me, loved me and promised me all."

Edwina's face glowed as she spoke, but then her expression hardened.

"She lost her bastard, so he went back to her again; I was broken … and I hated her for that. Then, your brother Ned and the rest of you were born; and I was left with nothing – well not quite…but a shadow of my love. As I told you … your half-brother."

Eleanor felt the slightest of tremors in her bottom lip as she listened; she didn't want to believe any of it, but then she thought how she had lived her own life and it seemed to ring true. She released her hold on Edwina and took the knife from her throat.

"Is that what you wanted to hear? Why do you think my brother was so swift to strike at your father when he got the chance? He never forgave your parents - and neither did I. You know it all now, but you'll rot on your own with that knowledge," said the prioress.

Eleanor was slow to register the change of tone and before she could react, Edwina had pushed her back hard; too late she saw the hand rush towards her head. Oh shit, where did she get the stone?

§§§

She woke up in a different cell which was damp, musty and much colder than her own. It was still dark and she had no idea how long she had lain there. She went to stand up but the whole of her head seemed to ache and she winced as she felt the pull of the small puncture beside her ribs. She scrambled with difficulty to her knees and began to explore the room with her hands; at once she found the stonework was crumbling away in places. She felt her way to the door and found an iron shackle fixed to the wall beside it. Using the iron ring she pulled herself to her feet; then walking away from the door she came up against a wall; she leant on it and then leapt away from it in terror as the top of it gave way and fell outward, crashing noisily to the ground below. She could feel a breeze on her face and turned to peer over the wall, but could see nothing.

When dawn came she was already wide-awake, staring in disbelief at the low walls of her cell. By daylight, she could see that the room had been built on a spur of the very rock upon which the whole priory rested. However, over time it seemed that part of the spur had sheered away and the walls built upon it had gradually been weakened. During the night she had pushed out part of the wall; she looked down at the stones which had tumbled to the valley floor below.

§§§

Edwina visited her after Prime. She was shocked to see how much more of the cell had been demolished – clearly it was more precarious than she had imagined – though no less suitable for all that. Eleanor, squatting on the floor, looked too tired to offer much resistance.

"Try not to destroy the whole cell, because it's the only one you'll ever see," said Edwina.

"It was all lies, wasn't it," muttered Eleanor, "everything you told me – and I fell for it."

"Would you know the truth if you heard it?" replied Edwina. Then she left her and locked the door again before making her way back to her own chamber. There Henry was waiting for her and she could see that he was pleased to see her. He kissed her cheeks and hugged her to him.

"You must be more careful, my dear," she said, "you were

seen, but tis no matter now."

"Good. Mother, you said that at the end of the year I'd be ready; now winter's come, I think it's time I went to take my inheritance. All those years in France have been wearing me down."

She touched his bearded chin. "More hair… you were just a boy when you left for France. You're so different now; older yes, and broader in the shoulder and tall, so tall."

"Yes, mother; I'm ready now!"

"Good, because we have a great deal to do; but you'll need to be patient, for you have many enemies – even if most of them don't know that you exist!"

"They'll soon know me and they'll need to watch their backs," he said with a grin, "both the Elders and the Radcliffes."

21

The Road South From Penholme, March 1460

They were encamped in a small wood, huddled around a smoking fire made with damp branches. Amelie studied the others: their mood was solemn, for all harboured their own fears and none welcomed time to dwell upon them - even Mags was subdued. They were a long way from Penholme now, a long way from where they had left Ned and Bagot. They had followed Will, frantically at first until they passed through the southern hills and out of the dales; then he had slowed his pace as they crossed mile upon tedious mile of rolling hills and valleys.

She was anticipating a miserable night, for they were tired and hungry; they had eaten only the game Birches had killed during the afternoon – and he'd killed precious little of that.

"What's this?" asked Holton, holding up a piece of bone with a shaving of brown meat on it.

"Don't ask and you won't be disappointed," replied Birches, putting an end to any further discussion about food.

Amelie hated sitting in the half-light, for it recalled memories of Mucklestone church; dark and dangerous. She felt her ribs where the knife had sliced into her; it was almost as if the cold blade was still lodged there. When she drove such memories from her head, her mind filled with thoughts of Ned: of his bloody power with the sword, of his kindness to the children. She knew she had been harsh with him, this fierce warrior with the soft grey eyes.

Mags sat down alongside her. "You're very quiet," she said with a knowing smile.

For once Amelie was glad of the cloak of night, which hid the flush in her cheeks.

"We're all thinking of him, not just you," said Mags.

Amelie stared absently into the smoke. "I don't know what I'm thinking," she said.

Mags pulled a face. "Then you're truly buggered!"

They hoped that Ned would reach them during the night, but he did not; nor did he arrive in the morning.

"Could he have missed us in the night?" asked Holton.

"Perhaps," said Will, though he did not sound convinced.

"We should wait for them," said Holton.

"We're not waiting," said Will firmly, "Ned told me to get you to Corve – and that's where we'll wait for them."

Amelie could see that everyone else disagreed and, left to their own devices, she thought they would probably have waited there all day, but Will forced them on and they sullenly rode south again, scanning the horizon behind them in vain. The clouds closed in and freezing March rain cut across them in wild bursts; it did nothing to raise their spirits. It took two more long days for them to reach the familiar gatehouse of Corve Manor. Mother Betwill clucked and fussed around them, but Betwill himself seemed much more concerned by the absence of Bagot and Ned.

Will led them all straight into the Great Hall, stepped up onto the dais at the far end and there on the lord's high table he placed Ned's battle sword, still smeared with dried blood from the struggle at Penholme.

"Let it rest here until he claims it himself," he said solemnly.

Betwill had been following at his heels. "When do you expect him?" he asked.

"Well, in truth Master Betwill, he may not come..."

"May not come? May not come? What do you mean: 'he may not come'?" demanded Betwill.

"God knows ... you must understand how it was – we were fighting for our lives! We parted in haste."

"I don't care how it was!" cried Betwill, "are you telling me that your lord is dead?"

"No!" he snapped. But they could all see that Betwill had already made up his mind: no lord meant that until another one appeared, Corve was once more his to command.

"I'll give him till Easter; if he's not here by then ... well, surely he won't be coming at all."

"Very well," Will agreed, for even he knew that they could not wait forever.

But two weeks later the refugees from Penholme found themselves summoned to the Hall by Betwill. On the high table Ned's sword still lay unclaimed and only one conclusion seemed possible.

Amelie voiced the question in everyone's mind. "What happens if he doesn't come?"

"Our lord told us to wait at Corve; and that's what we should do," said Holton simply.

"But for how long?" asked Birches, "You can see we're a burden on this house..."

"Surely 'our lord' must be dead, or he'd have been here by now," said Betwill.

"He's not dead!" declared Holton, "so we should wait."

"It doesn't feel as if he's dead," agreed Will.

Betwill shrugged. "Dead is dead – there's no feeling in it, boy."

In a breath, Will drew his sword and laid it against Betwill's neck.

"Steward you may be, but until Ned comes, you'll answer to me," he said.

"You?" Betwill was outraged. "I'll not be told by you - barely a squire! You've no power here."

Will moved his sword a hair's breadth nicking the skin on the steward's neck. "Just now, I've all the power here."

Betwill sweated, but he was no coward. Amelie rested her hand on Will's sword arm and gently pulled it away.

"Will, I am sure that Master Betwill understands well enough what Ned would want – there's no need for your sword here; we have seen enough blood already."

Obediently Will sheathed his sword. "Your pardon, Master Betwill; I acted in haste," he said and walked stiffly from the Hall.

"He's worried - we're all worried," said Holton.

"And I don't need advice from the likes of you," retorted Betwill, "any of you! Easter, I said – and Easter I meant. Three weeks, and after that, you can all go as beggars for all I care!"

On Easter Day Amelie rose early; she was not alone, for many of the women on the manor were already about, eager to watch the sun rise. She had shared some of their despair during the icy winter months; now she intended to share in their embrace of a new hope. They had come to accept that the husbands and sons who had left the previous summer with Thomas Elder would not be returning and Amelie felt some kinship with them. Thus she did not go to the private castle chapel with the Betwills, nor to the battlements with Will and the others; instead she walked through the fields with the young village girls, drinking in the early rays of the sun with them as they made their way to the small stone church half a mile from the Manor. The priest, born in the year of the great victory at Agincourt and worn out from years of hardship and penury, dutifully led his congregation in prayers and hymns for a new beginning.

She watched the women in admiration; they are beaten down to their knees each winter, she thought, and yet on Easter day they rise up again in hope. She recalled the lavish celebrations at court and the feasting that followed; but how much more this beacon of Easter meant to these folk, so far removed from the royal court. She watched and wept; later, in the evening, she wept some more for she did not find what she sought that Easter morning. She did not find renewed hope.

The day after, Ned's comrades gathered once more in the Hall, obliged to face the fact that he was not coming back.

"If our lord is dead, then there's nothing for us here; Betwill's right about that," observed Birches.

Will looked as if the spirit had been torn out of him. "I've been with Ned since I was eight; I shouldn't have left him, I should have died by his side."

"I can't believe it," said Holton, "dead, and my debt to him still unpaid…"

Only Mags seemed to notice his words, but for once she remained silent.

"We escaped with our lives, so we're all in his debt," said Birches.

"We've Amelie to thank for that," said Mags quietly. Amelie looked from one drawn face to another and said nothing.

"I can't just sit and wait," Will said, "I'm not made like that. There are things he'd want me to do, if … he couldn't. And, if he's gone, we'll not be safe here for long."

"What then?" asked Birches.

"I'm going to find Ned's sister, Ellie – it's something I can do for him and well, for me too."

"I'd be willing – if you want company; I'm not bound to any lord now," said Birches.

"What of you, John? What will you do?" asked Will.

"I suppose I must look for work in Ludlow; I had a liking for the place before," he replied.

"God knows why, I hated the filthy hole," Birches retorted.

"Yet, it's nearby – just in case…"

Whilst the others made plans, Amelie looked on feeling utterly lost – Ned had stolen her away, breathed new life into her and then left her; now she didn't belong anywhere. When they dispersed, only Will remained with her.

"You won't be safe here for long; come with Birches and me," he said.

She shook her head. "I thank you, Will, but I've had enough riding; I'll stay here, if Master Betwill doesn't throw me out."

"He'll not do that I promise you! But Ned would want you

safe; I can't leave you thus."

She put her hand lightly on his arm. "Will I be safer on the road with you? I pray you can find Ned's sister – he'd want that. But I'll stay here - I am content."

§§§

Will and Birches purloined the two fittest horses to travel to Shrewsbury whence they planned to follow a laborious route from one religious house to another until they found the Lady Eleanor; it seemed to Amelie a hopeless task from the start.

In the wake of their departure, Holton set off for Ludlow to obtain employment as a worker of metal. Amelie was pleased, though a little surprised, to find that when the time came for him to leave, Mags was outside waiting to accompany him.

Holton looked nervously at Amelie: "I'm hoping to get work at the forge – or the castle – I'll send word, so if you should need us, you'll know where to find us."

Mags hugged Amelie and said softly: "I'm sorry dear sister, but I had to choose…"

Amelie smiled. "I think you've chosen well."

In a brutally short time the manor had become a lonely place, for soon even the women who had moved in during the heavy snows had returned to their cottages. Amelie slept in the north tower chamber where she had first been taken many months before. It was small and cold, for Betwill considered a fire unnecessary, but no-one troubled her there – until the day after Holton left.

Something disturbed her just before dawn, for she was a light sleeper. She struggled awake and scanned the darkness of her room from the small hearth to the narrow window: there was nothing. And then, part of the nothing by the fire place, moved - or so she thought.

"Who's there?" she asked huskily. Now her eyes had adjusted she could see a small crouched shape by the unlit fire. Trembling, she seized the knife from under her pillow and moved warily towards the window.

"I can see you," she said, "and now you can see that I am armed. So, come out and show yourself!"

A thin figure shuffled towards her.

"That's close enough, stop there!" she ordered. "Who are you?"

The figure kept coming. "I meant no harm, lady – only to watch over you."

"Stop, I said! Who are you?"

"I'm Hal."

"Hal?" She breathed a sigh of relief, for it was one of the estate urchins; she had seen him about the manor, usually hanging back in the shadows.

"What are you doing in my chamber, Hal?"

"Guarding you, my lady."

In the gloom she smiled. "Are you armed?"

"No, my lady…"

Her smile broadened. "Come to the window," she said.

The boy looked at most fourteen years old and he had the fairest hair she had ever seen – almost white.

"You don't look old enough to be a guard, Hal."

"Hal's short for Harry – I was named after the King."

"Yes, I see." She thought fleetingly of the King, who was a familiar, yet aloof, figure to her. This boy bore little resemblance to his royal namesake – fortunately for le pauvre.

"And it's my dad's name, but he's gone now."

"And where is your mother?"

"She died, two winters ago; then my dad looked after me but he left with Sir Thomas last summer and didn't come back, so Betwill took me into the household."

"So does Betwill know you are guarding me?"

"No, my lady; he'd kill me if he knew I was here."

"Why do you call me 'lady'? I am just a servant."

He inspected her carefully. "You look like a lady to me and you aren't from around here."

"But still, I am not a lady."

"I could be your page," he offered enthusiastically, "I could fetch things for you."

"Hal, I don't own anything for you to fetch!"

Undaunted, he suggested mischievously: "perhaps I could fetch something you don't have yet?"

She laughed, relaxing for what seemed like the first time in months and, for a while, he lifted her flagging spirits and though she sent him on his way, she did not try too hard to discourage him. Had she still been at court then the notion of her having a page would not have been so fanciful; but in the bitter reality of her present station, it was nonsense – and she knew it.

The moment the youth left, the dark shutters closed once more and her bleak memories stirred again. Hal was right though, she probably needed a guard, for she must still present a threat to whoever had killed Marie Sainte – perhaps Edmund Radcliffe, perhaps not. She thought she had pieced together why she was such a threat and, if she was right, then she possessed a very dangerous secret indeed – one that the Queen might just be willing to kill for.

22

Penholme, February 1460

It was the hardest thing Ned had ever done: scraping out the earth and gently laying down the white faced bodies in the long shallow grave outside the village. It was all they could do, but it took a heavy toll on all three of them.

"If you don't give it up, we'll be putting you in this ditch as well!" declared Bagot harshly. "Leave us to finish it."

Ned stopped working and lay down on the bank of earth beside the grave; he noticed idly that several of his wounds were bleeding again. Nevertheless he leaned forward and grabbed Bagot's arm.

"We must follow Edmund and save the girls," he said

"By Jesus' wounds! You can hardly move, let alone ride! If those girls are still alive, he's not going to kill 'em now, is he? And if they're not, we'll be too late anyway."

By the time the other two had finished their task, it was late in the day and the light was fading too fast to contemplate travelling anywhere. So they camped for the night in the cold, blackened shell of Penholme. It was a sombre night.

"I should never have come back, Bagot. What madness I've caused; I think God has truly forsaken me,"

"You think too much – just rest!"

The following morning, Ned was weary to the core, his side and shoulder so severely ravaged that the flesh was now as torn and cracked as an old hide of leather. Bear had seen a hundred battle wounds in his time and he persuaded Bagot that they must stay put or lose their captain altogether.

"We must get a few miles done, we're still too close," argued Bagot, "Radcliffe's sure to send men here to search the woods."

"I can ride," said Ned and got awkwardly to his knees.

Bear spread his hands and left the decision to Bagot, who immediately saddled the horses.

Ned shook off Bagot's arm and attempted to mount, but the pain in his shoulder and ribs was so intense he nearly passed out; he turned back to Bagot.

"Perhaps I do need a little help."

Once mounted, he was determined to show that he was fit enough to complete the journey to Corve, though he noticed that his two companions rode close on his flanks lest he should fall. After half a day's ride at a slow pace, he knew that Bear was right: for he was still losing blood as the motion of riding opened up his wounds and the slightest movement wracked him with pain.

They were passing through a small wood when he slid from his saddle and struck his wounded shoulder as he landed. They propped him up against a tree whilst they build a primitive lean to shelter under the trees. It was cramped and damp, but it hid them well. They laid Ned inside and tried to bind up his wounds again to staunch the bleeding.

"That arrowhead has got to come out, Ned; it's festering in there," said Bagot.

"Can you do it?" asked Ned.

Bagot shook his head. "I've seen it done in France, but I've nothing to take it out with; I'd be ripping you to shreds."

"Wait!" said Bear and rummaged in one of the bags that was slung over his saddle; he took out several carved, polished pieces of wood.

"Ah, spoons," said Bagot, "can you do it?"

By way of an answer Bear jabbed his fist onto Ned's jaw to render him unconscious and doused the wound with wine. Then he deftly inserted the wooden implements and retrieved the arrowhead with ease.

"My God, but you're a man of skills," said Bagot, astonished how such large hands were capable of such delicate work. Bear poured on a little more wine and drank the rest from his flask whilst he sewed the torn flesh together; then he dressed it with a simple poultice. Finally he turned to Bagot: "now, you pray," he said with a grin.

They remained in the wood for several weeks, living off the sparse game and hoping Ned's condition would improve. It didn't. Bagot himself was barely able to walk; the struggles of the past few months had taken a heavy toll on him and the certain knowledge of his own decline hit him hard: he knew he would never again be an effective soldier.

"Leg," he indicated the offending right limb to Bear, "buggered!"

Bagot was surprised that the mercenary had stayed with them for so long, yet he seemed content to remain. One morning they both looked at Ned and shook their heads.

"He's beyond our help now, Bear."

§§§

"Lady, lady, lady!" Hal ran through the manor yard at speed.

He hurtled through the main door, knocking an alarmed Betwill aside in the process, and thundered up the stairs.

"Don't run!" Betwill called after him, "and stop calling her lady!"

Hal was already at Amelie's chamber door. "Hal! Calm yourself, now what is it?"

"They're coming, lady; they're coming!"

Amelie went ashen faced. "The Radcliffes?"

"No, Bagot and the others!"

"Bagot? Is Ned there?"

"I couldn't see him, but surely he must be ..."

Amelie ran down the stairs, tracked by Hal; they joined Betwill, who was already at the gatehouse looking over the rampart.

"Are you sure it's them?" he asked Hal, "I can't see our lord there."

As they watched the two riders come closer it was clear to all that neither of them was Ned Elder. Amelie let her head rest gently down onto the stone wall.

"Well, it's good that Bagot has come back," she said brightly.

"Open the gate!" ordered Betwill.

It was the sharp-eyed youth who noticed first. "They're dragging something," he said.

Amelie looked at the riders barely fifty feet way and she could see that Hal was right: they were supporting a rudimentary litter between the two horses, but she could not see who was on the litter.

"Some help here!" called Bagot and she raced down the steps and ran out to them with Hal.

When she first saw Ned's body on the litter she thought he was dead: his unshaven face was as grey as slate and he seemed to have aged ten years or more in the few weeks since she had seen him. Between them, they carried him in to the Hall.

"Take him up to my chamber in the north tower," she ordered, "we can light a fire in there." She glared at Betwill, daring him to disagree. But Betwill was pointing a trembling finger at the giant mercenary, bristling with weaponry. "And what is that?" he asked.

"That's Bear – feed him; God knows he deserves it!" Bagot clapped Bear on the back. "We'd all be rotting in the forest without him."

Bear and Hal carried Ned up the stairs, whilst Bagot, almost spent, sat down wearily in the Hall.

"We are pleased to see you, Bagot," said Amelie.

"There were a dozen times I thought we wouldn't make it," he said.

"How is he?" asked Amelie.

"You can see that yourself. I'faith, he's not good, not good at all. Where are the others?" he demanded.

"They waited a long time..." said Amelie.

"A long time! It was a bloody longer time for us!"

"They didn't want to be a burden," explained Amelie, eyes flashing crossly, "or they'd still be here waiting – none went lightly!"

"Why are you still here then?" Bagot was in no mood to be gentle.

She turned to him with glistening eyes. "Where would I go, Master Bagot? You've all spent the last months telling me how dead I'll be if I leave!"

Bagot was dog tired. "I shouldn't have spoken thus, and I'm sorry for it," he said.

Amelie shrugged, but noticed that she was not the only one whose eyes bore a tear. She went upstairs briskly and found Ned already laid out on her straw bed, Mother Betwill bending over him to examine his wounds, and Hal loitering near the fireplace.

Amelie thought Ned looked dreadful; it was painful just to look at him.

"He'll be stiff and dry as brushwood by morning; there's nought to be done for him now," concluded the old woman.

Bagot came and sat for a while on the bed, shoulders hunched in defeat, and then went out again. Mother Betwill followed him out wheezing noisily. Amelie got up to leave too, but at the doorway she hesitated and looked back towards Ned. She went to his bedside and began to examine his wounds, initially curious and then increasingly shocked by what she found.

"Holy mother, they have butchered you, Ned."

"Is he dead?" asked Hal.

"No, not yet."

"What are you going to do?"

"I don't know ... I thought perhaps I would look at his wounds."

"Can I help?"

"Yes. Fetch me some water, dear page – and some wine."

He raced off down the stairs grinning widely.

She began to strip off Ned's shirt, stiffened and encrusted

with blood, some of it still caked onto the dark matted hairs of his chest. When Hal returned with a half full wooden pail, she began to wash Ned's torn body - apprehensively at first, afraid of doing more harm than good, for his grip on life seemed tenuous. His skin was cool to the touch and she wondered how he had lasted this long; but then, as she washed the blood from his thin beard, he stirred a little and she sat back in surprise. Hal hovered at her shoulder.

"Alors," she said aloud, "if you are to be dead by morning anyway, I cannot make it worse. Hal, give me some room please."

She explored Ned's wounds with more determination and washed them thoroughly, ignoring the occasional moan that passed his lips. She discovered four separate wounds: three had begun to heal but one in his shoulder had become blackened and swollen. When she had finished her inexpert probing, he lay still; she would have been happier if he had shown more reaction.

The cheerless Mother Betwill returned to the chamber and observed her for a while, without offering any support, for she clearly thought it a lost cause.

"What's that boy doing in here?" she enquired disapprovingly.

"Hal's helping me," said Amelie shortly.

"He'll be no use; further he's away from that one, the safer he'll be too!"

"Can you please get me something for him to wear? And it's too cold in here, we need a fire burning."

"Ha! He won't last the night, I tell you. It's a waste of logs – and we've few enough of them. You're not at court now – we can't keep our fires burning all day and night as we please!"

"Even so, he's your lord, not mine; and we need a fire. Hal, please fetch me some dry logs."

Mother Betwill departed, grumbling to herself, as Hal sped recklessly past her, pleased to have another errand to carry out.

When he returned he brought a woollen tunic that Mother

Betwill had thrown at him as he carried the stack of firewood up the stairs. Amelie had flushed and cleaned Ned's wounds with wine and then covered them with rough linen dressings, torn from her own shift. Hal handed her the tunic – it looked filthy and smelt of wood smoke, but it would do.

"Come, help me lift him," she said, "but don't lift him by the shoulder or he might wake up and strike you!" Hal grinned, but took very great care.

When they had clothed Ned – no mean feat given his injuries – they laid him back on the straw and Hal was despatched to dispose of the blood-soiled clothing.

Bagot limped in and shuffled uncomfortably at the foot of the bed.

"Mother Betwill tells me he'll be stone cold by dawn."

Amelie frowned. "Well, we'll see."

"God knows I've seen wounds like his often enough, but not all at once on the same poor sod. It was hard, bringing him back like that, but he just wasn't healing. If he dies, it'll all be for nought," he said and trudged out.

Hal stayed with her long into the night; capturing her mood, he sat quietly beside her until, as the fire began to die down, she sent him away. By the dim light of the dying embers, she studied her patient again, but there was no change. An unexpected tear traced a lonely path down her cheek; another followed, and then another. She wiped them hastily away with the back of her hand, then she knelt down beside him on the matted straw and laid her head upon his chest.

"Are you going to die, Ned?" she whispered, "because if you are, I think I'd like to know; I have done my very best for you and now it's really up to you – oh, and I think also, it's up to God."

Then she lay down on the bed beside him, pulling the heavy woollen blanket over them both and drawing his icy body close to her.

A sudden thought caused her to stifle a laugh. "Do you think I can trust you to behave yourself tonight?" She closed her eyes and smiled in the darkness.

23

The Abbey of Valle Crucis in North Wales, November 1460

"I really thought I could find her," said Will, "but there are abbeys, priories, nunneries; I'd never have believed there were so many - it's hopeless!"

It was deep into November and they sat in the grounds of the Cistercian abbey of Valle Crucis in the northern marches of Wales. Above them towered the east front of the abbey church where the monks were singing mass.

"We've been searching for half the year and more," said Birches, "it's time to give it up, Will. We should go back to Corve before winter really sets in."

Will nodded with only a token show of reluctance, for he knew well enough that their fruitless search must end. "South, it is then," he agreed, "and back to Corve."

The monks had proven most hospitable and one in particular, Brother Thomas, had taken a kindly interest in their search. After mass he came to bid them farewell, his white habit flapping around his legs as he strode along the cloister. He looked a good deal more animated than usual, Will thought.

"It came to me after Mass," said Brother Thomas breathlessly, "so I can only think that God's hand is at work."

"What, Brother?"

"Mind you, they keep to themselves up there…"

"Who do, brother?" asked Will.

"Came right into my head after Mass - it's truly the inspiration of the Lord!" declared the excited cleric.

Will groaned. "Brother, what was it that came into your head?"

"Well, I've thought of a place you might try," he explained, "if you were to ride up the valley, you'd find a small house of nuns further up in the hills."

"It's not really on our way…" said Birches.

"But thank you, brother, all the same," said Will.

With the cold November winds already starting to blow, it was taking a risk to go further west, but the monk's words now gave them a reason to do so. Will could hardly contain his excitement as they rode out of the abbey. "She could be there; she could be there! This is the sign we've been waiting for!"

"Don't even dare to hope, Will. We've no reason to think she's there," warned Birches.

"But what if she is? We have to look - it can't be very far."

Birches shook his head. "Very well, but we must move fast. We don't want to get caught in the hills if winter blows in."

So instead of making their way back south to Shrewsbury, they took a detour to the west and followed a narrow track along the river valley before climbing onto higher ground. They had ridden barely five miles before Will began to regret his decision, for the temperature dropped like a stone and they wrapped their cloaks tightly around them as the weather closed in. Yet Will was reluctant to turn back and they continued for the rest of the day until, in the late afternoon, they saw a dour black gatehouse ahead. Will pulled up a hundred paces short, staring at the edifice ahead; it looked grim, he thought, and eerily unlike a dwelling place of the Lord.

"This could be it; it looks miserable enough," he said.

But when the gate was opened to them, they were met by a nun with a round kindly face who could not have been more welcoming. They were led at once to the guest house, which was smaller than some they had seen at the larger abbeys, but it had a hall with a good sized fire and along one side of the hall were screened off bays for sleeping. One of the nuns brought in a bowl of water for them to wash off the journey's dust and shortly after they were provided with a much-needed hot, if simple, meal.

Birches leaned across to his young companion and whispered: "It just shows: you can't always tell." Will nodded, for he too was reviewing his own hasty estimation of the priory.

"After we've eaten I'll ask the question, but I can't see Radcliffe sending her to a nice little place like this." At every house they had visited he had posed as a concerned brother and he had asked the same direct question, but the answer had always been the same: no-one had accepted an inmate resembling Eleanor Elder.

"Still, we've had a hot meal, we've got a bed for the night," said Birches, "and if we make an early start tomorrow then we might reach Shrewsbury by nightfall."

§§§

Edwina watched thoughtfully as the young man approached her chamber; he was really rather attractive for a pilgrim. Sister Margaret admitted him and Edwina waved her away before turning to study her guest admiringly. If he's a pilgrim, I'm a fishwife, she thought. He's wickedly handsome with a real swagger to him; he's a fighting man, but he has sad and weary eyes.

"My lady prioress, we're most grateful for your hospitality," he said.

"Few travellers reach us here in this remote place; are you on your way to the coast?" she enquired.

"My lady, I'm on a quest to find my sister Eleanor Elder who I believe may have been brought last year to a house such as this."

Her heart seemed to stop for a moment – hearing the name

from his lips. Her mind raced through the possibilities: could he really be her brother? She had never set eyes on Ned Elder, but this youth had red hair like Eleanor. Could he have been delivered to her so easily? It seemed unlikely. Suddenly she realised that her silence had given him hope.

"I'm sorry, but I can assure you that she isn't here," she said hastily, "you suggest your sister was taken against her will?"

"I'm sure of it," he replied, "she would never have submitted otherwise."

"How distressing for your family," she said.

"Well, it wasn't very likely," he conceded, "I thank you once more; we'll leave you in the morning." He looked beaten, drained of hope.

"I shall pray that you are soon reunited with your sister," she said earnestly.

Will thanked her again and withdrew to the guest house once more. When he had gone, she silently rejoiced, for she had done what her brother and nephew had failed to do: she had Ned Elder. If she could destroy him, then half her work would be done. Yet these men were both armed, so what was she to do with them? Perhaps, after all, it would be safer just to let them go on their way.

§§§

"Well, if nothing else we've had a good night's rest," said Birches, handing Will his cloak.

Will smiled ruefully. "Aye, we'd best make a start; we've a long road to Corve."

Birches pulled at the door to the guest house. It didn't move.

"It'll be stuck; just give it a kick," said Will, but a hefty bang from Birches' boot did not free the door.

Will shrugged his shoulders. Birches began pounding on the door, but soon gave up. They both tried shouting, but to no avail.

"It must be locked, so what's going on?" asked Birches

thoughtfully.

"I don't know. I could understand it if we'd found Ellie." He glanced at Birches. "You don't think…?"

Birches shook his head. "No, we've seen no trace of her. I had a good look around last night while you were talking with the Prioress."

"But why lock us in then?"

"Perhaps they just don't trust us; they're all women, we're both armed…"

"Alright, let's give them a while and see what they do next."

In the end they had to wait until the evening; then the door was opened, but before they could get to it, a pitcher of water was slid in and the door was slammed shut again. This time they heard the key turn in the lock, which prompted Birches to recommence kicking the door.

"Let us out in the name of Christ, you fools! We mean you no harm!" he shouted.

When he finally stopped, all was silent and the door was not opened again that night. By the following morning they were both beginning to feel very ill at ease.

"Listen," said Will, "they're only nuns! When they bring us more water, we'll seize the door and force it open; they'll run away screaming and we can just walk out."

"Yes, but they're afraid of us already; that'll just make things worse. And what if one of them is hurt? These are holy women."

"Well, they're not acting like holy women!"

They had no choice but to wait, but it was not until sometime after noon that the lock turned and the door creaked open three or four inches. No water was pushed in but they heard footsteps retreating back across the courtyard. At once they pushed the door open and ran out into the yard: it was empty. They stood still, watching and listening; they stared at the buildings that backed on to the yard.

"I don't understand; are they letting us go now?" said Will quietly.

"None of it makes much sense," said Birches.

"Perhaps it was all a mistake."

"Don't be a fool, Will."

"Come on then, the stables are in the next courtyard."

They walked to the far side of the yard and tried the door in the wall, but found it locked. There was rain in the air and the wind was getting stronger.

Birches sighed unhappily. "You know Will, I've always thought myself a patient man, but these nuns are starting to bloody annoy me."

They turned back to retrace their steps across the yard to another gate.

"Success!" said Will, as they passed through onto a narrow grassy path with high walls on either side. They seemed to be on the outer fringe of the buildings and followed the path through an iron gateway and on into a stone walled passage.

"This seems to be leading us back inside again," said Birches doubtfully.

As they passed under a wooden walkway a foul smelling liquid was suddenly dumped down onto Will. He moaned in disgust. "It's a pot of piss!" he declared, outraged.

"Hah! Nun's piss!" laughed Birches, but he stopped laughing when another generous helping drenched him from head to toe. "By Jesus; I've had enough of this!" he said.

At that moment a shrill scream echoed along the passage. Will turned towards the sound, his face dark with anger. "It's her," he cried, "she's here! Ellie! I'm coming!"

He drew out his sword and raced to the other end of the corridor, passing through an unlocked door into another lighter passage beyond.

"Will, wait! You don't know where you're going!" called Birches. But he saw that Will wasn't stopping and so ran after him, putting an arrow to his bow as he ran. A further, weaker cry increased their urgency and they wrenched open several doors along the passage until only one final door beckoned.

All was quiet as they paused before the door. It was bolted shut.

"Be careful," whispered Birches.

Will drew back the bolt and pulled open the door; he was met by an icy blast of damp air as he looked into what was not really a room, but rather a floor with two crumbling walls. Wind and rain drove into their faces as they stared at a sheer face of rock about thirty feet away from them. Then there was a whimper from the floor to the right of the door. The trembling figure wore a dirty brown habit and her face was cut and bruised. Will hardly recognised her.

"Ellie?" He knelt down to raise her up, but she shook her head vigorously and sobbed at him.

"We need to give her some water, lad," said Birches, "she's in shock; she can't speak."

Will picked her up and she screamed once again and passed out. He was distraught as – too late – he saw her left leg trailing at an odd angle. He gently put her down again on the floor.

"I'm sorry, Ellie; I'm so sorry!"

At that moment, the door to the passage slammed shut and the bolt was rammed home. A quiet, satisfied voice said: "Now you've found each other – you can all rot there together!"

"We've been played for fools," said Birches bitterly and kicked the door.

Further along the passage another door echoed shut and there was only the howling of the wind against the stone. Birches looked down at Will crouched beside Eleanor on the damp floor.

Come on," he said, "let's have a look at that leg."

24

Corve Manor, April 1460

A faint glimmer of dawn showed at the narrow window. Amelie was dozing, not really awake, but gradually she became aware of Ned's body against her and she remembered. Her body felt as stiff as an oak board and her back was cold; she disentangled herself from him and rolled clumsily off the straw mattress onto the dusty floor several inches below. She got quickly to her feet and straightened down her shift, feeling oddly embarrassed; then she knelt down beside the bed to study his face: a little less pale perhaps, she thought. She stroked his ragged black beard with her fingers: he felt warmer to the touch. She felt tears welling up again. "You see, one night in your arms and I can't resist you."

Her palm lingered for a moment against his cheek, but from Ned there was no response. She moved over to the window, but it was barely light enough yet to make out the terraced strips of land beyond the curtain wall. She leant against the stone embrasure, letting the cool air wash across her face.

"It seems so long ago you found me in that church," she said aloud, "I should have thanked you for that, but I got so … angry with you for a while."

She paused and turned to look at him, but he had not stirred.

"We should never have gone there, but mother was so stubborn. He was waiting for us in the dark of the tower.

I don't remember the moment he stabbed me, but I must have dropped the torch… and then I awoke with you and Mags and the others. My lady was not as fortunate as her daughter."

She fell silent then, watching the first threads of dawn creep slowly towards her as they lined the clouds with red.

"And now I am alone," she concluded.

"Never think that, my lady, you have me!" said Hal.

Amelie spun round from the window. "Hal!" she scolded, "how long have you been there? You are a very rude boy to listen to a private conversation."

"But there's nobody here, my lady - no-one who's listening anyway."

"But you were listening – and you shouldn't have been!" She unleashed a furious torrent of abuse in her own tongue, which fortunately for Hal he didn't comprehend at all.

"Go away! I never want to see you again." That he did understand, but before he could leave she stopped him, "No wait – what did you hear me say? Tell me at once!"

Hal did not, however, answer straight away; he was a clever lad so instead he considered what he thought Amelie would best want to hear.

"My lady, I only heard you say you were alone and it upset me to think that you were lonely."

Amelie studied the boy's face: it was surely a face that could not lie, though she thought that boys probably lied very skilfully indeed. Yet it suited her to end the matter, for to discuss it further would only excite his interest no matter what he had heard. Besides, she didn't really want to send him away for, as he had pointed out, he was the only company she had.

Hal studied the floor intently.

"I believe you, Hal, and I forgive you; but please do not call me 'my lady'."

He knelt at her side. "Thank you, my lady! You'll see I'm a loyal servant."

"Hal, I want only a loyal friend, not a servant."

"Then I'm that friend, my lady."

Amelie could not stay cross with Hal for very long and she smiled at him indulgently. "I think perhaps you are."

She turned her attention to Ned once more, lightly touching his forehead.

"He's colder again," she said and began to lay a fire in the tiny hearth, whilst Hal hurried off to fetch more logs.

Once the fire was lit Amelie stayed constantly by Ned's side: when he sweated, she soothed him with cooling water and when he shivered, she engulfed him in a blanket warmed by the fire. From time to time, she dribbled water down his throat in the hope of keeping him alive. The longer she spent with him, the more she became aware of the tiny milestones of progress he was making. In the early afternoon his eyelids flickered open for the briefest of moments. At first Amelie thought she had imagined it, but later it happened again and this time she fancied that Ned's grey eyes seemed to meet hers before they slowly lost focus.

In the evening he came to for several minutes and Amelie was able to coax some potage into his mouth. He was so weak that she was relieved when at last he swallowed a little. That night she slept alongside him once again and Hal stayed in the room with her, curled up on the floor before the cooling fire.

The following day the same pattern was repeated; Bagot was much heartened and spent more time in the chamber with Hal. Ned's body twitched and trembled as he lay unconscious.

"His wounds hurt him still," said Hal.

"More likely Mother Betwill's potage," observed Bagot, "I wouldn't give it to my horse!"

In the evening, Amelie sat on the bed and leant over him to feel his forehead; without warning he spoke to her, his voice like gravel: "You swing your hips when you walk."

Amelie nearly jumped off the mattress in surprise. Then she replied, tearfully, "Yes, I think I probably do." She hugged him and then when he gasped with pain, quickly released him.

"I'm sorry," she said and got up to brush away her tears. "Welcome back, Ned."

He looked hard at her. "You're looking better," he said, his low voice cracking as he tried to grin at her.

She laughed. "Well, it's good that one of us is!" She lay down beside him and stroked his head.

"They said you would die," she whispered softly, "I hoped perhaps not."

"I feel like I've died," he muttered as his eyes closed. Amelie put her arms around him.

"When I was small, in Anjou; if I was ill, my mother would lie down next to me, hold me and speak softly to me. She would say: be still; close your eyes; let your body melt away as I hold you to me and, when you wake up, you will hurt no more."

And she held him gently until he was quiet and, after, she drifted off to sleep too.

During the night she awoke; something felt different. She was holding him as she had done each night, but he was also holding her – his arms folded around her. In the darkness she felt him stir against her and smiled: some parts of his body were clearly a little less injured than others, she thought, before slipping back again into sleep.

§§§

Ned awoke in the middle of the morning as Amelie was cleaning his wounds again. He smiled up at her, admiring the shape of her body and the curve of her breast in the bodice she wore.

"You do this every day?" he asked, studying her face intently.

"Most days; Hal sometimes helps me, as you see."

"You sleep in my bed?"

A hint of a smile crossed her lips.

"You were cold... but I think you are quite warm enough

now to sleep on your own. I am certain that Hal will stay with you at night in case you have need of anything."

"I would stay with you most willingly, my lord," offered Hal at once.

She took Ned's hand and looked at him with a serious expression.

"Ned, I am not a physician, but I know your wounds are bad; if you try to move around too soon you will undo any good work I might have done. Will you promise me that you'll take care with this poor broken body of yours?"

"I will so swear," mocked Ned, "as long as you promise to look after me until I can walk on my own."

"Very well, my lord."

"Am I your lord then?"

"Well, let us say that I don't have any other lord – at the moment."

§§§

It was not until Lammas tide, several months later, that he ventured outside the walls of the manor house for the first time, clutching Amelie's arm tightly for support. It was the first of many walks and sometimes Hal would accompany them, for Ned had come to regard the boy like a younger brother.

"I am sure that Bagot would be only too willing to take you for these walks," teased Amelie.

"Bagot would only nag me for not recovering sooner. Do you mind then, spending your time with me?"

"I have nothing better to do, but perhaps I should go to Ludlow to find work. Can you walk on your own yet?"

"No," he said quickly, "and I'm sure I'll need your help for some time yet – if you're willing, of course."

"If I wasn't willing, I'd have given up on you a long time ago."

But as the brittle October leaves began to fall, even his troublesome shoulder wound was slowly healing and he knew that soon he must return to the troubles he had set out to overcome the year before. More than half a year had passed with no word of Will or Birches and Ned felt guilty that he had done nothing about it. So he started to spend more time with Bagot, working to strengthen his wasted muscles. Hesitantly at first, he tested out his shoulder: anxious to reassure himself there was no permanent damage. Bagot retrieved his battle sword, which had been left untouched in the Hall. His shoulder felt stronger, although it throbbed painfully when he exercised and ached for hours afterwards. Nevertheless, he soon regained much of his previous dexterity and strength.

Hal followed him everywhere and soon found a new role for himself in Ned's service.

At first Bagot was appalled. "You can't make him your squire! He's not of worthy rank."

"Do you see many others for the position?" asked Ned, making a show of looking around the manor courtyard. Bagot huffed a great deal for a day or two, but he saw the lad's genuine worth and soon came to regard him as his own protégé.

Hal spent much of his time sparring with Ned; they practised with wooden swords until Hal, who was an excellent learner, mastered some basic techniques. Ned also encouraged him to spend more time practising at the archery butts in the nearby village, for he had shown more than a hint of promise with the bow. With his time thus committed, Hal saw less and less of his beloved Amelie.

"I miss her," he told Ned one morning as they practised.

"So do I," said Ned.

"Aye, and if it weren't for her, then you'd have been dead long ago."

"I know, Hal; I owe her my life – and she has had her own troubles."

"You mean when her mother was killed," said Hal. Ned lowered his sword and looked at him curiously for a moment.

"I know nothing of her mother Hal; but it was her Lady, Marie Sainte, who was killed."

Hal dropped his weapon. "Oh, I'm sure you're right," he said hastily, but something in his manner aroused Ned's interest. He stared at the youth; there was an awkward silence.

"Are you telling me, Hal, that Marie Sainte was Amelie's mother?"

"I've probably got it wrong," said Hal, but Ned had already deduced enough.

At that moment Amelie walked into the courtyard and Hal started as if he'd been caught stealing.

"Hal," she said laughing, "do I frighten the brave squire so much?"

Hal darted out of the gate without a word. She frowned and looked inquiringly at Ned, who was still holding the wooden sword.

"You have upset him! What have you said to him?" she demanded.

"It's what he said to me, but please don't blame him."

She looked at him uncertainly.

"Come, let's go inside." He ushered her up the stairs to the solar and shut the door behind them.

"Ned?"

He told her what he had guessed, waiting for the emotional torrent he expected would shortly engulf him, but her reaction surprised him: she merely sat down heavily on a chair, with her head resting in her hands. Then, looking up, she said: "It was not Hal's story to tell, but now that you know, perhaps it's as well that you do. And, to be able to talk to someone about her ... you would have loved her – everyone did."

"I saw her once: she was a beautiful lady."

"Yes, my mother was beautiful; a girl of good birth, but she made one mistake: when she was fourteen she fell in love. She had me and we were both punished for it. I was taken from her and brought up in an abbey near Angers; she was in disgrace, unable to marry. Then a few years later she was sent to England as one of Queen Margaret's ladies. The

Queen was young too and not the easiest person to befriend, but maman became very close to her in those first years."

"How did you come to England?"

"When I was about ten, I was brought here. I hated it: the nuns at Angers had always treated me well; I was sad to leave them and I had no idea why I was here. Then maman told me; but it took years for us to become close."

She paused and Ned took her hand, squeezing it gently; she didn't snatch it away.

"Both of us have lost those we love," he said. Amelie placed a finger against his lips.

"Hush, for I have something else to tell you - and while I can tell it, let me – tomorrow I may not want to."

Ned waited, intrigued.

"The Queen was a lonely woman in those times and there were many handsome courtiers that flattered her, wanting through her to gain favour with their king. Now," she stopped for a moment, her throat suddenly dry, "and this is the thing – the thing why she was killed, I think. The Queen's son, Edward, was born about a year after I came and my mother told me that during all the time before he was born, for well over a year, the Queen had no … liaison with the King, but sometimes she did meet another ..."

Amelie reached under her shift for a small leather pouch which she wore around her neck and extracted from it a tightly folded piece of cloth. She passed it to Ned, who unfolded it carefully: it was a piece of exceptional silk embroidery depicting a lady seated with a garland of flowers in her hand as she receives a ring from a kneeling knight; in the bottom corner of the cloth were two names. Under the name Margaret was another name; but it was not the name of her husband Henry. Thoughtfully, Ned passed it back to her.

"She asked maman to make it for her – the Lord knows why, but the Queen kept it – and kept it well hidden. But just before she died, maman took it from the Queen's private chamber and gave it to me. She told me to keep it safe, for it might protect me; but she never had time to explain how."

"Put it away – safely," said Ned sternly, "it's certainly something the queen might kill for."

"Alors… now both of us know."

"Never, ever show it to anyone else, even a friend, for knowing about it alone might be a sentence of death."

"But how can it protect me if I don't show anyone?"

"It's a weapon, but a weapon you can only use once and at the right time."

She looked at him, her wide eyes radiating concern. "But, what is the right time?"

"Who knows? Perhaps next week, perhaps never; but for now, you mustn't let it out of your sight."

There was a sudden banging on the solar door and they both jumped – and then laughed self-consciously.

"Come in, Bagot," ordered Ned with a grin. The grin faded when he saw the bleak look on Bagot's face.

"Lord, Holton has returned from Ludlow!"

"I love the man well enough Bagot, so why such gloom?"

"I'm sorry my lord; but he brings news: terrible news."

They hurried down to the Hall where an agitated Holton waited with Mags.

"My lord…"

"What, man? What's the news?"

"There's been a bloody battle, lord; York is killed, his son is killed, Salisbury too and countless more."

Ned quickly gathered his companions up in the solar and his mood was black. It seemed Holton knew few details, but the details mattered little.

"What does it mean?" asked Amelie.

"It means we're done," he said, "our cause is lost. It was a poor hope to wed our fortunes to those of York; but now York is gone and my estates with him. More than that: there's no power in the land that can stop our enemies now: we'll not be safe here for long."

"As soon as you're fit, my lord," said Bagot, "we could slip away into Wales, or the south west."

"What would you have me do, Bagot, lead a few more folk

to the slaughter? Do you want another Penholme!"

The others looked up at this and the room fell silent.

"Ned, what happened at Penholme?" asked Amelie.

But it was Bagot who answered: "You all know what happened: Ned nearly died - and others did die! That's what happened at that damned village."

"They should know the rest," said Ned quietly, and he told them.

"All killed?" said Mags incredulously, "but some were mere girls?"

"We didn't find all," said Ned, "perhaps Becky ... Margaret, one or two others – we didn't find them, so they may have been taken."

"Well, what if they weren't taken," said Mags, "what if they were hiding and scared. Why didn't you go after them?"

"I scoured that land round the village myself!" declared Bagot, "there was no sign of them and Ned was almost done by the time we'd given them a burial - he couldn't ride anywhere!"

Ned looked across at Amelie, who averted her eyes: he knew she would never forgive him for the loss of the children. Holton held Mags close and Bagot stared at the floor. Ned knew they could have done no more, but he carried a fierce anger in his soul that he had not even been able to avenge the dead.

"The fault is mine," he said, "and God will judge me harshly for it."

He snatched up his sword, walked out of the room, ordered his horse saddled and then, wrapping his cloak around him, he struck out into the hills above Corve. He had no idea how far he would ride, but far enough to be alone.

25

Goodrich Priory, early December 1460

Birches dozed against the door. Eleanor lay on the floor with Will cradling her head in his lap. Not for the first time she was staring up at the bell tower that overlooked their decaying prison.

"Will, are you any good at climbing?" she asked finally, "only I think there's a way out up there."

She pointed up to the remains of the broken masonry that jutted out from the wall above them. Where the roof had fallen away, it had left several broken timbers in the stonework.

"I don't know; it looks as if it could fall anytime," said Will.

"Perhaps, but I've had more time to think about it than you and it hasn't fallen down yet! I was going to have a go myself, but now with my leg ..."

"Well, your leg looks a lot better since Birches set it," he said, "though your legs always looked pretty good to me..."

"If you two hadn't come, I'd be dead by now anyway."

"If we hadn't come, she wouldn't have broken your leg," he pointed out, but she just grinned at him.

"Well, I'm still glad you found me."

Will thought they would all be dead soon enough, though whether from thirst or exposure to the elements he wasn't sure.

"Here, you may as well finish this between the two of you."

She handed Will the last of the barley bread left for her several days before; he lobbed half to Birches and then tried to chew his way through the hard crust. They had survived several freezing nights – just, and tried to lift each other's spirits with each successive dawn. Now the water and barley bread were both gone and they didn't expect to be given any more.

"We need to get out of here – before we're too weak to do it," Birches said. "She's right, Will, I could climb up to the opening in the upper floor of the tower; then come back down and let you two out."

Will stared at the masonry and timbers above them. "Those timbers look rotten to me."

"It's better than sitting here freezing our arses off till we starve to death!" said Birches.

"Alright," Will conceded, "but I should go – I'm younger and fitter than you."

Birches laughed at that. "I'm a forester for the love of Christ; so I'm damned sure I'm a better climber than you are; and… you should stay with Lady Eleanor."

The latter looked at him. "Yes, Will – he's right, please." Will was doubtful, but acquiesced.

"When's the best time, do you think?" asked Birches.

"If you wait till the bell rings for Vespers, they'll all be at prayers," said Eleanor, "but it should still be light enough to see your way up; then by the time you come back down here, it'll be dark."

"Good enough," he agreed.

So they sat and waited through the rest of the drear, sleet laden day until the light began to fade. By the time the Vespers bell finally sounded to call the nuns to worship, the sleet had petered out but they were soaked to their frozen skins.

Birches got up stiffly and stood before the daunting tower wall. He wiped his hand over the stone.

"It's wet, but not icy," he said.

"If you can get to the first window ledge, you'll be fine,"

said Eleanor.

"Are you sure about this?" asked Will.

"Come on, let's get on with it. Start me off."

Will pushed him up so that he could reach the overhanging beams and, clinging to one of them, he clambered up onto the ruined outside wall of the cell. As he did so, crumbling pieces of stone slipped from under his feet and almost sent him skidding over the edge.

"Watch out," he hissed, "cover your heads!"

He hoisted his feet up onto the protruding stonework, and grabbed the beam, hoping that it would hold his weight. But at the last moment it cracked and splintered so that he slipped back down the wall. He lunged an arm across to the adjacent timber and just managed to cling on to it; he prayed it would hold.

"Birches?" Will called up.

"Keep your voice down – I'm alright," he whispered.

Not far above the slippery beam was the narrow window on the next floor of the tower. He levered himself up to crouch on the beam; he was committed now and if it cracked he would fall. His cold fingers slipped as he reached up, but he got his hand on the stone sill of the window. The light was dwindling fast and he knew that he couldn't maintain his hold on the greasy sill for very long. The timber was still bearing his weight, so he reached up and, using all the strength in his right arm, he strained to raise his body up to the sill. With a mighty effort of the muscles honed over half a lifetime he clamped his arm over it and pulled his head and shoulders up to the opening.

"Thank Christ for that," he muttered, but his relief was short lived, for when he tried to slide in through the window, he realised with horror that he could not fit between the stone mullions. Now, precariously balanced holding onto the stonework, all he could do was try to find a way up the outside of the tower to the top. He crouched on the sill and began to ease his way up onto the stone lintel above the window and to his immense relief he discovered that when he stood on it he could reach the stone coping on top of the tower wall. He gripped the stone and inch by inch hauled himself up, his arms screaming at him to stop, to let go.

§§§

Sister Ursula rang the bell for Vespers; it was she who always rang the bell, no matter what time of day or night. She had seen sixty previous winters pass and at her age she slept little and had no difficulty in rising at the required hour. The small bell to call to prayers was located on the second floor of the tower. Having rung the Vespers bell, she was overcome by a sudden weariness in her legs and sat down to rest on the wooden bench nearby. She dozed for a while, but when she came to she was looking across to the window. It slowly dawned on her that there was a pair of brown booted feet standing on the window sill. Her candle provided only a dim light; she turned away and then looked back again: the boots were still there but even as she watched they swung up out of sight.

"Oh dear," she said, knowing she would have to raise the alarm; she eased herself up from the bench, took her candle and started to descend the spiral steps to the ground floor. At the foot of the steps she paused to catch her breath, the air wheezing and rattling through her chest; then, with an effort, she continued towards the chapel.

§§§

Birches finally heaved himself over the parapet and landed with a loud thump on the wooden boards that formed a walkway around the tower roof. For what seemed an age he lay still, gulping in lungfuls of cold air and trying to get his breath back. Eventually he sat up and looked around him; he could see almost nothing, so was forced to navigate by touch, seeking the small door he knew must allow access to the bell floor below. He was still struggling to locate it when a square shaft of light pierced the night only a few paces away from him. Instinctively he turned away, flattening himself against the low wall as a cloaked figure held a torch aloft and then walked away from him along the boards to the other side of the tower rampart.

He seized his chance and dropped through the opening on to a straight flight of wooden steps down to the bell floor. When he reached the landing below it was in utter darkness; he took a tentative step forward and was struck hard in the small of his back

"Jesus!" he roared. He felt as if he'd been hit by an iron bar and he fell forward onto the floor. As he was falling, a short blade prodded weakly at his chest, but barely scratched him. His back was already numb from the force of the first blow, but he stood up and drew his long knife, slashing blindly to left and right until he could manoeuvre his back against a wall – shrill cries in the darkness told him that he had struck home.

He held the knife out in front of him while he investigated his lower back; it felt wet, so he had been stabbed, not hit; already he could feel the weakness creeping into his legs.

"God's blood! You murdering bitches," he muttered. He heard them moving in front of him.

"Murdering bitches!" he shouted. "Back away or I'll cut you all!" He shook his head angrily, knowing that he did not have long if he was to release the others.

Then the door above him opened and torchlight flooded in; Birches took in the stark scene around him: several nuns had crawled to the far side of the room and in front of him there were another two who looked very much alive. The light descended the steps and he saw that the prioress was holding it. He lunged forward at her, striking the torch from her grasp. She stumbled and it rolled onto the floor and went out, suddenly plunging the room into darkness once again. The brief flare of light had given him the edge he needed, in particular the location of the steps down to the floor below. He made a dash for them, but took several more cuts on the way. He half ran, half fell down the spiral of steps, but someone had followed him down and at the bottom she jumped on him and stabbed him again in the back. Pain lanced through him and he threw her off onto the floor; he could see her now, for a small oil lamp in the wall threw a shallow glow of light upon them both.

She was more agile than he expected and she sprang at him again; he lashed out, slicing his knife across her chest. He must have cut her badly, for she fell back and lay breathing heavily at the foot of the steps.

He got up unsteadily and made for the cell door to release Will and Eleanor. When he reached it and slid back the bolt, he leaned against the doorframe, knowing he would go no further. Will, sword already drawn, pushed open the door and stared aghast at Birches who was covered in blood.

"Sweet Lord! Are you alright?"

Birches gritted his teeth. "No, of course I'm not alright! Now get moving; these bitches are armed with knives!"

He slumped down onto his haunches leaving a smear of blood on the wall. Will saw it and offered his arm.

"Don't waste your time," urged Birches, breathing hard, "I'm spent; just take the Lady and go - oh, and take my bow too, it's a fine bow; I don't want it rotting here with me."

Eleanor limped to the doorway and gasped when she saw him. Then she screamed as Edwina, who had clambered down the steps, launched herself at them with a dagger in her hand. Will hesitated for a fraction of a second – reluctant to cut her down with his sword. She stabbed him in the side as she ran past him and lunged at Eleanor, transfixed in the doorway. Birches was already on his feet by then, and pushed Eleanor aside to make a grab for Edwina. He took her knife blade full in the chest as he wrapped his arms around her and pulled her through into the cell. Edwina's momentum carried them both up to the low crumbling wall. Too late she saw the danger and struggled to release Birches' hold on her, but he locked his arm more tightly around her. She frantically twisted the knife in his chest, but the archer's arm held the shrieking prioress in a vice-like grip. His last conscious act was to throw his weight backwards over the wall so that the pair of them teetered briefly on the brink and then, with Edwina open mouthed in shock, they fell.

Will and Eleanor hobbled to the edge of the drop and peered over, but the black void revealed nothing.

"He's gone," she said.

Will hugged her close. "Come on," he said, "let's go."

"Do you think he might …?"

He shook his head.

"His bow!" remembered Eleanor. She picked it up and they turned to go, but facing them on the threshold was a trembling and bloodied nun. Sister Mary's habit was slashed and blood-stained, her bruised face was impassive; she planted her feet and brandished a broad bladed knife. "You'll never leave here," she declared.

But this time Will did not hesitate: he sliced his sword down across her shoulder and breast before she could even move, almost cleaving her upper body in two. Bright blood gushed from her heart and she was dead before she struck the stone flags. Eleanor leaned against the wall, shaking; he put his arms around her and picked her up.

"Come on, there may be others. I swear if I come across another nun, I'm going to kill her just for being here. Do you hear that?" he shouted at the walls of the passage as he limped along it, "If I see any of you, I'll kill you, as God's my witness!"

They walked unsteadily through the cloister; there was a lamp burning at the gate but otherwise all was dark and silent.

"What are we going to do?" she asked.

"We'll have to stay here till it's light. We can't go stumbling about in the dark – besides, we'd freeze."

"Alright, but I'm not staying here a moment longer than I have to!"

They made their way to the cellarium to search for provisions, but found little of use, although they discovered a large tallow candle to light their way to the kitchen. Being

January, there was little food to be had but in the kitchen they scavenged the remains of a barley loaf, some cheese and several soft apples. They sought out a refuge for the night in a corner of the refectory and huddled together on the rushes under two woollen blankets. They hoped to steal a few hours' sleep, but they found it difficult to come by.

Will could scarcely believe that he had found Eleanor; for all the misery she had endured, he thought, her shimmering beauty was untarnished. All the feelings he had for his young love suddenly surfaced again as he lay down beside her. She stirred against him, welcoming his warmth with a gentle kiss; for both of them it revived happy memories of their former intimacy.

"Of all the things I've missed over these many months, the very worst was not being with you," she whispered, pulling him closer and running her hand down his thigh.

"I thought you had a broken leg …"

"Do you not lie with girls who've a broken leg then?"

He shook his head. "I'd forgotten how wicked you are."

"I'm sorry, I am wicked … and poor Birches not yet cold; but I need you, Will."

"If I couldn't resist you before, do you suppose I can now?"

§§§

It was not the first time Henry had heard a scream at Goodrich, but several in the space of a few minutes gave him food for thought. Edwina's explanation was sure to be diverting, so he went to her chamber and waited. All was quiet so he assumed that the natural order of the Priory had been restored but when, after an hour, she had not returned, he began to wonder. He walked out onto the path that led to the chapter house. He could hear several of the sisters inside and voices were raised; when they emerged, he followed them and watched in shock as one by one the corpses of the fallen nuns were brought into the infirmary.

After laying out the bodies, the nuns retired to the

dormitory and Henry went in search of the Prioress. He inspected each of the corpses in the infirmary with trepidation and it was a relief that Edwina was not amongst them; but if she was not amongst the dead, where was she? And who had so brutally despatched the nuns?

He completed a furtive search of the rest of the Priory, with the aid of a small beeswax candle which he shielded as much as possible as he moved around the buildings. The bell tower was appalling: there were traces of blood everywhere, especially on the steps at the bottom – it looked as if they'd butchered a pig there. He paused by the open door to the damaged cell and glanced in, but there was less blood there. He stood in the passage outside, puzzled by what he'd found; then he continued his search.

Even before he entered the refectory he had seen the glow of candlelight, but did not at first notice the pair huddled together in the far corner of the room. However, when he set down his candle on the table, they awoke with a start and he ran back down the short corridor towards the lavatorium before they could follow him. He returned much chastened to Edwina's chamber, where he found Sister Margaret wringing her hands. She was the only one of the inmates who knew who he was.

"Where is she?" he demanded.

"I can't find her anywhere in the buildings," she said, terrified.

"Neither could I, so she must be outside – but Christ knows why! Get some torches!"

"But, the nuns have only just retired…shouldn't we wait till morning?"

"Wait? No, we won't wait! Get the bloody nuns out with torches – now! Do you think I care a pisspot for any of you? We must find her!"

He drew his sword and ran down the steps to the cloisters, seizing a torch from the cloister wall as he went. There was no sign of anyone in the stables and he even peered apprehensively into the fishpond, but Edwina was nowhere to be seen. By then Sister Margaret and several others had joined him; most looked at him in wide-eyed shock. The night was bitter, but he cajoled them to go with him as he searched the grounds inside the wall, stumbling where the cobbled yard was uneven, but still they found no-one.

"What about the ruined part?" he asked.

"You can only get there from the postern gate," said Sister Margaret.

"Come on then!" he bullied them.

By the time they reached the rear gate to the abbey, several more of the sisters had arrived with torches. Once through the gate, he walked forward and the rest spread out in a line either side of him; he made his way carefully across the rock strewn ground and at first he did not see the bodies. Then by the flickering torchlight he saw a different shape amongst the stone debris and crouched down beside it. He was relieved to see that it was one of the Elder men.

"More light here, damn you!" he shouted and all the nuns gathered around him.

He noticed the point of a blade protruding from the dead man's back and investigated more closely by rolling the corpse over. He shuddered when he saw that Edwina lay crushed underneath; she still gripped the knife that had killed her assailant, but the hilt had been punched into her chest. The back of her head was bloodied and broken where it had struck a block of masonry. Sister Margaret gasped, but he pushed her aside and pulled out Edwina's body, already cold and stiff. She seemed so frail, her chest covered with sticky, half frozen blood and a look of shock engraved on her white face.

"You stupid, stupid bitch," he said quietly, "we still had so much to do…"

"Let's take her inside," said Sister Margaret, "she must be honoured in death as befits the prioress of this house."

Henry nodded absently, his mind racing ahead to consider other consequences; but he gently picked up the broken corpse and carried it back to Edwina's chamber. He laid her on the bed and Sister Margaret covered her with a large linen cloth.

"She must be properly attended to," she said, her voice trembling.

"Not now." Henry was already preoccupied with what he must do next.

"But…"

"Not now! Get out woman, or there'll be another dead nun in here!"

With solemn dignity, Sister Margaret withdrew.

He tried to see his way forward: he couldn't stay; he must go while he still could, for those in the refectory might decide to search the place more thoroughly in the morning. He took a long, deep breath and then got up and went to the bed. Recalling Edwina's instructions he knelt down and reached under the foot of the bed. There was a loose stone in the floor, exactly as she had said; it was just possible to slide the stone out from under the bed. Beneath the stone was a small iron key which he retrieved and turned over in his fingers.

Next to the bed was a small cupboard recessed a little into the stonework; he opened the door and in the cavity behind it was everything that Edwina thought of value: mainly documents, though a few pieces of jewellery too. He cleared it all out and quickly skimmed through the documents, seeing enough to know that all he needed was there.

He closed his eyes for a moment to think, then he sorted through the documents again more carefully and when he had finished he replaced them all in the cupboard which he then locked. They were far too precious to carry about with him. He did not return the key to its hiding place but instead took it with him. He was tired, but he gathered up all that he needed and lifted the sheet to take one last look at Edwina; he kissed her cold forehead.

"Don't worry, mother; they'll pay."

It was nearly dawn when he went down to the stables; he found three horses and took them all with him when he rode out into the frozen valley. It would be a terrible journey for him, but much, much worse, he thought, for those without mounts.

§§§

Will roused a sleepy Eleanor. "Come on beautiful, it's not a long ride to Valle Crucis – we can be there by noon!"

The monks had been helpful before and Will had little doubt that they would provide some much needed care for Eleanor's leg. But at the stables, he was devastated.

"We needed those horses, Ellie."

"If you're trying to persuade me to stay here…"

Will knew that fierce look of old. "No, of course we can't stay here, but if you've learned any prayers, you'd better start saying them."

"This is going to be a struggle, isn't it?" she said.

"Come," he said, mustering a cheerful tone, "we'll follow the stream; that way we won't get lost."

But after less than a mile, he called a halt and they stopped to rest by the water's edge, for every awkward step Eleanor took brought a more audible gasp of pain and confirmed his worst fears. Then for what seemed like hours he carried her, and it felt good to cover a little more distance, but as he tired the rests became longer and more frequent. In the early afternoon he groaned when he saw a chill mist drifting up the banks of the stream and in no time it had engulfed them. The temperature fell sharply and they shivered under the shelter of a fallen beech.

After a long, cold night, Will basked in the early morning sunshine and gently woke up Eleanor by massaging the cold and cramp from her legs.

"Careful!" she warned, as he laid his hands on the injured leg.

"Sun's out," he said, "everything feels better in the sun."

She smiled and kissed him. "I do too."

Will led her once again along the riverbank, where the ground was softer and did not jar her leg and they started to put more distance between themselves and the priory. At last

Eleanor wore a cheerful smile and their youthful joy in each other's company was reawakened. Will kept up a slow but steady pace.

"We've done well today; we should stop for the night soon."

"Oh, we won't make it tonight then?" He heard the disappointment in her voice; she seemed to slow and lean on him a little more. He hugged her close for a while, taking the weight off her leg.

"You're too tired; we should stop now."

"I can go on for a bit longer," she said more brightly and stepped away from him. She reached behind her for his hand, to pull her with him but missed him and lost her balance. In a moment she had slipped off the bank and fallen onto her knees into the cold water. The stream was flowing fast and Will had to stoop down swiftly to lift her up before the current took her; he held her tightly to him and there they clung together as her pain gradually subsided and the water dripped from the hem of her cloak onto their muddied boots.

That night there were fewer clouds and the ground beneath them froze. Will managed to light a small, smoky fire, and gathered sufficient wood to keep it replenished for a few hours. They lay cocooned in their two thick cloaks, hoping to shut out the worst of the freezing air.

The next morning brought no encouraging sun, only a driving, freezing sleet which swept through the threadbare trees over the cold embers of their fire. Though they were awake at daybreak, they could not summon up the strength to move their limbs. But Will knew, tired though they were, if they sat for much longer in the stinging blizzard they would freeze to death where they lay. With an effort he got to his feet and raised her up; he carried her for a few yards, but the ground beneath his feet was now treacherously slippery with a thick layer of wet ice.

"Let me try," she said, "or we'll never get there!"

She took a few steps, pain searing through her calf; then she stumbled, caught her foot on a tree root and fell forward, sliding off the edge of the bank and into the freezing water. Will lunged out to catch her, but she slipped from his grasp and plunged into the deeper water, where the current immediately dragged her downstream.

"Ellie! Hold on, Ellie!" Scarcely seconds had passed, but already she was gone.

He tore off his cloak to dive in, but it was impossible. The stream rushed down through a narrow ravine, the water chasing over shallow pools and rapids before it dropped to the valley floor. He couldn't get down to it for the tangle of small wiry trees that clung to the steep slope.

"No!" He drew his sword and hacked at the thin branches, as the angry blizzard tore into him.

"No!" He blundered along the bank peering through the sleet for a glimpse of her, stumbling from tree to tree, until he reached another sequence of falls. He scoured the pools and overhangs but could see no sign of her. He searched on as the sleet turned to snow until, cold and bitter, he could barely walk and his hands were frozen and sore. Finally he stopped and fell to his knees, allowing the large white flakes to smother him.

§§§

The ice cold water crushed the air from her lungs as she fought against the freezing current. The first of the rapids rolled her onto her back; still she flailed her arms to reach the overhanging branches, but they were already too far away. The chill torrent numbed her limbs until she couldn't move them and, as if bound and gagged, she was buffeted over rock and ice, spun around, raised up, dropped down, turned over and raised up again. The cunning river stole her will to resist and her helpless body was dashed against the bedrock.

PART THREE: WAR

26

The Hills above Corve Manor, January 1461

There was a light covering of snow on the high ground and the tarn appeared black and shiny against the white speckled rock and moss. It looked very different from the first time Ned had stumbled across it riding up into the green hills above Corve. How long ago was that? Barely a month, perhaps less... before the first hint of snow at any rate. He dismounted awkwardly, still feeling some stiffness in his shoulder, and sat down on a large rounded boulder by the frozen margin of the pool. It was a lonely place, but solitude suited his mood well enough. He picked up a handful of small fragments of stone and one by one threw them into the water. When he tired of that he leant back against the stone and closed his eyes.

After a while - he wasn't sure how long – he realised he wasn't alone. He slowly opened his eyes: across the other side of the water a figure stood against the sun. Ned rubbed his eyes, thinking at first it was a trick of the light, but there was someone there, leaning on a sword in a halo of sunlight. He seemed unusually tall, perhaps taller than he; his hair had an amber hue, or was that just the glow of the sun? The newcomer strolled several paces out of the line of the sun and Ned could see now that he was young, perhaps about his own age.

"You don't rush to take up your sword?" the stranger

observed.

"My sword's slung over my saddle and if I can't get to it before you reach me, I deserve to die," said Ned, closing his eyes again. Just for a moment he'd been foolish enough to imagine that he had seen something more than just another roaming sword for hire. He was past caring – let the fellow do his worst.

But the swordsman did nothing and the hill top went quiet once more; curious, Ned opened his eyes again and found the stranger was sitting on a rock on the opposite side of the tarn.

"What do you want?" asked Ned, ignoring the usual conventions of politeness.

"Good day to you too - you're on my land: this is Mortimer land."

"I don't give a shit whose land it is," said Ned.

This prompted the knight to walk around to him and perch on an outcrop nearby.

"I used to come up here as a young lad."

"Listen, I don't want to talk to you, so why don't you just go."

"You're a miserable bastard," said the knight, "but whatever you're so miserable about, I'm damned certain I've more cause to mourn than you!"

"I grieve for many!" snapped Ned getting up, for it seemed the knight was not going to leave him alone. He wrapped his cloak tighter around his shoulders and went to his horse.

"Who then?" the stranger challenged him, "Who do you grieve for?"

Ned turned to face the knight, warning him with his eyes; the man was beginning to annoy him – did he think mourning was some sort of a contest?

"I mourn the execution of my father," he said.

The knight shrugged, clearly unimpressed. "I can match that; try harder."

His response took Ned by surprise. "And the murder of my brother," he blurted out.

"Aye, I can match that too – say again."

"…and the seizure of my estates."

"Aye, well that goes with it of course!"

"I'm attainted for treason!"

"Oh, and I," the tall knight replied laughing.

"You mock me!" said Ned, placing his hand on his sword hilt. "My sisters were abducted too!"

The tall stranger paused. "Now, that is truly a cause for grief," he said and his face creased into the most engaging grin. "Enough! You've outdone me for, as far as I know, my many sisters are safe and well."

Ned found himself smiling too, though he had no idea why; he was drawn to this knight, whose charm and easy manner were blunting his hostility so effectively.

"But I'm guessing that none of those is the reason you're up here," said the knight abruptly.

Ned was inclined to argue, but it made him think for the first time why indeed he was up there on the isolated hilltop.

"Tell me," invited the knight. They sat down together beside the freezing water's edge and wrapped their cloaks around them. Ned related the grim story of his past year and when he had finished, it was the turn of his new acquaintance.

"We have common enemies, it seems; I too am Edward; the sometime earl of March. A few days ago I returned to the Marches of my boyhood, only to learn that the Duke, my father, is slain and our cause is in ruins."

"Yes, I've heard that – it was the final blow, I think."

"Final?" said Edward, "nothing is final while you still breathe, Ned. Like you, I've lost much that was dear to me, but I'm not going to accept it without a fight. I will spill every last drop of my blood to get back what I've lost and I'm going to replace my lost estates with a kingdom!"

Ned shook his head. "I'm done with fighting; it brings only misery: I was willing to shed my blood, but I ended up spilling everyone else's. I fought for your father once, but he ran away – and so did you, for that matter. And many died because of it!"

"I'm not my father."

"But you'll take up arms again and more blood will flow!" said Ned.

They both fell silent then for several minutes before Edward spoke again.

"These common folk, the families you spoke of – did you force them to join you?"

"No, but they had little choice."

"They had every choice: you said that one betrayed you, but the rest didn't; they stayed with you. And why do you suppose that was? Do you think they relished the prospect of serving this Radcliffe for the rest of their lives – and their children's lives? Of course not! They knew the risk, but they stayed with you; no-one could have expected this butcher to act as he did – not you, nor they."

"But still, I failed them."

"You fail them more by your weak words now; you still have a duty to those who live on your estates. It's a God given duty and it doesn't end when you get fed up."

Ned looked up sharply at this: here was a youth his own age reminding him of his responsibilities.

Edward put an arm on his shoulder. "Ned, being the leader means you keep going when all others have lost the will to carry on; when they have no more hope, they must still have you - in the front rank, where they can see your steel and hear your voice!"

Edward's words hurt him, but he knew his companion was right: he had lost sight of his duty. If this knight could fight half as well as he could talk then it would be something to behold.

"I confess, you've forced me to think again," he said.

"Nothing is by chance, Ned! God has thrown us two together. If I'm right, then God will see me become king; if I'm wrong, then He will bear down hard upon me and sometime, perhaps in a week, or a year, a headsman's axe will split my head from my body and I shall burn in the eternal fires of hell – but right now, on this hill, I have faith in my cause! I'm mustering an army at Wigmore; join me! I shall sweep all before me - I swear it."

Edward staggered to his feet, shaking the cramp from his long legs; he grasped the reins of his horse and swung himself into the saddle.

"Come to me at Wigmore and we'll crush the buggers together!"

He rode off swiftly down the slope without looking back and Ned stared after him, as the sound of the horse's hooves slowly faded away. He'd heard a lot of fine words, but still they carried some hope – and he did feel hope. If the hand of God was in their meeting, then it was about time, he thought.

§§§

By the time he returned to the manor at Corve he'd had more than enough time to think. The mood at Corve had been bleak since his revelations about Penholme and he was determined now to lift the gloom. He cantered into the courtyard and jumped from his saddle, running into the Hall without breaking stride.

"Bagot!" he shouted, "I've been adrift for too long; it's time to rejoin the fight!"

He went to the dais and sat down at the high table.

"By St Stephen! There's a wondrous balance in the Lord's work!" exclaimed Bagot, descending the stairs into the Hall. Amelie and Mags followed him down and the others came in from outside.

"Well, I haven't seen much balance in it yet," said Ned with a grin, "but I intend to do something about that."

"You're back!" said Mags, smiling.

"I've only been gone a few hours!"

"Your body perhaps, but your spirit has been away for a lot longer," said Amelie quietly.

"Well, it's back now," he declared.

"Good," she said, and kissed him lightly on the cheek. "For I took much trouble to keep you alive!"

"Well, tomorrow I'm going to war again," said Ned.

Her face clouded and the others greeted his announcement with stunned silence; he could hardly blame them, for they were bound to imagine the worst. Amelie and Mags looked downright miserable and the others were worried what their part would be. But he didn't indulge any of them.

"Now leave me friends to speak with Bagot," he said. Amelie and Mags pulled faces at him but left with Holton and Hal.

"Forgive me, lord – but how has this come on so suddenly?" enquired Bagot.

"I've met the Earl of March and he's mustering an army at Wigmore – I believe he can succeed where his father failed."

"Mustering an army for what?" Bagot looked at him doubtfully.

"To take the throne - and when he does I'll get my lands back and the power to free my sisters; and Yoredale will no longer be governed by the Radcliffes."

"All well and good, but don't forget this youth was one of those who left us to fend for ourselves in Ludlow. What makes you think you can trust him now?

"Something about him – he convinced me; if I think too much about it, I don't know why."

"Well, I suppose that's what trust means. When do we leave then?"

"First light."

Bagot nodded approvingly and scuttled away to make the necessary preparations.

A few minutes later, Holton came in bearing a full harness of plate armour and carefully put it all down on the rush strewn floor. He bent down onto one knee.

"Lord, my skills are poor, but I was able to fashion this for you when I was in Ludlow. I wasn't sure that it'd ever be used, but I'd be honoured if you'd wear it."

Ned stared at the polished plate pieces; he was speechless.

"I hope it will serve you well enough, until you find better," Holton continued, "of course, you may think it not good enough…"

Ned felt the smooth curved finish of the burnished steel breastplate.

"John Holton, you're a master craftsman! This is fine work, a thing of beauty; some of it looks almost Italian in quality!"

"Well lord," Holton hesitated. "That's because some of it is Italian; I used old bits and damaged pieces I found here and in the town… I had some help and I took advice from the armourer at Ludlow castle about the weight and style. Pray try the helm, my lord, for I've been worried about the fit."

Ned picked up the round polished helmet and ran his finger along the solid steel ridge that ran from the broad plate of the neck to the forehead and the sharp point on the front of the hinged visor. Inside it was lined with doubled strips of linen.

"I only tinkered with it, that's your finest Italian basinet that is," Holton said.

Ned put the helm upon his head; it felt wonderfully light. He opened the visor. "Holton – it's perfect!"

"It's little enough, lord, to repay the debt I owe you."

Ned removed the helmet: "Holton, I'll wear this harness gladly and none on the field will be wearing better, but you've no need to repay me any more for deeds done many long years ago."

"I do what I can, lord," said Holton.

Ned smiled. "John, I know you'll want to serve with me, but with all of us gone Corve will be poorly defended and if the battle goes ill for us, I want a man I can trust with Amelie; a man who, whatever happens, whatever the danger, will be at hand to see her – and the others - through it."

Holton nodded gravely. "I remember well what you said to me those months ago in the forest; I'm no soldier, but I'll do all I can to keep them safe."

"I know you will," said Ned, grasping Holton's outstretched hand. As he watched him swagger from the Hall bursting with pride, he hoped most fervently that the young smith's undoubted bravery would not be called upon.

A few minutes later, Mags ran in; she had clearly just spoken to Holton.

"Thank you, Ned," she said, squeezing his hand; then she hastily drew back, suddenly conscious of her excessive familiarity. "But he's worth more to me here than he is to you there." She turned, embarrassed, and left the Hall as fast as she had come in.

Whilst Ned was admiring the rest of the harness, Amelie quietly came in from the buttery.

"It is very pretty, my lord." He heard the sadness in her voice and smiled at her.

"It's a work of great skill," he said.

"Yes, and it's also a work of great love," she replied softly.

"I know why you're here."

"But still I will say it: Ned, this is not your fight! You've sworn no oath to bind you to this cause. It's different for the local people – they live here and they'll be fighting on their own lands. I understand that."

"Then understand this, my dear: my father and brother both died in the service of Edward's father; and I *am* local. These estates at Corve are the only estates I have left and they'll fall to the Radcliffes with all the rest if I don't fight for them."

"But what if … what if it goes badly for you? What then? What if I were taken too…"

"Then I would never forgive myself. I'll fight for York because I must, but I will come back to you."

He stood close to her, searching her glistening eyes and taking her hands in his. He wanted to say that he had fallen into those deep brown eyes the first moment he'd seen her in the church tower, but he knew that after Penholme she couldn't feel the same about him. So he stepped back and let her hands go.

"However the battle goes," he said, "there'll be men all over the Marches so stay within these walls till I return. God will watch over you. I know how much I owe you and, wherever you are, I'll be with you."

§§§

Wigmore was the Earl's stronghold in the Marches: its thick stone towers thrust up from the forested slopes and dominated the small village below. The sight of such a majestic edifice lifted their spirits as they approached in the late afternoon. There was clamorous activity in every corner of the castle: every space, however small, was crammed with weaponry of all kinds and a host of men, all imbued with a sense of urgency.

"Bear – see to the horses; Bagot, find somewhere to bed down for the night and I'll find out what's happening," said Ned.

There was a crackle of activity in the castle yard as captains marshalled the men, their nervous breath merging with the chill mist that clung around the base of the fortress. Ned made his way through the broad doorway into the Great Hall, where he was astonished by the wealth of blue and yellow banners bearing the Mortimer arms and with them also some white rose badges of York; these no doubt were the trappings of the Earl's lineage. But stacked in every corner of the Hall and the small chambers off it were the means of waging war: a vast stockpile of weapons and armour.

He found the Earl of March holding council in his great chamber on the first floor – heavily bedecked with yet more banners and badges.

"My lord," he announced himself as he crossed the threshold and knelt, "I have answered your call to arms."

"Ah, Ned!" the Earl embraced him like a long lost comrade, much to the surprise of the others in the room who greeted him with a silent and uncomprehending stare. The men assembled in the chamber were Edward's closest adherents: Marcher men, loyal to the cause and fighting on their own soil; now they wanted to know who this young latecomer was with the northern tarnish to his voice.

Edward raised Ned up and put a welcoming arm around his shoulder.

"Ned is the only man I know who's lost more than me in this business; he was commended to me by no less a man than my noble cousin, the late Earl of Salisbury."

All seemed suitably impressed by this announcement, not least Ned himself who had no inkling that the Earl had spoken for him. Several rose to clasp his hand and Edward ushered him to a seat near him.

"Ned, we're talking through our plans - join us."

For Ned it was an unlooked for invitation; he had thought only to pay his respects to the young Earl and then withdraw, so he took his place reluctantly at the Earl's council table.

Ned made no contribution at all to the business of the council, but listened well and learned much. In particular, he learned that the north of England, his homeland, was almost entirely in the Queen's hands. His own position was thus starkly clear: in Edward's success lay his only chance of challenging Radcliffe power in Yoredale. It seemed though that Edward had a strong ally in Richard Neville, Earl of Warwick, the son of the late Earl of Salisbury. He had captured King Henry and had assembled a large force of men in the east so Edward's position was not as weak as he had supposed.

Edward summed up the situation for his captains: "Before my father, the Duke, was killed, it was agreed in parliament that when King Henry died, it would be my father, as the rightful heir, who would succeed him and not Henry's own son, the Prince of Wales. Margaret rejected this accord because it disinherited her own ... son."

His companions around the table chuckled at the Earl's hesitation and Ned could guess why: most of them believed that the birth of a son to the Queen at a time when the King had lost his wits was a touch too convenient. Whilst he joined in the laughter, he felt a chill inside knowing that Amelie carried knowledge that could destroy the House of Lancaster. He should have taken it from her, for he could not tell whether the item she held would protect her or condemn her.

The Earl was continuing: "Thus it is Margaret's stubborn opposition that brings us to the present state. As long as we have Harry of Lancaster in our hands, we can act in the

King's name; but whatever we do here, if we lose Harry, then we'll all be condemned once more as traitors. And mark this well: there'll be no pardon; we must win here or we'll die."

His words were greeted with unanimous enthusiasm with much thumping of the table in agreement and Ned, who saw himself as an outsider in this close Yorkist circle, was caught up in the mood of optimism that the Earl generated.

"Now to the plan for battle: there's a crossroads by the river to the south of here where the Hereford road meets the road to Ludlow; that cross is at the heart of my forebears' lands – Mortimer lands – and it'll be a most fitting place to vanquish our enemies."

Ned wondered at the confidence of the young Earl, scarcely more than a few weeks older than he was; he recalled his own agonising decisions on a lesser scale during the previous year and marvelled at how strong this man's convictions must be. He could be an awesome power in the land – a man actually worth fighting for.

Edward dismissed them to their camps having ordered a muster before dawn the next morning, but he asked Ned to remain with another older man who had sat at his right hand in council.

"Well, Ned, you've met my allies – and this is the best of them, my good friend, Will Hastings."

"Sire, I'm grateful for the late Salisbury's kind words," said Ned.

"Ha! In God's name, Ned, Salisbury told me nothing about you, but they needed convincing and I thought he might do it rather better than me!"

He laughed aloud, immensely amused, as did Hastings who had clearly suspected the deception.

"Will here is one of the few men I'd trust with my life; you, Ned might be another, but in case I'm wrong I'm going to send you into battle with Will, for if you betray me he'll certainly kill you."

Ned was unsure whether this was another jest or not, but his doubts evaporated when he looked at the serious expression on Hastings' face.

"You may rely on my loyalty, my Lord," he said.

"Be assured, Ned," emphasised Hastings, "that I'd kill without a thought any man who threatened the Earl, even if it were my own brother; or for that matter, even if it were the Earl's own brother!"

"And he means it," said Edward, "but it won't come to that. Now, to work; for we still have much to do."

Ned went outside to find Bagot and Bear; they awaited him in the courtyard. He appraised them as he walked towards them: two men, his whole contingent; it was something of a joke really. Yet the pair might still strike fear into their enemies. Bagot would never be the soldier he once was, but he still had power in his sword arm and Bear, he looked relaxed – and why not? For him this had probably been a way of life since his youth. Never short of a sharp implement or two, he seemed to have acquired even more weapons: now he carried an ugly short handled halberd. Noticing Ned's enquiring glance, he grinned enthusiastically. "We fight horsemen? I'm ready!"

27

Yoredale Castle, January 1461

Emma stood in the Hall beside the high table, perplexed. With Edmund bedridden from his wounds and Richard and his father called to arms by the Queen, she had become accustomed to sitting alone at the high table. She took only small meals: often a little meat and bread with some cheese; but tonight the table was loaded with an array of platters and bowls of food.

She looked around the Hall; she sensed an oddly subdued atmosphere amongst the servants. True, it was hardly riotous at any time, but it had been more relaxed without the Radcliffes and the best part of the castle garrison. Now she sensed the apprehension again; something was different. It was more crowded too: almost all the castle servants were there, even the brewer, who was rarely even sober at this time of day. In recent months he had never been there, but tonight he was. What did they all know that she did not?

Halting footsteps echoed on the stone flags in the passage beyond the Hall and her heart sank. Edmund entered from the far end of the Hall and the assembled household fell silent, as if some sorcerer had cast a spell upon them. Edmund looked around him, scrutinising every sullen face and then laughed.

"There are rumours abroad that I'm a dying man; that's why you're all here for, as you can see, I'm recovering very well!"

Polite applause greeted his announcement and continued whilst he made his way to the dais to join Emma.

"A sisterly welcome would be appropriate," he said quietly. She brushed her lips lightly on both his cheeks in turn. He looked pale, she thought, and his usually neat thin beard had grown untidily.

"I'm relieved to see you so well, Sir Edmund," she said, raising her voice.

He leant heavily on the table for support and smiled at her tight-lipped; then he replied in a low voice: "Careful you don't choke on your words, lady. And it's no thanks to your shit of a brother; but I dare say he's as badly off as me – or worse."

They had barely spoken at all since their first brutal meeting and she would have preferred to keep it that way, but appearances now dictated otherwise. He took her hand and led her to the table, sitting her down beside him, as if she were his lady.

"Bit of a show this evening," he said, "to celebrate my recovery."

He offered her wine; but she refused and did not touch her food.

"Drink," he instructed; he was still smiling, but his tone was cold. She sipped the wine and he leant towards her, putting his hand on her knee as he spoke: "drink, dear sister, drink." He gripped her knee until the pain of it brought tears to her eyes. "Drink and eat, so that all can see how pleased you are to see me."

So she drank, and she ate, though she felt sick with fear for the rest of the evening. Edmund gorged himself with eels, wildfowl and several cheeses; all was washed down with a generous quantity of French wine, specially fetched from the cellar for the occasion.

He leaned into her again and reached down to caress her thigh, his hand slippery with grease from the cooked game. "I remember our first meeting with pleasure," he said.

"I don't," she replied, trying to prise his hand from her leg, "and I beg your leave to retire."

"Beg? In time you will, but you don't need to tonight – I'm tired now, too tired to sport with you; you may go."

She got to her feet with as much dignity as she could muster, but he seized her hand and pulled her back for a moment.

"I won't be tired forever," he said with a drunken grin.

§§§

Later, in her chamber, she lay fretting in her bed; it was a freezing night and Yoredale Castle was, as always, bitterly cold. Becky came in with an extra woollen blanket and wrapped it around her, but it offered little warmth – or reassurance.

"So, he's out of his bed then," said Becky.

Emma nodded. "Just keep out of his way if you can – easy to say, I know."

Becky shrugged. "I'd like to stick him, and he knows it - but he also knows he just has to mention the girls and I'll lick the shit off his boots. Ellie would do it though; she'd cut his throat while he was thrusting into her!"

Emma frowned. "I'm not sure I remember my sister as you do," she said coolly.

"I'm sorry, lady," said Becky, "I got a bit … I'm sorry."

"Let's hope it won't be as bad as we fear," said Emma and Becky left her.

Would Eleanor do that? Becky probably knew her better than she did. How sad a figure the young girl was now – Becky had been such a bright thing in the old days when she was at Elder Hall with Ellie. Now she was a bitter vessel filled only with bile.

§§§

In the night she woke up with a start. She sat bolt upright and looked around her chamber; something had disturbed her, but there was not a trace of moonlight and she could see nothing. The chamber was above the main body of the Hall linked by a short passage – a passage which only one other had access to: Edmund, whose chamber lay off the other side of the Hall. It had grown colder during the night and her nervous breath hung in the air before her.

"Did I wake you, my dear?"

His words from the darkness shocked her and she shuddered with fear, holding her breath tight in her chest. She heard him come closer and she reached under her pillow.

"Perhaps it was when I took this?" he said, lightly hefting her dagger.

She slumped back against the wooden board.

"I suppose there's no point in asking what you want," she said, unable to keep a tremor from her voice.

He sat down on the bed. "You mistake me lady; I want nothing from you, at least not tonight with this poor wracked body of mine."

"I am not your lady," she said.

"Well, let's agree that I'm the only Radcliffe who's had you. And I'll have you again – and again – whenever I please. My father wants an heir from you and he's not too particular which of his sons sires it."

"Richard…"

"Richard what? Richard's far more interested in a certain sleek haired stable boy than you. But … for now, my body's rusted up from lack of use – like this knife blade of yours. But make yourself ready. One way or another you'll be my lady soon enough. You'll be my lady in body and you'll be my lady in soul."

He buried her knife into the pillow and left her. She did not sleep again that night.

§§§

She stared at the great Radcliffe banner on the west wall of the Hall behind the high table. Crimson red, that was appropriate enough; and a square of yellow to hold that hideous black hawk with its talons outstretched. She had hated it from the first moment she saw it. It struck her though that despite all that blaze of colour, Robert Radcliffe's

Hall was a miserable place when it was empty. She examined the rushes on the floor: they had lain there unchanged for a month or more and they smelt of everything foul. Every morning the servants did their best to brush the dog turds outside, but those smells, and others, lingered.

She set down the basket containing the last of her dried lavender on the high table. Then she walked up and down the room scattering stems of the herb as evenly as she could. When she had emptied the basket, she stopped and rubbed the last few pieces between her hands, breathing the perfume in deeply. How splendid the plant was, she thought: strong, steely blue and heavily scented – she was intoxicated by it, and the Hall would smell all the better for it.

"We have servants to do that, don't we?"

She sighed with resignation; it had been too much to hope that Edmund would leave her in peace for long and it had already been a week since his nocturnal visit.

He was observing her from the entrance to the Hall; between them lay the two long tables and benches set out for the evening meal.

"It passes the time, lord, until my husband returns," she replied, remaining on the dais.

"I can think of better ways for you to pass your time, sister." He began walking slowly alongside one of the tables. She was disappointed to see that he was hardly limping at all.

"Are you feeling better?" she asked, avoiding his eyes and dreading the answer. She picked up her basket and started walking down the other aisle towards the door.

"I would speak with you," he said.

"You are speaking with me." She kept walking; he stopped and turned to walk back parallel to her.

"I've much to do," she said and continued walking.

"You've nothing to do!"

They reached the panelled screen to the buttery and kitchen at the same time and he took her by the elbow.

"You're missing my touch - I can tell and I'm not so tired now." He leant towards her and inhaled.

"Ah, the lavender – I remember it…"

He took a step closer, forcing her back against the screen, then he reached down to stroke her upper leg with his hand. She clutched the basket to her breast as he moved his hand higher.

"I think you'd like to lie with me again," he said.

"No, brother; leave me, please! There'll be servants nearby." She tried to push past him, but he seized her arm and the basket fell to the floor.

"What do I care about servants? It's been far too long," he said, still holding her arm. She shook herself free, but forced herself to face him.

"You took me once and I was foolish enough to let you; but it won't happen again – whatever you do. I'm your brother's wife - and I expect you to respect that!"

"Well dear sister, you're going to be very disappointed then."

He took her arm again and threw her across the nearest table; she rolled over the board and fell onto the rushes, striking her head on the edge of a bench on the way down. He sauntered along to the end of the table and made his way around to the other side; she could see for herself that his old swagger had returned. She got to her knees, blood dripping from her cut head onto the rushes. She had barely stood up when he reached her but she surprised him with a savage slap to his face; he hardly flinched, but it gave her a chance to run, and she did.

"Excellent! By God's breath, I need some exercise!" he shouted.

Emma dashed up the staircase to the floor above, but found herself in the small gallery overlooking the Hall: a dead end. Immediately she returned to the stairs; Edmund almost caught her there but only managed to pull at her skirt, ripping the hem. She lifted her skirt higher, continuing up to the guest chambers on the next floor; none were occupied, but none were secure either. She ran into Lord Radcliffe's private chamber in the North West tower, thinking from there she could reach more guest chambers on the floor above. She climbed the spiral stair in the tower, hearing Edmund's footsteps close behind her, but if she carried on blindly going up she would find herself out on the battlements with nowhere to go.

Then suddenly she fell – a damned trip step; and it worked only too well for she missed her footing and fell forward striking her forehead on the stone, another bleeding cut. The breath was knocked out of her and Edmund was coming. He was near; very, very near. Suddenly her foot was being dragged back and she had only the smooth stone to try to hold onto. He was pulling her back down the steps and she had to break her fall onto each step with her hands. In desperation she kicked back with her other foot and was rewarded with a grunt from Edmund and he let go of her foot. She picked herself up and ran on up to the guest chambers, speeding through them both along the west wall, hoping there was access to the other stair at the south end. There was, but now where? Up or down?

The chapel – she seized upon the thought, for it had a bar across the door as a last redoubt. But the chapel was on the floor below, so she ran down the stair, almost tripping again but just recovering her balance as she lurched through into the empty solar. The chapel was on the south wall, only a short passage away. She paused, breathless for a moment, but heard no sound of pursuit; she could only hope her kick had injured him seriously. She passed along the passage and found the chapel door open; she rushed in, slamming it shut. With her back against the door she looked around for the wood to bar it shut, but could not see it.

She took some deep breaths and tried to calm herself, straining to hear any noise that would warn her of his approach: no footsteps, nothing; she imagined that the whole household must be listening too. She must bar the door just in case; there was an iron candleholder that might do the job. She hesitated, then left the door to fetch it, glancing back anxiously while she dragged it to the door and leaned it at an angle so the iron wedged under the horizontal cross frame of the door. She wasn't sure it would hold but it was the best she could do.

She liked the chapel: it had tall windows which allowed in plenty of light; the figures in the glass made for a fine array of colours and created a beauty which she treasured, especially in such times. She went to the front pew and knelt before the altar rail. She bowed her head, closed her eyes and began to pray: "Thank you Lord -"

"...for delivering the lady Emma safely to me," said Edmund.

Her eyes flew open and she jerked her head to the left: there was Edmund lying nonchalantly on the front pew. Then he stood up; in his hands he was holding the length of wood used to bar the door.

"The chapel was a pretty obvious choice really; by the way, your kick hit my wound, it hurt..." he said and struck her on the shoulder with the piece of timber. She cried out in pain, then he hit her on the back and then the head, and again on her shoulder. She screamed at him, trying to crawl away from the blows as he casually followed her, kicking her and prodding her body with the wood. When he tired of that he discarded the bar and lifted her to her feet, clutching her breasts and pushing her back against the side wall.

"Please, Edmund, I beg you!" she cried, her mouth bloodied and sore.

"Yes, we talked about begging the other evening, didn't we?" he said.

"Please! This is God's place!"

"Well, it was you that led me here - it's a first for me too. Besides, God can have it back - I'm only borrowing it."

Then he lifted her skirts and took her; but she didn't care because at least the beating had stopped. And as he thrust into her, Becky's words echoed around her bruised head; but she was not her sister.

§§§

It was late. She should have arisen by now – most of the household were up and about their daily chores and normally so was she; instead she lay in her bed as if paralysed. She had missed the evening meal; Becky, bless her, had found her in the chapel and somehow helped her stumble back to her chamber. She had cleaned her up; winced at the countless cuts and bruises she bore and dressed her in a clean linen shift before wrapping an abundance of blankets around her.

She had lain awake for hours after Becky left her; to be a wife was expected, but to be the whore of her husband's brother… It was not enough for Edmund to have stolen her maidenhead; he had to humiliate her further. When finally she got up, she washed her face and put on her dullest, most unattractive clothes, choosing a head piece with a veil which covered most of her face and hid her bruised cheeks and cut lip, but it could not hide her shame.

When she next saw Edmund he was relentlessly practising his sword strokes with one of his men at arms, sweating hard to rediscover his fighting strength. With an effort, she nodded to him and then walked quickly by, for he had impressed upon her that she must behave in every way as his lady or she would receive a greater beating than before.

§§§

That evening she lay restless once more in the cool darkness of her chamber, the heavy scent of lavender making her head swim. She drifted into a light sleep but was awoken by noise from further along the passageway. She arose and walked cautiously out of her chamber, staring across the upper level of the Hall to the small chamber where Edmund slept – except, from the sobbing she could hear, he was not asleep. On impulse, she ran across and burst into his bed chamber to find him beating Becky who was stripped to the waist, her back and breasts already scarred by stark red weals. He was angry at the interruption and pushed her roughly back out of the door.

"Young Becky here is meeting all my needs tonight. If I want you, I'll tell you; so don't come in again unless you're told to!" He smiled, but there was menace in his tone.

Becky met her eyes, shook her head gently and waited for the next onslaught.

Dismissed and humiliated, Emma retreated, shoulders hunched, to her chamber. The worst feeling was that of relief – relief that tonight it was Becky, not her, on the receiving end of Edmund's own special brand of loving. She sat on her bed, angry with herself for her weakness and stupidity. She resolved that never again would she succumb to Edmund, no matter how much force or guile he used.

But her new resolve was not tested, for the following day he left without warning to join his father and brother on campaign. She should have felt elated to be rid of him, but she knew he would return and she would once more have to play his lady and what would Richard do about that?

28

Brecon Castle, Mid Wales, Late January 1461

"At least it's stopped snowing," remarked Jasper Tudor, Earl of Pembroke, slamming shut the door to the Great Hall at Brecon Castle.

"It's still bitter out there," said his father, Owen, "and that precious army of yours that you've just dragged all the way from Pembroke will be shitting ice out there tonight!"

"Didn't have much choice, did I?"

Jasper was King Henry's half-brother and a trusted member of the extended royal family who had pledged himself to Queen Margaret's faction early in the struggle. His dubious reward from the Queen was to be ordered to put an army in the field in the middle of winter and take it into the Marches to finish off the remaining Yorkists on their own territory.

"She should have waited till the spring!" Owen said.

"You could have stayed at Pembroke!" sparred Jasper.

"I may be over sixty now, but I can still fight well enough."

"If our enemy's mustering, so must we."

"I don't think the Earl of March is going to invade Wales!"

"It might have been easier if Wiltshire had got himself moving!" said Jasper.

The Earl of Wiltshire's tardiness in bringing much needed reinforcements from abroad had irritated him immensely, for it had delayed their expedition. By the time he had at last arrived from Ireland the weather was a great deal worse. Nevertheless, Jasper told himself, they had reached Brecon intact, now they must plan what they would do once they arrived in the Marches.

"If we move on Hereford," argued Jasper, "we can control the southern Marches and counter any move the Earl of March makes."

"What is at Hereford?" asked Owen, "March will be at Wigmore – we know that. If I was him, I'd come out from Wigmore and take you head on as soon as you set foot in the Marches."

"Well he won't act like you. He has little experience after all – he's still a boy."

"True, but when I was his age I took many risks; if I hadn't taken risks I'd never have bedded a king's widow! You don't expect to fail when you're young."

"And did you fail?"

"Mostly, but not with your mother!" laughed Owen.

"We could do with recruiting a few more men on the way - you've seen what Wiltshire's brought us?"

"A rough mix, Irish obviously, French and Breton too – a noisy lot."

"All I know is they'll be speaking half a dozen different tongues, so I hope they all know how to fight!"

"Can we rely on Wiltshire, do you think?" Owen asked.

"You've reason to doubt him?"

"There've been a few rumours, but nothing clear – just talk."

"Well, the Queen has promised Lord Radcliffe will join us – perhaps that'll give us some local men."

"Ha! No point in worrying about Wiltshire if you've got Radcliffe with you – if it comes down to his life or ours, he carries his own shield highest."

§§§

The horses snorted irritably in the freezing mist that cloaked the courtyard, for the sun had yet to rise when Edward of March led his vanguard out of Wigmore Castle. He slowed to allow Ned to draw alongside him.

"I trust you're not seeking any solitude this morning Ned," he said with a grin. "I'm pleased you've come – we'll be few enough. But you won't forget this day, for your fortunes, as well as mine, will rise up from it."

He cantered off to the front of the column leaving Ned to reflect that his fortunes could hardly sink much lower. Will Hastings joined him. "Confident, isn't he," he said.

"It's strange, but I must admit I feel good about it as well, though I can't think of any reason why I should."

Hastings nodded knowingly. "He does that to people. Watch out if he asks you for anything – before you know it you'll have agreed to lend him your wife!"

"We'll be across the river Lugg soon?"

"This mist is doing us a service now, but if it stays much longer we'll be in trouble."

It was past dawn when they crossed the river, but the mist still obscured the sun. Ned and Hastings joined the other captains as the Earl explained once more his battle plan, but their attention was quickly drawn elsewhere. In the eastern sky a glimmer of sunlight was breaking through the drifting patches of icy mist, lending a pale, golden hue to the frosted fields.

"The sun!" said Edward. "About time!"

"What in God's name's that?" exclaimed Hastings, for above the mist another smaller sun had emerged beside the first. The assembled host fell silent, then gasped in unison as yet another sun appeared before their eyes. Many knelt in fear and crossed themselves; others stood rooted to the frozen earth, terrified by the three suns shimmering side by side in the winter sky; the light was so intense that none could bear to look at it for long.

"What does this mean?" breathed Hastings, already on his knees; but Ned had no answer.

He was no stranger to the glories of an icy dawn: he had seen an ice shower falling like a crystal blue curtain across the rising sun and he had witnessed the angry, red fingers of sunlight reaching out from the east along the river Yore to melt the ice by its banks, but he had never seen such a thing as this.

He watched open mouthed as the dazzling blaze of light spread like fire across the sky; a large bright sphere in the centre, tinted blood red at its outer edges and flanked by a pair of stunning blue white orbs. A rainbow of colours radiated up through the mist, filling the whole of the firmament with every hue imaginable; surely if there was a way that God appeared to man, this must be it.

In many men's hearts the initial wonder was already turning to fear and the eerie silence was replaced by a low anxious murmuring; then Edward's voice thundered out across the fields of kneeling men at arms.

"Friends, be calm! This is but a sign from our heavenly Lord! For these three suns are the Father, the Son and the Holy Ghost, and therefore be not afraid, for you should know, all of you, that by this vision we go forward against our enemies in the name of Almighty God!"

The moment he finished speaking, as if on cue, the three suns merged gloriously into one and the cool mist melted away before its power.

"It shall be my sign!" shouted Edward exultantly, "my badge shall be the sun in all its splendour!"

He raised his great battle sword and received the spontaneous acclaim of his men. Ned, intoxicated by the power of the vision, was caught up in the wild fervour and he too brandished his sword aloft and like all the others he believed he was invincible.

When the uproar subsided, Edward set his army for battle and addressed his commanders.

"That's the way they'll come," he said, with simple certainty, "over the rise and down the slope towards us."

"What if they don't give battle and slip by to the south of us, to Hereford?" asked Hastings.

"They won't. I've men watching every move Jasper makes and they tell me he's coming this way. Jasper doesn't want

Hereford or Ludlow, he wants me; if he can crush me, then his war is won. We'll sit here and wait for him to come down to us. When he does, we'll unleash the barbs of hell on him – and he'll wish he'd ignored his Queen and stayed put in Pembroke! Will, you'll have the van on our right flank; you must hold against their first charge down the hill – it'll cost some blood, I fear."

"We'll hold, my lord," said Hastings, taking Edward's outstretched hand and clasping it like a brother.

"And Richard," said Edward, addressing Sir Richard Croft, "you have the rearguard and you have our lives in your hands – do not commit your men until all our enemies are in the field."

The Earl smiled warmly at his captains. "Friends – you know what comes now. Go to your men and fill their hearts with steel. And mark me on the field, for I'll be where the most blood is being spilt."

§§§

Jasper took his troops through the thin leafless trees at the top of the rise and saw the waiting Yorkist army spread out below him. It was no more than a gentle slope but it would give his men at arms some encouragement when they charged the Yorkist line. He was a little surprised that his adversary had not chosen a better defensive position; with his back to the river, the untried Earl of March had surely made a fatal mistake.

"We must take our chance and drive them straight back into the river," he said to his father.

"Pray Wiltshire is close at hand, for we can't do it alone," said Owen.

"He should be on the far side of the coppice by now, ready to cut loose; if he bleeds their flank, then their centre will fold and you can throw in your mounted knights to rout them."

"What of Radcliffe? No trace of him yet!"

"We don't need him - we'll be drinking King Harry's health in Hereford tonight!"

But now that the moment was near, Jasper hesitated; he had expected that by now Wiltshire would be in position with his Irish levies, but they were not yet in sight.

"We can't wait any longer," he said.

"God be with you, son," said Owen, gripping his hand firmly.

§§§

Ned waited nervously with Bagot and Bear close beside Hastings. Bear looked as if he'd come out for an early morning stroll, Bagot was fiddling with the straps of his breastplate, but Ned just wanted to get on with it. He stared up the slope: there was a mass of men at arms in green and white livery to their left but ahead of them the ground was clear; surely there must be men in the broad coppice still swathed in chill morning mist? Had he seen a glint of sun on metal? He stamped his boots on the cold earth; the February sun was struggling to warm the ground and the soil was still as hard as iron.

"What are they waiting for?" he muttered.

Then suddenly the Lancastrians were on the move, gathering momentum as they charged at the Yorkist centre, bellowing Welsh oaths at the waiting ranks led by the Earl of March.

Hastings held his nerve, resisting the temptation to support the Earl with either his men at arms or his archers. The latter were hidden in a fold of land below the coppice where he expected the left wing of the enemy to appear at any moment.

Ned found himself sweating, despite the cold; he'd thought he knew what to expect by now, but to wait idly whilst the Earl's men bore the brunt of the assault was hard. He scanned the coppice again but saw no-one; then he heard them: it started with a single tortured wail and reached a crescendo of wild unearthly screaming. And then they were there, racing down the hill towards them; they looked as fearsome as they sounded, hurling short handled spears as they ran. Countless spears flew through the air howling like wounded hounds and Ned stood, his heart pounding in his chest as the frozen ground reverberated to the cacophony of sound.

"Irish," Bear informed him casually, "no armour."

Ned trembled with anticipation; all he could think of was his last combat: the ill-fated duel with Edmund – what if he had left his nerve in the forest at Penholme?

"Hold steady!" shouted Hastings above the din as the spears pierced his lines. One struck Bear full on the breastplate but splintered at once and he brushed the remains aside with disdain, for the primitive spears were no match for mail or plate armour.

Then the Irish kern, rabid for battle, closed upon them, wolves coming in for the kill.

"Loose! Loose!" cried Hastings and his waiting archers released a deadly shower of arrows high into the sky. The archers' volley fell like thin slivers of ice onto the lightly protected Irish and cut them to shreds; but, though the force of their attack slowed to a walk, they kept coming.

"Christ's Blood! Those Celts have got fire in them!" said Bagot.

"Meet them at the charge!" shouted Hastings, waving his men at arms forward.

Close beside him ran Ned, bearing his heavy battle sword on his shoulder, tracked on either side by Bagot and Bear, the latter's deep guttural bellow driving their men on. The two armies met with a shrieking crash which resounded across the valley to the far side of the river.

Hastings threw himself into the thickest part of the fighting and Ned was never more than five paces away, punching and jabbing his sword into the crush of flailing bodies. The Irish, mostly without even chain mail, leapt upon them ferociously, for they had to get in close if they were to drive their long daggers into the weak spots in every man's armour. But Hastings' seasoned men at arms broke up the Irish line, turning their battlefront into a series of melees where they could find the space to slash and club brutally at their lightly armed opponents.

Ned was born to fight in a melee and he cut a bloody path through waves of bewildered opponents, hammering the Irish back sideways across a slope already littered with their dead and dying. Ned's onslaught tore the heart out of Wiltshire's shattered vanguard and forced it across into Jasper's flank.

"Hold your lines! This isn't won yet!" shouted Hastings, as some of his men broke ranks to pursue the retreating Irish.

Ned looked across to the centre of the field, where the young Earl of March was being hard pressed in a close quarter struggle. He knew it would be sapping the energy of the well armoured men at arms on both sides; but, inch by inch, yard by yard, it looked as if Edward was dragging his men forward and compelling Jasper to give ground.

§§§

Watching from the top of the rise, Owen saw the welsh dragon banner moving back up the slope and he knew his son was in trouble – that much was obvious. To throw in his entire rearguard too early would be suicide, yet to do nothing would risk his son's utter annihilation. He was still awaiting the arrival of the English contingent with Lord Radcliffe, a man he recognised only by his notorious reputation. Now he was increasingly fearful that the English would not arrive in time. He summoned his youngest captain and gave him his orders:

"Ride east along the Hereford road; if you meet Lord Radcliffe, tell him that Owen Tudor requests his aid at once. Say it clearly in such a loud voice that none can deny it was said. Then, tell him softly that he may gain little honour from the victory if he delays."

The young man looked nonplussed for a moment, but nodded and turned to leave.

Wait!" ordered Owen, "you understand what you must

say?"

"Of course, my lord."

"Listen to me lad, if he won't come to our aid, don't hesitate: flee for your life for he'll not spare you. Do you understand me? Get yourself home to the other side of the marches!"

The captain nodded with easy confidence, then mounted and rode off recklessly fast down the icy slope to join the road to the east.

Owen swallowed hard as he watched the young captain leave and then turned to face the battlefield once more.

"Where are you, Radcliffe?" he grumbled, watching his son's men at arms slowly leech blood as they fell back up the slope; every minute he delayed saw more butchered Welshmen fall.

Finally, he knew he could delay no longer; he drew up his mounted knights and urged them forward to launch an audacious and, he hoped, decisive attack at the Yorkist left flank. Edward's centre would have to turn and deal with his horsemen and when they did so, their line would be weakened and Jasper could press forward once more. At that point, he would throw in the remainder of his rearguard and hope to God that the enemy rearguard was already engaged.

§§§

Robert Radcliffe fixed the Welsh messenger with a look of open contempt. He was not one to be summoned by the likes of Owen Tudor; yet nor could he reject his ally's loudly voiced request for help.

"You tell me that your master expects me at once; but you can't tell me the current state of the battle – do you expect me to ride in blind, boy?"

The young captain had no answer.

In fact, Radcliffe already had trusted men scouting ahead and he fully expected a reliable report at any moment; but he wished to crush the offensive young Welshman first. He knew well enough why the youth had raised his voice upon arrival and whilst he could not chastise Owen Tudor, he could at least punish his messenger.

"Well, I'll stay on the road and judge for myself," he said and turned to the horseman at his right hand. "Mordeur, reward this fellow for his words."

Mordeur smiled and nodded. Lord Radcliffe rode on slowly with his main force, whilst Mordeur put his hand lightly on the youth's shoulder and drove his dagger hard down into the Welshman's neck. The youth clutched speechlessly at the wound unable to stop the blood pouring freely from it; by the time he slipped from his saddle, the life had already drained from his body. Mordeur moved on to re-join his master, casually wiping the blood from his blade.

Radcliffe ambled at a snail's pace along the Hereford road until his scouts confirmed that the Yorkist force was almost encircled and seemed certain to be destroyed; then he moved with speed, eager to secure his share of the victory spoils. As he neared the ragged fringes of the battle, he saw at once that Owen Tudor's attempt to surround Edward of York had actually stalled badly and his mounted knights were being all too successfully countered by Edward's bill men. He smiled with grim satisfaction, for this suited him very well: his intervention would now be decisive and the victory would belong to him.

"Do we go in my lord?" asked Mordeur.

"No, we'll wait just a little longer - but have the men ready."

§§§

Sir Richard Croft, commanding Edward's rearguard, had been waiting for a call to arms for the best part of an hour and his small force was becoming restless. He was eager to respond, and when he saw Owen Tudor's charge he thought surely this was the moment to rouse his freezing men at arms and attack.

"Sir Richard!" A scout arrived breathless. "A mounted

column coming in at speed from the east!"

"The east? Who in God's name's in the east?" he muttered to himself. It was certainly none of Edward's army.

"Make ready!" he shouted. His mind was in a whirl, but he kept his head and waited to see where these fresh troops intended to strike. He watched then in horror as Lord Radcliffe's mounted knights galloped around Owen Tudor's tangle of men and horses, and swept right round the rear of Edward's lines.

"Sweet Lord, they're going to take Hastings from behind!" cried Sir Richard.

Even as Radcliffe rapidly dismounted his men to launch a brutal assault on foot into the rear of unsuspecting Yorkist right flank, Croft at last mobilised his men at arms to join the battle.

"But where?" he said under his breath, "where?" for Edward's army was now beset on all sides.

But there could be only one answer: Edward came first; Hastings would have to look after himself.

§§§

Ned's arms and breastplate were dripping with Irish blood; he had never seen so much blood. With the resistance of the Irish kern broken, Hastings' vanguard was hacking its way towards Jasper Tudor's beleaguered Welshmen.

"Push on! Push on!" Hastings exhorted his men amid the clamour. "Turn them!"

Ned harried the Welsh line with Bear alongside him but he suddenly realised that Bagot was not with them. He dared not turn from the fight, for Blore Heath had taught him what ruin a moment's inattention might bring; he could only hope the old warrior was not hurt badly.

He pressed forward, unaware that the rear of Hastings' vanguard was being scattered as a wave of panic swept through it. Soon, despite the noise all around them, even the front ranks could hear the cries of their fallen comrades and

Ned could make out a familiar haranguing voice. He glanced back to see Bagot cajoling and harrying the troops in the rear ranks who were being scythed down by Radcliffe's sudden attack.

"Hold, damn you!" Bagot roared at the men at arms as they fell back in disarray. "Turn your back again and I'll kill you myself!" he railed.

Hastings looked back in horror and watched the ranks carrying his own badge of blue and purple dissolving into bloody chaos.

"Will!" Ned shouted, "keep going! We'll watch your back!"

Ned turned and took Bear and half the men in the rank behind to go to Bagot's aid.

"Give me some room there!" he shouted and fell in beside Bagot who had formed up a ragged line to slow the enemy's progress.

"Who the hell are they?" yelled Ned.

"Look!" said Bagot, "look at their badges and pennants!"

He could hardly miss the red and gold pennants he'd last seen flying at Yoredale Castle. He cast around the men that faced him: most were encased in mail coats or metal plate, but in the centre he picked out Mordeur's ragged black hair and there, next to him, stood Richard Radcliffe, wearing a liveried tabard over his armour and another knight who by his build and similar livery could surely only be his father, Robert.

So be it, thought Ned: his life was back in his own hands. This was not a struggle for power; this was personal – this was about his father, his brother, his sisters – this was about blood.

He took a long stride forward, flanked once more by Bagot and Bear, and cut his way towards the three well armoured knights he had identified. The two sides closed upon each other with renewed vigour. Ned pounded the Lancastrian men at arms to a standstill, carving a bloody arc through their ranks. He allowed no mercy, fighting in a spray of blood and crushing the dying beneath his steel shod feet as he drove back the living. The Radcliffes did not know him, he realised exultantly, for he was fighting with visor lowered, under Will Hastings' blue banner and soon they were only a few yards away. He could see that Mordeur was pointing him out to Robert Radcliffe who then battered his way towards him, chopping men aside in his haste. At last Ned blocked Lord Robert's path; all around them metal rang and bones shattered. Ned raised his visor, the better to see his opponent. To his left Bear had taken on Richard Radcliffe and on his right Bagot was laying into Mordeur; but for the two at the centre of the melee there was an impasse. Ned barely moved a muscle, his sword held unwavering in front of him.

"One mistake, boy; and I'll kill you!" barked Robert, "if you had trouble with Edmund, you'll have more with me!"

Ned held his stare impassively, and said nothing. His anger must remain ice cold for he had no intention of trading insults; merely blows.

His silence seemed to unnerve his opponent and in one swift movement Robert lifted his sword and swung it hard at Ned's head. Ned swayed back to avoid it but the tip of the blade grazed his visor, causing it to drop half shut and obscure his view. Radcliffe followed his first strike with another at Ned's head and then drove his sword at Ned's shoulder joint; but Ned had regained his balance and parried both blows. Another shuddering exchange ensued leaving Robert back on his heels.

"Some help here!" he shouted, looking to Richard and Mordeur, but both had trouble enough of their own. Nevertheless, several of his men at arms came quickly to his aid; one struck Ned on the back with his sword, but Holton's fine armour did its work and deflected the blade. The other aimed a pole axe at his neck, but the blow never landed. Bear – still pushing back Richard with the battle axe in his right hand, used his left to snatch the short handled halberd from his belt and bury its spike through the base of the man's helmet, severing the top of his spine. Ned punched the hilt of his sword through the other assailant's visor and turned to face Lord Robert again.

"You'll have to do better, my Lord!" he shouted.

The latter clearly knew that he was on his own and put everything into a desperate assault, cutting at Ned's legs to unbalance him, but to no avail and little by little, Robert Radcliffe was forced to give ground.

Ned glanced to left and right: Mordeur was struggling to hold Bagot and one glimpse of Bagot's savage face was enough to tell him the outcome there; Richard Radcliffe was hanging on against Bear, but wouldn't last long, for his large adversary was pounding him into the slippery turf and there was nothing he could do about it. Then suddenly, to Ned's astonishment, Mordeur turned and ran for the horses. A ripple of alarm spread through Lord Robert's battle line as others followed Mordeur.

Ned shouted to Bagot and Bear on either side of him: "Finish them! Drive them back into the river!"

He watched as Lord Radcliffe's company retreated in disarray and was scattered from the field. Richard and his father stood their ground and were soon joined by Owen Tudor and the remnant of his men, routed by Croft's rearguard.

The survivors were surrounded and refused to yield, but Lord Robert was tiring and a heavy blow from Ned's sword knocked him to the cold earth; the plate armour on his right side cracked and misshapen. He staggered to his feet only to be felled by another hammer blow – this time to his head. He was up on his knees but his helm was so damaged that he could no longer see through the visor; he twisted and swayed as Ned struck him from one side and the other, knocking the sword from his hand and battering him to the ground.

With every blow Ned saw only his brother Tom, bleeding to death in the forest clearing. Radcliffe was on his knees and ripped off his dented helmet, cutting his head in the process. Ned shaped to take off his head, but Richard stood over him to parry Ned's blow.

Richard's intervention reminded Ned of Emma and at the last moment he checked the stroke.

Lord Robert picked up his sword again and pushed his son aside.

"Do you think you can prevail over me?" he scoffed breathlessly.

"Yield!" cried Ned.

"I've seen your like before and crushed them all!"

"Finish it," urged Bagot, returning to his side.

"Yield!" ordered Ned.

"You're a traitor, like your father! Nothing you do to me will change that!"

"By St Stephen, finish him!" shouted Bagot.

"Yield," ordered Ned once more, for the bloodlust had left him and he felt only weary and empty.

"Do you think that by setting your muddy foot upon my neck, you can so easily get back your lands?" said Robert.

"Richard," said Ned hoarsely, "for Emma's sake, if you yield I'll spare you; but your father must yield to me what's mine — and he must answer for what he's done."

Lord Radcliffe angrily tossed his sword aside.

"Very well! I'll be ransomed within a week and then I'll have my day!

Ned leaned forward on his sword, exhaustion suddenly overtaking him. "No, my Lord," he said, "your day is done."

They watched the sorry remnants of Jasper Tudor's dismembered army being driven across the fields to the east into the freezing and turbulent waters of the river Lugg.

"Poor bastards," muttered Bagot, "they'll not get the chance to yield!"

29

North Wales, January 1461

Fire - that was her first thought. She tried opening her eyes. There was smoke in the air and her eyes were soon stinging. There was a yellow glow before her - surely that meant a fire? Shit! They were right: they'd all told her she'd be damned for the way she lived and here she was in the fires of hell. She shut it all out and it drifted away for a while but slowly she became aware of the fire again, inhaling the smoke and choking. There was another pungent smell, of leather or some other animal hide. She opened her eyes again and stared at the fire for a long time, mesmerised, searching its core until in its very heart she saw a shadow and the more she fixed upon it the larger the shadow became, until it loomed above her. She screamed and struck out at the dark figure with her hands, but it fought back and pressed her down, squeezing the life from her.

A grim hair encrusted face leaned over her. "Be calm, sister! Be calm! You're safe!"

The words were beating at her, wearing her down. She didn't know the face, nor the deep, gruff voice that went with it; but gradually Eleanor understood that she was no longer in the river, nor was she in any spiritual world; and she accepted that, for the moment at least, she was indeed safe. She stopped struggling and lay still, breathing heavily.

After a few minutes her eyes became accustomed to the dim light and she lifted herself up, exploring the space around her: it was not a room; it was a cave. She was lying on a firm bed of heather and rushes with a heavy woollen blanket wrapped over her. In front of her were two squat, oddly shaped candles giving a wavering cream light. On the ground within a circle of round blackened stones the small fire burned; she looked up, following its smoke as it disappeared into a narrow fissure in the roof. An odd mix of animal skins and wool blankets were draped on the rock walls and dry, but dirty rushes lay on the floor.

On the far side of the cave, the owner of the gruff voice and hirsute face stood impassively. His abundance of facial hair was liberally streaked with grey; he was tall, built like an oak and dressed in a cloak and hat made of animal fur – he seemed enormous. He came closer and she saw that he was indeed enormous. How long had she slept, she wondered? It seemed to her very warm inside, then she tried to recall what it was like outside. She gasped out loud as she remembered the icy stream; yet her habit was dry.

"I'm Gruffydd ap Thomas," he announced.

"You pulled me out?" she said, her voice trembling, her throat dry and tight. He nodded slightly. "How long ago?"

"You've been here a while, sister," he said, "thought you were dead for a time..."

"My clothes .... They're not even damp."

"Took your wet clothes off; wrapped you up warm; set your leg; dried your clothes and put them back on you again."

Eleanor took a few moments to absorb the implications of his simple, staccato account, but she was too tired to discuss it and since she was clearly alright there seemed little point.

Then she remembered Will. "The young man with me - did you see him?"

"Yes."

"Well, where is he?"

"Don't know, and I don't want to know."

"Well I do! I do want to know."

"More fool you! He should never have led you where he did – he as good as killed you. Forget about him, he's probably lost himself anyway."

"Don't say that! Surely I've borne enough."

Her rescuer remained silent, brooding. She collected herself and tried to think clearly.

"Is it still sleeting?" she asked.

"No," he replied shortly, adding after a wicked pause, "it's snowing a blizzard, sister!"

"Why do you call me sister?" But before he could answer she quickly realised that the habit she still wore would have been enough. "I'm not a nun."

"If you say so."

He was staring at her hair. She'd forgotten: she was no longer exactly an eye catching beauty and her roughly shorn hair would mark her out as a woman of God.

"I'm not! But I'm too weary to argue. My name's Eleanor; can you find Will for me? Please?"

"No." It was said with emphatic finality.

"If you're not willing to find him then why did you bother to pull me out of that stream?"

"Already sorry I did!" With that, he gathered his cloak about him, turned and left the cave, allowing a flurry of white flakes to blow in. One of the candles guttered and the warm glow went with it; suddenly the cave seemed a lot less welcoming.

She felt bruised all over, but when she tried to move her troublesome leg, she found to her surprise that it had been expertly bound up – so much so that she could move it with very little pain. Whatever she thought of her rescuer, she mustn't lose sight of his kind treatment of her, nor the small fact that he had saved her from certain death.

She got up and wandered around the cave, seeking something to reveal the essence of this unusual man. From his accent, he seemed Welsh, yet his command of courtly English was far too comfortable for a man of the country. He had, she felt sure, lived at court at some time in the past, but she was disappointed to discover little in the cave to provide any clue to his identity. Her leg began to ache again, so she lay down once more on the bed and swiftly fell asleep – all thoughts of the stranger and Will passing from her mind.

§§§

When she awoke Gruffydd was framed in the entrance to the cave and she laughed to see him.

"You're covered with snow! A man of snow!"

He stamped his boots and shook the snow off his cloak. She hopped off the bed and gave him a spontaneous hug which took him utterly by surprise.

"It's a long while since anyone did that," he said quietly.

"I must have seemed ungrateful before," she said, "but I'm just worried about Will."

"Well, it's been too long to find him and, in any case, you can see nothing out there now."

"Is it so bad?" she asked.

"It's worse than before - a wild north-easterly. You could lose a man and his mount in those drifts."

"Well, I thank you for trying." She squeezed his large hand gently and then limped back to rest her leg upon the bed. "And thank you for binding my leg. Oh, and thank you too for dragging me out of the river!"

"Well, whoever set your leg did you good service," he said.

She bowed her head and closed her eyes. "Indeed, he did more; he did me a great service and I shall always remember him for it."

Gruffydd seemed lost for words, but she filled the silence with her story. Every detail tumbled out as she told of her capture and imprisonment; her despair and pain; how Birches had lost his life in freeing her and how Will had cared for her and how much she cared for him.

"I watched you two for a day; wondered about you – a nun – walking across the land with a young man."

"Then why didn't you come to help us sooner?"

"Don't talk to folk very often and when I do, I usually regret it! Women have gotten me into trouble since the day I was born and it's still happening now, sixty three years later. Interfering always leads to trouble."

"Yet, you didn't leave me to drown?"

"Saw you floundering in the water – just couldn't walk off and leave you. Reached in my arm and plucked you out, I did.

Anyway, now the weather's closed in again. Saw it coming a few days ago, that's why I've stocked up my larder." He gestured to the game hanging in the cave.

"I'm grateful for the warmth of your cave," she said.

"Doesn't amount to much."

"But it's dry, safe and warm."

"Aye, it's dry, safe and warm; but it's still just a hole in the rock. Oh, ignore me; I'm just a sorry, self-pitying old bastard!"

She looked across at her rescuer and her face broke into broad smile; he looked away sheepishly.

"What do you think has happened to Will?" she asked.

"Well, if he's what you say he is, he'll likely have looked for you up and down the river; he won't have found you – 'cos you're here – and when the snow got worse he'll have given up and gone back down the valley. Valle Crucis – that's where he'll be! It's the nearest place. He'll have gone to the monks there – if he's still alive, that is."

"Can we get there?"

"Not in this – and even when it clears, the deep drifts will still be there. And you'll need to give that leg a chance, or I'll have wasted my time." Gruffydd appeared to wear pessimism like a second skin.

"You'll get me out, though, won't you? I'm sure if anyone can, you can."

She lay back on the bed and soon tiredness lulled her to sleep again.

§§§

Despite Eleanor's persuasive powers, the elements were unwilling to release her as quickly as she hoped. The snow continued unabated for another day and soon she could see that even Gruffydd was perturbed by the heavy falls – the heaviest snow he could recall in all the years he had lived there. They were going to have to wait some days yet, he thought, before they would be able to make an attempt to reach Valle Crucis.

In fact it was another two weeks before he judged that they

could head down the valley; it was a long fortnight for Eleanor and she supposed for Gruffydd too. His cave was hardly large enough for him on his own, let alone the pair of them. She astonished him by her daily ritual of stretching and exercising her limbs and torso; it was a practice she had begun at the age of twelve and in the depths of loneliness and despair at Goodrich, it had given her a routine to help her survive each relentless day. She was always aware of her effect on men and she watched him squirm uncomfortably as she went about her exercise. Her sister had often told her she had no shame and this must surely fit that description: bare legged in front of a lonely hermit was about as unacceptable as it could get.

"Not bad for a nun," she said, holding a leg in mid-air, teasing him.

Under his beard he blushed. "I'm starting to wonder if the Lord himself didn't throw you into that stream," he said, "and I can see well enough now that you're no woman of God!"

"I think you've just kept me here to look at – you should buy a tapestry instead!"

Her leg was healing very well and she was anxious to be on her way; and she could see for herself that the land was passable.

She was surprised but pleased when Gruffydd agreed to accompany her until she was reunited with Will but when they reached the abbey of Valle Crucis, they learned that Will had already left in the belief that his young love had perished in the river.

"Well lady," enquired Gruffydd, "whither now?"

She had put so much faith in the belief that Will would be at the abbey, that she had no immediate answer to Gruffydd's question. Will had spoken of Corve, but she didn't know where it was and he had told her that Ned was no longer at Yoredale. Her leg was throbbing from the effort of the journey down the valley from Gruffydd's remote refuge.

"Gruffydd," she said finally, "take me back to the cave."

30

Hereford, February 1461

Edmund had ridden hard, hoping to join his father before the campaign in the Marches began. Only when he passed the dregs of the defeated Lancastrian army straggling north from Hereford did he realise he would arrive too late. A mile from the gates of the town, Mordeur was waiting for him – he looked tired, as if he had been there for many hours.

"We expected you sooner ... sire," he said.

Edmund ignored the rebuke. "Where's my father?" he demanded.

"The town's not safe for you; it's full to the rooftops with your enemies."

"My father?"

"Your father is taken. He'll be executed tomorrow; nothing can be done."

Edmund absorbed Mordeur's terse assessment; he would have taken it worse if a favourite horse had died.

"And my brother?"

"Still lives and he has some of our men with him."

"What's our own strength?"

"A dozen can ride, nine can fight."

Edmund shook his head: not enough men to make much difference.

"What about the French girl?"

"We're still interested in her then?"

"I am still very interested in her – therefore, so are you."

Mordeur shrugged. "Before the battle, I made enquiries and I know where they went last winter."

"Last winter's a very long time ago." Edmund preferred not to think about it.

"Your brother, soon to be the new Lord Radcliffe, is also camped north of the town…"

Edmund took the hint. "Very well; we'll meet one problem at a time."

"You've had a long ride - don't you want to rest?"

"If I'd wanted a rest, I wouldn't have come! Now let's get moving."

§§§

Richard's camp was hidden in a small copse near the Hereford road. It was cold on the road but the welcome in the camp was colder still.

"You took your time!" said Richard, "you'd have been more use before the battle."

"Why are you sitting here on a pile of leaves, when our father is about to have his head struck off?" asked Edmund, dismounting.

"Ask your friend – he started the rout! I don't want him here."

"Still, you don't seem to be preparing a rescue."

"I can't stop the execution, but you can't be too bothered about it or you'd be in Hereford not here!"

"You yielded - you should have fought to the end!"

"That would have pleased you, wouldn't it? You'd have become lord, with no effort on your part at all! Anyway, Ned Elder could have killed me, but he didn't for Emma's sake. We should end the feud here: he's lost a father and a brother … and so have we."

"You can do what you like, but the feud won't end until every last Elder is dead."

"Even the women?"

"Your wife, you mean? She just a woman, Dick; there are others about," he smiled darkly, "although I suppose you might not have noticed."

He must have betrayed his thoughts at that moment for Richard suddenly stared at him.

"You've had her, haven't you?"

Edmund grinned. "What could I do, Dick? She was a desperate woman, and ...I didn't think you'd mind – after all, someone's got to put an heir in her belly." Baiting his brother was a pastime he had sorely missed in the past months. "Don't tell me you care for her, Dick; we both know that you only care for that lad with the black silky hair."

"I care ... about her," said Richard.

"Do you now? That's what she said! Tell you what: if she turns out to be with child, I'll marry her!"

Richard took a step towards him. "She's already got a husband!"

Edmund embraced his brother, but murmured: "not after today; you should have let Ned Elder kill you..."

"Must everything you do end in blood?"

"So the good Lord seems to ordain," said Edmund with a smile; he reached to his saddle and snatched up the poleaxe that hung upon it. In one swift movement he whirled around and aimed the spike at the side of his brother's unprotected head. Richard had been expecting treachery from Edmund, but he reacted too slowly and the spike caught his shoulder and lodged there. He tried to reach for the hilt of his sword, but his arm hung useless by his side. Several of his men at arms quickly drew their swords and formed a protective shield around him.

Edmund took a step back and leaned casually against his mount. He smiled at them: "If any man still has a weapon in his hand when I've finished talking, he is a dead man. I say my brother is a coward and a traitor; and I declare that I am my father's true heir – now sheath your swords or be ready to use them."

To his surprise, half a dozen of Richard's most loyal adherents remained around their stricken lord – clearly his brother was better appreciated than he imagined. But the rest had no intention of going against Edmund and they now joined his own men in a ragged circle.

Richard gritted his teeth and slowly pulled out the poleaxe from his shoulder.

"Thank you, brother, for the loan of your weapon," he said.

"Much good it will do you – you won't be leaving here alive," said Edmund. Nevertheless, he cursed silently, for he knew that he was facing Richard's most durable knights and they would not sell their lives cheaply; besides, they knew now that no quarter would be given.

§§§

Not long after first light Ned stood in Hereford market place staring at the execution block on its low makeshift scaffold hastily erected the previous day. He wore his mud stained grey cloak carelessly over his armour, for the morning air was crisp and chill and there was a thin covering of gritty snow on the cobbles. Already a large crowd was gathering, funnelling through the web of narrow streets that led into the market place; it wasn't every day that such an event occurred in Hereford. He saw many of Earl Edward's soldiers mingling noisily with the townsfolk who had defied the bitter February weather to bear witness to the executions.

He watched with grim fascination as the condemned prisoners filed out into the square from the nearby inn with their escort. He drew closer to the scaffold where Bear and Bagot awaited him – the latter scanning the crowd nearby for any hint of trouble.

Owen Tudor walked at the head of the sombre procession followed by Robert Radcliffe; these two stood tall and proud, whilst the gentlemen who accompanied them stared wide-eyed at the means of their destruction. Tudor seemed almost relaxed until the headsman unceremoniously ripped off the collar of his red velvet doublet. Then he turned to the Earl of March and called softly, but audibly enough: "Is this head, that once lay in the warm lap of Queen Catherine, now to lie on that cold block?"

"The head that lies in the lap of someone else's queen deserves to be struck off!" replied the Earl tersely.

But Owen responded with dignity and resignation: "You'll see one day young man that love doesn't always run the course you expect."

As Owen ascended the scaffold, Robert Radcliffe waited at the foot of the steps, only a few yards from Ned. Owen walked the few remaining paces to the block with a fierce dignity. There were a few shouts of abuse from some quarters of the square, but it was all rather half-hearted and only a muted cheer greeted the blow of the headsman's axe, as Tudor's head rolled off the scaffold onto the snow flecked ground below. Ned had never witnessed an execution before and although he had known well enough what would happen, it still shook him.

Thus he was already unsettled when Radcliffe called to him: "You'd better start pleading with your new master for my life, or you'll never find your sister; I'm the only one who knows where she is, I promise you."

Ned returned his cold stare with interest: "The Earl isn't going to pardon you, whatever I say."

Radcliffe eyed the block thoughtfully and then spoke again: "I know the secret upon which your life and fortune will hang; if you give me my life, I'll give you yours."

"There's nothing I want to hear from you – secret or otherwise."

"Get on with it!" ordered the Earl of March, gesturing for Lord Robert to be taken onto the scaffold, but Radcliffe shrugged off the guards.

Ned knew that the Earl would administer the same summary justice to his prisoners as had been meted out so recently to his own father and brother.

"Give it up," he said, "there's nothing in all Christendom that'll make the Earl forgo your death."

"Does the noble lord require assistance to climb the steps?" asked Edward, impatiently waving forward one of his men at arms to take Lord Radcliffe up to the block. Radcliffe watched as Owen Tudor's severed head was rammed onto the market cross and saw his brief moment of opportunity slipping from his grasp.

"Ned Elder's life may depend upon the knowledge I have!" he called out to the Earl.

"Well tell him now, before you die!"

Radcliffe pulled away and pointed angrily at Ned. "This feud is not over. If I must die, I'll tell you half a tale and let the doubts fester in you!"

He was pushed down to his knees and his neck was thrust down hard onto the rough block, still wet with Tudor blood. As the executioner's axe traced its upward arc, Lord Robert raised his head and shouted to Ned: "a bastard brother!"

The axe hesitated at the apogee of its journey to the block.

"You've a bastard brother! Of Radcliffe blood - and he'll come for you!"

The headsman looked at the Earl, who gestured for him to proceed.

"You won't even know him," said Robert and laughed bitterly as the headsman's axe fell with a dull thud onto his half raised neck, and the hollow laugh lingered in the air.

The headsman was sweating, for Radcliffe had lifted his head at the vital moment; the axe did not sever the head and instead skidded off the top of the skull. Ned winced as another hurried blow hacked at the still moving head: blood and brain dribbled from the split head but spine and artery remained intact.

"In the name of God man, finish it cleanly or expect no payment from anyone here!" shouted Edward at the unfortunate headsman.

Finally Lord Radcliffe's head was parted from his thick, muscled neck, but his death gave Ned little satisfaction, for he knew it wasn't the end. On the scaffold the remaining prisoners, five gentlemen, were fitted with nooses, since their status did not merit the headsman's axe.

Bagot clapped him heartily on the back. "One less Radcliffe

to worry about then!"

"I'm not so sure; perhaps there's one more Radcliffe to worry about."

"He was trying to save his head - you could see that."

"It may be," said Ned, watching blankly as the last of the condemned men dangled from the scaffold; but in his heart he was not so sure.

The onlookers had already begun to melt away into the warren of lanes, but Ned remained beside the blood soaked scaffold with Bagot.

"The Earl goes to meet his cousin, the Earl of Warwick," said Ned, "and he's given me one month to put right my personal affairs; then I must attend on him in London."

"And what do you hope to do in a month?" asked Bagot.

"I could take back my lands; the Earl has promised to remove the attainder and give them back to me."

Bagot smirked, despite himself. "Are you going to?"

"No! For as you well know, the Radcliffe brothers still sit in Yoredale castle and ... what Edward gives can easily be taken away by the Queen."

"So, his generous bounty is worthless!"

"Bagot – I still have Ellie to find; there's enough to be done."

"Aye lord – let's get on with it then."

31

Corve Manor, February 1461

Amelie shivered in the lee of the curtain wall at Corve Manor, cloak wrapped tight around her against the bitter wind. She started as a small bird fell out of the chill sky and fluttered helplessly against the cold stone: she knew how it felt. Maman would be so very cross with her for feeling this way; how desperately she missed her.

Mags hurried out of the Great Hall doorway and joined her.

"It's good to know it's colder out here," she said, "I was beginning to think it was just as bad inside. I swear Betwill would rather we froze to death than use any more logs."

Amelie lifted her chin in response. Mags glanced at the pale face and red eyes; Amelie turned away.

"Missing someone?"

Amelie wiped her moist eye lashes with the back of her hand. "It is nothing – I'm just cold."

Mags smiled. "Mmm, nothing; but you keep fretting on it all the same. Let's go inside, before we do freeze!"

They went up to the north tower, but it was little warmer in there. They stood at the arrow loop in the wall and Mags looked down at the large figure of Holton on the rampart below.

"He'll be worrying away down there," she said.

"At least you can see him worrying."

Mags felt only a fleeting pang of guilt. "I've learnt a lot about John Holton these past months."

"He's so loyal to Ned - almost beyond loyal - the armour he crafted…"

"Hah! I carried some of that to Ludlow! I gave him such a battering over that – it near finished the two of us. I didn't see the point of taking it all that way."

"But he did?"

"He more or less said he'd rather leave me behind than all that broken plate! I could've hit him; but then he just came out with it. Told me how his life changed when he was twelve years old; how he met Ned."

"How?"

"His father's mill was burned down and his parents in it – he just said it, as if it happens all the time; and when he told me his tale it was as if he was back there in the mill house, hearing the cries and smelling the smoke. I shan't forget it in a hurry.

"The cracking timbers woke him before first light; the smoke was already thick in the mill when he got out. Then he went back in and dragged his parents out one after the other, as the thatch crackled above him. He watched the flames running along the great wheel until it fell into the millrace. When the roof beams snapped and fell the blaze must have lit up the valley."

"And Ned?" asked Amelie, intrigued.

Mags grinned, looking down to the ramparts once more.

"Believe me; it took a goodly time to get that much from him! But, like you, I wanted to know how these two were bound so close. The mill didn't catch fire by itself; when he left the mill, he saw the village youths coming; they chased him through the woods into the open fields where he fell over baulks and into ditches – poor sod, they'd tried him for years, it seems: the miller's fat son."

Amelie held Mags' eyes as a tear squeezed out.

"Then he came to the steep slope down to the river, he half ran, half fell down it; came to rest by the water. He could hear them shouting; then he simply gave up and waited for the blows to come and they did. He told me he knew he was going to die and just hoped it wouldn't take long."

"But he didn't die…" Amelie said quietly.

"Aye, the blows stopped and he was lifted up, eyes still shut tight; when he opened them he saw the village youths running back up towards the woods. And there was Ned Elder. Ned had no need to help him; he was nothing to him. He was the fat son of the local miller – who everyone hated - but Ned saved him."

"He feels a debt then…" said Amelie.

"It's a debt John thinks that nothing can ever pay."

"I think I know what he means…"

The shadows were lengthening as the blood red winter sun died in the western sky.

"Surely the battle, won or lost, must now be over by now," she said, "but what if he is lying wounded in some cold field, only this time I cannot mend him?"

"Horsemen!" The shout from Holton crackled across the courtyard. "Earl Edward's livery!"

The two women sprang up and raced down the steps to the courtyard as the gates were opened, but it was not Ned. He had sent a detachment north to bring news of the victory and to send word that he and the others were safe. Holton's relief was almost tangible: he could not stop grinning. His worst fears that the battle would be lost and he would be defending Corve against an army of ferocious Welshmen would not after all be realised.

"The Earl's army has moved on to Hereford," said the knight in command.

"Good! Then I will go to Hereford!" announced Amelie. Holton stopped grinning and his heart sank: the thought of escorting Amelie to Hereford filled him with horror.

"Surely it won't be safe?" said Mags, sensing his disquiet.

"I must go! The Hereford road should be safe enough to travel on and perhaps if I go alone no-one will notice me."

"Lady, if I let you wander the marches alone, our master will never forgive me!" protested Holton.

"Nor me!" said the knight. "If you're set on travelling, I'll gladly escort you when we return in the morning."

"Good!" said Holton, "but I'll go with you of course."

"And I!" said Mags at once.

"Me too," added Hal.

The next day they did not leave Corve as early as they had hoped: ice and flurries of snow hampered their preparations and by the time the company was ready, the knight escorting them was beginning to lose patience; but, eventually, they set off.

To reach the Hereford road they had to pass through a heavily wooded valley where several icy and meandering tracks wound through the trees making it difficult to keep the group together. As they rode on, Amelie's levels of anxiety increased – how she hated these dreary winter forests where she had already seen so much misery. She stared accusingly at every tree, devoid of leaves, their black branches dripping ice. How could she even have contemplated journeying alone to Hereford? But she comforted herself with Ned's words: 'wherever you are, I'll be with you.'

§§§

"Two women amongst them, I think," observed Mordeur as they tracked the small group winding along the valley floor. Edmund's triumph over his brother had cost him most of the men at arms and he could ill afford to lose any more. Yoredale had already been stripped bare and his small force was hardly likely to wreak havoc in the Yorkist controlled Marches. Mordeur had taken him to Corve Manor, where after several hours they had seen the small party set out.

"Is she there?" asked Edmund.

"I think it's her, but it is a big risk; we didn't expect an escort; we're too few."

Edmund ignored his advice and took them higher up the slope amongst the trees where they could stalk their quarry with less chance of being seen. He studied the group closely: seven – no, eight harnessed men and two women both shrouded in their cloaks. He really needed a closer look.

"When they get into the trees, we'll start to even up the numbers," he said.

The Frenchman nodded and they rode forward briskly so that they could get ahead of the riders below. Soon they were far into the trees and Edmund ordered them to dismount and make ready their bows.

32

Hereford, February 1461

After the executions Ned set off for Corve Manor, but not before he witnessed a remarkable scene. As they rode slowly out through the square, the severed head of Owen Tudor still remained on the market cross, but around it a circle of countless lighted candles had been placed. In the centre of the ring stood a well-dressed woman, her face streaked with tears, lovingly combing his hair. Ned watched in fascination as she gently washed the blood from his chin and caressed his lifeless cheeks. It was at once both touching and obscene.

The sight of Lord Radcliffe's head still skewered on a pike with the rest reminded Ned that he had much unfinished business; Robert Radcliffe's revelation on the scaffold - for all that Bagot dismissed it - called everything into question and he could not banish it from his mind. Yet for now, he was exhausted and just wanted to return to Corve. The victory had brought him closer to success than he had ever imagined, but he had only a month to finish the task.

The journey from Hereford was more dangerous than he had expected, for everywhere there were small desperate bands - remnants of the defeated Welsh army - who lingered hopefully seeking plunder in the Marches before they began the long arduous journey across the mountains to their homes.

He underestimated the time it would take them to reach

Corve and by nightfall they were still on the road to Ludlow and had yet to negotiate the bleak expanse of thick woodland that lay to the south east of the Corve estate. For a moment he hesitated on the margins of the forest, conscious of the darkness descending rapidly and the freezing air clinging to the trees. He wheeled his horse around and dismounted.

"It'll be dark as pitch soon and we'll be blundering around in circles. We'll camp on the edge of it tonight, then push on to Corve tomorrow."

§§§

Mags clung desperately to the horse's neck as it plunged through the trees, lurching this way and that, shaking the ice off the branches to sting her face. She sobbed breathlessly as the horse carried her on through the forest; though she tried to rein her in, the mare thundered on regardless. Mags knew the animal was hurt but if she turned to investigate the wound she risked being tossed from the saddle, so instead she hung on to the horse's mane. Then, to her surprise, the beast began to slow down until it ran, gradually, to a canter and finally broke into an uncertain trot. Briefly she was relieved, but then she looked up to see several horsemen approaching her through the trees and her heart sank. The riders ahead of her slowed and she tugged on the reins to turn her own horse, but the beast was done with running. She steeled herself for the inevitable, slipping her small knife into the bloodstained hand that had held it earlier. If the others were dead then it mattered little; she would do her best to take one with her.

"Mags?"

She dissolved at the sound of Ned's voice and dropped her head onto the horse's neck.

"Mags!" he called out again and rode quickly to her. He seized her bridle and helped her dismount; she leaned her weight against the mare's warm flank, her body trembling.

Ned stared at her and a chill swept through him.

"What are you doing here? Why aren't you at Corve?" he asked.

"We were going to Hereford."

"Why? You were supposed to stay at Corve!" he said angrily.

"Who was going to Hereford?" asked Bagot gently.

"Amelie wanted to go and ... well, most of us."

"So where are the others?" demanded Ned. "And where's Holton? He was supposed to be looking after the pair of you!"

Mags suddenly remembered the moment.

"He's dead," she said softly, "he's dead; he told us to go... so we did; but he took such a terrible, terrible blow. I saw him go down, so I rode; I just left him..."

"How long ago?" asked Bagot.

"I don't know ... the horse just ran and ran!"

Bagot wiped his hand across the mare's back and looked at Ned: "This horse hasn't run so very far."

Ned jumped into his saddle. "Come on! We may still be in time!"

They rode through the forest, eyes piercing the ragged trees around them. They saw no movement, but it was not long before they came upon the place where most of the fighting had occurred; the dead still lay where they had fallen.

"Search nearby," ordered Ned, "and be careful." He drew his sword, but soon Bagot discovered Holton's body. He lay still, felled by a savage cut to the head; Mags flew to his side, but gasped to see him and turned away. Even the veteran Bagot winced when he saw the wound: the force of the blow had splintered the teeth and broken his jaw, slicing the flesh from the jawbone itself so that the lower half of his face was a mass of blood, shattered bone and teeth. He must have died in agony thought Bagot; but when he touched Holton's arm, he was astonished to find it still warm.

"By St. Stephen's breath! He's still alive!"

Mags scrambled over to him and tried to hold him.

"Careful!" warned Bagot, "we don't want him coming round – the pain'll be too much."

Ned stood over the motionless body. "How has he survived

such a wound?"

"No-one could bear such a blow and live," said Bagot, "he's hardly breathing."

"Can you save him?" asked Mags.

"Save him for what? He'll be in such pain, he won't be able to talk, or eat for that matter. No, it's better to let him go."

"But can you save him?" asked Ned.

"With the right tools I suppose I might. I've done patching up in the field, but never anything like this. You need a surgeon - and I'll not put him through the fires of hell for no purpose!"

At this, Mags ran out of the clearing sobbing.

"Bagot, if he can be saved, I want him saved – he's earned every help we can give him."

Bagot shook his head. "I've seen wonders achieved on men after a battle, but without the right tools, I would just butcher him even more. If he's earned anything, it's the right to be spared that."

Nevertheless, he sat beside Holton, for he did not want the youth to die alone.

Mags returned breathing heavily and thrust into his arms her battered brown bag, the contents of which none of them had ever been allowed to see.

"Do your best," she said in a breaking voice, "you'll find what you need in there; I'll help you."

She sat down beside him. Nonplussed, Bagot opened the bag and examined the articles inside; he found, carefully and individually wrapped in cloths, the instruments of a battlefield surgeon.

"They're my pa's," she said, in response to the unasked question.

Bagot shook his head in disbelief and then prepared to work on Holton. He hesitated, undecided where to start.

Ned and Bear made a thorough search and found several more bodies, but of Amelie or Hal there was still no sign. Ned said nothing. God was supposed to be watching over her, but then God seemed to be making an example of him.

He walked across to Bagot and Mags bending over Holton; the big man's face was almost cut in half and his lower jaw bone hung uselessly; Ned shook his head: he could not see how such damage could be repaired. "It'll take a miracle," he said.

Mags looked up at him. "Then for the first time in my life, I'll pray for one."

As Bagot had expected, Holton was now spinning in and out of consciousness: every time he came to, he tried to speak but he could form no words and razor shards of pain caused him to pass out again.

"If we can bind him up, get him fit to travel," said Bagot, "that's all we can hope for - it's too cold to work on him for long out here."

"Get him back to Corve," agreed Ned, "Bear can go with you; I'll scout around a bit more and join you later."

"I should stay with you," argued Bagot.

"Your skills are worth more to him."

"What if the attackers are still near?"

"Then they'll feel my loss. Now, get him to Corve!"

Ned was not about to leave whilst Amelie might still be nearby, perhaps hurt; but after five or more hours of riding circuitous routes through the trees towards Corve, he had still found nothing. So, as darkness fell, he completed the final miserable miles to the castle, where he found Bagot at the gatehouse anxiously awaiting his return.

"How is he?" enquired Ned. "Have you asked him what happened?"

"He's barely breathing, anyway he can't speak, so don't expect to get anything out of him."

"He doesn't need to speak: he's a miller's son; he's been taught letters."

"Go to Betwill, he must have parchment and ink. Quickly!"

Ned sat down beside Holton, whose face had been bound together so that he could not move his jaw. He was barely conscious, but seeing Ned he gamely tried to raise himself from the straw bed.

"Don't you move, John, please. I'm sorry for your pain, but I must know what happened: you need only nod; can you help me?" Holton nodded slowly, grunting as he did so.

Ned took a deep breath: "Has Amelie been taken?"

Holton's eyes welled up with tears and he nodded again.

"Do you know who has her?"

He inclined his head slightly, every movement causing him agony.

Ned gave Holton the parchment and quill. "I want you to write the name for me, if you can."

He held the horn of ink steady, whilst he supported Holton with his other arm and watched as he painstakingly formed the letters one by one. Ned could read well enough to decipher the name Holton had written. It was the name that he feared most, but he gently helped Holton to lie back down again. He took the smith's hand and clasped it in both of his own. "John, when you are well again, you'll be at my side. For now, you may be sure that we'll hunt down this butcher."

He strode into the Great Hall and kicked out angrily at a stack of logs by the hearth, scattering them across the rushes; then he went out into the dark, freezing courtyard and kicked the wall repeatedly. Then for a long while he stood in silence, until Bagot joined him.

"It's him, isn't it?"

"Edmund bloody Radcliffe," replied Ned.

"Hardly a great shock though. So what now?"

"The Earl's given me a month and I've given my oath to that. Do you think that'll be long enough?"

"Well, we've had no news of the Lady Eleanor for over a year; not to mention young Will and Birches. You could search for all your years - never mind a month. On the other hand, we've a good idea where Amelie will be – but we can't take Yoredale castle!"

"I know. You're right, but I can't just leave her – not with Edmund of all people!"

Bagot put his hand on Ned's shoulder. "Ned, if you don't keep your oath to the Earl, he'll not forgive you. You think you've done him great service – and you have – but if you're forsworn, what you've done will count for nothing. You've got a chance, a chance you couldn't have dreamed of a few weeks ago – it won't come again."

"I'll not abandon her to Edmund – not even for the Earl of March!"

"Then you're a fool. What do you think your new master will make of it? Do you think he has any regard for such women? I've heard women are but trifles to him - of no importance! If you desert him over this girl, he'll bury you."

"He has a careless way with women, true enough; but his way is not my way. Is it worth regaining the manor, if I have to sacrifice Amelie to get it?"

"Your father wouldn't have risked all for a servant girl!" retorted Bagot.

Ned turned on him angrily. "My father's actions cost us our estates in the first place so don't lecture me with stories of what he would have done! If you don't want to get involved then go – I release you again from any fealty you think you owe me!"

Bagot dismissed his offer with an angry gesture.

"I've already told you: where you go, I go and that's not going to change – however foolish you are!"

For a while Ned remained silent, not wanting to argue further with his mentor.

"What you say makes sense, I know, but she's … in trouble – and not just from Edmund."

"Well, it's in God's great balance now," said Bagot, as if that made sense of all, "sometimes we can't understand God's plan."

"I tell you Bagot, I'm getting weary of 'God's balance', for it has not favoured us of late!"

"He's kept you alive so far."

"I'm not sure that God is as keen to keep me alive as you think."

"God's balance weighs the good and the bad that we do; it's not about what the Lord does, but what we do."

"Then surely, Bagot, we're already lost: for we've killed so many between us that truly the scales must be heavily tipped against us."

For a time both men were quiet again. Bagot fidgeted uncomfortably.

"When I was at Castillon with Talbot..."

"Please, Bagot; no more war stories."

"Very well, but you're not the green lad you were when all this began: you've proved yourself a great warrior – I've seen some, so I know – you've a chance now of getting back your lands, your honour. You can still perhaps win over Lady Emma and you may yet find Lady Eleanor, but this maid ... she will drag you away from those things."

Ned dropped his head wearily into his hands. "Why the devil didn't she just stay here?"

At that point Mags pierced the air with a squeal. They looked at each other in confusion as she ran past them. There at the gate was a scruffy but familiar youth.

"Hal!" Ned greeted him like a lost soul, embracing him warmly. "It's good to see you, lad; but where have you been?"

"Lord, my lady told me to ride ... and I did; I thought she was with me...and then I turned round and I was on my own ... I wandered through the forest; I've never been so far away before ... I was lost."

He told them all he knew of what had happened, which was little enough; then, remembering one last act to be carried out, he reached inside his tunic, took out a crumpled piece of silk cloth and handed it to Ned, who recognised it at once.

"She said you must have it and I shouldn't give it to anyone else."

"What is it?" asked Bagot.

"It's the end," said Ned, "she's given up the only weapon she had."

He felt the curious eyes of the others upon him.

"Well, we know where Edmund will be; I'm going north and, if I survive that, then I'll go to London to keep my oath to the Earl."

33

Ludlow, February 1461

Will stopped at the lower bar in Corve Street and sat on the stone wall that marked the frontage of the cottages on the east side of the road. He was cold and his feet were sore and blistered where his boots had worn through. He looked across to the house of the Carmelite friars and put his head in his hands, for he was back on the very spot where he and the others had been almost a year before. He pulled his leather jerkin tighter around him and stumbled on up the street through the Corve Gate where a watchman eyed him suspiciously. Just inside the gate was the Bull Inn; he went in and sat down at a table in the dimmest corner of the room, exhausted. He examined the contents of his purse – enough for a pot of ale or two, but not a bed for the night. The ale did little to lift his spirits, but he was dog tired and soon slumped forward, letting his head rest on the rough wooden table; he quickly drifted off to sleep.

He was woken up by a deep woman's voice.

"If you're falling asleep here, you can pay for a bed – or buy some more ale!" she said loudly.

Will stirred briefly, and the hostess turned to a burly figure seated by the door.

"Wake him up for me, Wellman," she instructed, "as if trade isn't bad enough as it is. I'm not having 'em sleeping in 'ere."

Wellman lurched to his feet and went to Will, seizing a handful of hair to lift him up; at once he recognised him.

"You!"

"Me?" Even if Will had not absorbed a little ale, he would have struggled to recall the man who now pinned him to the wall by his neck.

"I've been hoping to run into you one day without your well harnessed friend. Don't remember me, eh?" He wrenched Will's sword from its scabbard and dropped him on to the rush floor. Will grunted, the breath knocked out of him.

"On your own now – and only one sword - you had two when we last met and you had 'em across my neck. Full of it then, weren't you!"

"Wellman!" cried the hostess, "I told you to wake him up – he can't pay me much if you half kill him!"

He felt Will's purse. "He's got no coin left!" he called out and proceeded to throw Will from one wall to another; the disturbance attracted the other occupants of the hostelry, who left their drinks and gaming to watch the two protagonists. They laughed as Will landed heavily on the rush floor and stayed there, inhaling a heady mix of dog's piss and ale.

"John Wellman, you're far too big for him!" shouted one cheerily and then drifted off like the rest to continue his ale and conversation. Wellman himself, tiring eventually of his sport, lifted Will to his feet, carried him to the door and threw him into the gutter that ran down the centre of the street.

"Stay there with the other turds," he said and retrieved Will's jewelled sword, grinning broadly as he caressed the blade.

Will struggled to his feet in the filth of the gutter. He swayed for a moment in the cool air, leant against the tavern wall and then slowly slid down onto the cobbles. He didn't care if he never got up again.

A tall figure emerged from the shadows opposite the Bull.

"Well, well," he said to himself. He bent down to Will and, having established that he was still alive, he lifted him up and carried him over his shoulder. Will stirred, but said nothing; it was not far to carry him.

He banged loudly on the house door and it was opened cautiously.

"You weren't gone long. Oh, the saints! Who've you got there?"

"A friend - open the door, Lizzie, so I can get him by the fire!"

§§§

When Will awoke he was propped up in a large chair next to a fire that threatened to roast him. There were two other chairs in the smoky room: in one sat Felix of Bordeaux and in the other sat a young woman.

"Felix!" said Will, still groggy, "you're back in Ludlow?"

"So I am!" agreed the Frenchman amicably, "but I have not often left it since last I saw you – and very glad I am to see you again; though I find you in a poor state, young Will."

Will stared blankly at the woman, then the room; there were two large chunks cut out of the cob wall filling.

"But this is where you were held isn't it? Pinned to the wall? Do you live here?"

Felix shrugged. "Why not? I don't blame the house for what happened. This is Lizzie, widow of the late wine merchant, Geoffrey of Ludlow, and now the owner of this house. When I first came to the town, it was to collect a debt from Geoffrey, whose wine business was, shall we say, failing."

He looked at Lizzie who smiled at him fondly.

"He drank more than he sold," she said with a grimace.

"And then they found him dead in the town ditch after last year's troubles," added Felix.

"So I had to persuade Felix to let me carry on the business myself," she continued.

Felix chuckled. "Lizzie was very persuasive but the business should have been doing well in this town and I'd rather sell wine than not. So, here we are."

Looking at the pair Will felt that there was another story to be told, but he was too tired to hear it.

Suddenly he noticed his empty scabbard.

"My sword! Was it taken?" he asked, dimly recalling the beating he had taken.

"Rest easy, it's on the chest over there," said Felix.

"But how did you get it?"

"Indeed, it was no great labour, for Lizzie supplies the Bull with all their imported wines – the innkeeper did not care to give me offence, so he soon 'found' it for me; though there was a fellow who seemed a little put out about it."

"It's good to see you again, Felix."

§§§

In the morning, Will awoke to find himself upstairs in a comfortable bed chamber. When he arose he discovered a pitcher of water in his room and quickly splashed his face. Then he ventured downstairs and found Felix in the wine cellar.

"The widow's wealthy," said Will, admiring the crammed cellar.

"She's a good woman, Will, and she suffered much last year; if she's wealthy now it's through her own hard work. A good woman is beyond price."

Will smiled, but there was no humour in it.

"What of you, my friend?" asked Felix, "come, we can talk at ease here; tell me what's brought you to this."

"I found her, Felix… found my beautiful Ellie and then I lost her."

And though he had sworn to himself that he would never speak of it to another, he poured out every detail to Felix. For a long time afterwards they remained in the cellar in silence.

"So, what are we to do with you now?" asked Felix finally.

"There's nothing to be done."

"You're not a lost soul, Will."

"I'm beyond lost."

"You're a fine young man…"

"No, not even that."

"Tell me: does Ned know about his sister yet – or Birches?"

"I've not seen Ned; for all I know, he never got back."

"No, Ned came back! Holton told me before he left to go back to Corve Manor."

"Well, I'm glad of that at least."

"You owe it to them all to tell them, to bear the news of Eleanor's death, of Birches' death – or how will they know?"

"What if there is no-one left at Corve to tell?"

"Then we'll find that out together," replied the Frenchman resolutely.

"But surely, you have business here?"

"Will, I'm a vintner; as long as I can pursue my business, I can be wherever I want to be."

34

Yoredale Castle, February 1461

Edmund Radcliffe stood behind Amelie watching her hunched body racked with pain; her silence was unnerving him. She had been stripped, searched, beaten and interrogated; but still she had given him no more than the occasional involuntary cry. He knew that the girl must hold an item of value to the Queen, yet they had found no trace of it.

Mordeur waited outside the small store room, leaning against the doorway.

"It would help," he said, "if we knew what we were looking for."

"You're sure that she's got nothing hidden about her at all?"

"Nothing, I even got one of the women to search her – very thoroughly – and she has nothing! Can we not be done with her now?"

"Are you certain?"

"My lord, she has been searched in every way a woman can be searched – I assure you, every way!"

"Very well then."

"But…"

"Well?"

"There is one more thing you might care to try," said Mordeur.

"Yes?"

"She knows the Standlake brats…"

Edmund nodded and the Frenchman went to fetch them.

He turned back into the room and laid his hand upon the top of Amelie's head. He smiled as he felt her stiffen in anticipation of the blow to come, but his touch could be unnervingly gentle.

"You were with the Standlakes for a time weren't you?" he said quietly, stroking her hair, "You must have become quite…fond of the children, quite … close to them. Three of them are still here on the estate. I thought you might like to see them."

To his disappointment she showed no immediate reaction, no emotion.

Mordeur brought in the three girls: Margaret, Sarah and Jane; all were in their early teens, but thin and stunted from under nourishment; their hair was dirty and matted. The girls were terrified even before they saw the welts on Amelie's face; once they had done so, they began to wail and weep, as they fully expected to meet their end.

Edmund, however, was watching Amelie as she stared at their scared young faces and at once he knew that all the agony she had endured so far would count for nothing, because now she would tell him everything she knew – and, when the girls were taken out, she did. Even so, he struggled to make sense of it.

"You tell me you had this piece of embroidery which your mistress gave you, but you don't have it anymore? You gave it away…"

Edmund paused to allow the full significance of his incredulity to sink in.

"Your mistress entrusted this to your care, so you just gave it away; you know that doesn't seem very likely to me."

"I have told you all I know," she said, "it was a simple piece of silk - a small gift from my mistress – that's all."

"But, if it was such a 'simple piece of silk', why didn't you tell me all this before? Am I to believe that you put up with all that pain for a piece of silk of no importance to anyone?"

"I did not know what you sought..."

"The young girls... you wouldn't want any harm to come to them?" He toyed carelessly with her fears. "Mordeur, you know, he likes them very young: I think it's the small, soft paps he's partial to..."

"I know nothing more," said Amelie. "I gave it away – I did not think it was important. I gave it away! You must know I would tell you anything I could to save those girls..."

"Yes, I believe you – I believe you would tell me anything to save them, but can I trust what you tell me? You need to think again my little bitch because if you don't, I'm going to flay those girls while you watch their blood run into the earth beneath your feet!" He stalked out.

§§§

Amelie was lost: it was only days since her capture, yet it seemed like weeks; she had kept hope by denying Edmund the one thing she knew he wanted, but now....

Within the hour Edmund returned with Mordeur dragging young Margaret, stripped naked and hands bound. He threw her thin body over a wooden bench, where she shook with fear.

"I cannot tell you anymore!" cried Amelie at once.

Mordeur began to thrash the girl with slow deliberate strokes using a scourge of hazel and thorn; no part of her thin body was spared. As Margaret bled, she screamed without cease and Amelie screamed with her, for she could think of nothing more to say to satisfy her captor. When Margaret passed out, Mordeur threw a pail of ice cold water over her which revived her agony and started her screams once more. Then the whipping began again, rhythmically shredding her skin to the bone; until each scream became a whimper and finally Mordeur rolled her onto the blood black straw where she lay still.

Amelie stared unwaveringly at Edmund; she had never hated anyone before.

"Her miserable little life is over," said Edmund, "but yours, on the other hand, is not."

§§§

Edmund and Mordeur mounted the spiral stair up to the Great Hall.

"So much for that idea; we've learned nothing! Take her down to the house near Saxton, and make sure she's secure," Edmund ordered. "Then join me at York; pick a few of your best men to take with you to guard her and make sure you can rely on them – I don't want just any scum!"

"They're all scum and we need them all with us," Mordeur replied, a hint of rebellion in his tone, "it's a waste of men-at–arms."

Edmund couldn't risk Ned Elder finding her at Yoredale and he couldn't spare the men for a garrison at the castle. Within days he was due to meet up with the other royal armies from the north; he needed every man he had, but still he didn't trust the girl.

"Be sure you understand me: I want her safely locked away and I want her still to be there when the fighting stops. Perhaps if she lies in a stinking cell for a while, she'll give me what I want. Lock her up tight and let no-one see her. Remember, as far as anyone's concerned she's dead – and as far as the Queen's concerned she's been dead some time!"

"As always, my lord," conceded Mordeur grudgingly, "I will do what needs to be done."

He left and Edmund returned to his chamber, pondering the intricacies of court politics. He realised that his star would not be in such a lofty position for long. There were other lords who were desperate to supplant him in the Queen's affections, for the King was a mere cipher; the real power lay with her. So, he must watch his back, for once the present danger receded, all the young noble bucks would begin scrapping for the rewards their loyalty to the Queen merited. He was already calculating what he would accept by way of patronage and considering who his closest rivals were; above all he feared the influential young Henry Beaufort, Duke of Somerset. The Duke's favour with the Queen could be a powerful obstacle to his own advancement.

He supposed he must wed the recently acquired Emma; then again, if she did not give him a son she might very soon need to be replaced by a more productive spouse. He had certainly moved on from needing any sort of alliance with a family of as little consequence as the Elders and he had no intention of rotting in parochial Yoredale for the rest of his days. Yes, he must marry her quickly.

The return of Mordeur interrupted his thoughts.

"There is someone I think you should see, my lord."

"Well, who is he?"

"He is one of many we've indentured, my lord."

Whenever Mordeur uttered the phrase "my lord" it always seemed to Edmund as if he was mocking him.

"Surely I don't have to speak to every one of them?"

"This one seems different."

Exasperated by the Frenchman's excessive economy with words, Edmund ground out a response.

"Mordeur, either tell me what concerns you or get out."

"He does not seem quite… correct."

"Correct? What does that mean? Does he have too many arms? Speak man!"

"There's something about him that is different from the others."

"Different?"

"He holds himself differently from the others." Mordeur struggled to phrase his concerns in English. "He is too … confident."

"I like my men to be confident. Who is he and where did he come from? He's not one of my brother's tiresome youths is he? Does he bring any knights?"

"He calls himself Henry of Shrewsbury and he says he's from the Welsh marches – he has no knights of his own. He's down in the courtyard now." Mordeur pointed the youth out.

"The bearded one by the brew house? Yes, he looks as if he

owns the place, but if we question everyone we recruit too closely we won't have an army at all – there are no innocent men out there!"

Nevertheless, Edmund knew Mordeur well enough to recognise that he was a good judge of men.

"Well, send him up to me; I'll judge for myself."

A few moments later Henry of Shrewsbury strode into his chamber.

Edmund studied him carefully; he was a little intrigued despite his other preoccupations. His visitor was young, dark and well built: impressive.

"I am Lord Radcliffe," he announced, anxious to stamp his authority on their conversation.

The youth looked puzzled.

"And you are..?" prompted Edmund.

"I'm Henry, Henry of Shrewsbury... I expected you to be older."

"You expected perhaps to find my father, or my brother?"

"Well, I've heard of your father, my lord."

Edmund thought it unlikely, but let that pass. "Why did you come here to join me?"

"I didn't know your father, but my own father did, so I thought I might seek service in your household."

"Can you fight?"

"I can fight well with sword or hammer, my lord."

"Good! I need men at arms. You bring no other men with you?"

"I think you must have recruited them all but my own sword arm is a good match for most."

"Indeed?" He could see what Mordeur meant: the youth had all the answers, but perhaps too perfect.

"So, you have no land of your own?"

"No, my lord; all I bring stands here before you – it's in the indenture."

"And you are from Shrewsbury?"

"Yes, lord – born in the town."

"I've been to Shrewsbury," said Edmund, "so has my horse

and I think he might be able to tell me more about Shrewsbury than you can."

For the first time Henry looked uncertain.

"Well, I think I'll have to keep you alongside me, Henry,"

"I'd be honoured, my lord."

"Don't be. Standing next to me can be dangerous."

"I'll welcome it!"

Edmund gave up trying to have the last word and dismissed him. He watched him go, still not sure about him. There was something he'd seen, some nuance of look or voice that had jarred a memory, but what he didn't know. He could certainly use every fighting man he could find; heaven knows he was leaving the estate bare enough: no labour would be done, except by the women and the older boys who were left behind. No doubt in his absence some of them would be stealing from his demesne and hunting wantonly through his forests.

§§§

Henry stood in the cold, damp courtyard below. The walls around him rose sheer and unwelcoming – like their owner, he thought. He could feel Edmund's eyes upon him but at least he had been accepted, after a fashion; his first task was complete. With a few well-rehearsed lies he had entered the world of the Radcliffes.

35

Elder Hall, Yoredale, February 1461

It was just after dawn. Ned stared long into the valley of Yoredale to the west, so shrouded in morning mist that little could be discerned even on the upper slopes above the trees. The three of them stood on the tower ramparts of Elder Hall - or what remained of it, for Lord Radcliffe had reduced the walls of the once heavily fortified manor house, torn down its great oak gates and laid waste to the interior beyond recognition. The sight of it had shocked Ned at first, but there had been far worse in the past year; in the end, a building could be rebuilt.

Beside him Bagot shuffled uncomfortably: Ned knew he thought they were on a fool's errand. The struggles of the past year would have exhausted a much younger man that Bagot, and they both knew that he had few battles left in him. Now he fretted whilst Ned scanned the horizon once more.

"What exactly is it that you expect to see?" asked Bagot, "it's barely light."

Ned frowned. "I expect to see what I used to see whenever I rose early and rode through the valley: people - at least a few of them, men and women starting their day's work. Where are they, Bagot? Why is no-one doing anything?"

Bagot then began to take more interest.

"Well, they could all be dead – from plague or famine – or

they're just too cold and miserable to come outside, or...
they're no longer in the valley."

"Exactly!"

"By St Stephen, he's already gone hasn't he? He's stripped
the estate! Radcliffe's taken every man jack to the Queen."

"Perhaps, come on; let's see what's left at the castle."

He descended the tower steps at a run and strode out
through the house. Bagot and Bear exchanged a brief glance
and then followed in his wake. They rode out through the
damaged gateway along the track which led up the northern
slopes from the valley floor. Before them in the distance, its
square towers just visible above the mist, was Yoredale
Castle.

For the first time since they had set off from Corve Manor
several days earlier, Ned was feeling optimistic, for if
Edmund had already mustered the men of the estate and left
the castle only very thinly garrisoned, he might have a chance
of success. Several miles further on, the track began to ascend
uphill to the castle. A hundred yards or so from the fortress,
he reined in his horse.

"Of course," said Bagot, "you could be wrong. In which
case we'll be cut to pieces the moment they see us!"

Ned nudged his mount forward again, taking a direct and
confident path up the hill, for no-one atop the battlements
could have any hope of discerning who they were until they
were a good deal closer. He noted silently that the steep track
was not its usual thoroughfare of activity and the high towers
showed no sign of life at all. When they reached the open
gateway they did at last encounter a sentry, though he did not
seem very committed to his task.

"God give you good morning!" Ned greeted the man
cheerfully, but he was met with only a sullen stare. "Is Sir
Edmund here?"

"Lord Radcliffe," corrected the guard, "isn't here."

"Lord Richard Radcliffe?"

"Lord Edmund Radcliffe."

"Where is Richard Radcliffe?"

"Dead."

Ned was swiftly reconsidering. "We'd like to see Lady Emma?" he asked with forced politeness.

"Lady Radcliffe isn't here either."

Bagot's horse shuffled impatiently in the gateway, accurately reflecting its rider's frustration.

"Who is here?" persisted Ned.

"Who else do you want to see?" enquired the sentry making no attempt to conceal his lack of interest.

Ned's conciliatory manner began to desert him.

"Fellow, I see only you. What is to prevent me and my heavily armed comrades simply riding past you into that courtyard?"

The gatekeeper's obstruction clearly did not extend to barring their entry and he stepped back to lean lazily against the gatepost. "Go on then."

Ned thought his willingness to concede entry did not augur well. They walked their horses into the courtyard and dismounted. The lower walls of the yard were green with damp in places from the persistent wet weather and absence of sunlight. The great courtyard was deserted and Ned contrasted its appearance with his last visit when it had been choked with people, horses and wagons.

He eyed the ramparts warily, but still could see no other guards; he began to wonder if there was anyone else left in the castle at all. They walked cautiously towards the staircase which they knew would lead them to Emma's chamber. As they made to enter, a young girl suddenly appeared in the doorway and recognising Ned, stopped dead.

"You!" she spat out the word hot with anger. She ran at him and struck him across the face so hard that he took a pace backwards.

"I thought you were long dead!" She shrieked and slapped him again on the other cheek. "I've wished you dead and cursed you for this past year!"

She went to strike him once more, but Bagot stepped in and seized her arm.

"Enough!" he said.

"Enough?" replied Becky Standlake, struggling to free herself from Bagot's grasp, "it could never be enough! You did for us all!"

She hurled her words at Ned like sparks snapping out of a roaring fire.

"You left us to die! You left the children to die; cut down after they'd watched their fathers and mothers hacked apart in front of them! And where were you? Or you, Bagot, come to that? Where were any of you so called fighting men – fleeing for your lives – that's where!"

"Peace, girl!" ordered Bagot, for Ned was still in shock from her tirade, "you're blaming the wrong man!" He pushed her back into the nearby kitchen. "Ned almost died!"

"He should be dead!"

"We did all we could! No-one could have done more!"

"It wasn't enough though, Bagot, was it?" said Ned quietly. "We were too late; we saw them in that bloody beck, where they fell and we gave them good burial, but it wasn't enough."

She showed no sign of noticing his words, so he went to her and lifted her to her feet.

"I can't change what happened, but I've come here to put an end to his butchery."

"You can't put an end to it!"

"Have you seen Amelie at Yoredale? We think Edmund brought her here."

At the mention of the French girl, Becky's sullen expression turned to tears and she looked down at her feet.

"I didn't know it was her, but she had a tough time; she's as good as dead. Poor little Margaret..." she choked on her tears. "Poor little Margaret died for her; the poor little sod. He doesn't spare anyone."

"What happened?"

"I buried what was left of Margaret; a scrap of blood and bone..." She shook her head, for talking to Ned had brought back the horror of it all.

"And my sister? How fares she?"

"I told you, he spares no-one. He's taken her with him too; he wouldn't leave them here – almost every man's gone with him."

"Do you know where?"

She shrugged her shoulders in reply. Ned was bitterly disappointed: he had hoped that the women would have stayed at Yoredale, but he should have known that where Edmund was concerned it would not turn out to be so easy.

Bagot swore wholeheartedly. "He could be anywhere! At least now we should abandon this and make all speed to join the Earl."

"I suppose," said Ned almost to himself, "that wherever the Queen is, Radcliffe will not be far away.
Do you want to come with us, Becky?"

"What, to another war? No, the other two girls are still with me and I've to look out for them now – we're all that's left of my kin..." She paused for a moment then said: "Have you news of Ellie – the Lady Eleanor?"

Ned shook his head: "nothing; nor from Will who went to find her."

"Poor Will; if any man can find her, he will."

She turned away as they walked out, but then turned back and called to Ned: "I liked Amelie; for her sake, I hope you find her."

Then she returned to her work and the three men made straight for their horses and rode, without another word, out of the gates.

The lone guard watched them go then he went into the castle to find Becky.

36

Corve Manor, February 1461

"It is not very big, is it?" said Felix, looking up at the less than imposing walls of Corve Manor.

Will shrugged. "Everyone says it can't be defended, but it served us well for a time – not that we were ever attacked..."

"Who are you?" bawled a voice from the gatehouse above them.

"Master Betwill," Will called up, "it's me, Will - you know who I am! Let us in, we've come out from Ludlow."

"I don't care where you've come from! Young Elder isn't here and I have charge of this manor; I don't have to let you or anyone else in – and I don't know who he is anyway! This isn't an inn – go back to Ludlow and stay there. We've had enough extra mouths to feed these past months!"

Felix sighed and considered that wherever he travelled there were folk like this Betwill; it was wearisome, but inevitable.

"We can pay you well enough for your trouble," he said and reached into his purse to toss a silver coin up to the startled Betwill. The speed with which the gates were thrown open suggested that Betwill hoped further coins might be forthcoming, but once inside, Will and Felix were swept away by Mags. She hurried them up to the north tower, sat them down and brought them what food and drink was still to be had.

As they ate their meagre feast, each told his own story. When all had been said Will could find no small shaft of hope in what he had heard.

Hal brought in Holton and Mags glowed with pride. "John's a walking miracle," she declared, "he shouldn't be alive, but he is. He can't talk yet – but in time I know he will."

Will didn't know what to say, but merely stared at the torn face; Felix smiled and gently shook the young smith by the hand.

Later, when Felix and Will were alone, there were decisions to be made.

"Are you still going to follow Ned?" Felix asked.

"I'm hardly a free man, Felix; I'm bound to Ned by the oath I swore when I was fifteen – I belong with him. And … it should be me that tells him about Ellie."

"True enough, but Ned's trail will be cold now and by the time you reach Yoredale he'll likely have left again, for he too is bound by oath and it seems he must attend the Earl of March in London."

"Well, I can do no other than follow him."

Felix hesitated, weighing up an idea that had occurred to him only that morning.

"A week or two ago I was in London on business; the city's in uproar! The merchant guilds have favoured March and Warwick over the Queen and now the merchants are shitting themselves, for any day they expect the wolves to fall upon them from the north."

"Wolves?"

"The Queen's raised an army in the north to recapture King Harry – and the London folk fear the worst."

"Northerners aren't savages!"

Felix smiled a broad Mediterranean smile. "Ah, but they've not met you, Will; or they wouldn't be so worried."

"Well, it's no worry of mine either way."

"Peace! I'm telling you. The Earl will go to London and thus Ned must go to London to join him. We too could ride to London; when you find the Earl, you'll find Ned."

"I'm not sure, Felix; surely London is bigger than Ludlow? I can't just wander around London! I've no coin and no trade -

how would I live?"

"Well, I've thought about that: you have a sword."

"I had two once, but they've not brought me much good fortune so far."

"Well, they may do in London: there are people there who have sacks of coin and much power; they would pay for a sword arm like yours. Believe me, you could make a living there."

Will grinned at the Frenchman. "Well, I've nowhere else to go."

"I've never been to London," said Hal, putting his head around the door.

Felix scowled at him. "There's nothing for you in London."

"There's nothing for me at Corve! I wanted to go with Ned, but he bade me wait to see if Will came back – and now he has."

Felix was inclined to dismiss the notion out of hand, but then he considered more carefully: Hal was a strong lad and Will might need a willing hand - perhaps it would be good for both of them.

"Will?"

"In truth, I'd be glad of his company."

Hal grinned and came into the chamber bearing a thin tightly wrapped bundle, which he held out to Will.

"Ned left it for you … just in case."

Will removed the wrappings and stared at the sword he had given Ned at Penholme.

"Thanks; this belongs with its brother." He fell silent for a moment.

"Now, Will, when we get to London I've a position in mind for you with a goldsmith – it'll give you some employ while you're waiting for Ned."

"But I know nothing about gold!"

"You'll not need to: you won't be working it, you'll be guarding it. The alderman owes me a debt or two and he needs a good man to help him to keep his gold store safe for a few weeks; I thought it might do for you."

"Surely if he's that wealthy, he can afford to hire any number of local men."

"In times past perhaps, but now many of those who bear arms have joined one of the armies and he's left to choose between those who can't fight and those he daren't trust: gold is a powerful reason to betray your employer."

"You think I'm up to such work?"

"Well, you'll need to be willing to use those swords if need be – so now's the time to tell me if I ask too much."

"No, it'll suit me well enough; I'll be glad of something to do."

The following morning they bade farewell to Mags and Holton and set off on the road to London, or at least what passed for a road in the Corve valley. It was little more than a rough track until they neared Hereford but from there they picked up the old road to the south east, which though in disrepair was a good deal firmer than sodden fields or mud churned tracks.

At Cirencester they lodged at an inn Felix remembered from his visit to the town's wool fair several years earlier. Then they headed further east, where they found more and more travellers on the road; many had heard the same rumours as Felix of a wild and ill-disciplined northern horde robbing, raping and killing their way southwards. They encountered men of Dorset and Somerset – indeed there were contingents from all over the south west – all hoping to stop the raiders before they laid waste to their own lands.

"It's going to be damned crowded in London, with all this lot!" said Will.

"There'll be more than this, I'll warrant; many folk will be looking for a safe haven behind the city walls," said Felix.

It took them a further three days to reach the outskirts of London and by then the landscape began to change: the large wide fields giving way to smaller holdings. The rutted lane they had been following all morning joined a wider firmer road and several more rough tracks merged with it like the tributaries of a great river. Soon the broad way ahead divided into two: one road to the south and the other north. Hal stared in awe at the great stone cross at the junction.

"That's the biggest piece of stone I've ever seen!"

"It's fine work," agreed Felix.

"What folk'll do to honour the Lord, eh?" Will commented, "it must have cost a year's wages."

"A good deal more than that, I think, but the Cross is not there to honour God," said Felix, "it's there to honour a Queen, a lost love called Eleanor. Does that make it worth the expense, do you think?"

Will fell silent and they moved on.

Ahead of them rose the tall spire of a church so large they could not see the end of it.

"They say St Paul's is the biggest church in the whole of Christendom," said Felix.

"How can it stand so high?" asked Will, "is all of London so big?"

The Frenchman smiled. "It is big, but you'll get used to it. Come on, we'll go in at Ludgate."

The modest town of Ludlow had not prepared Will for the crowded streets of London: countless people on the move, animals - pigs in particular – seemed to roam wherever they pleased and down every narrow lane and alley, someone was selling their wares.

He opened his mouth to speak, but Felix silenced him swiftly.

"For all our sakes don't talk too much or too loud; that uncivil grunting you use for speech may not be very welcome in the city at present - they may take you for a thieving northerner. The same goes for you, Hal."

"But, I'm not a thieving northerner!"

"No, you're a thieving southerner!" said Will.

"Peace!" said Felix, noting the stony stares of passers-by.

"Are there many goldsmiths in London?" asked Hal.

"Hundreds! But this one is an alderman of the city, so he's very important! Now listen, if you are to be of any use to the alderman, you must get to know your way around quickly.

It'll be hard at first but, between the two of you, it shouldn't take too long."

The road widened and Felix announced: "This is Cheapside, and anything you might want to buy, if you had any coin - which you don't – can be found in and around this street somewhere. You'll likely be running errands down here a lot."

The two youths looked at each other blankly, for they were already lost.

Felix ushered them down a side street and stopped outside a large, half-timbered house.

"Wait here," he instructed when the door was opened and he passed quickly inside. He was not gone long and was soon introducing them to their new employer, Alderman John Goldwell, a tall ruddy faced man with a jovial manner.

"Alderman Goldwell will tell you your duties and you'll carry them out until I return in a few weeks' time. That's the agreement, and when the Earl's army arrives Will, you can try to find Ned – when you're not working. You will not, though, leave the alderman's service until I return."

Their new master was surprisingly enthusiastic to meet them – though less so when Will opened his mouth to speak for the first time.

"Oh Lord," he said, "you're from well north of the Thames! You'll need to take care – still, no bad thing perhaps. Your job, Will, is to help me keep my goods safe and, sometimes, deliver quite valuable items to my clients. Felix has assured me on two counts: firstly, that you can handle yourself well enough, and secondly that you're an honest man – you'll understand that this is rather important to me!"

Felix looked uncomfortable and interrupted him.

"John, you are my good friend, but so is young Will, so you'd better tell him what happened to the last man."

"Ah...well, it's not so easy to find good men, especially now. And Felix is right: you should know that the last man was killed and some of my goods were taken. It was after curfew, but the watchmen in Cheap are idle good for nothings!"

"So, you see there may be some danger in this work, Will," said Felix.

"I'll do my best," said Will. Felix gave him a long look, wondering whether he was asking too much of him; but he clapped him on the shoulder and quickly took his leave.

§§§

Will was sorry to see him go, but at least he had Hal with him; even so he began to feel some responsibility on his own shoulders.

"Now, to business!" said the Alderman and he took Will, with Hal in tow, on a tour of his premises; he would not normally have deigned to do so personally, but he was much aggrieved over his recent losses and determined to ensure that his new servant was fully prepared. His establishment was extensive, for it housed not only his large family but also his two apprentices and several servants, not to mention providing space for his workshop, warehouse and strongboxes. At the back of the house was a high walled enclosure – nothing grew in it, but the walls helped to protect the rear of his property from intruders. Every gate and door they passed through was locked, which necessitated the same pantomime activity as Goldwell examined a large bunch of keys at length until he found the correct one.

"You'll take your meals in there with the apprentices," he said as they moved swiftly past the kitchen. "My daughter Sarah runs the house – my dear wife having passed to the Lord some years ago. Yes, I was blessed with eight fine children, but not a son amongst them! Still, three now married and five to go!"

At last, they were taken to the apprentices' room at the back of the solar on the first floor, where they were to sleep. The alderman left them to introduce themselves to the two young occupants who were not exactly fulsome in their welcome.

"What news do you bring of the war?" asked the elder one, Peter, who appeared to Will to be about his own age.

"Not much," replied Will, sensitive for the first time of his northern speech.

The apprentices exchanged amused looks.

"We'd thought to have heard by now of the Earl's army gone to fight the Queen – but no word comes," said the younger apprentice, Robert.

"The Earl of March?" asked Will.

"March? No, Warwick of course! You seem to know less than we do!"

"We've no news," said Will, mainly because neither he nor Hal had any idea who the Earl of Warwick was.

"He doesn't say much, does he, our boy from the north?" remarked Peter.

"I speak if I've a mind to," retorted Will.

"Oh, he speaks if he's a mind to," mimicked the apprentices in unison, chuckling.

Will gave them a murderous look and walked out stiffly.

Hal decided to have a little sport. He shook each of the apprentices by the hand and congratulated them. "You're brave lads," he said in a serious voice, "I'd never of spoken to him like that; it takes some guts."

"Stop your foolery," said Peter.

"You know who he is, don't you," said Hal, leaning in and lowering his voice, "and what he was brought here for?"

"He's here to guard the goods – we know – and if he's as stupid as the last one, he'll be in his grave before dawn!"

"You don't know then," said Hal, feigning concern, "it's only Will Coster - he's a born killer. Those swords on his back, and he's so fast: you've hardly time to say 'blade' before he's gutted you… Your master's brought him in after what happened with the last one."

The pair of apprentices looked at Hal doubtfully, but he had certainly seized their attention.

"I tell you, if he goes for one of those swords, you'd best run for all you're worth, for he's quick as a lightning strike - and he's not keen on being insulted."

§§§

Will wandered out into the unlit rear courtyard. He relished the darkness in the still cool of the evening and was quite content to sit alone. If everyone he spoke to was going to treat him so poorly, then he was going to be as miserable in London as he had been at Ludlow and three weeks would seem endless.

"Ah, here's our mysterious northerner." The soft voice came across the courtyard from the kitchen door.

Not another one, he thought, looking up at the owner of the voice, framed in the doorway with a lantern light flickering behind her. He couldn't make out her features, but he assumed it was one of the goldsmith's numerous daughters.

"Are you not cold out there, or do you northern men not feel the cold?"

Will did not know how to answer her, so he remained silent. "I'm Sarah - one of the many daughters! I think Papa's afraid you're going to carry one of us off! He told us not to talk to you, or at least only to be civil."

"Good!" said Will and walked away over to the warehouse door.

"Well he obviously didn't tell you to be civil!" retorted Sarah, slamming the kitchen door shut.

Will was relieved; he didn't want to talk to anyone much, but especially not to a young girl looking for a husband. The goldsmith had given him the key to the warehouse – though not the strongboxes stored in it. He tried the lock and went in. All seemed peaceful; he sat for a long while in the dark, then he carefully locked up again and returned to the sleeping quarters, where the others were already asleep on their straw mattresses.

Nevertheless, he could not settle: he regretted his behaviour towards the girl, for it was not in his nature to be so rude; he recalled the lively banter he had enjoyed with the village girls of Yoredale - how far away all that seemed now. So he lay awake and his thoughts turned inevitably to Eleanor; how long was it now? Not long enough to forget. She was dead and he had to accept it – so Felix had told him many times – but he could not see how. He tried once more to get off to sleep, but a gentle scratching noise now kept him awake: an animal outside perhaps - likely one of the bloody ubiquitous pigs! He got up and went to try to locate the source of the noise; as he stood on the first floor landing, there was a sharp, but distinct crack. So, it wasn't a pig.

37

Yorkshire, mid-February 1461

Ned rode hard, driving eastwards out of Yoredale then skirting Richmond and turning south to join the North Road. But when they reached it they wished they hadn't, for it was swarming with men and wagons.

"It seems that more than Edmund Radcliffe have answered King Harry's summons," said Bagot.

"Answered the call of his Queen more like," said Ned bitterly.

The result was that a vast royal army straddled the road to London, spreading out for miles on either side. He knew that he could never hope to track down Edmund in such a great host.

"But this is perfect for us," said Bagot, looking highly amused, "where do you hide three armed men where no one notices them?"

"I know, in the midst of an army," said Ned, "but we'd still best be on our guard."

"I don't see why," replied Bagot, as he waved an arm cheerily to a small knot of riders as they hurried past them.

"Sweet Jesus in Heaven! Is there anyone you don't know, Bagot?"

"I was in France a long time, lord; I fought alongside many," Bagot replied, aggrieved.

As they overtook the numerous bands heading south, it became clear that not all met with Bagot's approval: many were from the northern borders and beyond. he regarded the Scots with outright disgust: "they can barely speak; they're little better than beasts! It's a bad sign to see them this far south."

"Well I doubt they're here to support King Harry; they want only plunder."

As the day wore on, they joined a substantial column of men bearing pennants of white and red. At first they were relieved to have escaped the Scots, but Bagot's initial enthusiasm soon evaporated when he noticed the shields.

"Shit!"

"What is it?" asked Ned.

"The red bar across their shields…"

"What about it?"

"I've just remembered … 'Butcher' Clifford!" he muttered, "we'd best keep clear of him!"

"I take it you mean Lord Clifford? How is he any worse than the rest?"

"I heard that last year at Wakefield he killed the Earl of March's young brother, Edmund – though he yielded to him - and he hacked off the old Duke of York's head and set a crown of paper upon it."

"Mmm, soldiers' tales grow with the telling, Bagot."

"Men I trust told me; he's sworn to kill all the Duke's kin – and he's not a man to take lightly."

"Another pointless feud! God knows, we'll be at this killing till Judgement Day!"

He quickened his pace despite the wintry conditions, anxious to move on so that they could put some distance between themselves and the Lancastrian horde.

"Careful," warned Bagot, but too late Ned realised that they were bearing down on Lord Clifford himself at the head of the column. He slowed to a walking pace, but Clifford and his aides had already turned to see who was thundering towards them.

"Who is it that thinks I go at too slow a pace?" bellowed Lord Clifford, eyeing the three riders suspiciously. "Wait there, you two!" he ordered Bagot and Bear, identifying them as the heavily armed hired help. Ned fell in alongside Clifford and they rode forward at a more sedate pace.

"Your pardon, my lord," said Ned, "we meant no disrespect."

"And you are?" demanded Clifford and when Ned told him he replied: "Ned Elder? Why do I know that name?"

Ned's companions edged a little closer.

"Where are you going in such haste?" It was no polite enquiry.

Bagot intervened from behind: "We're hurrying to rejoin our men, my Lord."

Clifford did not turn but said to Ned: "Tell that crusted old man that if he speaks to me again I'll put my sword in his wretched mouth to stop it up."

Bagot heard well enough and wisely dropped back of his own accord. Ned shot him a warning glance nevertheless.

"My lord, we ride in haste to overtake our liege lord, Edmund Radcliffe," he lied hopefully.

"Edmund Radcliffe, now there's an interesting fellow; I know Edmund, though I wouldn't call him friend – not many do!"

Clifford's words casually disembowelled Ned's resolve: how much, he wondered, did Clifford know of Edmund's affairs?

"But surely he's still in York," said Clifford, "unless he went to his house at Saxton."

"That would be where exactly, my Lord?" Ned was gambling crazily, and he knew it, but if there was even the smallest chance of finding Amelie, he was going to take it.

"Mawfield Hall – but if you serve Lord Edmund, then you must have heard of it – the Radcliffes have been building it for years! But we're a long way south of that now, so you're not going there. Ned Elder?" he paused, "might I have known your father, do you think?"

"It's very possible, my Lord," replied Ned, praying that Clifford did not know his father or his fate. He dreaded the next question, but Clifford changed tack again.

"Perhaps Edmund mentioned you to me - might he have done, do you think?"

Ned could feel the sweat on his brow; he glanced behind him and saw that Bagot's hand was on his sword hilt.

"I'm a man of little importance in the shire -"

"You'd best be on your way then; wherever he is, I doubt he rewards tardiness."

Before Clifford changed his mind, Ned cantered off, followed by Bagot and Bear. Despite the Earl's reputation, Bagot could not resist sweeping past him so closely that his mount almost shouldered Clifford's horse to one side. The Earl was outraged but the three riders were already at the gallop as he hurled abuse after them about what he would do to Bagot when he came across him again. Bagot laughed enthusiastically, but Ned was less amused.

"Why go out of your way to make another enemy? I should've thought we had enough already!"

"He is the enemy; I just wanted him to mark me, as I have marked him, so that if we meet in battle he'll know who strikes him down."

Ned shook his head sadly, for he doubted that Clifford would be too concerned about facing Bagot.

"For God's sake man, you'll be lucky to stand up long enough to strike him! Still, at least we've found out something useful about Edmund."

"Mawfield Hall; but it's just a name and we've no idea where it is, except somewhere near Saxton!"

"Let's hope we find the Earl in London – he may give me leave to search."

Bagot shook his head, but said no more.

Ned had only one thought: every mile he rode south dragged him a mile further from Amelie.

On the road they encountered still more of the Queen's soldiers.

"It's endless," said Ned, "we're surely on the wrong side in this war."

They bivouacked overnight just beyond Northampton and

set off early the following morning for London, making good progress.

"We won't make it today," said Bagot, "but we should get as far as St Albans."

They rode on for several more miles before Bagot began to slow down to a trot.

"Look at the group ahead," he said. Something in his tone caused Ned to take him seriously, though he could discern nothing untoward about the large group ahead comprising many men at arms and archers on foot and a good number of mounted knights.

"What is it?" asked Ned.

"Look at the badges, three stags in a green field; it's Trollope, Andrew Trollope."

"Don't tell me: you fought with him in France."

"Not just that, but both of us should have fought alongside him at Ludlow. I remember being pleased to see him in that miserable camp, but he wasn't there in the morning when we were overrun…"

"And fairly obviously he now supports the Queen. Will he know you?" asked Ned.

"Better than you do, I fear; we'd best ride past with all speed!"

They quickened their pace once more and raced past Trollope's force at the gallop.

§§§

Trollope looked after them, deep in thought; then he turned to the knight alongside him. They were of an age, Andrew and Sir Henry Lovelace; made of the same fibre and steeped in the same bitter blood of the French wars.

"Perhaps it's time you left us, Harry," he said, "we may run into Warwick's patrols soon – better not be seen together."

Lovelace took his proffered hand and gripped it firmly.

"Be sure you look for me when the battle comes; I'll send news if I can."

Trollope nodded and drew the column to a halt as Lovelace led his detachment forward at speed.

§§§

It took them the best part of the day to reach St Albans and only a red glimmer of sun remained as they crossed the river to the west of the town and rode towards the great Abbey buildings. Ned was impressed by the fine large houses in the market place, but he noted that Bagot seemed more interested in the plethora of taverns they found in the area around the Great Cross.

"Have you been here before?" he asked him.

Bagot nodded enthusiastically. "Several times; we used to pass through on our way south to the ports. How could I have forgotten there were so many alehouses and inns? Old demons; I suppose I wanted to forget."

The town was bustling with activity despite the cold weather and late hour; there were many men at arms, archers and bill men in evidence.

"Looks like we've found another army," said Ned, noting the liveries of red and black.

"Aye, that's the red and black of a Neville army," said Bagot.

"Some wear a badge with a bear and ragged staff. Who's that?"

"They're Warwick's men, I think."

"March's great ally," said Ned, "so we're amongst friends?"

"Indeed, but they may take some convincing; don't forget they'll be expecting trouble from the north – they may decide we're it!"

"Bagot," ordered Ned, "stop staring at the taverns with your tongue out and see to our horses; they deserve a meal before you do. We'll be in this one – the Fleur de Lys."

Bagot did so, chuckling quietly to himself at Ned's murderous pronunciation of the French name; but other heads turned too: Ned's harsh Yorkshire tones were attracting unwanted attention.

Bagot took Ned's mount. "Don't get yourself into any trouble before I get back," he warned.

Ned shook his head in despair; sometime he was going to have to educate Bagot in how to properly address his lord. He entered the inn, secure in the knowledge that he had alongside him possibly the largest man at arms most folk would ever have seen. Unsurprisingly it was busy, with bitter cold outside and every man inside seeking to drown his fears for what might occur on the morrow. He used the last of his coin, lent him by Will Hastings in Hereford, to buy some ale, bread and cheese. There was a long table beside the wall, but no places left to sit, so they squatted on the filthy rushes on the floor; when Bagot came in he was appalled.

"What, lord!" he roared. "Sitting like a dog, when every bench has a knave on it?"

Before Ned could stop him he had cleared a space by tossing several of those at the table from their seats. The whole room went quiet as Bagot dusted off a seat for Ned and ushered him on to it. The men thrown aside slowly picked themselves up and there was a menacing murmur around the room. They're going to murder us, thought Ned; he looked at Bagot in disbelief. "I followed your advice," he said pointedly.

The wrath of the occupants was about to crash about their ears, when Bagot calmly announced: "This is the valiant Sir Edward Elder – hero of the great victory but two weeks ago in Mortimer country and favoured knight of the noble Edward of York!"

Silence greeted this announcement, for none there had been at the battle, though Bagot's words were well judged for no-one was too keen to give offence to Edward of York since most of them wore the livery of his great ally. There was an awkward pause.

Then two archers came up to Ned. "I know you," said one, "you were at Blore Heath with old Salisbury - a year or two back." The other nodded enthusiastically.

"Blore Heath? Is that where it was; it seems a lifetime ago," replied Ned.

"We were in the trees to your right; we fell back behind you when they came on hard - you and your red headed friend."

The mood in the tavern began to relax again as everyone resumed their conversation or took up their drinks and the unseated clients drifted off to other parts of the room. Despite the unpromising start, the evening passed most amicably; they exchanged much gossip, as Ned had discovered soldiers tended to do, and many insisted on buying him ale. He was surprised how long into the night the drinking went on. Yet the ale gave him little cheer, for he brooded quietly on the past. He missed Will terribly – his friend had always been with him and somehow they had got each other through every scrape. Then there was Amelie; he felt inside his jerkin for the small square of silk and turned it over gently between his fingers. Bagot would tell him that she was already dead, but he had to believe she wasn't; for if she was, she was yet another casualty of his attempt to regain what he had lost.

Eventually the ale took its toll and most of the archers and men at arms succumbed and crawled off to sleep. Ned remained at the table with several of the archers; Bagot and Bear were already slumped against the wall.

"You're all billeted in here then," Ned said.

The archers laughed. "This is our 'guard post', and not a bad one, eh?" said one.

"The Earl's got archers all over the town and by now there'll be barricades across the streets too," said another.

"It's just as well," said Ned, "our enemies are not far distant, barely a day's march – even in this weather."

"Let 'em come with all speed. We'll give those northern buggers a shock tomorrow," chipped in one of the men at arms and his fellows were equally bullish.

"Shriven on Shrove Tuesday they'll be!" Everyone laughed at that.

"We'll soon send those heathen Scots and robbers back

where they came from!"

Ned, remembering what he had seen on the road, was anxious to introduce a word of caution.

"Lads, there'll be some good men amongst the scum - they'll make a fight of it," he said.

"So will we!" roared a host of them cheerfully. He wished he could share their optimism.

He shook Bagot awake. "We'll get an early start again tomorrow," he said, "we don't want to get caught up in all this!"

"You woke me to tell me you want me to start early?" said Bagot irritably. "Thanks!"

Finally the Fleur de Lys settled into something resembling peace but it seemed to Ned barely a moment later when the bell in the nearby tower began to toll.

"It's not yet dawn, is it the end of curfew?" he mumbled to Bagot.

"No, they're raising the alarm: the enemy are already in the town!" Bagot shouted. "To arms, to arms!"

Ned stumbled up the stairs to a first floor window. Dawn was breaking half-heartedly through the leaden sky; visibility was poor, but there was no mistaking the columns of men running towards the market place.

"Shit! They must have marched through the night!" exclaimed Ned, "but it was freezing!"

"I should've expected it," said Bagot ruefully, "Trollope would do anything to get an edge."

They hurried to the uppermost floor where the archers were revelling in their deadly work, for they were putting up such a storm of arrows that Trollope's vanguard were hard pressed – trapped in the killing ground of the narrow streets.

"This is better than I'd hoped; we're making short work of them," said Ned.

"Trollope won't let this go on for long," said Bagot. And he was proven right, for soon the beleaguered Lancastrians started to pull back along the streets to the river; this prompted an exultant cheer from the town's defenders.

"They'll be back, I'm afraid," predicted Bagot.

And they were. Another assault came after an hour's respite, but the outcome was the same: Trollope's men again took heavy casualties and fell back in disarray. Men at arms rushed out of the buildings and finished off the survivors with bill and halberd; the archers too came down to retrieve as many of their spent shafts as they could.

"Come on," said Ned, "let's take a look at our lines."

"Our lines? Do I take it we're stopping here then?" asked Bagot.

"We can't just ride away now, can we? Can we?"

"Shouldn't we be pushing on to London?"

They stepped over the fallen bodies outside the inn and walked up the market place from the Fleur de Lys, crossing back and forth through the shuttered shops and merchants' stalls. It was still a grey drear morning and the southerly wind blew light snow on their backs as they headed up to the church. Bagot looked up at the houses gloomily.

"We're poorly manned up here; where's the rest of the army?" For beyond the church yard to the north he could see no men at all. "Trollope's sure to find his way in here."

They retraced their steps to the tavern with less enthusiasm than before, troubled by what they had seen.

"Still want to stay and fight?" asked Bagot.

"Come on, we're not leaving them in this mess," said Ned. They withdrew back to the Fleur de Lys; the archers there seemed to have little idea where the rest of Warwick's army was either.

"In the fields behind us," said one, gesticulating vaguely to the east, "or is it to the north, but I don't think we'll need 'em anyway."

"Well, we'll soon know the answer to that," observed Bagot, grim faced.

Sure enough, a warning shout came from the clock tower and within no time it seemed that the Lancastrians were appearing in every street and lane.

"He's found our weak spots soon enough!" said Ned.

"You've got to admire the man," said Bagot.

"I don't have to admire him just now!"

"Aye, the lads upstairs'll need all the help they can get!"

They barricaded the tavern door as best they could and waited for the inevitable; Bagot and Ned with swords drawn and Bear ready with his mighty poleaxe resting on his shoulder. There was a roar of noise from outside, but Ned could see nothing, so he went up to the first floor where the archers were firing down from the windows.

He stared down into the market place and then ran to look out of the rear window. Wherever he looked there was a host of soldiers. This is hopeless, he thought, and bolted downstairs again.

"We can't wait for them to come to us, Bagot: there are just too many. They're taking each house in turn – if we stay, we're dead. We'll have to fight our way out."

"Not again," said Bagot, rolling his eyes at Bear, "I'm getting too old for this."

Bear merely shrugged, for it was all the same to him.

Ned raced back up to the archers and told them to come down. At first they were reluctant to leave the vantage points from which they were wreaking such havoc, but the older ones knew he was right: they were still killing, but they were already trapped.

Down below, Bagot and Bear removed the barricade and stood ready. The archers had unstrung their bows and joined them, swords drawn.

"We need numbers, lads," said Ned, "so we'll fight to the tower and try to get our men out of there and then on up the east side of the market. Follow me and keep together! Remember, we're not running; we must fight our way out in good order or they'll butcher us!"

Ned charged out of the Fleur de Lys flanked by Bagot and Bear and followed by a score of archers holding their short swords at the ready. They punched a gap through the nearest group of men at arms and headed for the tower only a few paces away. They swept aside the attackers and were quickly joined by its defenders, almost doubling their number. Screams came from the nearby Red Lion tavern as several archers were thrown off the roof; if Ned's men needed any encouragement to move fast and fight hard, that was it. They were almost surrounded, but as they advanced up the street their numbers were swelled by others coming out of the buildings.

Ned was leading the men blind: he didn't know where Warwick was, or the rest of his army, and they were beset on all sides by greater numbers. They battled towards the church hard pressed, their enemies shredding men from the column as they tried to extricate themselves from the town. At the church Ned thought of seeking sanctuary, but the heavy doors were firmly shut against them.

"We're fighting a whole army here," he yelled to Bagot.

"Fall back?" mouthed Bagot and for the first time Ned knew it was utterly up to him. There was no time to plan – just staying alive was keeping him fully occupied. Bear's strength was invaluable, but even he was being driven back.

Then for a moment or two there was some respite and at first Ned couldn't work out why; then he realised that a small number of archers were covering their retreat from the roof of the Bell tavern half way up the street.

He was almost in tears, knowing that those men would soon be cut to pieces for their trouble, but in the midst of the melee he stood tall and raised his sword aloft to salute their courage. But how could he seize the slender chance they were giving him? He struck out to the north east, cutting through the houses and back alleys into the fields and away from the butchery of the market place. A hundred paces further on they reached a ditch and dived behind it for cover. It was not pleasant, being a receptacle for the town's rubbish; it was also exposed to the south wind which had drifted snow onto the bank of the earthwork.

"Bagot!" called Ned. "Do a tally and sort out the archers – we need them to give us some cover."

But the archers knew their work and, despite their ice cold

fingers, were already restringing their bows and soon pinning back any of their opponents who attempted to cross the open ground to reach the ditch.

Ned was joined by a well harnessed man who had commanded some of the town's defences.

"Well done, my lord," the newcomer said gravely, "most of my men at arms were cut down in the first few minutes; I thought we were finished, but a few of us have escaped - thanks to you."

"I'm no lord, just Ned; what do you know of the Earl's positions?"

"I've no idea where he is. We expected an attack from the north, so the earl's army was facing north. Of course, he could have moved his lines since we occupied the town but his brother, Lord Montagu, is at Barnards Heath to the north - just beyond the church."

"Then why didn't he come to our aid?"

"I can only guess that he was under attack as we were."

"Well the town's a bloody shambles – surely he has men to tell him so? God's death! All Trollope's force is coming through the town!"

"Then Montagu's army will be destroyed, for he only commands the van; the rest is not yet engaged."

"And where in God's name is the rest?!" thundered Ned. "And where's the Earl of March? Surely if he's in London, both armies should be in the field against the Queen?"

"I've not heard that March is in London – I was there two days ago and he wasn't there then!"

Bagot returned. "We're all of three score strong, lord; some wounded, but can stand."

"I'm not sure about the 'strong', Bagot," he snapped. "And do you know – the Earl of March hasn't got to London yet! We could've stayed in the north! I've left her there and I didn't need to!"

"You couldn't know that – and what difference would it've made: we don't even know where she is!"

Their new comrade stared at them in confusion and Ned

did his best to bury his anger.

"How well do you know this place?" he asked.

"A little."

"Well, that's more than me. Can you get us to Montagu's lines?"

"I think so; this ancient ditch runs towards the heath, but I'm afraid where it ends we may find ourselves in the open."

"It's gone quiet here," observed Bagot. Their pursuers, in the face of stiff resistance from the archers, had retreated.

"They're after a more important prize – Montagu's vanguard," said their new comrade.

"Bagot," said Ned, "we're going to try to join up with Montagu. Tell the men – and tell them well done too."

"They'll be bloody overjoyed to get out of here," he said, clambering away over piles of dung, putrid animal flesh and broken pottery.

Without delay they scrambled along the ditch until it petered out; by then they could all see and hear the clamour on Barnard's Heath where the full might of the Queen's army was now pounding into Montagu's men.

"Timing, my lord," Bagot advised quietly.

"I know. Divide the men into two groups: half the archers and half the men at arms in each party. One lot go and the other lot covers; then when the first group make it, they give cover to the second as they come in."

Bagot nodded without enthusiasm.

"What's your name?" Ned asked the young captain.

"Stephen Orton," said the other with a smile, Hertfordshire gentleman and proud to be!"

"Good. Let's hope you stay one for the rest of the day! You lead the first group," Ned told him, "and I'll follow."

Bagot was about to interrupt, but Ned silenced him with a glare which said: yes, Bagot, I know the second party might not make it.

"If we don't meet later, Ned Elder has been proud to know you, now off you go!"

Stephen nodded and took the first men out into the open.

Barely thirty paces to his left was the flank of the Lancastrian force already embroiled in a bloody struggle with Montagu's men. But it did not take long for them to spot the small group racing towards the Yorkist lines and some of the men at arms turned to pursue Stephen's men. A sharp volley of arrows from Ned's archers stopped them in their tracks.

The first group reached Montagu's left flank without further losses, but then had to make their way carefully through the spiked netting and caltrops that protected it. Having picked their way through, they turned to offer support to Ned. He was already on the move, but Trollope had obviously seen the first movements and was ready for him with a larger force. Ned knew that if they were caught before they reached the lines they would be cut to pieces.

"It's going to be close!" he shouted to Bagot.

Bagot glanced back anxiously. "If they're with Trollope, they'll be his best men!" he replied.

Stephen's bowmen sent volley after volley of arrows into Trollope's advancing Lancastrians, but they did not falter for a second.

Ned and Trollope reached the Yorkist front line at about the same time and a bloody melee broke out. Trollope had clearly marked Ned out and made straight for him. With their first exchange of blows Ned earned some respect from his experienced opponent but only for a moment; then Trollope bludgeoned him back with his heavy sword as the melee closed in around them. Ned had never faced such power and could only parry each blow and hope to stay on his feet. His men were just about holding their nerve, but he sensed that many had an eye on the struggle between the two captains.

Trollope kept coming, forcing him back; he was breathing hard – this man was too strong for him! Then he caught his heel in the spiked netting; he lurched backwards and there was nothing he could do to stop himself. He hit the ground heavily and felt a sharp length of steel brush his neck: shit, a caltrop. He lay flat on his back and couldn't get up; he couldn't even free his tangled foot. He looked across at Bagot and Bear; neither would reach him in time. Trollope planted one boot firmly on his sword arm, pinning it to the ground, and moved in for the kill, raising his sword to plunge it through his neck.

38

Cheapside, City of London, Mid-February 1461

Will remained still for a moment then stepped back into the apprentices' room to retrieve one of his swords. When he slowly descended the creaking stairs to the ground floor, the noise had stopped. There was no light in the house and the front shutters seemed to still be in place, as was the solid oak door. He turned and walked through the Hall which occupied most of the ground floor. At the rear of the Hall was the door to the courtyard; he looked out towards the warehouse – no sign of life there either.

Now he did feel tired, for it had been a very long day already; he turned to return upstairs but as he did so he noticed that one of the front window shutters was now open. He paused, silently scanning the darker recesses of the large Hall; then he edged slowly towards the open shutter. A man suddenly lunged up at him from the floor and knocked him over; he crouched on his haunches, holding his sword ready. He could see more shadowy figures coming through the open shutter.

He rolled to his feet and clubbed at his assailant with the sword hilt in his right hand, ducking swiftly as a knife flew past his head and thudded into the wall. He pivoted on the balls of his feet and stabbed up at an arm trying to withdraw the knife embedded in the cob wall. There was a cry of pain and a spurt of blood; before anyone else could get to him he slipped swiftly between the men, slashing from side to side as he went. There were a few encouraging yelps and grunts from the intruders.

"Get out now, or you'll get worse," he warned.

His terse announcement was greeted with laughter and he thought then that there might just be too many of them: several dashed past him and ran through towards the rear of the property, whilst at least two more went upstairs.

"Don't say I didn't warn you," he said under his breath.

He'd been employed to secure the goldsmith's goods, but he feared for the occupants of the house and decided he should look to their safety first. Thus he mounted the stairs two at a time, easily catching up the second of the men ahead of him. Hearing him the man half turned, but Will cut at the back of his legs, slicing through muscle and tendon, so that he collapsed screaming as he fell the length of the stairs and landed in a silent heap.

His companion met Will on the landing, waving a knife wildly at him in the dark; Will swayed back and seized the wooden rail to stop himself falling whilst he parried the swinging blade. He forced his opponent up to the landing, but a scream came from the upper floor; someone had clearly got up there first. The house was now in uproar; a voice came from behind him. "Will! Take this!" and Hal handed him his other sword.

"Thanks!" said Will, "Keep the lads inside; I can't see who's who – I don't want to run one of you through!"

Now the intruders had every reason to fear, for he knew they were no match for his swords. He quickly despatched the man before him and thundered up to the next landing. There was shouting and arguing from the back room which he thought was the ladies' bedroom.

"Are you all alright?" he shouted at the closed door.

There was a sudden lull and then more commotion from within.

Below him there were more footsteps on the stairs. He sighed in resignation.

"Open the door!" he called out; "it's Will!"

The door was flung open. On a table by the back wall a single candle almost guttered with the draught from the door. Its flickering light revealed the Goldwell daughters cowering in the corner with a roughly dressed figure standing over them. In the centre of the room sat Mr Alderman Goldwell himself with a knife held against his throat by another man. For an instant Will just stared, uncertain what to do, for those mounting the stairs had almost reached him. He could feel the anger rising in him; these men would pay.

He held up his two swords, one still dripping blood. "If you harm anyone in this room," he said, "you'll surely die in this house."

Then he surprised them all by slamming the door shut and he turned to face the men now at the top of the stairs. He was in no mood to show mercy and struck out savagely; soon there was so much blood on the stairs that he was in danger of losing his footing.

On his way down to the ground floor he had accounted for four dead or dying. He crossed the courtyard where he found two more and killed them efficiently, hardly breaking stride. One thief remained in the warehouse; having splintered the locked door, he was attempting to prise open the chests with an iron crow. He turned as Will entered.

"All your fellows are dead," lied Will, "I warned you before; will you now submit, or must I put you to the sword too?"

Nonplussed, the man lowered the crow for a moment and stood up.

"You weren't here this morning," he said, puzzled.

"No, but I'm here now."

"You're not from the city..."

"I'm tired, choose your path, man: either drop the crow or raise it; one way, you're taken, t'other, you're dead. Which is it to be?"

The robber lowered his arm to drop the crowbar and then swung it up hard, but before his arm reached shoulder height, Will's swords had eviscerated him and he fell to his knees, his guts spilling out.

Will shook his head. "Stupid bastard," he said, leaving the quivering body bleeding onto the floor.

Then he walked briskly back through the house, pausing only to secure the open shutter as he passed the window. He was trembling as he climbed the stairs once more, for if he'd made the wrong call he might find his employer butchered. As he reached the apprentices' room on the first floor Hal peered out, but Will pushed him back inside with a bloody hand and continued up the next flight of steps to the room where Sir John and his daughters were being held. Now for the difficult bit, he thought.

He banged on the door with his sword hilt. Sarah opened the door, gasping as the light from the candle showed Will covered in blood.

Before the captors could speak, Will set out his terms: "Your wretched fellows have spilled their blood all over this house and now there's just you two; I'll let you go downstairs, while I count up to six - I've only ever learnt to go as far as six, so I wouldn't wait too long, because when I get to six, I'll be coming for you."

The pair looked at Will and saw a ruthless, blood soaked killer; their escapade had failed more spectacularly than they could possibly have imagined.

"One!" said Will.

They fled through the door and down the stairs.

"Are you alright Alderman? Two!"

"Yes, Will."

"And your daughters are safe? Three! "

"Yes, indeed, they are of course most distressed ..."

"Four!"

"Are you alright?" asked John Goldwell.

"A few scratches sir, that's all; five!"

"You look most ... terrible," said the merchant.

"I'm sorry sir; please stay up here for now, sir. Six!"

Will shot down the stairs in pursuit and found the two robbers competing to unfasten the shutter they had expected to find open. They dropped to their knees, tossing aside their weapons, pleading for mercy. "It'd be a mercy to cut your throats, for you'll surely hang for this."

But instead, he clubbed them unconscious with his sword hilt and tied them up in the courtyard.

It took hours to sort out the house; the watchmen, who had somehow contrived not to hear the commotion from the goldsmith's house, eventually appeared on the scene when a cry went up for them for the third time. They looked with astonishment at the bloody corpses scattered around the house. With the apprentices' help they piled the bodies in the courtyard, along with the two prisoners. If Peter and Robert needed any evidence to support Hal's description of Will, they were staring at it.

Will sat in the warehouse, still plastered in blood; now the fighting had stopped, his hands were shaking. The chest and crow were still there but a bloody smear on the floor marked where the corpse had been dragged out into the yard. There was a rustling in the doorway and Sarah came in bearing cloths and a bowl of water.

"You can't stay like that," she said, "take off your shirt and we'll get it washed for you. Hal can bring you another."

"I don't have another," said Will.

"Well, I'm sure we can find one; anyway, let me clean you up."

"I nearly got you killed…"

"You're cut," she said, helping him to pull his blood soaked shirt over his head.

She touched his chest lightly and he winced.

"It'll heal soon enough," he said gruffly.

She did not reply but merely started to wash the blood carefully from his upper body with a gentle touch which did much to calm his mood.

"It's on your face too," she said, wiping it. Then she took his hands and washed them in the bowl, holding them in hers for longer than she needed to. He looked up at her and she flushed; her father entered the warehouse and Will quickly removed his hands from the bowl.

"Sarah," the Alderman said, "try to conduct yourself as a lady; there are servants who could have cleaned up Will – in fact he could have done it himself! Go back to your room please!"

Will was about to apologise, but John winked at him as he followed his daughter into the house.

That made Will even more apprehensive; he'd sooner have her father's displeasure, for he suspected where Sarah's thoughts were heading and he had no intention of following her there.

39

Barnard's Heath, February 1461

Ned tried in vain to pull his arm free, but Trollope had him firmly pinned; in desperation, Bear threw his long dagger at Trollope. The veteran swatted it aside contemptuously with his sword, but even so it unbalanced him and he had to adjust his stance to finish Ned off. Then to Ned's surprise Trollope suddenly roared with rage and fell sideways. Ned couldn't see who had inflicted the wound, but he seized his chance and disentangled himself from the netting whilst Trollope was helped up by his men at arms. Bear hacked his way across to Ned as Trollope was taken away, blood pouring from his boot; Bear looked down and pointed to the ground.

"Caltrop!" he said and with a booming laugh he thumped his fist onto Ned's chest. "Very lucky knight!"

Ned grinned sheepishly, clapped him on the back and together they shepherded the rest of their men into the Yorkist lines. Ned and his men passed through to the rear of the lines to regroup and, despite their immediate peril, there was much backslapping and cheering.

"Stay put here and rest awhile," he ordered them, "but don't get too comfortable, you'll be back in the line soon!" Their celebrations quickly became more muted and Ned, leaving Bagot to restore order, went with Stephen in search of the commander. In the command tent he found John Neville, Lord Montagu, a man close to despair who was arguing angrily with one of his fellow nobles. They stopped abruptly when Ned entered the tent.

"Who are you and what do you want?" Montagu demanded.

"I'm Ned Elder."

"So? What do you want, Ned Elder? I'm too pressed for idle words."

"So am I," said Ned crossly, "I've just fought my way out of the town with fifty or so of your men! I thought you might like to know that the rest have been slaughtered, but I'll return to the line until you've finished arguing!"

In any normal circumstances, Ned knew his outburst would have caused much offence to Montagu, but the commander took the rebuke on the chin and studied Ned thoughtfully.

"I remember you … at Middleham; you sought my father's help – and you were with us at Blore Heath."

"I've grown up a little since."

Montagu sighed. "So it seems. What's the news then of our men in the town?"

"You have no men in the town; they fought bravely and they bought you some time, but now you have a whole army against you – without help you're finished."

Montagu seemed undaunted. "I've sent word to my brother; he has the main force with him. If we hold out till he gets here we can push the Queen's army back and rout them."

"He'd better hurry up then, for you'll not hold much longer. Is the Earl of March not nearby?"

"No, last news I had, March was in the Cotswolds."

"Jesus!" Ned shook his head.

"Can I rely on you, Ned, to hold my left flank?"

"I'll stand for as long as I can. But if help doesn't come …"

"My brother will come - you'll see; if you need me, well … my pennant will be flying in our centre."

Ned hurried back to his men, noticing that, if anything, the fighting at the front line was more ferocious than ever. Bagot had the men in battle order, ready to re-join the fight, and Ned addressed them briefly.

"The Earl of Warwick is close by and soon fresh men will

swell our numbers. But until then, we must hold firm."

As he stepped forward, Bear put a restraining hand on his arm.

"Burgundies!" he said, "Wait!"

Ned looked blankly at Bagot, who merely shrugged his shoulders. Bear pointed to a contingent of hand gunners who had just moved forward to try to relieve the pressure on the Yorkist line.

"Burgundians?" asked Ned.

"Yes. Wait," repeated Bear impassively.

Many men crowded around the hand gunners to support them with bills and pikes, especially when the some of the first guns failed to fire, their powder dampened by the drizzling snow. Several of the gunners were cut down by the leading Lancastrians before they could fire their weapons at all

"If we hang back any longer the line will break!" declared Bagot.

"Wait!" repeated Bear once more.

"We can't wait!" said Ned and he would have moved off, but two small explosions came one after the other, accompanied by screams of pain and a haze of smoke. A piece of hot metal traced through the air and embedded itself in the turf at Bagot's feet. A gun had burst, Ned realised, sending a shower of shrapnel slicing through the front ranks on both sides. Where, moments before, a brutal contest had raged over a narrow stretch of ground, there was now only a heap of moaning bodies, with limbs bleeding and faces charred.

"Too hot!" laughed Bear, striding forward past the surviving hand gunners, who fell back as sword and axe began to contest the line once more. So it continued for hour upon hour; both sides continued to pound each other ever more wearily, but from the start Ned knew he didn't have enough men. He was conceding ground, yard by slow yard, and in vain he looked to the north for signs of Warwick's relieving army, but saw nothing.

It was mid-afternoon but the sky above Barnard's Heath was heavy with cloud, threatening more snow. As the day wore on, more of Ned's men fell and of the remainder their armour was cracked and dented, straps were broken and pieces of bloody plate hung uselessly. He scanned the ranks of the enemy, who seemed ever more numerous but then one of the many noble pennants displayed against them caught his eye: the gold square shape of a bird on a blood red standard. He cursed his moment of inattention as he was knocked off balance by a fierce blow, but Holton's armour held.

"Look to your enemy!" roared Bagot a few yards away.

Ned pointed to the Radcliffe pennant, but redoubled his efforts not to give ground.

"It can only be Edmund!" he shouted.

Bagot glanced at it briefly. "Too far away - forget it!"

Ned knew he was right, but it didn't stop the bile rising in his gullet and fuelling his anger as he drove into the enemy host once more, punching his sword point home again and again.

Soon the combatants had fought each other to a weary standstill and, as if by some unseen agreement, the two sides drew back, disentangling their axes and swords and leaving a ramp of bloody, shattered corpses between them.

Ned's men dragged the half butchered wounded back behind them and then took a moment to breathe, heads bowed, leaning on swords or bent down upon one knee. Many removed helmets and gorgets to mop the sweat from their hair and neck. Ned cast a weary eye around him: everywhere the men looked spent; a priest, his vestments soiled by blood and earth, wandered amongst the men offering solace and encouragement to the living and absolution to those with mortal wounds. Ned knew the respite would not last long, for the Lancastrian assault must resume at any moment and then, sooner or later, his line would fail; no quarter would be given and they would be overwhelmed. Their only hope – and it was a slim one - was to hold the line until darkness consumed the field.

Bagot limped to his side. "You see that banner, lord?" he said, his face clouded by worry.

Ned could see all manner of banners across the field, but he humoured Bagot. "Which?" he asked.

"The black and white one - it's been worrying me."

Ned was more worried about the Lancastrian men at arms who seemed ready to join battle once more.

"Bagot – be swift! What about it?"

"I've seen it before…"

"In God's name, can there be a banner you haven't seen before?"

He could see that Bagot was troubled, but the enemy was mustering for the charge.

"Come on, rouse the men," he ordered and donned his helmet, bracing himself to face the onslaught once more.

"To arms! To arms!" shouted Bagot, as the ragged swathe of enemy swords, bills and axes began to advance. Ned stood once more before his men and looked into their faces. How could he rally them yet again? For himself, he had only to think of Amelie to rediscover his anger; but these men were not fools and they knew the odds were impossibly against them, especially those who had fought their way out of the town with him. He brandished his father's great sword aloft and when he searched their eyes he still saw the fire there and it made him proud.

There was a deafening roar as the Queen's host stormed towards them once more, eager for blood, and Ned took his place in the front rank. He swayed as the point of a long bill stabbed at him, then fended it off and hacked the shaft in two; it's lightly harnessed owner had only a second to contemplate his fate before Ned chopped down through his shoulder and chest, carving through bone, lung and heart. So the slaughter began again and he marvelled at his comrades' resilience, at the blows they took and the blood they shed alongside him.

Suddenly to his right Bagot shouted a warning, but his

words were lost in the relentless din; all he could see was Bagot wildly waving his sword and bawling to the men around him. But he could feel it: something on the field had changed; then he looked to where Bagot was pointing once more to the black and white banner. A cold fear gripped Ned for, too late, he remembered where they had seen the banner before when they had passed Trollope's column north of St Albans. The men at arms under the banner were now turning their backs to the enemy, they were going to run! No, it was worse than that, for their shouts drifted along the lines to him: "Harry of Lancaster! Long live the King!"

Sweet Jesus - they've turned! His men, so strong until now, fell back in disarray and Ned watched, appalled, as they turned their frightened faces towards him and were hacked down by the dozen. Angry cries of "traitor!" rang out, but they were soon drowned by an exultant roar from the Lancastrians as they poured through the newly created chasm in the Yorkist lines: the defection had dealt Montagu's vanguard a mortal blow.

Ned looked across to Bagot and saw a sight he never thought to see: the old warrior retreating from the line and hobbling towards him.

"Let's just get out alive!" shouted Bagot, his face a mask of despair.

But Ned did not need telling, for the ranks around him had already dissolved into bloody chaos.

"Fall back!" he yelled, "face the enemy, but fall back!"

Stephen seized his arm. "Follow me; there are horses in the trees at the rear."

"Hold together!" shouted Bagot, but men were being scythed down as they ran and he retreated in a spray of blood.

"I'm not going down like this," said Ned, "Stephen, take the archers with you and get to the horses – we'll fight our way back to you."

Stephen stared at him blankly.

"Go!" insisted Ned.

He paused only to check that Stephen was racing towards the tree line behind them then he bellowed above the clamour: "On me, damn you! Ned Elder! On me! We fight or fall as one!"

He turned to Bear, who was snapping and snarling at a group of billmen.

"Stay with him," he ordered, pointing to Bagot, "he can hardly walk!"

Bear nodded, snatching up a long handled poleaxe as he moved back to stand alongside Bagot.

A corps of about two hundred of them battled to maintain a rearguard as they headed for the trees. Ned knew that if Stephen found no mounts they would simply be surrounded and slaughtered. All around them the jubilant royal army was hunting down the disintegrating vanguard and the screams told him that no mercy was being shown.

"Hold!" he shouted with every blow he struck at their pursuers until his throat was dry and hoarse; but his men did hold. And when they reached the stand of trees, Stephen had a ring of mounted archers set to support their retreat. The archers let fly at point blank range and did appalling damage: their bodkin arrows punching even into the armoured knights and the broad heads slicing through flesh.

Soon the retreating group were amongst the baggage train where a large number of the horses had been tethered. Ned seized some reins and mounted to survey the field: in covering the last hundred paces, they had lost half their number, but they had put up such a strong defence that many of the enemy had sheered away to pursue easier targets or pillage the defenceless wagons.

Half his men were already mounted and ready to leave but the rest, including Bagot and Bear, could not do so for they were still holding back the enemy horde. Ned spurred his horse forward.

"Come on!" he shouted, "with me!" and he drove his terrified horse straight into the enemy line and sliced his sword across the foremost men at arms; his own men were almost as stunned as their opponents. Behind him, many of his horsemen followed, repeating his tactic and despite their superior numbers, the Lancastrians fell back in the face of the mounted knights.

"To horse! To horse!" Ned shouted and wheeled his own mount to rake the enemy line again, taking advantage of the uncertainty his first charge had caused. By the time he had done so, his remaining men were mounted and he turned to lead them away across the heath and scrubland. They rode at near full gallop for several miles until finally they reined in their exhausted horses and slowed to a walking pace.

"Keep a lively watch!" he called out, though both men and horses were so spent that they would have little fight left in them. He took them north hoping to locate their elusive commander-in-chief, Warwick. It was a miserable ride by men drained of strength and spirit: their comrades had been slaughtered and many had families in the lands between St Albans and London where nothing now could stop the rampage of the ferocious northern army.

"What a disaster, Ned," muttered Bagot, riding beside him.

For a moment Ned did not reply, then he said: "No, Penholme was a disaster; this is a defeat, that's all. We went into battle knowing we might meet defeat or death but those poor little Standlake buggers didn't even know they were at war. If I start to feel sorry for myself, Bagot, just remind me of that."

And in the darkness the veteran of many campaigns nodded as they rode slowly on.

Ned sent out riders ahead to find Warwick's camp, but it was well into the night before they saw the dying fires of the camp and quickened their pace. They were almost too late: the Earl was already moving his army – or the remains of it – westwards.

When Ned tagged onto the rear of Warwick's departing troops he was astonished to find that he was leading several hundred of those who had escaped the field at Barnard's Heath. He looked at Stephen quizzically and the gentleman from Hertfordshire offered him a grim smile.

"Word of our escape from the town spread fast; these men followed the man they thought might just get them out in one piece."

"Quite a lot didn't get out," said Ned diffidently and rode on in silence, contemplating exactly what he would say to the Earl of Warwick when eventually the column halted.

As it turned out, Warwick was so far ahead of him that he did not catch up until a day and a half later when the Earl stopped at Chipping Norton to meet up with Edward, Earl of March. By then, Ned was exhausted, and since every possible space to sleep indoors had already been taken, he spent the night sleeping in the open, like the rest of his men, under a bitter February sky.

40

Cheapside in London, Ash Wednesday, February 1461

The house door slammed shut so Will supposed that John Goldwell had finally returned from his meeting in the City. The alderman came straight through to the warehouse to find Will and one look at his grim expression told Will that the news was not good.

"Sir?"

"Terrible news, terrible news."

"Sir?"

"A black day, Will!" said the alderman without offering any explanation.

"How so, sir?" asked Will.

"Our shield and protector, the noble Earl of Warwick, was routed yesterday at St. Albans ... and many good men were slain!"

Will had no idea who Warwick was or where St Albans was. "But what does it mean, Alderman?" he asked.

"What does it mean, Will? What does it mean? It means that nothing now stands between us and the Queen's northern horde of murdering cutthroats."

"So what's to be done, sir?"

"Ha! That you may well ask! The City's holding its breath but no one can agree on what to do. Some are for barring the gates but it seems to me that if we're defenceless we may as well submit to the Queen at once and sue for clemency."

"Well Alderman, I don't know much but I saw what happened when the Queen's army ran through Ludlow. If you're not killed, you'll be ruined: your gold'll be taken and your daughters raped. Once that army comes through the city gates, no-one will control it – so, you'd best try to keep it out."

"It can't happen like that here in the City of London? Surely…can it?"

"I've seen it once and I don't want to see it again," said Will.

"Well, I admit you're not the only one with such fears. We tried to send gifts to the Queen: some food and coin to sweeten her soldiers; but a mob of our own folk barred the city gates and wouldn't let the wagons out! They took the food for themselves – and the money too, I dare say!"

"They're scared, sir – and with good reason," said Will quietly. "The theft of a little food will be nothing to what'll happen if the Queen's army gets in. How far away is it?"

"Pah! A day, if that; the vanguard will arrive in no time. And that's why I came home to speak to you." For once he looked uncertain.

"To me? Is there something you'd like me to do, sir?" prompted Will.

"It's not what you were hired for and … you may not wish to do it."

"Best spit it out then sir and we can see."

"Very well. My mother lives on the Strand, outside the gates. As a rule she refuses to set foot in the City but now she really must be brought in."

"And you want me to get her?" asked Will.

"Yes, but it won't be easy - and I don't just mean the obvious danger. She's a woman who doesn't take very well to being told what to do."

"And she won't know me from the Queen's men!"

"Indeed! That's why Sarah must go with you – her grandmother will refuse her nothing – she's something of a favourite with her."

Will frowned. "Could I not take you, sir; surely she'd do as you say?"

"Perhaps Will, but that just isn't possible; I have my duties here - how would it look if one of the senior alderman was seen leaving the City just now – whatever the reason?"

Will could see the sense of that, but the last thing he wanted was to be thrown together with the alderman's daughter. He had to admit she had a certain attraction and in Yoredale he had fallen in love with a different girl every week – until Eleanor. But now Eleanor was dead and he didn't intend to fall in love again. So for his part he had tried to avoid Sarah and whenever that failed he had remained aloof and cool towards her.

"Now don't look at me like that, Will," said the alderman, "I have eyes! I can see you two won't want to take this journey together, but I can see no other course."

Will remained silent, so he continued hesitantly. "I ask this as a favour, Will, not a duty."

Will sighed audibly. "I'll do anything I can, sir," he said finally.

"Excellent! You can take my boat to the Strand; it'll be quicker. The whole journey can be done in less than a day."

"I don't like the sound of that, sir. I've never been on a boat so I'd sooner ride there," said Will.

"I'm sure you ride well and I know Sarah could ride, but I'm very sure that my mother couldn't ride even if the devil himself turned up at her door! Besides … I can't be sure they'll let you back through the gates at present. No, the river it has to be."

Will nodded reluctantly.

"Now make ready. You can be off by noon and you'll likely be back in a few hours."

"As you say, sir," said Will as he left, but he did not greet his new errand with any enthusiasm. He didn't want to venture outside the city, he didn't want to go on the river and he most definitely didn't want to go anywhere with Sarah Goldwell in tow. Yet how could he refuse?

Thus within the hour he dutifully went down to Trig Lane

on the river where the alderman kept a boat at his personal disposal.

"Is it safe?" asked Will, when he saw the small sharp prowed vessel bobbing beside the jetty.

"Nothing to worry about, Will," replied the goldsmith, "this is a wherry – the very latest thing. I use it all the time on business and these boatmen have proved themselves stout enough fellows in the past."

Sarah stood stiffly on the wharf with her arms folded. She stared out across the river to the south bank and said nothing either to her father or Will. The two boatmen stared doubtfully at Will, seeing him armed to the teeth, but said nothing. They helped Sarah aboard with all due courtesy for she had travelled with them before, but Will they left to clamber aboard as best he could – which was not with any particular grace.

It was cold on the river and a chill drizzle descended upon them as they made their way upstream. Their journey was carried out for the most part in silence for the boatmen were too respectful to make idle chatter and neither Will nor Sarah had anything to say to each other. He fixed his attention on the assortment of wharves, mills and warehouses along the river bank and the plethora of boats that plied their trade along the Thames. Whenever their wherry was caught in the waves created by larger boats and barges he gripped the side of the boat as if at any moment he might be thrown out. Nevertheless their progress was smooth and fast as they neared the great southward bend in the river towards Westminster. There the cramped City houses and grimy warehouses were replaced by large imposing houses and gardens, each with its own private mooring and jetty.

One of the boatmen called out: "Strand Lane!"

It was a surprise to Will how quickly they had reached their destination, but then the boatmen pointed further downriver where several spirals of smoke mingled with the low lying cloud. Will observed that there was also a haze of smoke over the houses near the Great Cross to the west.

The two boatmen exchanged a nervous glance. "We'll wait for you here," said one, as they secured the boat at the small landing stage. "Best not be too long, though," he warned.

Will and Sarah set off at a brisk walk up the lane.

"How far is it?" he asked, for like the boatmen he was worried about the smoke and what it might mean.

"The end of the lane," replied Sarah curtly.

He moved on swiftly, concerned that if there was trouble further west it would not take very long to reach them. Sarah struggled to keep pace with him but when they turned out of the lane into the broad Strand he waited for her to lead them to her grandmother's house. An elderly female servant gave them admittance and took them up to a chamber facing north onto the Strand.

Widow Goldwell seemed most surprised to see her granddaughter, but when Sarah quickly explained their purpose the old woman would not countenance for a moment leaving her house.

"It'll take more than a few robbing Scots to force me out. Why, in the City I'd be at the mercy of all the thieves and beggars! And who's he?" She eyed Will suspiciously. "He looks like a hireling, but you can't take your eyes off him, so what's he to you?"

"He's nothing to me at all," Sarah replied but her blushing cheeks told her grandmother a different story.

"My lady," said Will, "we're in haste. You must leave with us at once."

"If you're not her lady," the widow replied acidly, "then you're certainly not mine! Hold your tongue until you're spoken to! Sarah, surely your father didn't expect me to come with you?"

"He hoped you would, if I asked you."

As the two women argued Will's attention turned elsewhere as he strained to make out some noise from the street. He glanced at the servant standing near the window; she met his eyes and nodded slightly for she too had heard raised voices.

"Well, my dear," said widow Goldwell, "even though I love

to see you, you've had a wasted journey for I'd rather die here than move into the City."

As she finished speaking her servant was propelled across the room towards her and landed at Sarah's feet with an arrow protruding from her back. Blood flowed steadily from her body, as the life twitched silently from her.

Sarah screamed and her grandmother turned pale.

"Get down," ordered Will as he edged along the wall to the window. The two women crawled away from the pool of blood slowly expanding across the floor and sat on a small low cupboard in the far corner of the room.

"She'd served me all her life," said widow Goldwell softly.

Another arrow flew through the open window and hit the far wall.

"Is there a chamber at the back?" Will demanded.

Widow Goldwell nodded: "the solar."

"Go in there now," he told them. As they did so Will peered out of the window. There was a crowd of armed men in the street, but in several different groups and he could not make out whether they were together or not. He suspected from the dress of some that they were border men from the northern marches for he had seen one or two before in Salisbury's army at Middleham. These men were a long way from home, but then so was he.

A sudden explosion of splintering wood below brought his attention back to the present danger. He ran to the rear solar.

"They're in the house!" he said, but of course they already knew that and downstairs a young girl screamed.

"My serving girl, Jane!" cried Widow Goldwell, "she'll be in the kitchen."

"I'll see if I can get to her; stay here and keep quiet till I come back!"

Her grandmother was disposed to argue but Sarah took her hand and they knelt down on the floor where they began to pray together quietly.

Will left them and shut the door, striding across to the top of the stairs. There was much noise from below and the servant screamed again; he cursed knowing he could not leave her thus. He drew out both his swords.

"I'm tired of this," he said to himself, but he took a deep breath and thundered down the stairs, realising the moment he reached the bottom step that he was too late for the young girl, skirts lifted above her breasts, lay still by the smashed partition to the kitchen. He had endangered the others for nothing.

He took in the wider scene in an instant: there must have been half a dozen or more of them in the large Hall busily ransacking the room. He expected them to come straight at him but at first they simply assumed he was one of their own and asked him only what the pickings were like upstairs. Swiftly he adopted the role, but something, some nuance of speech or body language made them think twice. Then they did rush at him and forced him back up the stairs. These men were not like the thieves he had despatched so easily a few days before. They were no strangers to brutal killing and two dead servants provided ample evidence of their intent.

At the top of the stairs he stopped and turned to face them. At best, they could take him on two at a time and he wouldn't make it easy for them. The first two underestimated him; he slashed at them with both swords and kicked them back downstairs. Another pair attempted to dislodge him but he drove them back too. However, the next two men starting up the stairs were an altogether different proposition: they came at a steady unhurried walk for they knew he would fall back before them. And he did, for they were carrying long bills with murderous blades which far outreached his swords.

Shit, he thought: we're dead. He might parry them away for a short time but they would keep stabbing at him until one of their blows struck home. On the other hand, he reasoned, Scaroni did say he could be the best swordsman in Christendom...

When the bill men reached the top step, there was no sign of Will. They called up their fellows and moved cautiously across the landing. They knew well enough that the most obvious threat might lurk behind the door at the top of the stairs, so one kicked it in whilst the other lunged forward with his bill. Standing beside the shattered door, Will seized the bill shaft and pulled on it so that the attacker's momentum carried him onto Will's waiting blade. Then Will reversed his grip on the bill and darted out of the room, sweeping it from side to side, cutting two men severely and forcing the rest back down the stairs.

He retrieved his sword and glanced out of the front window again: outside, the local citizens were trying to storm the captured houses one at a time, but all was being pursued at such a slow pace, that it would be of no help to them. He heard footsteps on the stairs again but was too slow to return to the landing and cursed as they reached the stair head before him. He darted into the solar and slammed the door behind him. Sarah and her grandmother stared at him in alarm.

"Get behind the door and keep quiet!" he ordered, "they'll be in presently. I'll draw as many in as I can. You two must get to the stairs and get out; you'll find friends further down the street."

"I don't know, Will," said Sarah.

"Do as I say!" he hissed and quickly pressed his dagger into her hand.

"Courage girl!" said her grandmother.

Will set himself on the far side of the room opposite the door as the attackers crashed it open. They came at him hard, as he knew they would, for he'd already given them more than enough cause. He needed all his agility to survive the first onslaught and even so he felt a sword point pierce his leather jerkin in the first frantic exchange of blows. Yet with two swords he could occupy several opponents whilst Sarah and her grandmother fled. Now all he had to do was keep his assailants in the room. He worked his way around to the door and slammed it shut. That got their attention.

Five had entered the solar: one he'd accounted for at once

and a second he'd wounded so badly he sat whimpering against the wall, bleeding out onto the floor; so there remained only three. He was starting to feel confident again until a shrill scream from downstairs shook him to the core.

Was it Sarah who had screamed, or her grandmother? He couldn't tell, but he had to get down there! If he was such a bloody great swordsman, then he'd better start showing it! He went in close and ripped one blade across a chest whilst stabbing the other into a throat. He pressed on, parrying with one sword, slashing with the other and when he stopped moving, the last man turned to flee. Will carved a sword across his back and kicked him angrily to the floor.

He took the stairs three at a time. At the foot a wild eyed warrior raised his axe, but Will hit him so fast that his sword pierced the man mortally before the axe had finished its up stroke. Will wrenched out his blade as man and axe fell to the floor and then abruptly all was still. He could smell the blood as he stepped over the fallen man and edged towards the door. He couldn't see anyone except the kitchen girl who lay exactly as he had seen her before. He turned and went through the pantry into the kitchen; then he sank to his knees. Sarah and her grandmother lay together, unmoving, on the stone floor. Sarah had her arms around her grandmother and there was a single short handled bill embedded through them both; the floor was already wet with their blood.

41

Chipping Norton, mid - February 1461

The manor house which had been put at the disposal of Edward, Earl of March, was small but the Hall was laid out like a king's chamber. Edward, now using his father's title: Duke of York, exuded informality, seated casually on a large, but plain, oak chair. Ned observed those close to the Duke carefully: the nearer they were, the more influential they were. All stood in his presence save one. Richard Neville, Earl of Warwick, despite his lesser noble rank, possessed vast lands and power beyond that of his protégé so he sat just below the young Duke, facing all the others. There was an overbearing arrogance in the Earl's manner that brought out the worst in Ned. He recognised in Warwick all the features of a powerful man that he disliked most and he struggled to hide his distaste. Yet Will Hastings had already made him well aware that Warwick, though proud and arrogant, was a popular man with many others in the room.

Ned was pleased to see that Warwick, despite his lofty status, seemed to be under some pressure from Duke Edward. He had a lot of explaining to do, for aside from Ned's own complaints, his heavy defeat at St Albans had cost the Duke his most vital asset, King Henry, who was now reunited with the Queen. As long as the Duke could claim to be acting on behalf of the lawful, but witless, King, then he had the power of the law on his side. Now once again, he was a traitor.

Ned listened most carefully as Warwick reported to Duke Edward and the rest of the council how the debacle at St Albans had occurred. Ned chewed his lip throughout as his frustration grew, yet he sensed that the shrewd Duke was not entirely satisfied with Warwick's account.

"Cousin, you've described what happened, but I'm no wiser as to why the battle went so ill," said the Duke. Warwick must have been waiting for this point and he had his explanation well prepared.

"Your Grace, the root of it all was treachery: men not staying at their posts in the town, others fleeing the battle lines and even turning against their fellows. Thus, my brother's men couldn't hold their line until I could bring my own battle to bear against the enemy."

"God's truth!" exclaimed the Duke, "We've seen enough men change sides in this campaign already! And Trollope led some of them again, I'm told."

"Yes, and he surely persuaded others to turn against us," confirmed Warwick, clearly a little discomfited by the thought that the Duke might have other sources of information about the battle.

"So…" Duke Edward left the word hanging in the air for a moment, before continuing – "were it not for these acts of cowardice and treachery, you would have overcome the Queen's army?"

"Certainly!"

Ned almost intervened, but Hastings caught his eye and glared across at him, so he held his tongue as the Duke continued to press Warwick.

"Can we not root out these cowards? Are they known to you? Else surely we risk the same thing happening again?"

For the first time in his account the Earl seemed less sure of himself.

"Many paid with their lives, your Grace; others no doubt joined the throng of Lancaster in the town…; it's difficult to be clear. Who told you that Trollope was there?" he asked sharply.

He's a bit rattled, thought Ned, and so he should be.

"Someone I trust well," replied the Duke smoothly, and with only a slight hesitation, he added: "as I do you, of course, cousin!"

It seemed that Duke Edward was content to leave the post mortem there - just as Ned had feared, no-one was going to blame Warwick, certainly not the Duke.

"Lords, gentlemen, let us consider now the next move rather than the last one," said Duke Edward.

But Ned could not let the moment pass.

"Your grace!" he interrupted, "may I speak a word about St Albans?"

Duke Edward frowned at him and Will Hastings looked at him in horror.

"No, Ned, you may not," said the Duke firmly.

"But your grace, more should be said!"

The Duke's normally relaxed visage froze and the hushed circle of councillors waited with interest to see how he would deal with such an impertinent interruption. Warwick stared at Ned furiously.

It was plain for all to see that, for once, the decisive young Duke was unsure: could he afford to slap down a young knight such as Ned, for there were few of higher rank than knight amongst his chief supporters. But his easy charm soon returned and he smiled indulgently.

"Very well, Ned, as a gesture of the high esteem I hold you in."

Will Hastings was hurling murderous looks at Ned for he had instructed him very clearly to say nothing before the Council; but now Ned had everyone's attention.

"Your Grace, Lord Montagu's men fought bravely and laboured many long hours against a vast host of the enemy; they waited in vain for the Earl to come to their aid. Lord Montagu himself told me he had sent to the Earl for help, but after several hours none had come and we were spent. Yes, there was one knight who changed sides and his men broke our line, but by then the day was already lost."

Warwick was seething at the challenge to his account.

"And where were you in all this?" the Earl enquired. "You seem quite untouched by these 'long hours' of fighting."

"My Lord, I was in the town in the morning and then joined Lord Montagu's main force sometime after noon, so I saw what was happening for most of the day."

"So, you were one of those who fled the town, leaving it to the Queen's men," said Warwick.

Ned saw Hastings wince as he turned stony faced towards the Earl. Duke Edward was poised to put an end to the discussion, but too late.

"My lord," said Ned, the anger rising in him, "I took out of the town the bloody remains of the archers and men at arms you left there to die! They fought well for you and when they joined their comrades on the heath they fought well again there. Many died while they waited for you!"

Before Ned had finished, Warwick was already out of his seat, his hand on his sword hilt.

"What are you to speak of me? You speak of me as if I am some lowly dog?"

"Enough!" interrupted Duke Edward standing swiftly to get between the two.

"Come, we are all for the same cause in this house. There's no need for such words."

To Warwick he said: "Cousin, save your sword for the real battle!"

Then he turned to Ned whilst everyone held their breath. "Ned! Leave us! When I have need of your advice again, I'll summon you, or not, as I please."

Ned, still livid, flashed Warwick a disgusted look and stumped out of the room.

§§§

Hours later when Will Hastings caught up with him he was still angry.

"Are you so keen to die young?" Hastings enquired, "The Duke was most angry with you – and he rarely gets angry with anyone! He could hardly let you insult his cousin and chief ally in full council. You put him in an impossible position!"

"Not as impossible as the archers in St Albans!"

"Ned, he knows your mettle well enough; you didn't need to say anything. I'd already passed on your account to him – as I told you I would. You promised not to raise it; that was a condition of you being there at all. You betrayed my trust."

"Yes, and I'm sorry for that Will."

"Well, he wants to see you now. Is it safe to leave you with him?"

"I'm not a fool, Will."

Hastings laughed and clapped him on the back sympathetically.

"Well, I think the Duke's council would probably argue with that! Picking a public fight with Warwick? You've made an enemy of the most powerful man in the land; and he won't forget it, so you'd better take care. If he wants to, he'll snuff you out like a candle. Go – and receive your punishment!"

§§§

Edward was in his privy chamber, which meant the solar of the Chipping Norton manor house. Ned was admitted and, much to his surprise, Edward embraced him warmly.

"Ned! Good to see you again, though you've won a few more cuts and bruises since last time I saw you!"

It was as if the council meeting had never happened.

"Your Grace, I humbly crave your pardon for my offence this morning."

Edward shrugged his broad shoulders.

"Well, as for that, the offence was less to me than my cousin though I don't suggest that you try to ask his pardon! I'll keep the two of you as far apart as possible: you can join my uncle, Fauconberg, you'll get on very well together. Of course, he's also Warwick's uncle…" He laughed.

"Listen to me, Ned: you are without doubt one of my best

knights and there are few I'd rather have by my side. But, if we're divided, all will be lost – your dreams, as well as mine. The Earl is my cousin and a warrior that all men throughout Christendom either love or fear – except you. Thus, I need him more than I need you but I'd sooner have you both. You want your lands back and I'll give them to you and I'll give you more besides; but you must fight my enemies not my friends."

Not for the first time, Ned was overwhelmed by Edward's warmth and generosity.

"Your Grace, I'll do whatever you ask of me."

"Of course you will, Ned! Now, let's talk of it no more, or we'll become even more melancholy than we already are. What you need is a lively girl, Ned, and I'm sure we can find you one. I've had no trouble at all!"

Ned thought that very likely, since Edward's heady mix of good looks, power and easy charm usually caused women of all ages to fall under his spell – men too, come to think of it.

"I already have one, your grace - or at least I hope perhaps I do."

Edward shook his head sadly. "Now you see Ned: you're a valiant soldier, but I'm not sure you've got quite the right idea about women. Now, as it happens, I've a very comely wench waiting for me, so you'd better bugger off and find Fauconberg."

The man could charm a silver coin from a beggar, Ned thought, as he left the chamber.

§§§

Lord Fauconberg, Hastings told him, was the brother of the late Earl of Salisbury, who Ned had gone to all those months ago at Middleham. He greeted Ned enthusiastically and if he disapproved of Ned's outburst against his nephew Warwick, he did not show it. The Duke was right: they got on famously at once for Ned recognised in Fauconberg a no-nonsense leader of men who did not waste his time worrying about much else.

Ned, on the other hand, found he still had much to worry about. He was disconcerted to find that the men he had brought from St Albans had decided to throw in their lot with him.

Bagot wasn't so surprised. "These men are committed to the fight, but they also want to live through it," he said, "they think you're their best chance – poor buggers!"

"You've been signing them up?" asked Ned.

"Yes, of course – we need men! There you are, almost three hundred indentures for you to complete."

"What were you thinking?" Ned berated him in disbelief. "You'd no authority to get indentures from them!"

"Some of the captains have committed to bring men at arms or archers," Bagot continued enthusiastically.

"But how in God's name am I to maintain these fellows? I've not a penny's income!"

"I may have mentioned land to them…" murmured Bagot.

"My land?" Ned retorted indignantly.

"No, the Radcliffe lands you've been promised. Well, strictly speaking, you haven't got them yet – but you will! There'll be plenty to go round," he said airily.

"But it's madness!" declared Ned. "I can't maintain a small army!"

"You'll need them lad, if you want to get back what's lost," said Bagot soberly, "Oh, and we'll need some badges for them…"

"Bagot, there are times when I could cheerfully strangle you. Where in God's name are we going to get badges from?"

Bagot grinned confidently. "Well, I had an idea about that: I thought some might come from around your waist…" he indicated the torn, grubby banner which Ned still wore. Ned shrugged, unwrapped it and held it up: the light blue fabric was now streaked with the dried blood of many opponents. To see his father's banner again brought a lump to his throat.

"Well, if it can be used I suppose we should do," he said huskily.

Bagot took the cloth from him and looked upon it with something close to reverence.

"I fought under that standard for seven years – carried it once or twice, when we ran into trouble... I'll see what can be done with it."

Ned shook his head and ran his hands back through his hair: overnight it seemed he had become the master of a large force of experienced men at arms and archers. So far he had struggled to lead half a dozen effectively; the thought of taking responsibility for hundreds scared the shit out of him.

42

The Strand outside the City of London, mid - February 1461

Will steeled himself to look at them. Then he crawled across, leaving handprints in the blood, and removed the bill from Widow Goldwell's stomach. It was a grisly task but his hands and clothes were already plastered in blood so a little more made no difference. He lifted her and laid her out gently on the cold stone – so much for getting the old bird safely into the City.

Sarah looked peaceful, as if she was just asleep. He crouched beside her and touched her face: it was still warm. At once his eyes darted down to her midriff which should have been torn and bleeding at the very least – but it wasn't. Her grandmother must have taken the full force of the bill and Sarah seemed untouched. When he examined a cut on the side of her head, she stirred.

"Thank God!" he said and picked her up to carry her into the Hall away from her grandmother's bloody corpse. She came to in his arms and remembered.

"Oh, Will…" she sobbed.

He held her tightly to him. "I'm sorry, I shouldn't have sent you down, but it seemed the only way out."

She clung to him without speaking.

"We need to get you back to the boat," he said, "if it's still there."

"Is she?"

He nodded.

"I can't leave her, Will, I just can't! We must take her with us."

He sat her down on one of the few unbroken chairs in the room.

"Listen to me: we're not taking her with us. It would do her no good now and we need to get out of here fast. Wait here while I find something to cover her."

"No." She stood up, gripping his hand. "We'll both do it – I'm not afraid to see her but I don't want others to – and nor would she."

She winced as Will ripped down a wall hanging from the Hall and they carried it through into the pantry where they carefully rolled the body inside it.

"We'll come back, won't we, to look after her properly?" said Sarah.

"We'll come back," he agreed, "come on now."

He took her hand and led her to the door, where she looked back once before he hurried her from the house. In the street it was worse than before for the local citizens were falling back towards Westminster. They dragged their wounded with them whilst the raiders ignored them and returned to pillaging the houses.

"We can't get out that way," he said, "is there another path down to the river?"

"I'm not sure, I don't think so... not without climbing over fences and walls."

"Better fences and walls than bloodthirsty Scots!"

They passed swiftly through a rear gate into a small courtyard at the back of the house. Sarah's grandmother had only a very narrow piece of land and there was no access to the river, for along the rear of the property was a high wall, mainly of stone but repaired in some places by new brick.

"If we're to reach the river we'll have to work our way along through the other yards," said Will.

Sarah eyed the wall along the adjoining property. "This

one's not much lower," she said doubtfully.

"No, it won't be easy, but I think I can just about jump up to reach the top. I'll lift you up first - it's not going to be very lady like."

She shrugged her shoulders. "I'm not a lady, Will - just a merchant's daughter, that's all."

He offered her his hand as they approached the wall; she hesitated and then gripped it firmly. He looked back at the house but there was no sign of pursuit.

"Ready?" he said.

She nodded and their eyes met for an instant. He drew her to him and kissed her lightly on the cheek. "For good luck," he said sheepishly.

"I'm ready," she said and he lifted her up onto his shoulders, grimacing with pain as he did so. She clambered unsteadily onto the top of the wall, crouched for a moment and then, as she tried to straighten her clothes, lost her balance. As she lurched over, he reached out a hand to seize her foot and pull her back; she scrambled into a sitting position, breathing heavily.

"Never mind how you look! Just be careful!" he chided.

"I'm sorry," she said.

He moved back and then took a running leap at the wall but the days of icy rain had made it slippery to the touch and his fingertips failed to hold on. He tried once more but again could find no grip on the stone and fell to the ground. He stayed down on his haunches for a while, for he could feel the dampness around his wound that told him there could only be a few more attempts.

"Are you alright?" she called down.

"Yes, of course," he said, getting to his feet. "This time try to take my hand as I get up there; but if you think you're going to fall, let go."

"Let's try," she said, tight lipped. He tried again but although she easily reached his hand it slipped through hers and he fell back, winding himself as he hit the ground again.

She screamed suddenly.

"I'm alright!" he said to reassure her, but she was staring beyond him towards the house. There were two of them coming at him fast, one carrying an axe, the other with a broad bladed knife.

"Shit!" he cried. His swords slid out of their scabbards just in time to parry the first blows. He took a pace back, shutting out another scream from Sarah, as he gauged the power of his assailants. The axe man wore a mail shirt, his comrade did not. Will feinted to strike at the axe man and instead drove one blade through the body of the other man. His sword punched through leather, muscle and stomach before he ripped it up and drew it back out through the ribcage. As the stricken man fell, Will was already rolling to the ground to dodge the swinging axe blade. He stayed low and thrust both blades up under the mail coat. There was a wretched cry and a small river of blood; as his victim dropped to his knees. Will sprang up and sliced a sword across the back of the unprotected neck. As the lifeless body fell he sheathed his swords and glanced back at the house. He couldn't see anyone else.

Sarah sat quivering on the wall. She stared at him forlornly.

"Again!" he called up to her and he hurried to try the wall again. This time he took more of a run at it and planted one foot about a third of the way up to gain a little more height. Sarah once more seized his right arm and pulled for all she was worth, holding on to him long enough for him to hook his other arm over the wall and pull himself up. He paused half bent over the wall to get his breath back then he swung his leg over the top and sat facing her.

"You show no mercy..." she said in a small voice.

"We're still alive, aren't we?" he replied gently. She nodded and rested a hand on his shoulder.

They suddenly smiled at each other, like small children sharing some wicked secret, but a shout from the house reminded them where they were.

He jumped off the wall into the next yard and helped her down. He was encouraged to see that this property was much larger and extended further down towards the river.

"It's all bishops' palaces along here now," she said.

"Well, they'll be a popular target. They'll have plenty worth stealing!"

"There are river jetties all along here for the bishops are always off somewhere. There's sure to be a boat."

"Let's hope so, because we're getting further away from our own boat. Do you think they'll have waited?"

"Of course they'll wait," she said.

They hurried through the grounds, but he could not help pausing to look at the grand stone building.

"Perhaps there's help within," she suggested. Such hopes were quickly dispelled when a wooden chest crashed out of one of the broad glass windows on the first floor and plummeted to the ground, smashing itself to pieces in the bishop's fishpond. Flames then began to appear at the downstairs windows and they turned away towards the river. Again they encountered a high stone wall, but this time there was an open gate through to a landing beside the water.

They sat down disconsolately on the jetty and stared out across the river, for there was no boat. There were one or two small vessels in the murky distance towards the city, but far out of hailing range. Worse still, the light was fading and he suspected they would only have an hour or so of daylight left.

"The tide's turned," said Sarah, "there'll be few on the river now, especially in this weather."

Her shoulders sagged and she leaned against him; after a moment he curled his arm around her.

"There's something else," he said.

"Please tell me it's a bishop in a boat," she replied, refusing to look at the river.

"No, but shouldn't our boat be just a hundred paces or so up river? In fact shouldn't it be at that landing stage there?" He made her look along the riverbank where he was pointing. She stared at it for a moment and then wearily nodded: the boat had left without them.

"Let's take another look at the Strand," she suggested, "perhaps we could walk back. It's not so very far, is it?"

So they returned to the bishop's garden. Thick black smoke was unfurling from the doors and windows of the house where several fires had now taken hold. They picked their way warily through the grounds and out of a gate on to the Strand where a chaotic story was being played out. Several other houses on the south side had been put to the torch and across the broad street armed citizens in jacks and sallets took on the renegades from the northern army. Those not fighting were fleeing towards Westminster. Bloodied bodies lay on the ground and screams filled the air.

Sarah was horrified. "If there were no city walls, this would be our fate…"

"This is our fate!" he said. "Well, what now: river or road?"

"Staying by the river will get us nowhere if we can't find a boat…" she said.

Will had his doubts about both options. "But it must be a fair walk to the gates and they've been shut all day, so even if we made it before curfew, there's no saying they'll let us in."

"I'm an Alderman's daughter!" she retorted.

He smiled. "I thought you were only a merchant's daughter. Alright, let's give it a try."

"We have to make for the City gate, Ludgate," she said.

"Everyone else is heading west," he said.

"Home lies east, in the City! And that's where I want to go - through the Temple Bar and across the Fleet River. We can do it, Will."

He took her arm and they hurried along to Temple Bar where they found the gates wide open and unmanned. Sarah was out of breath and they stopped to rest for a while.

"We must be very careful," he said, "the watchmen have fled already and that's not a good sign."

He studied the street ahead thoughtfully. It was dusk and the light was going fast; on cue the city church bells tolled out the curfew.

They pressed on, crossing the bridge over the Fleet, but at

Ludgate they came to an abrupt halt: for in the street in front of the high gate was a raucous host of soldiers. They edged a little nearer, keeping in the shadow of the buildings, trying to make out what was happening.

"They're drunk," whispered Will, "or most of them are; they're taunting the City watch at the gate."

They looked on as a fusillade of insults was fired; some men urinated enthusiastically in the direction of the gate, whilst others let fly arrows into the darkening sky. The City watchmen played their part in the strange performance, hurling a selection of the city's ample supply of dung over the rampart onto the men below.

Sarah turned away from the gate. "All I want to do is get home," she said.

"Well you won't get in this way tonight," he said. "It's nearly dark. Come on, it's not safe here; let's find somewhere to wait out the night."

They retraced their steps towards the Fleet bridge, but a drunken soldier caught a glimpse of Sarah as her cloak billowed out and he seized her by the arm. Will pushed him away, dragging Sarah with him across the bridge, but the scuffle aroused attention and in no time it seemed a dozen or so were following them back towards Temple Bar. On his own Will knew he could easily have outrun them, but Sarah was flagging so he stopped.

"Will, no! There are too many of them!" she said.

Yes, there are, he thought. He reached down into his boot and took out his long dagger.

"Here – take this," he said, "just in case."

"But Will –"

"Wait there!" he ordered and, before she could protest further, he quickly pressed a kiss to her lips. Then he pushed her towards a large stone archway on the south side of the street.

He hoped that the confidence of their pursuers would be shaken when faced with the sight of a long blade or two, so he threw off his cloak and drew his swords with an extravagant flourish.

"Come on, then; if you're coming!" he called out cheerfully.

They came to a faltering halt, strung out around him – only the way to the arch was clear. He knew how this would go: they would hesitate, then they would egg each other on without taking a step further, then one of them would break the spell and attack. The rest would follow. There were at least a dozen and some were quite well harnessed, but would they all fight? Some looked nervous, but so was he. The uneasy standoff continued for several more minutes. Sometimes, he had learned, if you timed it right, opponents could be turned by a sudden show of aggression. They would fall back, uncertain of their own mettle. He looked from one to another. Not this time, he thought, not this time.

He was wrong about how it would go: several broke at him at once and it took all his skill to dance his blades around them. He whirled at speed, scything through jack and flesh with one sword, clubbing and thrusting with the other. He was cutting and slashing until they began to fall around him, leaving their blood upon his clothes. He felt their cuts too through his padded jerkin, each wound sapping his strength as they stabbed at him from this side and that.

Out of the corner of his eye he saw a movement by the archway, but the light was poor and he wasn't sure. "Sarah?" he cried.

The rough edge of a heavy blade scored the front of his jerkin and he was forced to defend himself again. There was a scream from the archway.

"Shit! Sarah!" he shouted, but there was no reply. He could feel the anger building in him and he swivelled then, raking both swords around to cut a bloody path to the arch. Then he saw her, backed against a wall. She'd let the dagger fall. The man in front of her was laughing, calling out to the others. He struck her head against the wall, but it was the last thing he did. Will's thrust went right through him. The best part of a yard of inch-wide Italian steel was sliced in and out before he could even blink. He dropped at Sarah's feet. But

Will took a cut on his back and as he turned a sword point pierced his chest. He fought back, his strength beginning to wane. Sweet Jesus, he thought, would it never end? And then suddenly it did. The remainder fell back leaving eight or nine dead, or as near as, lying in a bloody heap in front of him.

"Go on, run!" he bellowed, "or you'll all feel my swords in your breast!"

He lifted his right arm to brandish a bloody weapon in case they should imagine he was finished, but they were already melting away into the misty darkness. He stumbled to the arch and leant back against the wall, suddenly feeling dizzy and weak at the knees. He lurched sideways through the arch, reaching out for the wall and missing it. He fell to the ground and found Sarah on her knees.

When she saw him she held onto him tightly not daring to look at his bloodied body.

"I couldn't use the knife," she sobbed, "then he hit me ... and you struck him .... and the blood just ... flew out of him! I'm covered in it; but you're hurt!"

"I'm fine," he said as he slid from her arms; she tried to catch him, but her hands were slippery with blood and he lay down on the wet cobbles. She bent down to lift him but he groaned, so she sat on the hard stones beside him. "Will, all I can feel is blood - where are you hurt?"

He chuckled grimly. "Everywhere," he murmured.

"You're going to bleed to death!"

She sat him up against the wall and tried to examine him, feeling for tears in his jerkin.

"Bleeding is good for you," he slurred.

"Not this much blood!" she said.

"It's not all mine. We should get away from the street."

"You sound drunk! We'll find somewhere to rest," she said.

Together they got unsteadily to their feet. She picked up his cloak and draped it over his shoulders.

"Where are we?" he asked.

"Somewhere in the middle Temple. Lean on me. We'll go down this lane towards the river again."

"Alone with a pretty girl, but buggered full of holes," he mumbled, "it's not right, is it?"

"No," she agreed tearfully and squeezed his hand. They staggered along the lane until they reached a small jetty. It was dark, but the burning houses by the river gave a fiery glow to the waterside. They peered at the moorings and there, to their surprise and great relief, they found several boats. But when they looked more closely, they saw that all the craft were beached on a pan of Thames mud.

"Of course, we'll have to wait for the tide," groaned Sarah.

"Bloody tide! What next?" muttered Will.

"Come. We'll rest in the trees back along the lane," she said.

The night was cold and they sat down together with their cloaks wrapped tightly around them. There they remained for hours, absorbing each other's warmth and trying to sleep.

In the small hours, Will awoke, shivering; he was back in the valley of Goodrich Abbey. All the misery of the freezing hours he had spent with Eleanor engulfed him anew and mingled with the guilt he felt as he shared the warmth of the young girl beside him. He couldn't shake the images from his mind, nor could he share them with Sarah.

She leaned in to him and kissed his cheek; it was wet with tears. "Will?"

He shook his head. "I'm alright but when we go down to the river … just be careful," he said.

They drifted in and out of sleep for another hour or two, but it was not yet light.

"Let's try the tide now," she said, "it must've already been on the turn for a while. By now the boats might be afloat."

"Can we land in the City? I mean, before daybreak – with curfew?"

"Well, I think we've good enough reason for being out, don't you!"

At the Temple landing stage they found one of the boats now bobbing slightly in the still shallow margin of the river.

"It's a small ferry; that'll serve," she said. Will looked at it doubtfully, but they clambered down to board it and he cast off. They took an oar each and somehow managed to direct the boat into the centre of the stream. Will found the rowing hard for it opened up his wounds and tore them mercilessly. Their progress was slow and it was almost dawn when they approached Trig Stairs. If there was a quiet time to land there then this was probably it, for there was no-one stirring anywhere near the wharf. A thin mist drifted up the river, but one or two lanterns were still lit.

"Somebody's going to think it strange us landing here now," said Will.

"No-one round here is going to care either way – and the watch don't venture near Trig overnight!"

Will had heard that Trig Lane had a rough reputation but now, just before dawn, it was as quiet as a crypt.

She added mischievously, "they'll just think you've been out whoring all night on the south bank."

"They might think I've brought one back with me!"

"Well, you haven't … but you've had my breast next to yours all night none the less!"

At that moment the boat bumped into the landing and bounced off but between them they managed to steer it back alongside. Clambering out of the ferry, tired as mules, they stumbled on the uneven boards and fell in an ungainly tangle of cloaks and legs. They rose shakily as far as their knees and held each other.

"I thought we'd never get back," she said softly.

"Do you know, I've spilled more blood today keeping you alive than I've ever done before or ever want to again," he said.

"I can see well enough now," she replied, touching his chest with her hands, "that you've taken more hurt than you wanted to tell me of."

"Never mind that now… let's just get you home."

She took his arm, only partly to support him, as they made their way slowly up the steps from the river landing to begin the long walk back to her father's house in Cheapside. As they neared their destination two burly watchmen stepped into the street a few yards ahead of them. They took one look at the blood-stained pair and blocked their path.

"What's your business?" one asked Will, "being out before the sun this morning?"

His companion leered at Sarah.

"I don't care to say," growled Will, for whom this was very much the final straw, "but I warn you not to get in my way this morn or I'll cut you down for it."

"Will!" Sarah gripped his arm more tightly as a warning. "Be civil," she whispered, "we're not criminals."

The watchmen seemed to be weighing up their options.

"I'm Alderman Goldwell's daughter," said Sarah, "and this is my father's renowned watchman!"

Will could see from their eyes that they had made the connection, noting his swords and northern accent. Their faces now bore the look of fear.

"I'm sure you have your reasons" stuttered one of them, "God give you good day!" The two watchmen disappeared at speed into the mist.

"A 'Good day,'", said Will, "I could really do with one of those."

They were exhausted when they reached the Conduit house in Cheapside, but Will opened the stopcock and filled a wooden pail with water so that they could wash some of the blood off their hands and faces.

"Better?" asked Sarah, lifting her face for him to inspect.

"I liked it before…" he replied, then he grinned at her and kissed her wet lips; she started to pull away but then returned his kiss with interest. They remained locked together against the Conduit wall, until they parted to draw breath. He took her hand and led her away.

"This has been a very strange day, Will," she said and put her arm through his again as they walked on to the goldsmith's house.

"What are we going to tell your father? There's your grandmother… and we're in a state, the pair of us."

"Father likes the truth. We've done nothing wrong – yet."

"Nothing wrong? I've killed a dozen men!" he said, but he kissed her gently on the forehead before banging loudly on the house door. The nearby church bells tolled out the start of the new day.

§§§

Much later when their story had been told and retold many times within the Goldwell household, Sarah sought Will out. He had been put in her own room and she had moved in with her younger sisters. He sat bare-chested on her bed whilst Hal bound up his wounds.

"Thank you, Hal. I'll finish it from here," she said.

"I'm only too glad to help."

"I'll manage." She smiled at him as he left and she sat down on the bed to examine Will's cut and battered torso.

"How do you take such wounds without crying out?" she asked, bending over to kiss his shoulder. He put his arm around her and drew her to him.

"I told you it wasn't too bad and it isn't. I feel a fraud sitting here on your bed as if I'm courting death!"

"You are most welcome courting in my bed, Will, whenever you please."

"Sarah Goldwell, if your father could hear you now he'd beat you out of his house!"

"Well, I think I know my father a little better than you Will. I think he'd like me to be chaste and he'd like me to be content, but above all else he'd like me to be married."

"And you think that taking a young man into your bed means he'll marry you?"

"No," she said, looking into his eyes, "but I think that if I took you into my bed, then you would marry me."

"This much I'll say. I've a duty to my lord and great friend, Ned Elder. I expect to join him soon in the army of York."

She made to speak but he put his fingers gently to her lips.

"Aside from this one duty, I have no others and I'm committed to no maid who lives in Christendom. So you may be sure that, if I do come into your bed, I will marry you."

PART FOUR: THE BLOODY MEADOW

43

York, mid - February 1461

Emma bowed her head and retched into the bowl for the third time. A trace of bitter liquid dribbled from her mouth. She had clung to the hope that the uncomfortable ride to York would make the nightmare go away, but it hadn't.

What was the word Ned had used when his favourite hunting dog was killed?

"Fuck," she whispered. Ellie had explained the word to her later. She would know, of course. Ellie should be with child, not her. God knows she had lain with half the men of the manor – or so she said. Still, the word seemed apt enough now for she didn't want Edmund's child. Who would?

The door slammed open and the prospective father stood on the threshold. He stared at her distastefully.

"You look like a cheap whore, though I've had much better looking whores! If you weren't carrying my child you wouldn't be worth your keep."

"How did you know?"

"Christ! The whole household knows! The cook at Yoredale told me first – why do you think I brought you with me?"

"Why did you?"

"Because I need to marry you just in case I should perish fighting for our valiant King! Perhaps you hadn't noticed but there's no Radcliffe heir. God, I need a woman!"

She stiffened.

"Not you! Mary!" he yelled down the stairs to the maid, "get up here now!"

"Get some clothes on and try to look as if you're a lady," he told Emma.

Mary hesitated in the chamber doorway. "My lord?"

Edmund took her by the arm and bent her forward over the bed where Emma had just sat down. He lifted up Mary's skirts. The girl tensed and squeezed her eyes shut.

Edmund turned to Emma. "I told you to get dressed!" he shouted.

"Come on," he said to Mary, "put a bit of effort into it – or do I need to persuade you?"

She hurriedly shook her head and spread her legs wider.

Emma could see it wasn't the first time Mary had been called upon to provide such a service. She turned away. This was a new humiliation - normally at least he used a different room. She dressed herself in the most sober robe she could find whilst Edmund abused the maid energetically a few feet away. She brushed away her tears, not sure whether she was crying for herself or Mary.

When he had finished Edmund sent Mary out and barked at Emma: "I'll tell you the hour of the marriage – it'll be soon, so be ready."

She reflected that being chained to Edmund by the holy bonds of marriage could be no worse than her present state. He would still take whatever woman he wanted and continue to treat her as he pleased so either way she was in bondage and there was nothing she could do about it. She had imagined that the wedding would be a formal occasion attended by some of the lords in the Lancastrian host. Edmund, however, had other ideas. The wedding, he told her, would be as brief a blessing as the laws of the holy church allowed, for he was to take his men to London with all speed. So all was done in haste for a good fee and her involvement seemed almost incidental. The vows were made and a few more words were stuttered through by a priest who smelt of ale and then it was all over. God knows, Edmund must have spent longer inside Mary than he did in their wedding chapel. It occurred to her that the marriage might not be legitimate at all. Perhaps it was simply a charade by Edmund to embarrass her further.

Almost immediately after the ceremony Edmund was gone, on his way south with the Queen's army. Emma did not quite believe that he would go but even this absence it seemed was to offer her little respite, for he made sure that she heard the simple instructions he gave to his men.

"I don't care what you do with her as long as she and the child she carries are still alive when I get back!"

But the guards were none too sure whether Edmund was serious or not so they appeared to decide that it was safer to leave her alone. As the days passed and she remained undisturbed she even dared to hope that Edmund would not come back at all. Only a few scraps of news reached them of the great royal army's progress. She was desperate to leave him but she already knew that without a willing accomplice she could never hope to get out of York and therein lay her problem. Even before there was not a soul who would risk crossing Edmund to help her, but now that church and law had bound her to him, escape seemed impossible. Then, all too soon, news of a glorious royal victory arrived and a few days later Emma's freedom was curtailed once more.

§§§

Edmund's journey back from London had been unrelentingly dreadful. He was cold, wet, hungry, and, above all, bitterly disappointed. The whole enterprise now seemed an utter waste of his time, with the final straw being their ignominious retreat, empty handed, from London. His misgivings about the campaign in the south had become festering sores during the long days he had spent riding back to York.

He arrived back in an evil mood and Emma did not have to wait long to feel the effects of his anger. He raged about the

York house bellowing insults at the top of his voice. It was as well the house had stout brick walls when he launched into a particularly vitriolic and unrelenting assault on the Duke of Somerset.

"Spineless, weasel hearted Somerset!" he shouted. "Why did we not march on London? All was within our grasp and was just thrown away!" He wandered, incensed, from chamber to chamber.

"Now I'm back in York I shall have to see the Queen and attend the royal councils of war – all that bloody tedium!"

But despite all his misgivings, he knew he must attend if he was to exert any influence of his own. His rivals in the council were already positioning themselves to take most advantage when the final victory was achieved. It forced him to advance his own plans more swiftly and he had thus dispatched Mordeur to Mawfield to soften up the French girl for a final questioning. He needed to know what that wretched girl knew if he was to put any pressure on his royal mistress.

§§§

During Edmund's frequent tirades Emma tried to play the loyal, supportive wife; but to little avail.
Most of his rage was still directed at the Queen's commander.

"His highness Somerset! That puffed up clown! He couldn't find a shithole if he was sitting on it!"

His anger railed on uncontrolled as he paced around his Hall whilst members of the household did their best to keep out of his way.

"All he does is wait. Wait! Wait! Wait! He's waiting now until our foes can put together another army, I suppose."

"I'm sure the Queen values your counsel too," Emma said gently.

Edmund abruptly stopped pacing. "Hold your tongue! What could you know about such matters?"

He cuffed her savagely to the floor. She was stunned and embarrassed, though she thought she might have been used to it. Henry, who was standing nearby, was shocked. He bent to offer her his arm as she rose but Edmund pushed him to one side.

"Don't bother! She knows her own way up from there!"

Nevertheless Henry threw her a brief glance of support and in her utter misery it shone like a beacon.

During Edmund's frequent absences from the house he entrusted Emma's safety to Henry who thus began to spend an increasing amount of time with her. For Emma, the presence of Henry was infinitely preferable to that of Edmund for she found him quite companionable. Unlike anyone else she had met since her abduction, he seemed willing to listen to her and converse with her almost as an equal. She noticed that when Edmund was present Henry acted more coolly towards her and part of her was intrigued that he was willing to conceal something from Edmund. For all that, she remained circumspect, for anyone so close to Edmund was most definitely not to be trusted.

One evening, a few days after Edmund's return from St Albans, Henry came to her chamber and knocked on the door.

"I'm not used to people knocking," she said as she opened the door to him.

"May I come in, lady?" he asked.

The single beeswax candle on the small table by the door flirted with extinction.

"You may do as you please sir, since my husband tells you so."

"Your husband isn't at home tonight, lady. I thought you might like some company but if not, then I'll leave you alone."

The candle leaned towards the draught, almost guttering. She tried not to smile at him, but failed. "Should I entertain you alone, I wonder?" she asked mischievously.

He looked momentarily disconcerted.

"No, you may as well come in," she said.

In the half-light they looked at each other awkwardly for

what seemed to her a long time.

He studied her sparsely furnished chamber. "You live in a nun's cell," he said, breaking the silence.

"Knowing Edmund as you now do, would you expect anything different?"

"Perhaps not, my lady."

He sat down on the one substantial item of furniture in the room, the bed.

"Not a bed for a great lady either," he observed.

"If you feel you need to tease me in his absence, please don't. I've had enough of that from him."

"It won't always be like this," he said.

"No, it'll be worse! I think I know my new husband a little better than you," she said bitterly. "He'll wait until his child is born and then he'll quietly get rid of me; and if his child is a girl, he'll probably get rid of her too. This is the lord you've sworn allegiance to."

"It wasn't my wish to upset you, my lady."

"Upset me? It doesn't upset me. The only question for me is the same one I've faced since Edmund first took me: do I wait for him to kill me or do I do it myself?"

Henry moved to take her hand in his. "Don't speak of doing so!"

"Then don't toy with me. You'd better go now." But she didn't shake off his touch and he showed no sign of leaving. They sat on the bed.

"I'd like to trust you, Henry. Can I trust you, I wonder?" But even as she asked it, she knew the folly of the question.

"I wouldn't," he said with a grin, "but I'd trust the others even less!"

She relinquished his hand and moved to stand by the south window, shuttered against the cold night.

"What do you want of me?"

Henry stood up and moved to the chamber door. "I have eyes, my lady. I've seen how you're treated and I don't like it. It's beyond what any lady should have to bear."

Emma smiled bleakly but made no reply.

"I only wish to help you, but if you want me to go, I will."
But he turned at the door. "Without help, you can't escape
him."

"You think I don't already know that! You wouldn't stand
against Edmund - only a fool would and you're not that."

"A fool," he acknowledged, taking a pace back towards her,
"or one who cares for you."

She turned away from him again. "You barely know me so
please don't tell me you 'care' for me."

"Well, believe it or not, as you wish," he said and before she
could respond he had stepped out onto the landing and shut
the door behind him.

She was disconcerted by his words; but then surely he was
simply playing Edmund's game.

§§§

Later that bitter February evening, Edmund returned to his
York house after another bout of prevarication with the
Queen's closest advisers. His mood was dark when he came
up to see Emma and she feared the worst, retreating into the
far corner of the room.

"Oh please!" he dismissed her fears. "I can do a lot better
than you in the middle of a town this size. There are at least
three noble 'ladies' who wouldn't say no!"

"Well I assume you came to me for some reason, my lord?"
she said for there was never an easy option with Edmund.

"Yes, I'm going to move you out - out of the town ... down
to Mawfield."

Why now, she thought at once, but was sensible enough not
to ask.

"In your condition, you need a more ... restful place... out
of the way."

So that was clear enough, she thought: 'out of the way',
where no-one would miss her after the child was born. She
tried to think how to approach this sudden change: was it a
threat or might it provide an opportunity?

"Might I be allowed a visit into the town before I go?" she

asked. "Perhaps the market? I'd like for once to walk outside. Surely it can do no harm?"

She expected he would reject her suggestion out of hand, and at first he looked as if he was going to, but then he seemed to think better of it.

"Very well," he conceded, "but only for a short time. York is a dangerous place just now, full of aliens, Scots and the like. And you won't go alone: Henry and some others will take you."

She was astonished, but pleased, that he had acquiesced so readily.

"And I've changed my mind. I could do with a bit of diversion tonight." He pulled her to him and, having wrung such a welcome concession from him, she knew better than to resist.

§§§

The following morning Henry attended on her earlier than usual.

"Our lord commands me to carry you off to market," he announced cheerfully, "but whether I'm to sell you or buy another just like you, he didn't say!"

Emma looked at him and smiled. She couldn't remember the last time she had smiled so often but she seemed to be doing it rather a lot around Henry.

"All is prepared, my lady; you've only to summon me when you're ready."

He did not have long to wait for Emma was excited for the first time in months, though she wasn't sure whether the cause of her excitement was the market or her escort to it. The house on Stonegate was not very far from the market place and Emma resolved that they should go on foot. The smell of the market reached them long before they could see any stalls through the throng. Winter foodstuffs were in short supply, but still Emma gratefully inhaled the cocktail of aromas the market provided.

"Isn't it wonderful!" she said.

"All I can smell is spilled ale and horse shit," said Henry.

"Now, what do you want to buy?"

"Buy? I don't want to buy anything. I just want to be here, feeling alive for a change!"

"Well, I can understand that," he replied.

She doubted that he could but let it pass. Her other gaolers were already lagging far behind them, leaving the responsibility to Henry, which suited her fine. She was secretly pleased that he did not seem to mind.

"Come, lady. We'll make our way right around the square." He took her arm and then, when they were amongst the crowd, he dropped his hand to take hers and squeezed it gently. She smiled without looking at him, but pressed his hand in response. They wandered around the market place, Emma' cheeks flushed and not entirely by the cold February air. She stumbled once on the cobbles and he seized her around the waist to stop her falling, leaving his arm there as they walked on. After a moment she stopped and let go of his hand. Pretending to take a keen interest in the poultry hanging from a stall, she bent and spoke softly to him.

"Be careful, Henry; we must not be seen too close in public – if Edmund got to hear of it he'd kill us both."

"You're right. I've been foolish, I'm sorry."

"You don't sound very sorry. We must be more discreet - and patient," she said gently.

They walked on but then Emma stopped, staring into the distance. A look of disbelief was on her suddenly pale face and she swayed and promptly fainted into his arms. Shocked, he lifted her up and shouted to some of the others who were amiably drinking at a nearby alehouse. Reluctantly they dragged themselves away and came to his assistance clearing a route for him out of the market place and into the streets back towards Stonegate.

"Is she still alive?" asked one of them nervously, "there'll be hell to pay if she dies."

"Of course she's still alive! She's just passed out, you fool, not died!" he snapped.

It took only a few minutes to get her back to the house and

when he carried her up the exterior steps to her chamber she was already beginning to come round.

"Leave this to me," he told the others, "but send one of the servants up to her chamber shortly."

As he laid her on the bed she was muttering to herself and crying.

"I don't remember ever doing that before; perhaps God's trying to tell me I should just concentrate on having this child."

"The faint - does something trouble you?"

"I thought I saw someone in the crowd today," she said, sitting up on the bed, fear in her eyes, "but you must say nothing to Edmund! Swear to me you'll say nothing to him!"

"But, what's this about?"

"It was probably only a trick of my crooked mind, but I'll tell you no more unless you swear to me."

"Of course I swear it – do you doubt me so easily?"

Still she was unsure. "I doubt anyone who rides with Edmund! Swear on what you love most - it matters to me."

"Very well, I swear … on my mother's life."

"It's not easy to put trust in anyone; safer not to," she said. But when she saw how miserable he looked she took his hand and kissed him on the cheek.

"In the town, at the market, I thought I saw my sister – and, it was the shock I think. But now I've had time to think and I'm sure I was mistaken. All I actually saw was a wisp of red hair under a hooded cloak. It could have been anyone but, just for a moment, I hoped it might be her."

"Where is your sister?"

"Sent away. A long time ago it seems."

"You shouldn't lose hope that you'll see her again," he said squeezing her hand gently.

She looked up at him searching his eyes.

"Henry, I'm not going to wait for Edmund to send me somewhere to die. I need you to get me out of York now!"

There she had said it. She left the words hanging in the air.

"Lady, you run too fast!" he said.

"Today or tonight," she said, almost breathless at the thought.

"But where am I to take you? And how? There are too many problems. We just can't rush madly out of the town – and we certainly wouldn't get out of the gates at night."

"You won't take me then."

He moved to the door. "Lady, I must think on this; there's much risk to us both here."

"Forgive me, I know I ask too much," she said, "but you've already taken a bigger risk: we've both concealed things from Edmund – and he's an unforgiving lord."

44

Elder Hall, mid - February 1461

Eleanor and Gruffydd rode beside the river until they reached Elder Hall and there her elation at returning home quickly turned to desolation. They had ridden across half the country only to find an empty shell, for the high walls had been reduced to rubble. She looked at Gruffydd as they stood in what had once been the Great Hall.

"I'm sorry," she said, "I thought perhaps Ned or Will might be here. It doesn't look as if anyone's been here for a long time. It's so bleak here, who'd want to be here now?"

"Lady, I don't regret one mile of our journey, so nor should you," replied the Welshman. "But what'll you do now? I'd advise we stay here at least for the night: there are a few dry places you could bed down..." He realized that Eleanor was no longer paying attention. She was staring beyond him to the ruined wall where the door down to the cellars stood open. He turned to look over his shoulder and saw a young girl in the doorway, a servant by her dress.

To his utter bewilderment the two young women suddenly screamed and ran towards each other, embracing like sisters and talking excitedly in floods of joyful tears. When they had calmed down, they walked over to Gruffydd arm in arm. Eleanor was as animated as he had ever seen her.

She grinned wickedly at him. "Becky and I shared many years together and some very ... personal secrets: she was the only one that knew about Will as I knew all about Harry. Both our fathers would have whipped us if they'd known!"

Gruffydd nodded but fearing that more revelations might follow he left them alone and busied himself preparing a place for Eleanor to sleep.

Meanwhile the two girls squatted amidst the debris of the Hall, suddenly overwhelmed by the memories of the place.

"I come here sometimes," said Becky, "I feel closer to Harry here because this is where we spent our last weeks. It seems so long ago now."

"Not so long... Will told me what happened."

"Will didn't see the worst of it. After Harry died, it just got worse - a long, long ... misery. And it hasn't ever stopped."

"Tell me all then," said Eleanor, so Becky spared her nothing of what had happened at Penholme. Eleanor hugged her closer and they wept like children.

"When we parted all those months ago, I thought I'd see you here in an hour or so," said Becky, "then when I heard you'd been taken, I never thought to see you again."

"Have you seen Will or Ned?" asked Eleanor.

"I've not seen Will since Penholme, but..." she hesitated. "Ned was here about two, or three weeks past."

"Thank God! How was he?"

"Ellie, I flew at him; I was so hard on him. I know it wasn't all was his doing, but ... if he hadn't come back... all my kin, my Harry too, would still be alive."

"Where was Ned going, did he say?"

"He was going after Edmund."

"What about Emma? Where's she?"

"She's probably in York. Edmund took her with him - he keeps her on a very short chain!"

She looked at the darkening sky. "I should get back to the girls. I don't like to leave them alone; they've been through enough."

"Are they safe?"

"Safe? Well they're at the castle, but they're not safe - no-one's safe on this manor."

"Who's left at the castle?"

"Only us, a few other servants and Durston, the little turd that minds it till Edmund gets back."

"Gruffydd could get rid of him for you?"

"I could get rid of the little shit myself but Edmund will come back and, if I cross him, he'll bring hell down on us. I don't want that for my little ones – not again."

"Come with us then!"

"If it was just me, you know I would but with the girls... They're safer where they are for now."

"Then let's pray that Ned finds Edmund."

"He found him once before, but he couldn't kill him and we paid with Standlake blood. Not much changes for us folk."

Becky hugged Eleanor to her once more and then hurried out of the Hall running up the hill towards Yoredale Castle.

"I'll be back!" Eleanor shouted after her. "I swear to you! I swear it to you!"

She watched Becky disappear from view at the top of the rise and then turned to help Gruffydd build a fire in the large stone hearth. She was grateful for his company and she owed him much. She hardly limped at all now for her leg was healing well and it was all his doing.

They slept that night on the filthy remains of rags and rushes on the floor of the hall and when the following morning dawned cold and drear, they awoke stiff and bruised. But during a restless night Eleanor had come to a decision.

"I'm going to find Emma and Ned; I know it'll seem a fool's errand to you but I'm going to do it. And, who knows, when I find Ned perhaps I'll find Will too."

"You'll be needing some company then for all this 'finding' you're going to do?" he said.

She smiled and patted his arm affectionately.

"I'd be long dead – several times - without you, but I think you've come far enough. You're a long way from home, Gruffydd."

"Pah! You've seen my home, lady! It's hardly much to go

back to, is it? I've nothing better to be doing."

She suddenly beamed at him and threw her arms around him enthusiastically. "That's what I hoped you say!"

Gruffydd uttered a long sentence in Welsh in which she suspected he was most rude about the wiles of young women.

"Becky thought Emma might be at York so I thought I'd start there," she said brightly.

"There's some sense in that but poking around the town will be no task for a lady!"

Eleanor merely shrugged her shoulders. "Tell me truly Gruffydd, when you look at me, do you think straight away: 'Lady'?"

"Well, perhaps not in those ill-fitting common clothes I got for you, but you always look like a lady to me."

"Well you're no judge then because, believe me, I've never been much of a lady! But whatever York is like, it can't be worse than Goodrich!"

"It'll be stinking with men of war."

"I can take care of myself a little - apart from getting out of freezing rivers. For that I need help!"

"Even so, stay well cloaked and keep your hair covered; or we'll be fending them off with pikes!"

She smiled, but then remembered how she had been captured at the river all those months ago. He was right: speed and spirit alone would not be enough. As they mounted to leave she scanned the wreckage that had been her home since birth. If she did return it would not be to Elder Hall, for that time and place had gone.

They struck out first towards Middleham and from there took the road south to York but they encountered very few harnessed fighting men.

"It looks as if the armies have gone south already or we'd be seeing hundreds more men," observed Gruffydd.

Instead they travelled along with those who followed in the wake of the armies: the pedlars, beggars and whores. They made their precarious living on the fringes of the bloody civil war.

"Best not mention your name," advised Gruffydd, "for if your brother is a thorn in the side of Lancaster then the name alone might be enough to get us into trouble."

They arrived at York just as the Bootham Bar in the north wall was about to close its gates for the night. They rode swiftly under the portcullis, but Eleanor stopped in wonder at the massive cathedral on her left hand, illuminated by torches along its great length.

"It's so tall! And long! And beautiful…"

"Indeed my lady there is much to marvel at in a city such as this."

It was a city however, where every tiny street seemed at that moment crammed with people and wagons.

"Folk are keeping to the town for safety," said Gruffydd, "it's more crowded than I expected – God knows what it'll be like when the army comes back!"

The poorer folk she'd noticed did not even attempt entry to the town and instead had camped in squalid disarray outside the city walls and along the river banks; and from there their noise and stench permeated to the very heart of the city.

"We'll never find lodgings," she said disconsolately, "we'll be sleeping in the street and be carried off by the watch!"

"Oh, I don't think so." Her companion grinned as he picked his way expertly through a warren of narrow streets into the north east of the city. Finally he found what he was looking for and pulled up at an inn where a disorderly crowd were gathered around the doorway haranguing the innkeeper.

"Ah, thought as much," he said. "Stay here, if you please, lady!"

He quickly dismounted and began wading through the onlookers towards the door. As he reached it, the innkeeper was knocked aside by two wrestling drunks who burst out of the door, locked in an angry scuffle. The crowd briefly went quiet and then parted as Gruffydd seized the two miscreants, one in each of his generous hands and slammed them into the door post one after the other. Then he tossed them senseless into the gutter and turned to the innkeeper, who had picked himself up.

"A chamber for my lady tonight and I'll see there's no more disorder in this house," Gruffydd proposed.

The bruised innkeeper had clearly had enough from his would-be guests and leapt at the offer.

"She can have their bed!" he agreed, accepting Gruffydd's outstretched hand, "as long as you can clear these folk. The bells have tolled and I've no more space – I've already let the stairs!"

Gruffydd's intimidating size and his actions so far were enough to persuade the others to seek accommodation for the night elsewhere.

The inn was unpleasantly overcrowded and hardly peaceful, but they managed to claim a space at the long table and secured some lukewarm pottage and bread to fill their empty stomachs.

"This is a good place to start our search for there's plenty here who'd sell gossip," said Gruffydd enthusiastically.

"Gruffydd you may not have noticed but we have little to buy gossip with!"

"Don't you fret about the details, lady. You'd best go and find your bed before the landlord sells it to someone else!"

"And where will you sleep?"

"Wherever I please! If you get into trouble, just scream!"

She laughed and a scruffy boy led her up to her bed which was one of seven in a large room. She was not surprised for Gruffydd had warned her what to expect. Setting aside the appalling stench that drifted up from the cesspit in the yard below, the room was not as bad as she feared; the other guests however, were. Though there was a couple in the bed on one side of her, the inhabitants of the room were predominantly male and when she took off her cloak and uncovered her hair, it was as if a lamp had been lit in the room for the men immediately stared at her. However, she set out her position clearly by taking out her small narrow bladed knife and thrusting it hard into the wooden frame of her bed. She hoped her new admirers had taken note.

It was not a pleasant night and she was awoken several times: the first when the husband from the next door bed, having gone downstairs to relieve himself wearing only his nightcap, clambered back into the wrong bed in the darkness and attempted to copulate with Eleanor. She slapped his face and then kicked him so hard that he screamed and woke up the whole room. Eleanor had her knife at his throat when Gruffydd rushed upstairs followed by the landlord holding a smoking rush light.

"Lady, was that you"? asked Gruffydd.

"No, someone made a mistake," she declared calmly as the unfortunate man's wife looked accusingly at both her spouse and Eleanor in equal measure.

"I'll thank you not to get me from my bed at the smallest inconvenience!" the landlord announced to the room in general and departed back down the stairs.

"Lady?" enquired Gruffydd.

Eleanor smiled. "Gruffydd – if I scream, you'll know it's me."

As the room returned to pitch black, she grinned as it occurred to her that when the unfortunate man limped back across to the correct bed, he might have difficulty in repeating the attempt with his wife.

She did not get to sleep for a long time though, as several of the rudely awoken guests decided to urinate from the window into the yard and kept her awake with their lewd suggestions as to what they would like to do to her if she would only oblige them. In the end universal snoring assured her that, for a time at least, she might get some sleep.

In the morning Gruffydd told a bleary eyed Eleanor what he had learned during the evening, mostly from the hostelry's servants.

"They see all sorts that goes on in the town, and they get the stories from others in service," he explained. He dared not enquire directly the whereabouts of Ned Elder, but he quickly established that Edmund Radcliffe had been in York and was expected to return from the war soon – along with thousands of others.

"That's excellent! If Edmund is still away, and Emma is at his house, then we can get to her!"

"We mustn't leap into this, lady. We know nothing about that household – how many are there, whether they're armed? No, we must learn more before we act."

The following day he left her at the inn and went in search of Edmund's house. To his surprise, finding it turned out to be quite easy but beyond that he found out little, though no-one was prepared to say much about Edmund Radcliffe and some made off swiftly at the very mention of his name.

It was hardly very encouraging and the day after Eleanor was in no mood to stay behind.

"You're safer here, your red hair makes you stand out!" he argued.

"Stand out? Gruffydd! You're as big as a cathedral! Don't you think you might 'stand out' a little? Anyway, I like to stand out and I didn't come here to just sit around all my days! I must be doing!"

"Well do some … sewing then!" was his terse reply.

Eleanor looked him in the eye. "If I had such a thing as a needle, I'd be sticking it in you right now! I don't sit showing my wares and waiting for a husband; I have to be moving, if not with you, then on my own!"

He was about to interrupt her, but she silenced him: "You agreed to come with me, not the other way round!"

"Very well, but let's say that there are some places you'd best not go - and you must keep your cloak over your hair!"

She smiled at him; the smile that had brought him all the way from the Welsh hills. Then she took his arm and they set off on foot to watch the Radcliffe house, passing through the market on their way to Stonegate. As they reached the house, he murmured: "Keep walking!"

Further up the street he pulled her smartly into an alley.

"What is it?" she demanded.

"Something's changed; our friend is no longer absent."

"What!"

"Look around you; there are men at arms everywhere – the army's back! You can be sure the house'll be well guarded now; we'll never get near your sister. By God, a day or two earlier and we'd have had the chance!"

There was a pause while she reflected on the consequences of this development, then "Shit!"

Gruffydd's eyebrows shot towards the heavens.

"Let's just go in and get her!" she said, "come on, give me your dagger."

"No lady, there'll be too many with her. We must think on this!"

"I'll go on my own then for I've no fear of Edmund Radcliffe!"

"Well you should have! If I've learned anything about him, it's that. Now come away - if they see you, we're dead!"

45

London, Late February 1461

A light fall of snow covered the ground and February was almost gone when Edward Duke of York's army left Chipping Norton and headed south towards London – and not a moment too soon as far as Ned was concerned. It took them several days to complete the journey and on the way they gathered more recruits fired up by stories of the brutal pillaging carried out by the Queen's retreating army. The Duke made his encampment in the fields at Clerkenwell outside London's city walls and there Ned had his first experience of managing his own contingent of men: if it wasn't fights, it was bad food, or drunkenness or outbreaks of some vile fever or other.

As Bagot told him more than once, "fighting's the easy bit; it's getting your men there in any fit state to fight that's the trouble."

In the evenings he invariably sought out Will Hastings who could always be relied upon to provide a welcome distraction with his armoury of amusing stories and his boundless good humour. But at the end of their first week in the City, it was Hastings that came looking for Ned in the company of several other captains.

"Come Ned," he ordered, with a glint in his eye, "official business!"

"If it's about the money you lent me at Hereford, I haven't

got it." said Ned.

"Coin? I don't remember giving you any coin at Hereford but if I did it was most certainly not mine! It would have been the king's - I mean the duke's - Edward's!"

"The king?" said Ned, noting the slip.

"Enough idle chat, Ned. We're in haste - we'll miss it if we don't hurry!"

"Miss what?"

"You'll see - come on!" And he would say no more as they left the camp at speed. They rode only a short distance into the City to Baynard's Castle, the royal fortress on the river which Duke Edward had made his headquarters.

"What's going on?" asked Ned as he hurried after Hastings.

"Hurry up!" hissed Hastings.

They arrived at the Hall where Ned recognised a large number of the duke's leading captains; he could also see that there were a good many local citizens present. Whatever was happening had already begun. Hastings scrambled into a seat on the fringe of Edward's council, whilst Ned joined a large group of knights standing at the rear of the Hall.

The Earl of Warwick was speaking and glared at those who were tardy especially when he saw that Ned was one of them. Nevertheless, he continued to address Edward.

"Your Grace, I therefore put before you a humble petition of the Lords and Commons together. We are as one in begging you to accept the Crown of this realm, rightful heir as you are; and we call upon you to take up the mantle of King and rid the kingdom of the usurper Henry and his wife, formerly called 'King' and 'Queen' of this land."

As he spoke many voices were raised outside, as Londoners shouted "King Edward!" and "God save King Edward!"

Edward didn't hesitate for a fraction of a second, but spoke out in a clear, strong voice:

"I accept your petition solemnly and I pledge to you that I shall restore to this realm the justice and rule of law that we have so sadly lacked in the usurper's time. I also pledge to hunt down Henry and his wife to prevent them from waging further war against our subjects so that we may finally bring peace to our troubled kingdom."

The cries outside were taken up at once by members of the council led by Warwick and others in the Hall. Caught up in the enthusiasm of the crowd, Ned too embraced the moment and hailed the new king. Their shouts were echoed by those braving the cold outside until at last their grateful king held his arms aloft, thanked them and sent them on their way.

"Come on, Ned!" shouted Hastings, "We're off to the taverns!" But Ned shook his head. He decided not to go with them, for he knew their raucous celebrations would continue throughout the day and probably long into the night. He would not have been good company for his mood had turned sombre; instead he rode alone back to the camp at Clerkenwell - not without some trouble since he'd yet to get to know London's streets. There he found that news of Edward's acclamation had already arrived and his men were in celebratory mood.

"Things are looking up," said Bagot in greeting.

Ned shook his head. "Are they? It's all very well Duke Edward being declared King, but it doesn't mean much if he doesn't survive the next battle."

"Well, true enough, battles can be dangerous Ned," agreed Bagot with a wry smile.

"Dangerous for me too," said Ned, "for if I'm dead, I'll get back nothing!"

He reached under his leather jerkin and felt the small piece of silk he'd kept in a pouch since Hal had given it to him – how long ago that was he couldn't even remember. It seemed that all he could recall now was blood and battle.

"I could've been killed at St Albans, yet I've done nothing! The Radcliffes still hold my lands; Emma's lost to me; Ellie and Will – I've no idea where either of them are. And Amelie? Well, all I have is the hope that I may see her again."

Bagot grunted: "You're still bloody alive, aren't you? Don't be in such a hurry to draw your last breath!"

"But everything I touch seems to turn to blood!"

"God's teeth, Ned, you can be a miserable bastard at times!"

Ned looked at him in surprise.

"In Christ's name! You're still alive with power to put things right!"

"Do you think it can be done, then?" asked Ned.

"Kill Edmund, get back your lands, find Will, your sisters and Amelie and stay in one piece? Of course not; it's fucking impossible!" He burst out laughing and clapped a hand on Ned's shoulder. Ned shook his head and had to laugh with him; and he felt a good deal better for doing so.

"Ah! Almost forgot!" said Bagot, "this came for you." He passed Ned a letter. "And don't blame me the seal's broken – it wasn't me!"

Ned turned it over in his hands for a moment. "But you've read it no doubt," he said.

"Aye, well I looked at it… an unsealed letter's clearly not private."

"But it was sealed when it was sent! Well you may as well tell me what's in it then."

"Er,… can't read very well, so I don't know. From a wealthy man though, I'm guessing."

"I don't think I've ever had a letter before – who'd go to the expense of writing to me?"

He opened it, though he was still irritated by the broken seal. When he'd read it he was more puzzled still.

"One of the City Alderman has asked me to call on him," he said.

"Why?"

"How the devil should I know, Bagot? I don't even know who he is!"

"Are you going?"

"Why not? You can come with me; Stephen and Bear can cope here."

"If we go now, we might get back before the city gates close," suggested Bagot.

"Alright, get the horses and we'll take a couple of men with us – not too heavily armed. We don't want to frighten the locals! Oh, and find out how to get to somewhere called Cheap."

He put the letter inside his jerkin, picked up his arming sword and waited for Bagot to return.

§§§

Bagot had been clever: he'd chosen a Londoner called Edwin to accompany them and the local man led the way into the city. With the celebrations still in full swing the city was even more crowded than usual.

"Which gate is this?" asked Ned, trying to get his bearings, as they jostled their way through the crowds.

"New gate, lord," answered their guide.

"Ah, I've been here before," said Ned, "earlier today! God's breath I didn't even know it! We could be going round in circles and I wouldn't know."

Edwin took them on through a labyrinth of narrow streets and lanes choked with people and animals. Their horses stumbled around a group of pigs rooting for food in the gutters.

"Hurry up man, this is taking far too long," urged Bagot.

"I'm trying to avoid the crowds," retorted Edwin sullenly.

"Well, you're not doing very well!"

Ned understood Bagot's concern: it was late afternoon and once the curfew tolled they would be in the city till morning. However, it came as a surprise when eventually Edwin announced that they had reached the alderman's house.

"At last!" said Bagot.

"Bagot, see to the horses; Edwin, you'd better find me an inn for the night," ordered Ned.

"The Mitre's nearby, lord," answered Edwin quickly.

"Good enough... see to it with Bagot."

He was a little apprehensive. A sudden message from a wealthy man that he didn't know was strange to say the least. However, Alderman John Goldwell greeted him warmly enough and Ned took a liking to him from the outset.

"You'll no doubt be wondering what all this is about," the goldsmith said, "but there's no real mystery to it. I have a young man in my employ who I think you know, Will Coster."

"Will? Will's here?" Ned was astonished.

"Indeed, he is."

"Safe and unharmed?" asked Ned.

"Well, more or less, yes. He's taken some wounds in my service, but he's mending fast."

Many questions occurred to Ned at once but he set them aside for later.

"Well, since he's still in my service, I'd like to see him," he said.

"Yes, to be sure... of course," Alderman Goldwell reassured him, "but before you see him, I'd like to ask you something."

Ned listened impatiently as the goldsmith explained his predicament.

"So, given the attachment between them," he concluded, "I'm anxious to ensure that Sarah has put her faith in a young man who will stand by her."

For a moment or two Ned said nothing. Will did not know it, but Ned was well aware of his friend's intimate relationship with his younger sister – and he knew Will had gone in search of Eleanor. Since then he had heard nothing, yet here was this apparently honest merchant telling him that Will had made some commitment to his daughter.

"Your silence gives me some concern," said the alderman quietly.

Ned shrugged. "I think I need to speak to Will, sir."

When Will came into the solar Ned embraced him like a brother. "By God, Will, I've missed you!"

"Well!" said Will simply, grinning broadly.

Ned noticed that a young girl was hovering in the door way - Will certainly had an eye for a handsome looking girl.

"Will, there are things we need to speak of," he said, "on

our own, I think."

His friend nodded. "This is Sarah – but you can meet her after…"

Ned gave a polite nod to the girl and she went out with her father.

There were two tall wooden armchairs with deep blue velvet cushions upon them in the solar; Ned ushered his friend towards them and they sat down.

"Luxury, eh?" said Will, waving a hand at the fine panelling and tapestries that adorned the chamber.

"You look pale; you've taken some wounds, I gather," said Ned.

"Ned…" began his friend.

"Will, what happened to Ellie? Is she dead?" asked Ned bluntly.

Will nodded. "God, it was a mess, Ned. Birches was killed too."

"Tell me."

So Will did so and he left nothing out.

"Ellie, dead." Ned could not conjure it up.

"I thought to do you a great service Ned, but I've not done so."

Ned searched his friend's eyes and saw the misery there.

"You've no cause to blame yourself. You did something to save her – that's more than I did. And I know how you loved her."

"Ned, after Ellie I was lost. Felix brought me here and now, somehow… well, there's this other lass, Sarah. I tried not to get involved…."

Ned shook his head. "You tried? Ellie's been dead, what… two or three months? How hard did you try, Will?"

"I can't explain it…Ned."

Knowing Will, Ned could quite believe it, but he couldn't find it in his heart to forgive his friend so easily.

"Now the alderman seeks my recommendation for you," he said, "and I don't find it easy. He wants to know if you'll be faithful to his daughter – if you can be trusted."

Will's face reddened. "I know I've disappointed you, but you can't say I've been anything other than the most loyal friend and servant!"

"Aye, that's true enough, but ... I need to think on it. I've still not quite taken in that my strong, beautiful sister is dead. Jesus, Will... I didn't ever believe she could be dead. Of all of us, she had such life; I don't think I ever expected her to die."

"What do you want me to do?"

"Stay here for now; I'm going to the Mitre – wherever that is – send me Hal at first light. I'll speak to you tomorrow."

He got up to leave, but Will threw himself to his knees. "Forgive me, lord! I did all I could to save her! I'm in your hands, as always."

Ned put a hand on his shoulder. "Aye, I know."

Bagot and the others were waiting for him outside.

"The inn's only at the end of the lane – more of a tavern really..." said Bagot.

"I trust I can get a bed there," said Ned.

"Yes, yes; it's all agreed."

"Come on then, I need a drink – perhaps more than one!"

The moment he entered the tavern, he didn't like it. It seemed popular with soldiers though for there were a good many men from the new King's army there.

The food was the worst he'd ever had and it didn't improve his humour.

"This chunk of bread's like a roof tile! And the potage – it doesn't just look and smell like dog's piss, it bloody tastes like dog's piss too! I'm not paying for that," he told Bagot crossly.

"You're not paying for anything – you've no money!" retorted Bagot with a laugh.

"In Christ's name, Bagot, I hope the ale's alright."

But Bagot was no longer listening for his attention was elsewhere and he was frowning. Ned knew that look only too well: Bagot had sniffed out some trouble.

"What is it?" Ned asked softly.

"The two men we brought with us... see where they're

442

sitting?"

Ned glanced at Edwin and his companion who were drinking with another group of men at arms.

"What of it? I'm happy enough they're not sitting with me!"

Bagot nodded, though Ned could tell he was still concerned. Yet, despite Bagot's misgivings, the evening passed peacefully enough and he was taken to a small chamber on the first floor where a thin straw mattress lay. Bagot had to make do with a heap of rushes and rags on the floor.

It was still dark when Bagot shook him awake.

"What's the matter?" he demanded irritably.

"I smell treachery," Bagot replied softly. "Something's going on – Edwin's not asleep in the Hall where I left him."

"Oh, leave it Bagot – just for once, just go back to sleep."

"We should go now – whilst we can," urged Bagot.

"It's still dark!" said Ned.

"Have I ever been wrong, lord?"

"Yes! Countless times!" Their discussion was interrupted by a knock on the door. Bagot opened it swiftly and Edwin appeared in the doorway fully dressed.

"I heard your voices, lord. Do you want me to saddle the horses?"

"Oh, very well –it'll make Bagot happy at least. Let's move!"

"Shouldn't we wait until the bells, lord?" asked Edwin.

"Sod curfew, let's just get going. Bagot, go and knock up Hal."

"That alderman won't be pleased."

"Well, it's your fault! Just do it!" said Ned, as he pulled on his jerkin and picked up his sword and belt. He wandered down the stairs feeling his way in the dark for the rush lights had long since burned out. He drew back the heavy bolts on the door, walked out into the lane and promptly dropped his sword belt which rattled noisily on the cobbles. He sighed and bent down stiffly to pick it up. He felt a rush of air over his head and something struck the door post with a thud. Still bent double, he looked back to see a crossbow bolt embedded into the timber. He turned to dive back into the tavern but the door banged shut leaving him alone in the dark lane.

Where the hell was Bagot? Come to think of it, if Bagot had gone to the Alderman's house, then the door would have been unbolted already. So where was Bagot? Where too was the crossbow, for its user had now had time to reload? He had to keep moving, so he crouched low to the ground and edged away from the door. Across the street were private houses, quite well-to-do – surely it couldn't have come from there. He reckoned one more bolt and then his attackers would close in on him. He was right: the second bolt grazed his shoulder and buried itself into the wall, then several dark shapes came towards him.

They took their time, moving around him and keeping their distance at first. Then they rushed at him. A buckler would have come in handy, but he fended them off with his sword and drew out the dagger from his boot. Cutting his way through them, he ran along the narrow lane seeking some space to fight but they followed him closely. He twisted and slashed to parry their blows, but they were no fools! Then, like a hilltop beacon suddenly catching fire, a sliver of light appeared above the houses: the first stirring of dawn. The bells would soon toll and there would be more folk about. It gave him a little confidence until he saw another three men at arms running to join the fight.

Shit, he thought, this is going to be difficult. He swiftly manoeuvred his back against a wall and held his sword out before him. He could see that he had already wounded two of them, but it did not seem to have deterred their comrades.

"If you know me," he shouted, "you'll also know that I'll kill every last one of you unless you give it up!"

Several of them smiled – it was not very encouraging. They knew who he was alright and they didn't care because he was their intended victim. They came at him again but he was ready for them. Scaroni had taught him by the Italian method - a school of patience: take the blow and wait for the opening. He had been a good student. He cut the first across the shoulder; the second caught the backswing under his chin. He swayed to avoid a thrust by the third and struck him in the face with his sword hilt. The next came at him and he ducked under a wild slash to stab him in the thigh with his dagger – blood spurted onto the ground as his victim cried out and fell. Another two launched themselves at him together and he scored the hand of one whilst raking his dagger across the face of the other. It was Edwin and Ned stabbed him in the eye, leaving the dagger pinned there, as Edwin screamed and dropped onto the cobbles.

There were two left standing, but Ned watched in disbelief as four more men came down the lane – there was an army of them. He could not retrieve his dagger and backed away as the newcomers surrounded him. He tensed again for the fight, arms aching, and then he smiled. Another figure had appeared at the far end of the alley and it was light enough now to see him clearly. His assailants suddenly saw the man too and turned uncertainly.

Will laid into them with his swords full of anger. They could not match his speed and he sliced them to pieces without mercy. Ned joined him and between them the pair cut every man down. Hal was soon there too, helping along Bagot who was bleeding from a head wound. Then the church bells rang and all was still.

Ned embraced Will. "You seem to have got even better at that," he said breathlessly.

"Hal got me up," said Will.

"Good. Now pack your things… and say your goodbyes, for now. We're going back to camp. I'll speak to the alderman."

He turned to examine Bagot's bleeding head.

"Pah! It's a trifle," said the veteran.

"Well, Bagot, you were right – this time. While I'm talking to the alderman, take a closer look at our friends."

§§§

When they rode back through York's camp Ned paused outside the Earl of Warwick's tent.

"My lord of Warwick!" he shouted. At once there was a commotion both inside and around the tent as Warwick's men at arms gathered to see who insulted their lord by bellowing at his tent. The Earl himself emerged from the enclosure.

"Should I have come out armed?" he enquired coldly.

"No, my lord. I regret to disturb you at this early hour but I've found something that belongs to you. I was anxious to return it."

Warwick looked surprised - as well he might thought Ned. He handed the Earl a rectangular piece of cloth, bearing the livery of a bear and a ragged staff.

"Well?" said Warwick.

"Is it yours?" asked Ned.

"Of course it's mine – all Christendom knows my badge, though I can't say the same of yours." He turned to his watching men, who sniggered at the slight. "Now where did you get it?" he demanded.

"I found it with this," said Ned, throwing an identical badge at the Earl's feet, and then he threw another, and another, and another, until he had thrown down ten. Then he stepped up close to Warwick and said softly: "it'll take more than ten of your men to kill me."

46

York, Mid-March 1461

It was still dark when Emma's chamber door creaked open.

"Edmund?" she said to the darkness. The door closed with another creak.

"No, not Edmund."

"Henry? Are you mad?" she hissed.

"Probably."

He sat on the bed, felt his way to her hand and squeezed it, but it only heightened her fear.

"Edmund will kill you! He'll kill both of us!"

"Do you want me to leave then?"

She didn't answer.

"Shall I leave?" he asked again.

"No," she said softly.

He lay down beside her cradling her in his arms and her fear melted at his touch.

"Emma -" he began, but she pressed her fingers to his lips; then she replaced her fingers with her lips. She succumbed to his caresses, letting him lie with her and love her until she was overwhelmed by a rush of feelings, all of which were new to her.

They lay together in the small hours without talking but in the end she had to ask.

"Are you going to take me away from York, from Edmund?"

She knew the question would cool their embrace, but she couldn't stop herself asking it, all the same. Henry didn't answer at once.

"I'm sorry, but why did you come if you won't -"

"Yes, I will," he interrupted her.

For a moment she thought she had misheard. "You will?" she breathed.

"Yes I will, but let's slow our pace a little; we mustn't act in too much haste. We must prepare well or we'll fail."

"Yes, you're right; we both know he'll come after us like a hunting dog. Are you sure you're willing to do this?"

In answer he kissed her.

"Leave the planning to me; I have a friend with a house not too far from York. If he'll let us stay for a few days, we can ride out Edmund's anger and make our way from there."

She hardly dared to believe. "Yes, I can see that might work; but many fear him - you must be careful who you speak to."

She got up, walked to the window and opened one of the shutters. As she thought, the sky was lightening over the hospital by the eastern gate.

"It'll soon be dawn. You should go before the servants see you in here."

"Yes, we mustn't give him any reason to suspect us."

She watched him go but couldn't return to sleep. The excitement shuddering through her body was churning her stomach to jelly. At first light she got up and threw back the remaining shutters; it was a bright morning. She looked back at her empty bed with a guilty smile. She found it hard to believe that she had allowed Henry into it so easily, but it had felt good.

"God forgive me, I'm a bigger slut than my sister," she said aloud. But Henry had given her hope.

She gave a start when Edmund suddenly breezed in.

"What's the matter with you? I'm your husband, remember? Make ready to leave the day after tomorrow," he ordered. "I want you out of the city in a safe place before battle is joined again."

Her mind boiled with unanswerable questions; did he know already about Henry?

"I'm grateful for your concern, my lord."

"Don't be; you're carrying my son. I want him kept safe before and after he's born – you, I couldn't care less about but if you do anything to harm my son, I'll tear you apart - slowly."

Emma swallowed hard. "I know, I know you will."

"Good! Be ready!" He strode out of the chamber without a backward look and she stood as if set in stone. Had he found them out? Was this his reaction? No, surely he would have done much worse – unless he was sparing her because of the child; perhaps he had already killed Henry. She tried to calm herself, but when Henry did not come to her all morning she began to embrace despair. When, several hours later, he arrived breathlessly at her chamber, she clung to him in disbelief.

"I was afraid he knew," she whispered.

"No, but I must attend on him now or he will begin to wonder. Then we must move very fast, my dear."

"How soon can we leave? Edmund's going to move me the day after tomorrow!"

"I know; be patient; I sent urgently to my friend and I expect to hear from him very soon. Be prepared to travel at an instant."

"Will it be tonight? Or on the morrow?"

"It'll be soon, soon. I'll come for you - be ready."

Emma forced a smile. "That's what he said…"

"I will come for you!"

"I know you will." She released him from her embrace and let him take his leave.

For the remainder of the day she saw no-one: both Edmund and Henry were elsewhere in the city on Edmund's business. Her nerves were taut to snapping point. She jumped in alarm when a door was slammed and froze in panic when voices were raised in the street outside. When the sun dropped in the late afternoon, she began to fear the worst, for she knew it was now too late in the day to go anywhere. All through the evening and deep into the night Emma thought Henry might come to her but he did not. She lay wide awake for hours, until exhaustion forced her to drift into sleep.

Just after dawn she was awakened by Henry sitting on her bed.

"No time to talk!" he said. "Edmund's waiting for me. Noon! I'll come for you at noon. Be ready – and dress for a cold journey."

He was gone so quickly that after a moment or two she began to doubt whether he had been there at all. She thought the morning would never end but at noon he duly came to her chamber. Even then she found it hard to believe that he was really going through with it and as he took her arm to guide her down the stairs her eyes filled with tears.

"I thought only a fool would help me," she said, "but I was wrong."

He squeezed her arm gently as they went out to the horses in the cobbled courtyard at the rear of the house. At every point she expected Edmund to appear and strike them down but their departure from the house passed without incident. They rode through the busy centre to the south side of the city and crossed the bridge over the river Ouse to leave by the Micklegate Bar.

When they were out of the city Emma's relief was palpable even though she knew they would not be truly safe for weeks. Henry had assured her that the initial journey would not take long.

"By nightfall, if all goes well, we shall be amongst friends," he said, "then we'll hide out for a week or two in this safe house until Edmund stops looking for us and then we can head west to the Marches where my family are."

"As far as he's concerned I'm carrying off his son. He won't ever stop looking for me and if he ever finds us..."

"Let's not fall into such a black mood, my dear. I'm sure it won't turn out as you imagine."

He smiled encouragingly at her and they rode on as briskly

as Emma could manage. She tried to remain cheerful for she was touched by his tenderness and constant care for her comfort; it was a new experience for her.

True to his word Henry got them to the house just before nightfall which was as well for Emma for, despite her thick woollen cloak, she was beginning to feel the numbing effects of the bitter weather.

"I trust my friends as you trust me," he said, "but just to be sure I'll go in and see that all's well. Watch for my sign and I'll wave you in if it's safe."

He left her waiting out of sight in a grove of low trees, near the gate. She was apprehensive enough for both of them for had he not told her several times that these first hours were the most dangerous. The light was fading, but she watched the house carefully: it looked newly built, beautiful. To her relief he emerged almost immediately and beckoned to her. She smiled with relief and at once trotted her horse through the gates. It was now almost dark, but a pale square of light from the open doorway welcomed her.

She waited a moment, then carefully dismounted and walked through the doorway.

"You might have helped me, Henry," she said, "I'm feeling so tired now…"

Her voice faltered as the great door closed behind her. She stared at the two men in the room, biting her lip so hard she drew blood; her head dropped and the tears ran freely down her cold cheeks. Henry was smiling at her, but she couldn't speak for beside him stood Mordeur.

47

Mawfield Hall, south of York, Mid-March 1461

The cellar door slammed shut and another beating was over.

Amelie lay still, taking in shallow breaths to ease the pain in her ribs. Her head felt tender all over and her left cheekbone throbbed, perhaps it was broken. Her left eye would not open; the eyelid was bruised and swollen. Still, there was nothing to see in the dark and she certainly had no more tears to shed. She had wept for the children at Penholme and for Ned when his body was torn and broken. She had cried too for little Margaret, and she had cried for herself until her eyes were scarred red and dry. Sooner or later, the tears run out.

She shifted her position painfully on the stone floor where they had thrown her. She tried to gather her dress around her but it was so badly torn that her modesty was compromised beyond repair - not that it mattered anymore. Her thighs still ached from the relentless assaults by Edmund's willing troop before they beat her senseless.

She must have been there for weeks now and it had been bearable at first; the solitude and hunger she had borne easily enough. But then the nightmare of abuse had begun: the core of her body had been so violated she was past caring what happened to her now. When she had given Hal that tiny, hateful square of silk she had made all this inevitable. Whatever Edmund still wanted from her, she had nothing left to give him.

In the darkness someone started weeping; when they'd

taken her out there had been no-one else in the room – in fact there had been no-one else in the room at any time. She lifted herself up on to one elbow and tried to focus her open eye onto the far side of the dark cellar.

"Who's there?" she croaked, her throat dry and hoarse. The pitiful weeping faltered for a moment but then resumed. She lacked the will to do any more and lay down again to give her aching body some rest. After a while the weeping petered out and she made another attempt.

"I am Amelie," she said, "who are you?"

There was some incoherent muttering, then silence once more.

"Won't you tell me who you are?"

The voice that broke the silence was small and sad: "Emma."

It took Amelie a moment or two to make the connection. "Emma? Ned's Emma?"

There was a rustling and scraping as Emma came over to her and seized her hand.

"Ned? My brother Ned?" she whispered.

"Yes, Ned: your brother, Ned."

"Ned's alive then." Emma sat alongside her and on impulse Amelie put her arms around her and held her as she told her in short, stumbling phrases how she knew Ned and related all that had happened since Emma had seen him at Yoredale Castle.

"Ned… always fighting on," said Emma, "but he would be."

"You're Richard Radcliffe's wife?" said Amelie.

"Richard's dead and gone - yesterday's husband. Richard's widow, Edmund's wife and now everyman's whore - a weak and stupid whore."

"You're Edmund's wife, and he's put you in here?"

Emma gave a grim, hollow laugh. "Better to be one of the dogs; he loves his dogs. They're well fed and he never, ever hits the dogs."

"What happened to you?"

"I don't want to talk about it - any of it."

They both fell silent then, exhausted and lost in their own miseries.

The following morning when the cellar door was opened, Amelie feared that another beating lay in store, but it didn't come and instead Emma was taken out. She was relieved for her, thinking that her incarceration had only been a passing mood of Edmund, but in the evening they brought Emma back to the cellar.

"I didn't think to see you back in here," said Amelie, hugging her close.

"Oh, I'm not forgiven – he made that very clear," said Emma bitterly. She flinched when Amelie stroked her cheek.

"I'm sorry," said the French girl. In the poor light she had not seen the bruises on Emma's face.

"A gift from my loving husband, who was not very pleased with me," Emma muttered, "and soon he'll kill me for my pathetic little act of defiance."

They took themselves to the corner of the room furthest from the door and sat in a huddle on the floor.

"Ned will come for me," said Amelie softly, "I know he'll be looking for me; and he'll find us, I know he will."

"It'll take him a lifetime to find this place. He'll find two dead, unlucky bitches - that's all he'll find," said Emma harshly.

"But we have to have hope ..."

"I had hope, but not anymore."

"You mustn't let Edmund break you," said Amelie.

"He broke me the first time he saw me. I amused him: he just loved doing his brother's wife. He's beaten me, raped me and with Henry's help he's broken me body and soul. I'm not even worth his trouble now."

"Who's Henry?" asked Amelie.

"Henry? I dared believe that Henry would help me, but all the time he was playing with me – just like Edmund. Why did he have to do that to me? Am I wearing a slate around my neck with 'slut' chalked upon it? Do I have 'whore' carved across my forehead!"

Amelie took her by the shoulders. "No woman should be treated as we have been," she said sternly.

She thought that nothing Emma could say now would shock her, but she was wrong.

Emma took her hand and placed it on her belly. "I have Edmund's child here ..."

Amelie shivered. "You're carrying his child and he keeps you like this?" she breathed.

"Oh, he'll make sure I don't starve; and if the child dies, so will I. You can't win against Edmund; but you know that already. I forgot it for a while ... I should have known better."

Emma pulled away from her and scuttled to the other side of the cellar to sit alone.

Amelie had run out of reassuring answers. She took a long, deep breath, though it hurt her chest to do so. She craved sleep, but every time she moved, her aching body woke her soon enough. Lying awake she thought of Ned, Will and the others, but there was little to cheer her: Will and Birches had never returned; and she herself had seen Holton struck down - poor Mags would be lost in grief. And what had become of Hal, her loyal Hal? He must have got away, or Edmund would already possess the little prize he sought.

Still, there was Ned. Surely he would come for her. She leant back against the unforgiving wall and dozed fitfully until the morning when the gaolers came again, but not for Emma.

48

Ferrybridge in Yorkshire, March 1461

Bitter, sleet laden winds swept Ned's company along the river Aire. They thundered across the old bridge at Castleford and then followed the much swollen river east past the fulling mills working feverishly by the chill waters. Within an hour they had reached Ferrybridge and Ned was heartily relieved to find the wooden bridge still intact.

"Well, there it stands," he said, "now all we've got to do is keep it that way until the 'noble' Warwick and the rest of the vanguard get here."

There had been rumours of a Lancastrian raiding party along the river and he didn't intend to be caught out. "Keep a good watch out!" he shouted.

"This isn't going to let up in a hurry," said Bagot, wrapping his cloak tighter around him. Ned glanced at the grey sky: he supposed Bagot was right. It was only early afternoon and the light was already poor. The journey from London had taken several days but somehow it had seemed longer in the wintry weather and he knew his men were tired and fed up.

"We'd best get the men doing something useful," he said, "Bagot, take half of them across to the north bank and set up camp there. Stephen, secure this side with the rest."

He had found much to admire about Stephen Orton since St Albans. He had a calm way with him that the men prized highly. Bagot had not moved and Ned was not slow to recognise the signs.

"Well, what is it?" he demanded wearily.

"The north bank's a poor place, lord – we'll be in the open and the trees to the north give every advantage to our enemies," he complained.

"Even so, we daren't leave the bridgehead unguarded. But you're right, we'll take everyone across and send out double the usual scouts."

Bagot nodded a little more cheerfully and started to lead the men at arms and archers across.

It was almost dark when the Earl of Warwick arrived. He merely glared at Ned and ordered his command tent to be erected. He left the deployment and organisation of his own men to his capable aide, Lord Fitzwater, and by nightfall the last of the baggage and spare horses had been brought across the bridge. In the evening the temperature plummeted and they settled down for another freezing night in the open, for the vast majority of the men did not share the luxury of Warwick's of a tent.

Ned could see that Bagot was still edgy.

"We've done all we can," he said.

"I know," replied Bagot.

"You still sound worried," said Ned, "should I be?"

Bagot nodded. "The forest is so close…"

"I might take a ride into those trees," said Ned.

"The scouts have reported nothing out of the ordinary," said Stephen.

"It can't do any harm though," said Will.

Ned paused for a moment. "Stephen, Bagot: stay here and keep a lively watch. Come on, Will; let's take a closer look."

They rode off to the north, taking their time. Their horses snorted unhappily as the wind tore at them from the north east and Ned could already feel that his cloak would not be thick enough.

"We'll do a circle from west to east," he said and he picked a line into the trees where they got some shelter from the wind. They threaded their way westwards walking their mounts carefully and quietly. They had spent half their young lives in the forest of Yoredale and they knew every woodland sound; if there was any trace of man or horse they expected to find it. After a while Ned pulled up and Will stopped close by; they listened but there was only the wind teasing the branches.

They set off again but their sweep to the west and north discovered no evidence of trouble and, when they had finished the easterly leg of their circuit, Ned gratefully turned south to return to the river. He was tired and they had taken so long they'd have little time to rest before dawn.

"It's a damned cold night for this," breathed Will, "but at least the wind's on our backs now."

But after a few more yards they stopped. They had both heard it, carried to them on the wind.

"Horses, moving through the trees!" said Ned sharply, "behind us to the east."

"Run for it?" asked Will.

Ned considered for a moment. "No, we'd better see how many there are first. There's no point in panicking if it's only a small patrol."

He drew his horse further back to wait where the trees were thin but tightly packed. Soon they could hear the familiar rattle of harness but, though they scanned the dark trees for movement, at first they could see nothing. Then Ned spotted the leading horseman - the first of many and even through the trees he could see that the men were harnessed for battle. They watched the column of riders pass slowly by less than thirty paces away and it seemed to take an age to pass. This was no small patrol.

"There must be hundreds of them! Could they be ours?" asked Will.

"What? Sneaking through the woods in the early hours of the morning? No, they're not ours but they're heading for the bridge."

"Shit!" said Will.

"Can't argue with that," said Ned, "come on, we'll have to

cut south and ride along the riverbank to warn the others. As long as they keep up the same pace, we should reach the bridge before them. They'll be aiming to attack at first light."

But the forest to the south was dense and overgrown and it took longer than Ned expected to reach the banks of the Aire so that as they raced westwards towards the bridge, the first glow of dawn was already on their backs.

"It's going to be bloody close!" Ned shouted, urging his horse on. He could see the bridge, but he knew that the trees lay so close to the river that the enemy could fall upon the sleeping camp with the suddenness of a lightning strike.

As they neared the bridgehead in the dim early morning light they began shouting at the top of their voices but their voices did not carry. At first glance the camp looked deserted for most men were asleep on the ground, swathed in their cloaks or blankets. It was the sentries on the bridge who first saw the pair thundering towards them. Ned was gesticulating wildly and the guards started running towards Warwick's command tent.

"Never mind him, wake the men!" bellowed Ned, still fifty paces or so away.

He looked across to the north. "Oh, shit! They're coming, Will!"

They burst into the camp, cajoling the men awake as they went through.

"To horse!" shouted Ned as he rushed past Bagot. "Bagot! Get the men up!"

Even as he heard Bagot bark out his orders he saw the mounted Lancastrians emerging from the forest and arcing down towards the camp. Warwick came out of his tent, with a squire trying to harness him as he moved.

"What treachery is this?" he demanded.

The attacking horsemen drove right through the shocked Yorkist men at arms using their lances to bloody effect. Many of the men wore nothing but their padded gambesons or leather jerkins and dozens fell in the first charge.

Another wave of horsemen came in and Ned paled when he

saw them.

"Mounted archers!" he warned, but it was to no avail as a storm of arrows poured into Fitzwater's men as they struggled to get themselves into some sort of battle order. Men dropped to their knees, breeches half raised, swords still in their scabbards.

"Rouse yourselves!" barked Fitzwater as he and Warwick struggled to rally their men; for the archers were taking a murderous toll of those not yet harnessed.

"We have to do something!" Will yelled. "I'm taking them on!" He rode directly at the archers.

"Jesus, Will!" muttered Ned, but he was obliged to follow his friend or abandon him. Together they hacked their way into the shocked archers and sliced their blades into the lightly armoured bowmen, halting their charge. Some turned aside and scattered back towards the trees but elsewhere on the field the fight was turning into a massacre.

"Will!" Ned shouted, "We must rejoin the men! We can do no more here!"

They turned about and cantered to the bridge where a swirling melee had formed around the defenders; the blue badges of Fitzwalter were heavily outnumbered by the white ones of the enemy.

"Oh, Jesus!" Ned exclaimed. "I've seen those badges before: it's bloody Clifford again!"

They had to force their tired horses through the Lancastrian ranks to get to their own. Then they quickly dismounted and joined the ragged line hastily drawn up by Stephen and Bagot. On the ground there were countless wounded including Fitzwalter himself who had not had time to don so much as a breastplate. He had been dragged behind the line bleeding horribly from a chest wound.

"We need to get to the bridge!" Bagot shouted. Ned realised then that the first wave of Clifford's men had charged straight through the camp and taken the bridge making short work of Warwick's guards.

"They're already taking it apart!" said Stephen.

"We have to retake the bridgehead anyway or we'll be cut to pieces on this bank!" urged Bagot.

Ned searched the chaos for Warwick; the main assault had come at Fitzwater's men, many of whom had perished in the first few minutes. Warwick's men were on the left flank and with relief Ned saw that the Earl was rallying his soldiers. They were driving a wedge through Clifford's force to join the remainder of the Yorkist force.

"Stephen, get your men moving back to that bridge!" ordered Ned, "Hold the line here, Bagot, but be ready to fall back."

"Ned! You go on to the bridge," Bagot called to him, "Bear and I can hold them here for a while!"

Ned waved his sword in hasty acknowledgement and then turned to club down a man who had broken through. He hurried with Will to the north end of the bridge which was still held by Clifford's vanguard. Stephen's men were already trying to batter their way through. Ned brandished his sword aloft, yelled out his name and thrust himself forward to face the front rank of the enemy Around him the cries of "For Ned!" and "Ned Elder!" rang out from his own men at arms and he swung his sword with all the venom he could muster.

Soon he found Warwick beside him in the thick of the fighting. It was the first time he had seen the renowned Earl in battle and he was a powerful warrior. Together they carved a brutal path through their enemies and retook the bridge, but at a bloody cost. The boards at the north end of the structure were wet with blood and the dead lay in piles on the river bank or tumbled into the water to float away downstream. Bagot and Bear joined Ned having led a brave rearguard, but their losses too were heavy and almost every man carried a wound.

Warwick quickly took command.

"We must hold the bridge – at any cost!" he ordered. "King Edward will have this bridge or I shall die here upon it!"

For all the contempt Ned had hurled at the earl, he had to admit that he certainly did not lack courage. But just as it seemed they had wrested the initiative from the enemy, a deadly shower of arrows fell upon the men at the bridge. Ned heard Warwick curse and turned to see him go down on one knee having taken an arrow in the calf – and he was by no means the only casualty. Warwick raged at the heavens and cajoled his men mercilessly but when the arrows stopped Clifford's men at arms pressed forward once more.

"We must hold the bridge! Hold the bridge! Stand with me!" Warwick bellowed, though he could hardly stay on his feet. The ranks around him were being prised apart, punched into from two sides and forced back upon each other so that those who were not cut down fell back into the freezing river, where they succumbed helplessly to the cold.

"Hold the bridge!" Warwick still screamed, though most of his men lay dead or bleeding around him. The survivors looked desperately towards Ned: they knew there was an all too obvious escape route across the bridge but at the price of surrendering it to the enemy who would surely then destroy it. Ned took a risk and clambered quickly up onto a timber rail of the bridge to survey the field; an arrow thudded into the wooden joist by his head and he jumped down again. He had seen enough: they were hopelessly outnumbered: it was retreat or be butchered at the bridgehead.

"Bagot!" He roared above the clamour, though Bagot was almost next to him.

"Get as many back across the bridge as you can! I'll get you some time."

"But the Earl said -"

"I know what the Earl said but it can't be done. Now, do as you're told!"

Ned hastily gathered some of his strongest men around him.

"Bear!" he shouted, "make a hole!" And Bear did, swinging his long handled battle axe in a great bloody arc slicing across three men at arms in one terrifying blow. Ned moved to his right flank and they hacked their way deep into the enemy ranks in a blizzard of blood until Clifford's men were forced to give ground. Just for a moment Ned thought they might do more but all too soon their surge forward came to a halt. Ned recognised the black armour of Lord Clifford in the centre of a powerful knot of opponents but he could not reach him. They had bought a little respite but that was all.

He snatched a glance behind him and saw that the orderly retreat across the river was under way despite the angry presence of Warwick who threatened to cut down any of his own men who set foot upon the bridge. Now that Bagot's men at arms were crossing Ned's tight group of warriors had to get out before they were cut off.

"Fall back!" he ordered, "And keep your order!"

When he reached the bridge Warwick staggered to his side in a blind rage.

"You bloody fool! You're giving them the bridge!"

"Fall back, my lord, or we'll all be killed!" said Ned coldly.

For an instant he thought Warwick was going to hit him with the heavy battle sword on which he leant but the Earl conceded and stumbled back across the bridge angrily shrugging off those who offered to support him.

Ned shepherded the brave men of his shattered rearguard onto the bridge. He looked back and as soon as he saw Clifford's men stop short of the bridge he knew what was coming.

"Arrows!" he shouted and drove his men on faster though some of the wounded could only hobble. There was a sudden moment of quiet when all he could hear was the desperate thudding of boots on wood and then scores of arrows tore into the bridge and those upon it. Men dropped all around him whilst others tried to weave their way across. Ned was almost to the other bank when he turned to see how the others were doing and an arrow struck him full in the face, knocking him off his feet and jarring his skull on the timber floor of the bridge. At once Bear gathered some men around Ned to get him up and carry him off the bridge.

"Archers to me!" Bagot growled and formed up a group of bowman at the southern end of the bridge to return fire for long enough to cover their retreat.

Gradually the wounded were taken to the rear and the front rank dug in at the tree line south of the river: they could stop the Lancastrians crossing, but could not prevent them from destroying the bridge timbers on the north bank.

Bagot swiftly wrenched off Ned's helmet and examined him. The arrow point had pierced the slot of his visor and lodged a tiny distance from his right eye. Ned brushed him aside and tried to stand but fell at once onto his knees, still dazed from the blow. His head was throbbing and his ears ringing.

"I'm all right!" he snapped, "thank God - and Holton's skill!"

"Sodding lucky – as usual!" announced Bagot and there was a muted cheer from his men.

Ned looked around at the survivors in disbelief: it was a disaster and the mood in the ranks was murderous. It was scarcely an hour since they had been asleep on the north bank – where all their meagre resources still lay. More importantly, they had surrendered the bridge. Across the river beyond the dismantled north end of the bridge he could still see several pennants, including Warwick's and Fitzwater's, fluttering forlornly over the corpses.

"What are our losses?" he asked.

"About half," answered Bagot gravely.

"Half? Jesus!"

"The Earl's not happy," said Stephen.

The Earl was in fact incandescent with rage as Ned discovered when summoned to a new command tent that had somehow been hastily erected south of the trees where the remainder of Ned's own men now rested.

"Yes, my lord?" said Ned testily as he entered.

"When I was wounded, you gave up the God damn bridge! Why? That bridge is the only reason we came here!"

"We couldn't hold it, my lord, there were too many."

"Too many?" sneered Warwick, "there are never too many! You just have to kill more of them!"

"They were too strong and the rest of my men would have

been slaughtered to no purpose."

"Your men! Your men? They're the king's men, not yours!"

"I fight for the king, and they fight for me; either way there'd be fewer of us to fight for him!"

"Your loss of nerve may cost this new king his throne!"

"Clifford had us cold."

"Clifford? Clifford? Clifford's a mere mortal like the rest of us! You should have fought harder, not run before him... I can see now how it was before!" He glared at Ned.

"Don't talk to me about St Albans!" Ned raised his voice. "I will never fight alongside you again... my lord!"

He stormed out with a livid Warwick roaring after him: "What do I care whether you fight or no? I shan't forget this further insult! You may be sure my cousin, the king, will learn of your cowardice! You'll hang by morning!"

49

York, Late March 1461

Eleanor hated York. It was crowded, noisy and dirty – in fact everything she disliked was wrapped up and enclosed within its thick city walls. Once more Gruffydd had left her at the inn whilst he kept a watch on the Radcliffe house on Stonegate. It was the fourth day and Eleanor's patience, easily tested at the best of times, was wearing perilously thin. She had walked out in the morning through the busy market and right up to the east gate but the cold wind and sleet had driven her back to the inn during the afternoon.

That evening Gruffydd returned cold and sodden to the inn where he found Eleanor hungry for news.

"Well?" she demanded.

"Yes, lady, thank you for asking: I'm quite chilled to the bone."

"I'm sorry Gruffydd but I just need to know!"

"Well, let me tell you then. Did I see your sister? Yes. Did she look well? No. Was she heavily guarded? Yes. Was I seen? Most likely, yes. I think that covers my day's work well enough!"

"You make it sound as if she's a prisoner," she said glumly.

"If she's not a prisoner then she certainly doesn't get out very easily."

"And you think you were seen?"

"Perhaps and, if repute is anything to go by, the power of this Lord seems to reach a very long way so we must be on our guard. Still, as long as they only know about me, there's no reason for them to imagine that you're here so we still have an edge."

"Not much of one! What next then?" asked Eleanor.

"We must expect they'll be watching me so it might be better if we aren't seen together."

Eleanor gave him a look of disdain. "I can take care of myself," she said.

"Probably," he conceded, "but I saw you in the town today and I thought we'd agreed you'd stay here."

She felt as if a favourite tutor had scolded her. "I went only to the market so don't worry."

"I know, I saw you there."

"Why were you there?" she demanded.

"I was following your sister – she was in the market place too. Did you see her?"

Eleanor saw the concern in his face. "No, I didn't."

He nodded thoughtfully. "It would be a rare stroke of ill fortune if you were seen. If you didn't see her then it's most likely she didn't see you."

"If only I had! We need to get to her somehow. We must find a way to talk to her - perhaps if she's out again. But she's well-guarded you say?"

"Well she had an escort if that's anything to go by."

"I should try to get in to see her."

"No! For God's sake, girl! You've only just escaped from them! If they find out who you are, they'll grab you straight away and then where will our fine plans be?"

"Gruffydd ... we haven't really got any fine plans, in fact we've no plans at all! Whatever I thought I'd do when I found her it doesn't seem so easy now. I've no idea what to do. Perhaps I should just go to her – even if I'm taken, at least we'll be together."

He took her by the shoulders. It surprised her for she couldn't remember him ever laying hands on her before.

"Listen to me, lady," he said solemnly, "I didn't drag you out of that stream so that you could give yourself up to your enemies so willingly! Swear to me you won't do anything so rash!"

She smiled at his concern. "Emma would say everything I do is rash!"

"All I've heard about Edmund Radcliffe is bad and it'll do us no good to give him another prisoner."

He still looked horrified at the thought, so she rewarded him with a tiny smile that softened his grave face.

"Believe me, Gruffydd, I'm very, very happy to be alive but I've never been very patient. Let's think on it and decide what to do tomorrow."

He nodded and she climbed the stairs to her crowded bedchamber. Normally she would have been irritated by several irksome new arrivals, but her mind was elsewhere. She had not cared to tell Gruffydd of another impetuous act when she had lain with Will the night they had freed themselves at Goodrich. In the past few days she had been feeling unwell and she suspected she knew why. It could of course be a fever she had acquired at the inn but she doubted it. In her heart she knew she was carrying Will's child and she was overjoyed but she dare not tell Gruffydd for he would never let her out again. But if she was with child she would bear the child with strength and pride, not fear. She knew that plenty of the village girls had continued their regular heavy work – she'd even heard of some who hardly paused to give birth!

In the morning Gruffydd was adamant that he would observe the Stonegate house once more and if he saw an opportunity he would try to get Emma out. Eleanor was feeling wretched, so she reluctantly agreed and did not stray far from the inn all day. The same happened for the next two days, but in the evening he returned once more to the inn he seemed more tired and despondent than ever.

"No sign of her at all today, lady. I'm beginning to wonder if she's still in the house at all. I haven't handled this very well," he confessed as they sat down at the long table to eat.

"I'm sorry, lady. I was foolish enough to think that I could get your sister back but in God's truth I'm not up to the task."

He looked worn out and she felt guilty that she had so utterly taken advantage of his devotion. She laid her hands on his across the table.

"Don't vex yourself so. I've pressed your loyalty too hard and it's me who should be sorry."

"This isn't my strength," he said bitterly, "give me a mace or an axe and I could fight better than most but this skulking about is not for me."

She squeezed his hands again. They remained downstairs for much longer than usual, sitting at the table for hours after they had finished their potage, bread and cheese. The inn was choked with travellers, and Eleanor did not relish taking to her bed too soon. So they talked all evening but they resolved nothing.

"Time I retired," she said, seeing that many of her fellow guests had already done so. He reached for the pot of ale on the table in front of him and raised it to his lips to drink her health. She smiled broadly for it was a gesture typical of this warm hearted giant. The landlord nodded to her and handed her a rush light, but as she turned to go up the stairs the inn erupted into chaos.

At first she assumed it was the usual drunken patrons but then she realised that Gruffydd had been set upon by several men armed with clubs. Platters of food and jugs of wine were sent spinning across the room as he was knocked down onto the table. Then two men came towards her and she knew this was no random attack. She swiftly drew her knife and stabbed one under the ribs as he tried to grab her but the other seized her wrist forcing the blade from her hand. She slipped from his grasp and banged his head against a wall timber. Another now faced her – one she had seen before, many months ago, in another world.

"You?" she breathed, as the fleeting memories from Goodrich leapt suddenly into her head. He moved fast and put his knife to her throat. Gruffydd wrestled back his assailants and succeeded in disarming one of them but then he turned towards her and gasped. Reluctantly, he dropped his weapon and someone cracked him hard on the skull.

§§§

There was a glimmer of light from under the doorway, but it slowly dimmed and the darkness returned. Amelie leaned back against the wall again. The room was ice cold but her body was burning, burning with pain as it had been since they had tossed her back into the cellar a few hours before. If Mordeur was not there the men made no effort to question her; they were content simply to beat and rape her. Amelie could not remember ever hating anyone but she hated these men - really hated them and wished the worst kind of brutal punishment to fall upon them.

Emma stirred, her sleeping head rested in Amelie's lap. They had been given a blanket but Emma had insisted on wrapping it around Amelie. They both knew that it did nothing to ease her suffering but it was an act of love and it was the first one she had encountered at Mawfield.

Footsteps sounded outside the door and then the bolt was drawn back noisily. Her body tensed and she held her breath. The door opened and a flicker of torchlight intruded into the room. With it came several of Edmund's men at arms who between them dragged a large, bloodied man in chains and a young girl. The girl was unconscious and they bundled her none too gently onto the stone floor. The man seemed dazed but the soldiers treated him warily and before they left they secured his chains to a beam in the ceiling, leaving him hanging by the wrists.

Amelie stared at the men who had beaten her earlier; they looked unusually nervous.

"What the fuck are you looking at?" growled one of them. "Do you want some more, then?"

She shook her head and turned away to stare instead into the far corner of the room. They went out, slamming the door behind them.

Something had changed. They made threats but they didn't do anything – why not? It was as if they were waiting – but what for? Amelie shook Emma awake and crawled over to the body of the girl. She was out cold and her breathing was shallow.

"Lady?" said a gruff Welsh voice.

With difficulty Amelie got up, unsteady from the cramp in her legs, and moved to where the other new prisoner hung from the beam. Finding him by touch, she clasped one of his large hands in hers and then ran her fingers over his face and hair. Her fingers felt sticky and she could smell the blood on him.

"Who in God's name are you?" he demanded, "you're not Lady Eleanor!"

"I'm Amelie and I'm trying to find your wounds. Are you in pain?"

"Of course I'm in bloody pain!" grumbled Gruffydd.

"I'm sorry. Who's the girl?"

"The Lady Eleanor, is she alright?" His tone at once became tender and concerned.

"I don't know, I can't wake her yet. How have you come to this place?"

"It's a terrible mess," he choked the words out, "and the fault is all mine."

Emma had been listening and went to crouch beside the girl. "Ellie?" Emma caressed her sister's face and sobbed. "Not my Ellie, please – I would wish you anywhere in all Christendom but here..." She moaned like a wounded animal and cradled Eleanor in her arms. Her sister came to and sat up, eyes slowly adjusting to the light.

"Emma, but how can it be you?"

The two sisters embraced and their bodies merged in the shadows, laughing and sobbing all at once. Neither could speak coherently and when they tried to talk, they couldn't find the right words. Instead they leant against each other, heads resting together.

It was a cruel concoction, thought Amelie, joy and despair. Emma was drained but the younger sister sounded stronger and soon she started chattering nervously through random fragments of what had befallen her. At first she left them to each other but later she joined them and they huddled together like small children.

"Ned will come for us," she said to the others with quiet confidence.

"I doubt Ned will come for me after what I did last time," said Emma.

"Nor me," said Eleanor, "for he'll think I'm already long dead."

"Well lift your spirits then, sisters," declared Amelie, "because Ned will come for me – of that I have no doubt! And when he comes, I want us to be ready."

She hugged them both to her and in the darkness she gritted her teeth and smiled; the first time she had smiled for many weeks. Gone was the despair and resignation for now determination was etched into her ravaged face and she began to consider the possibility of fighting back.

50

Ferrybridge, Late March 1461

Ned saw Fauconberg coming and steeled himself for the worst. The Earl regarded him stonily.

"You've been annoying my nephew again!"

"He was wrong, my lord," replied Ned.

"Well, he's told the king that you're the greatest fool and coward in the whole of his army."

Ned chewed at his bottom lip. "So, do you agree with him?"

"Well, I thought, considering the army's size, the charge was a little unfair." He chuckled amiably.

Old Fauconberg seemed to regard Ned's on-going dispute with his nephew as an entertainment laid on for his personal amusement.

"And what else did the great Earl say?" asked Ned.

"He told the king you should be hanged to set an example."

"And what did the king say to that?"

"Oh, he said: 'let's retake the bridge first' – he likes to deal with one problem at a time!"

"So I take it I'm not to be hanged then?"

"Hmm, I wouldn't say that exactly, and I certainly wouldn't stand anywhere on the field within a sword's length of Warwick!"

"So, what then?" asked Ned warily.

"Well, since you've angered the most powerful earl in England – again – you'll only survive if the king backs you.

He's already turned a blind eye once to your feud with Warwick and he won't be keen to do so again. You need a success, lad – some triumph that can't be ignored."

"So, we retake the bridge?"

"You don't – you've lost half your men! The King will retake the bridge, whilst you and I will be riding around to cross the river at Castleford and take Clifford by surprise – well that's the idea. So get mounted with the men you've got left and be ready to ride within the hour."

Fauconberg strode off and Bagot emerged from the nearby trees.

"A bit of luck, that!" said Bagot cheerfully.

"What? Not being hanged?"

"No! Not having to take that damned bridge – it'll be a bugger!"

"Well let's try and put our men at arms back together – they were in pieces last time I looked; and we still have tough enough task ahead of us."

§§§

By early afternoon they had arrived in the heavily forested area on the north bank just to the west of Ferrybridge, undetected by Clifford. Once again, despite the hour, the sky was dark grey with sleet. Ned glanced at the riders around him: their faces were set in grim determination for they all had some unfinished business with Clifford.

On Fauconberg's signal Ned led the charge down onto the Lancastrian position, racing through their lines striking hard with sword and poleaxe. Clifford made no attempt to continue defending the bridge and took off in a hasty retreat.

"After him!" shouted Ned and leaving Fauconberg to retake the bridgehead, he followed hard on Clifford's tail all the way through the breadth of the forest and onto the plain to the east.

"Catch Clifford and I doubt they'll hang you!" Bagot shouted with a grin.

"He's slowing," said Will, "we have him!"

"No, look at his front runners. We'll soon be slowing too," observed Bagot.

"Oh God - we're in the mire!" yelled Will, almost coming to a stop as his horse stumbled, its forelegs gripped by the marshy ground. Like Clifford, they were obliged to slacken their pace and soon Fauconberg caught them up.

"We're not gaining on them!" said Ned.

"Take the left flank," ordered Fauconberg crisply, "head north, get clear of this wretched bog and try to get ahead of them."

Ned was about to leave when Fauconberg added: "He'll be heading for Towton where we think Henry of Lancaster has his camp. Cut him off before he reaches Sherburn, Saxton or Towton and you may save your neck!"

It took Ned a moment to register the name. "Saxton, my lord?"

"Yes, now get a move on, lad!"

"Bagot!" shouted Ned and pulled away, followed by the rest of his command. As soon as they left the marshland behind they made much better speed across the scrubland and rolling grasslands to the north east. They raced down into a long broad valley and followed a small stream, which took them due east.

"Be watchful!" Ned called out, "there'll be more enemies than friends around here!" But he was thinking only about Saxton and how he might get there. His horse stumbled and it gave him a sharp reminder of where he was and what he was there for. He must concentrate or he would never get to Saxton.

"I see him!" shouted Will.

"You've sharp eyes then, young Will," said Bagot, "for I can't see anything."

"He's right," said Ned, for soon the pennants of Clifford's small retreating army were clear for all to see and Ned drove them on harder.

"We're gaining on them now!" said Bagot, warming to his task.

"He's pulled up!" Ned was startled to see Clifford's whole force suddenly turn about and ride towards them.

"His horses must be nearly spent! He's risking all here," said Will.

"Get your arses on fire and your weapons in hand!" bellowed Bagot.

"Spread out!" ordered Ned.

"By St Stephen, they've the numbers on us," said Bagot, "where's Fauconburg?"

"God speed!" Ned yelled as he sped towards Clifford.

§§§

Andrew Trollope stared down into the neck of the valley. Somerset's command tent certainly afforded them an excellent view of the approaches to the camp from both south and west.

"There!" he said, "See! He's there, just coming into Dintingdale," and he pointed out the distant riders of Clifford's force.

"There you are then - he's nearly here," replied the Duke of Somerset.

"Well he won't get here," said Trollope, "not without our help."

"It's not so far," said Edmund.

"He's got a fight on his hands! Surely we must go to his aid?" Trollope insisted.

Somerset frowned. "The army's not ready; it's too great a risk. He'll be alright – this is Clifford we're talking about."

Trollope was silently furious with his commander. "I'll take a few archers and men-at–arms to support him. Look! He's had to turn and face his pursuers. He'll be trapped!"

"Are you going to limp down to him?" asked Edmund.

"Lord Radcliffe has a point – however rudely he's put it - you're still not fit enough," declared Somerset, "and I need you here."

"Clifford can take care of himself," said Edmund, "he may lose a few of his men though I suppose it'll just give him more cause for his endless complaining."

"Sir Andrew," concluded Somerset, "you'd do better spending your time getting some intelligence on where York has his main force. We must know how close he is."

"Your grace, I shall see to it personally!" said Trollope and left his noble commanders.

How much longer, he thought, must he be ordered about by men with no grasp of warfare at all? Very well, if they wanted him to go and look, he would – but he would look where he damn well pleased! With a smug grin on his face, he quickly roused half of his men and led them down towards Clifford's beleaguered company in the vale of Dintingdale.

§§§

Ned drew his sword and rode directly towards Clifford's banner, hoping that Fauconberg would not be too far behind them. It would be tight. The two lines crashed into each other. Ned struck down Clifford's standard bearer, but Clifford was upon him fast and their swords clashed once before Ned's momentum carried him through the line of horsemen. He wheeled his horse around sharply to make a charge back again and saw Fauconberg in the distance.

"The Earl!" he shouted, "he'll drive them back to us!"

"Form up!" Bagot ordered, "Hold your lines and we'll have the bastard!"

Just as Ned was congratulating himself that Clifford would be trapped, he heard the thunder of hooves behind him and turned to see that a relieving Lancastrian force was hurtling towards them.

"Where the devil did they come from?" demanded Will.

But Ned wasted no time in wondering for now they were the ones who were trapped and his men were caught in no man's land. He turned to face the new threat behind them closer now than Clifford. Some followed his lead and turned but others were still facing west where they watched Clifford's force hurrying towards them. Caught thus, the men of York were struck hard.

"Trollope!" shouted Bagot, as he was nearly decapitated by the knight's poleaxe. He swayed in the saddle enough to avoid the full force of the blade but it still caught him a glancing blow on the shoulder and knocked him from his horse. Bear, quick to see the danger, used his mount to muscle Trollope away from the fallen Bagot.

Ned recognised Trollope's badges at once – he was hardly likely to forget! He also remembered the caltrop and prodded his sword at Trollope's wounded leg. Then he darted away to help Bagot remount his horse. Trollope roared with pain and tore after him, cutting aside a knight in his path as if he were made of straw. Ned kept moving and it was all he could do to avoid being surrounded and hacked down in the confusion. Then to his relief Fauconberg's men joined the fray and the two sides fought themselves to a standstill. Exhausted, some tore off their helmets and gorgets in a vain attempt to cool their sweating bodies and force new air into their lungs.

Ned glanced up at the nearby ridge to the east to see the fluttering spikes which marked out the front lines of the Lancastrian encampment. The whole chaotic melee was edging closer and closer to it and if he could not break the deadlock his quarry would escape.

"On me!" he shouted to his men, "form on me! Ned Elder!"

"An Elder! Ned Elder!" several others took up the call. Having rallied to him as many as he could, he suddenly wheeled them away from the fight and drove east towards the Lancastrian camp. Bagot gave him a quizzical look but rode with him none the less. Ned looked ahead again at the Lancastrian flags and tried to judge the distance accurately.

He turned to Bagot. "Bow range?" he asked.

"No further!" retorted Bagot, "we're almost in range now!"

Ned pulled up sharply and turned see Clifford and Trollope escaping from Fauconberg and heading his way. But he had time to steady his men.

"Archers! Dismount and make ready!" he yelled, then

realised in some alarm that only a dozen or so of his archers had left the skirmish with him. Well, it would have to do.

"Men at arms to the rear!" Bagot cried.

The archers formed up in a ragged line, all too aware of the horsemen charging towards them. A few tried to ram a couple of spare arrows into the turf but it was too hard. Then they were all tight with concentration, muscles straining as they pulled back on their bows.

"Loose!" shouted Ned and watched a dozen arrows fly on a low flat line and bury themselves into the front rank of the approaching horsemen. By the time the leading horse crashed down, cracking its head on the ice hard ground, the next twelve arrows were in the air and there would be no time for any more.

"Archers to the rear!" Ned yelled and urged his men at arms forward.

The two lines of horsemen were barely fifty yards apart when the last arrows struck their targets. Ned had learnt that in the charge there was no time for finesse and you lived or died by a capricious combination of raw instinct and sheer luck. In the few short seconds it took Ned to ride through the Lancastrian line he aimed a swingeing chop at Trollope which the veteran expertly parried, he heard a shriek of agony from one of the horses and he saw Clifford fall. Then the fleeting moment of impact was gone and so was Trollope, taking the remnant of Clifford's force with him to the safety of the Lancastrian camp.

"Damn me! Trollope's got away!" complained Bagot bitterly.

But Clifford had not: he staggered wide-eyed towards Ned and leant against his horse, blood pumping out from a wound in his neck where the stub of an arrow still protruded. He stared blankly at Ned, until recognition slowly dawned.

"You?" he said in a low, growling voice. Then he slid slowly to the ground and said no more.

"After all that 'the butcher' dies from a stray arrow," said Bagot, "still, I don't suppose they'll be hanging you now…"

51

Chamber of State, York Castle, Late March 1461

The Council chamber was full and Edmund lounged on the fringe of the assembled group. They were all there: King, Queen and Jack – yes, even the boy, Prince Edward. He still found it completely beyond belief that the King might have fathered an heir – especially one who looked and acted as if one day he might actually rule the kingdom! It intrigued him though he doubted the scurrilous view spread by York's followers that the Queen's late favourite, Edmund Beaufort, was a more likely father. He certainly believed the Queen capable of seeking an heir from another source. If it was Beaufort then his son, the Duke of Somerset, had certainly done alright for himself – commander of the King's army, no less. Presumably the post required no serious understanding of military tactics for Somerset had shown little enough so far.

He cast his eyes around the crowded room. Most of King Henry's greatest subjects had answered his - or rather his wife's - call to battle. None doubted that when they engaged with Edward's Yorkists this would be, for the first and probably the last time, a chance to end the whole wretched struggle in one day. He watched Margaret closely: she radiated confidence and why not? They had every advantage: greater numbers, the backing of most of his fellow nobles and a far superior field position at Towton. Nevertheless, he doubted that it was quite as much in his interests as the Queen's to settle the dispute too swiftly for he intended to wring every possible advantage from the carnage that would follow victory.

Henry, Duke of Somerset, was addressing them now and bemoaning the loss of Clifford. What a pathetic little shit he was, thought Edmund. He felt a small pang of regret about Clifford, but only a small one - battle was after all a risky activity. If Somerset was so upset then perhaps he should have tried a little harder to save him. Edmund had witnessed the slaughter of Clifford and many of his command within spitting distance of their own lines. Apparently Clifford's young son had survived – tragic, and yet an opportunity perhaps, once things settled down again. There would be a young local widow mourning her loss at Skipton Castle which was not so very far from Yoredale. Perhaps tragedy would also lie in store for his own recently acquired wife Emma.

Somerset was still talking but he seemed to have moved on whilst Edmund's attention had wandered and was now outlining the battle plans for the following day. It was hardly an original plan: stand still on the high ground and wait for the enemy to come to you. Surely, he mused, Ned Elder must be in the field again and, if so, then all was at stake and this time he would put an end to it. He must ensure that he got a command on the west flank of their array for Mawfield would prove a handy bolthole if the battle went badly - not that he imagined it would.

The room had gone quiet and he looked up to find everyone staring at him.

"My dear Edmund," Somerset was saying, "I'm sure you have much to occupy your mind but if you could possibly answer my question?"

Edmund was mortified. He could feel the sweat running down the back of his neck as he sought for a coherent response to a question he had not heard.

"Well?" demanded Somerset, clearly furious. In other

circumstances Edmund might have been pleased to have provoked the Duke to anger but he had not intended to embarrass himself before the whole council in the process.

"Of course, your Grace," Edmund stalled, knowing that whatever he said now he would probably appear a fool. He glanced at the Queen, fearing the worst, but to his surprise she was smiling. She gave him an almost imperceptible nod and then looked away. Could he trust her?

"I agree, your Grace," he replied hoping desperately that the Queen had not set him up for a mighty fall.

"You agree? You agree then to lead the reserve force in the woods on Castle Hill?" There was a hint of surprise in Somerset's reaction.

"I shall be honoured," Edmund squeezed the words out, relieved to have extricated himself, but he cursed his inattention for he had only a sketchy idea where Castle Hill was. Also, commanding the reserve would not help him to outshine his young noble rivals which was exactly why Somerset had given him the command.

"Excellent," continued the duke, "and you understand the importance of your position? You'll need to be ready to join the fray at a moment's notice – but only on my express order."

"You may rely upon me utterly, your Grace."

Now he smiled for this was better than he had hoped. Somerset had intended the command as a slight to keep Edmund away from battlefield honours, but he would take his reserve force wherever he pleased without waiting for any advice from Somerset. None the less, for the remainder of the meeting Edmund paid rather closer attention. When it broke up he was keen to make a swift departure, but Somerset called him back. He waited until the others had left before he spoke.

"I see through you, Edmund Radcliffe. Pity it was that wayward arrow hit Clifford and not you!"

Edmund regarded him coldly. "I'm not some feeble client of yours! I don't answer to you."

"On the field, you will! Mark what I say or I'll see you hanged."

Edmund grinned. "The axe, not the rope surely, as befits my noble status."

"Your 'noble status' is but a harness that can be stripped from you as easily as it was put on!"

Somerset swept angrily out of the chamber and Edmund was about to follow when another voice stayed him. The Queen came forward from the shadow of a broad arras; her face shone in the golden glow of the torches. The chamber suddenly felt smaller, more intimate and the atmosphere closer.

"If you're going to kill each other," she said, "could you at least wait until after tomorrow? What news have you for me … of our friend? Tell me she is dead and gone."

"She is dead and gone. You can forget her, your majesty."

"You said that once before."

"I wouldn't fail you twice."

"And?" The Queen asked.

"And?"

"Don't sport with me Edmund! Don't mistake my favour for anything more than self-interest. Did she give you anything which belongs to me?"

"No," he replied, enjoying the novelty of giving an honest answer. "She gave me nothing, your Majesty."

Queen Margaret nodded, seemingly reassured. "And as for Somerset, you would do well not to provoke him for he'll hold much sway after tomorrow."

"Of course, your majesty," he acknowledged and bowed as he left her. But, he mused, Somerset would only hold power if he made it through the day.

Mordeur awaited him impatiently outside stamping his boots on the icy cobbles.

Edmund took his arm at once. "Where in the name of Christ is Castle Hill wood?" he demanded.

Mordeur shrugged. "You ask me, a Norman? I don't know."

"Well, find out – and quickly! We need to have a look at it

now! What's the news from Mawfield?"

"All is as it should be. You have all the Elder women now."

"Get anything out of the French bitch?"

"No and I'm certain now that she has nothing for you. What do you want to do with them?"

"Oh God, I'm so weary of the Elders. We'll take 'lady' Emma back to Yoredale; then we'll have done with the others."

52

South of Towton, Yorkshire, 29th March 1461

A thousand small fires scarred the heath around Sherburn in Elmet where the army of York lay sleeping in the bitter cold, but Ned was not asleep. He sat in the shadows away from the glow of the campfire, where his breath made white spears of freezing mist. He was facing north to Towton where the enemy lay and somewhere in between, probably little more than a league or two away, was Amelie. The day ahead would be the day of days: he would resolve the wrongs done to him, or fall. Just now the latter seemed the more likely. Sleeping nearby were his closest friends and comrades and all around him lay the men who had made indentures with him after St Albans – though there were fewer since Ferrybridge.

He saw that others too were awake. Hal, no longer a boy but a young man - yes, perhaps it was time for Hal. He called softly to him and Hal came swiftly across and sat down. He looked nervous - and why not? Ned remembered how he had felt at Blore Heath. It was hard to believe it was scarcely eighteen months ago.

"I've a task for you tomorrow, Hal - an important one," he said.

Hal pulled a face. "That's what you say when you want to keep me out of trouble, lord."

In the darkness Ned smiled. "True enough I suppose in the past, but this task won't keep you out of trouble – in fact it'll likely put you into a great deal of trouble and … you'll be on your own."

Even as he said it he started to have doubts.

"Tell me," said Hal, interested at once.

"You said once that you'd do anything to help me find Amelie -"

"And so I would!" said Hal.

"Well I want you to track her down for me."

"You do think she's still alive then?"

"Yes I do, but if she is and I fall tomorrow..."

"You want to know that someone's still looking…"

"I think she's at a house Edmund Radcliffe has south of York called Mawfield Hall. I want you to find that house."

"Where do I start?"

"I only know this much: it's near Saxton and you could hit Saxton from here with one of your arrows – so it's close. At first light I want you to head into the village and start asking folk, but go gently for there'll be no trust there, only fear. Be very careful and, after the battle is won, come looking for me."

Hal nodded. Ned clapped him on the back and the youth went to sit down, then he turned back and said: "Lord, what if… the battle is not won?"

"Then Hal, it'll be up to you. I pray God keeps you safe and guides you in your search. Now get some rest."

Hal moved off but Ned noticed that on the other side of the flickering fire Will too was sitting awake, staring into the flames. Ned went to sit down beside him but for a time neither spoke.

"It'll be tough tomorrow, won't it?" Will said at last.

"Aye," said Ned, "it'll be bloody so you needn't bother with those fancy swords of yours."

"I know. Bear's given me a poleaxe – it gives me a chance!"

Ned gave him a wry smile. "A chance to kill one of us, I should think. When did you ever use an axe?"

"Bear's shown me a few moves..."

Ned grunted, unconvinced. "Better stay near Bear then."

"I'm not a child, Ned! I've seen battle before."

"Just get through the day in one piece, that's all," he said, punching him lightly on the shoulder.

Will glanced at him and in that sudden glimpse of his friend's face Ned knew there was something amiss.

"You're troubled, my friend," he murmured.

Will nodded. "I'll always be troubled, Ned. Every time I close my eyes I see Ellie slipping into that stream ... and my hand stretched out to her, never reaching her."

Ned took him by the shoulder: "You have to try to forget..."

"I don't want to forget her ... do you?"

"She was a spark of life that touched us all, Will, in one way or another. Be grateful for that and, if you live through this day, start a new life tomorrow. Wherever you want to go you have my blessing. Go and marry that Sarah and live your life - leave Ellie behind." He suddenly grinned. "If you're going to do all that, as I said, you'd best stay close to Bear!"

§§§

Dawn arrived accompanied by an icy blizzard. The fires had died down to the last white embers but a few early risers were stoking them up again if they could find the fuel. Ned couldn't be bothered but he watched Bagot throw on some filthy straw and the fire flared briefly. Then he added some none too dry wood and the flames protested, spitting sap, but they still burned.

"You've hardly slept. Not the best way to prepare for today," said Bagot.

"Sleep doesn't cure everything."

"By Christ though, it's not a bad start!" retorted Bagot.

"I'll sleep when this is over," said Ned.

"Do you think we'll fight in this?"

"I think that if our new king isn't going to wait for Norfolk to get here with the rest of the army, then he's not going to wait for the weather either."

Bagot shook his head sadly. "I've never seen such armies – in France yes, but not here in our own land. If we go at this hard today … we'll slaughter each other!"

"Then slaughter it'll be, for nothing can stop it now and the blood will flow like water."

He watched several priests pass amongst his men, leading them in short prayers or conferring hasty blessings whilst the men donned their mail or plate. The snow had eased a little and a few streaks of red stained the eastern sky. Orders began to ring out across the meadow as pages ran errands hither and thither and squires helped their frozen knights to don their armour.

"There'll be little quarter given today," said Ned, getting stiffly to his feet. "Pass the word to the men: it's time to move."

He embraced Hal and sent him on his way to Saxton then he walked from man to man with a word of encouragement for each, embracing them all – and the last was Will.

"God protect you, brother," he said softly.

53

Sunrise, Palm Sunday, 29th March 1461

Hal mounted his horse and picked his way carefully through the sprawling Yorkist host to begin his search. He wondered at the vast size of the army as it seemed to unfold around him and begin its slow advance northwards into Towton Dale. The village of Sherburn was choked with the many hangers-on that the army had attracted: as well as the priests, there were pedlars and whores aplenty amongst the throng. He ignored them all and rode on through, glad to be rid of the familiar stench of the camp. He trotted towards the far end of the lane leading out of the village. A solitary figure was riding towards him and there was something strikingly familiar about him. He stopped and as the rider came closer he shook his head in disbelief.

"You're just about the last man I'd expect to see up here!" he said with a grin.

Felix folded his heavy cloak more tightly around him.

"This is not an errand I sought, I can tell you! I have a warm young widow waiting for me in Ludlow - what do I care if you all get yourselves killed?"

"Then what are you doing here?"

"I shouldn't be here with all these priests and whores! I swear there are more priests and whores in this village than men at arms!"

"So, what in all Christendom could have made you come

here of all places?"

"Well, a friend."

Hal smiled knowingly. "The 'friend' wouldn't be a certain goldsmith – or a certain goldsmith's daughter?"

Felix nodded sheepishly.

"So, are you planning to watch over Will?"

"No! My only 'plan' is to keep myself from getting killed! Then, however the battle goes for Will, I can... give an account," said Felix. He paused, looking warily at Hal. "Why?"

"Because you could help me," said Hal and explained his own task.

Felix sighed. "Come on then. It sounds safer than the battlefield and it must be warmer riding than standing still. I wasn't born to such weather, you know - it's not good for me."

§§§

In Towton Dale the snow returned with mischievous intent, driving across the field. Ned peered to the north where he expected to make out the pennants and standards of the enemy, but he could see nothing. He glanced around at his own men, drawn up on foot in Fauconberg's vanguard which formed the left flank of King Edward's army. The snow swirled around them blowing into their faces and at once he could see even less.

"Where in God's name are they?" he yelled at Fauconberg who was standing beside him.

"They have the high ground ahead – there's a low meadow between us!"

"We can't fight in this!" declared Ned.

"We can! And we will, though I can't say I've fought in worse, because I haven't!"

His hollow laughter was snatched away by the wind.

"Our king has told us to give no quarter," he continued, "so there'll be no ransoming of gentles or lords after this battle. Don't fall down Ned or you won't get up again!" He was not laughing this time.

Suddenly out of the driving snow King Edward appeared, tall in the saddle and resplendent in his gold burnished plate armour with a coronet on his helm. He shook Fauconberg's hand then raised his great sword aloft and rode along the lines speaking to the men, though his words of encouragement were borne up the hill behind them by the biting wind. Finally he turned to Ned putting a large steel clad hand on the young knight's arm and bending closer to make himself heard.

"Palm Sunday, Ned! This is our day and it's men like you and me that'll win this battle. I'll look for you on the field at the end of the day. May God protect us both!" He clapped him on the back and rode off once more into the snow.

Ned wondered if on Palm Sunday God wanted a battle quite as much as Edward seemed to, but at that moment the snow abated a little as the wind dropped. Then to his surprise the wind swung around so that the blizzard blew at their backs and the white veil was suddenly lifted from his eyes. At last he could see the massed forces of Henry of Lancaster arrayed on the slope that rose ahead of him. It was a fearsome sight for as his scouts had reported, Henry's army was larger than theirs.

Ned jumped as Fauconberg beside him bellowed: "Archers forward!"

"The breeze is fickle, my lord," cautioned Ned.

"Let's see, shall we?" replied Fauconberg calmly. "One arrow only!" he shouted.

His archers drew back on their bows as one then let fly their volley which flew like a vast flock of falcons curving through the air. Lifted by the wind, they dived murderously down to wreak bloody havoc on the Lancastrian front ranks, the long bodkins punching through mail and flesh.

"They must return fire," said Bagot, on station beside Ned.

Every man in the ranks behind them stood taut as a bowstring as they awaited the inevitable Lancastrian response. Somewhere nearby bowels were evacuated noisily.

Then they glimpsed it – a storm of arrows burrowing towards them through the snow. They braced themselves for the impact, but incredibly the arrows dropped like stones fifty yards short, robbed of all momentum by the blizzard wind. A large, spontaneous cheer of relief resounded along their lines.

Fauconberg urged his archers further forward where they retrieved many of the enemy arrows. They then let fly another volley high into the air and watched their arrows hit home into the very midst of their opponents. Another cheer rang out and another volley was launched. Another reply fell short prompting another cheer. Another volley, another cheer and so it went on.

"It can't be this easy," said Ned.

"No," replied Bagot, "it won't be – look, they're on the move. They have to come at us or die where they stand!"

"Archers withdraw!" came the roared command from Fauconberg and quickly the men fell back to loose their bowstrings and take up their swords and bills.

"Make ready!" shouted Bagot, "No quarter lads, no quarter!"

"Stand fast!" yelled Ned from his place in the front rank.

Their opponents were coming down off the ridge quickly and then starting up the low incline which Ned's men defended. Their line was led by heavily armoured men at arms bearing sword, poleaxe and mace, followed by every sort of soldier armed with bill, hook or halberd. Ned felt the sweat begin to build even as he shivered with cold. The enemy were twenty paces away, raging at the snow which blurred their vision. He scanned their line, seeking out the most formidable opponents. Ten paces away and he fixed on a target. Then they struck Ned's line and the very ground shook beneath his feet with the impact of axe and sword on plate and bone.

Ned thought he was ready for it but even he was knocked backwards by the force of the onslaught. All around him men were giving ground before the enemy assault and those who fell were crushed at once as the two opposing ranks of steel clad warriors trampled over them. Fauconberg's words of advice thundered in his ears: 'don't fall down Ned'.

Above the bewildering din he could hear shouts of "King Harry" ringing out and the screams and cries of the wounded rang in his head. He tried in vain to hold the line but, snatching a look to his left, he was horrified to see that even the mighty Bear was being thrown back. Dear God, if he couldn't hold them, then no-one could! He took a glancing blow on the right shoulder from the broad end of a poleaxe blade. It split his pauldron in two so that it hung with his padded jack exposed but mercifully his skin was barely grazed. In cold fury he punched the blade of his sword through his opponent's visor feeling the damage it wrought and driving the knight back. But it was a timely warning to him to concentrate on what was in front of him or he'd die there and then.

Still his men were conceding ground, being flung back, step by step up the gentle slope. If they were pushed much further they'd be turned in on their own centre and the battle would be lost before it had scarcely begun! Then to his right, he glimpsed the king's gold helm. Edward, two yards tall and powerfully built, was clubbing his way through the enemy ranks and inspiring those beside him to greater deeds than any of them could have imagined possible.

Fauconberg to his left launched a similar counterattack and Ned knew he must find the strength to do the same. Somehow Bear had moved to his side and with Bagot on his right, he took a giant pace forward, changed his sword grip and brought his heavy weapon hard down on the man opposite – chopping mortally into neck and shoulder. Then he took another brutal step forward crushing the fallen man's arm under his foot and forcing back his next opponent. Bagot and Bear on his flanks matched his power and at last their line was edging forward. Still they had already lost much ground and their enemies seemed without number. Every man that fell was at once replaced by another with fresh energy firing through his limbs.

Ned's arms felt like lumps of lead yet he fought on doggedly, his helm and breastplate plastered with the blood of the unknown men he had butchered. The slaughter went on for another hour and had the sun been visible it would have been approaching its zenith but it wasn't and the gritty snow continued to fall on the blood soaked dead and the breathless living.

Then as if by some preordained agreement both sides pulled back. They had to draw breath and rest their weary limbs. For a moment Ned dropped to his knees and leant on his sword but he could not linger there. In the short respite he, like every other commander on the field, had to regroup his company. He shouted at them to take heart, to watch him, to stand together and hold the line. He saw with anguish amongst the dead and dying some who had followed him from St. Albans. A few of the wounded were dragged back behind the lines and he called for some of the reserve to step forward.

Then, as abruptly as it had stopped, the battle recommenced all along the front. Some were slower to return to the fray than others, their resolve already weakened and their worst fears confirmed.

Ned began with a determination not to give another inch of ground, but almost at once he was conceding yards of it and judging by the shape of their battle line, even the King was retreating before the superior power of their enemies. Doubts crept into his mind.

"Shut them out!" he shouted, willing himself to resist. But the struggle had become a wrestling match with each side trying to shove harder than their opponents. There was no room to swing a blade and all he could do was hold his father's great battle sword in both hands and bludgeon with it, fending off the punching blows aimed at him. He was exhausted already but to stop was to die.

As he feared, the whole left flank of their battle was being twisted back on to its centre. He fervently hoped that the right flank was holding its own or the whole army would be folded up and surrounded - there was only one outcome if that happened. In the midst of bloody chaos he realised what was going wrong: the extreme left of their line was visibly crumbling as men retreated across behind Ned's part of the line where they hoped to be safer. And as the far left was driven back further so the rest of the line was being pulled backwards.

This is the moment, Ned thought. This is where we must stand firm and he parried yet another chopping blow and staggered, dazed with the effort. He saw the next hammer blow coming, but was too slow to meet it with his sword and was knocked sideways. His vision blurred for a moment. Jesus, don't fall down Ned

54

Castle Hill Wood, Noon, Palm Sunday 1461

Edmund waited with a smile on his face for he couldn't believe his good fortune. The wood had turned out to be an ideal position: on the fringe of the battleground and not too far from Mawfield. It afforded him some very desirable options no matter which way the battle went. He commanded a force of nearly three hundred horsemen and the trees sheltered them from much of the ice storm which was engulfing the other combatants.

The men at arms contesting the field were all on foot and by the time his mounted knights charged at them out of the trees they would be utterly exhausted and he would sweep them from the field. But as the peevish Somerset had said, rightly for once, the timing of his attack would be crucial – not that he would let the Duke decide it. He had his own observers in the trees and he would probably have a clearer picture than Somerset who would likely be glory seeking in the centre of the field.

With the enemy routed he aimed to capture some important players who would pay much to regain their freedom – perhaps even Edward himself. All this 'no quarter' nonsense might be good for kings, but what a waste. Of course Ned Elder was an exception: he must be despatched for this was the best chance he would ever have to do so. Now he had the two sisters under lock and key; it just remained to finish off the last male of the Elder clan and his father's bold strategy would finally be completed.

"My lord," Mordeur broke into his thoughts, "the duke has ordered us to attack now."

"Really?" He was genuinely surprised. "Well, it seems a little early to me. Let's have a look shall we?"

They mounted and rode cautiously to the edge of the wood where the thinning trees provided much less cover. Edmund stared towards the field but much of the action was obscured from his view, not only by the driving sleet and snow, but also because Castle Hill Wood was in a slight depression. Thus though the sounds of the battle reached him clearly enough, he could not see exactly what was happening.

"Mordeur, find out from the men in the tree tops whether either side has broken through yet."

The Norman rode back down into the wood and returned a few minutes later.

"Well?"

"They don't think we've broken through the Yorkist line yet."

"They don't think? This isn't a game we're playing out here for want of something else to do! All our lives hang on this day!"

"It's difficult to see clearly, my lord."

"Difficult?" muttered Edmund, "then we wait. Make sure they tell you when they 'think' we are breaking through – and keep the men ready!" He wanted his arrival to be decisive and he certainly did not want Somerset to triumph without him.

"What about the Duke's messenger?" asked Henry.

"What messenger? I don't recall any messenger – perhaps he fell into the beck?"

§§§

Felix pulled up. He was cold, wet and miserable.

"We're getting nowhere, Hal! We could've ridden to York and back in the hours we've spent – someone there must know. I'm beginning to wonder if Mawfield Hall exists at all!"

They had skirted north through nearby Saxton and Towton, giving a wide berth to the latter where the Lancastrian camp followers were anxiously awaiting the battle's outcome. No-one they dared speak to had even heard of Mawfield Hall. It was far from promising.

"Perhaps Ned's got it wrong," said Hal, "what do you think I should do?"

"Let's just keep riding around to the south west as we said we would. We'll have gone full circle soon and you can do no more, Hal."

They rode on for another mile or so before Hal spoke again.

"You'd think God could just give us a bit of help on this, wouldn't you?" he said disconsolately.

Felix was reluctant to risk irritating the Almighty by passing comment but he thought Hal might have a point: without divine intervention they seemed destined to fail in their search. He stared south towards Towton Dale where the battle still raged, hidden from them by the driving snow. It was so hard to see that he doubted they would notice the Hall even if they passed beside it.

They tracked westwards until they reached a beck, which seemed much swollen by the recent rain and snow. The course of the beck would keep them safely away from the battlefield, but Felix rode watchfully along the soggy bank, his horse slipping nervously on the ice and mud beside the water. The beck ran through a deepening gully which sheltered them from the whining wind but Felix knew they were not going to find a large manor house there.

They rode on saying nothing and soon they came to a bridge across the beck. They had to cross it since following the gully would lead them back towards Towton Dale. A slippery track took them across and on to the higher more exposed ground above the beck. For the first time the snow became lighter and as they turned south the wind changed again and came at their backs.

Felix came to a sudden halt for he saw Towton Dale below them to the east and witnessed the appalling carnage taking place. He had never seen the like of it before and could scarcely believe his eyes. After only a few moments he began to understand the positions of the two armies and grasp what was happening.

"We're losing, aren't we?" said Hal, drawing alongside.

"Well, I don't know much about such things but it certainly looks as if the Queen's armies are pushing them back – dear God, what a slaughter!"

They were torn by the grim fascination of watching the battle and the need to press on.

"If Ned loses, Amelie will likely be killed – if she's not already dead," muttered Hal.

"Well, come on then Master Hal, let's make more speed!"

They set off again and followed the contour of the land above the beck rounding a hill which brought them squarely into the wind again. Immediately their horses shied away from the freezing wind and turned in towards the slope to face downwind.

"Look!" said Hal. He pointed to the top of a tower which he could just make out further up the slope. They rode on up the slope to try to see the rest of the building but it was too steep so they returned to the track along the ridge and lost sight of the tower.

"Just because you see a large manor house, doesn't mean it's the one you're looking for. Even if it is, you can't just ride in – you must be careful!" advised Felix.

But Hal was desperate and urged his horse on along the ridge hoping to catch a glimpse of the house but where they thought the house would be trees now obscured their view. Frustrated, they turned back towards the battlefield again and stared across the ravine down to the beck and to the meadow beyond where the bloody struggle was being played out.

"They're definitely falling back aren't they," said Hal, his voice breaking.

"You can't be sure yet," said Felix, anxious to reassure him, "the left flank might be in trouble but the right is holding."

Nearer to them, just across the ravine, was a small forested area and Hal suddenly noticed the men and horses milling around in the trees. He pointed and Felix followed his gaze.

"What are they doing there?" asked Hal.

Felix sighed long and hard. "I think you know that, Hal."

"They're going to join in at the right moment, aren't they?"

"Yes, they are."

"They're going to hit the left flank aren't they?"

"Yes, they are."

"Ned's on the left flank…"

"Ned could be dead already, boy."

"I don't think so."

"You don't think so?

Hal shook his head. "God'll keep him safe."

"Well, God can be a little … inconsistent … in such matters."

Felix looked across again at the writhing battle line and he was puzzled why the Lancastrians in the woods had not yet intervened, for they were numerous enough to make a difference and Ned's comrades must be completely unaware of them.

"Can we warn them?" asked Hal.

"Well, we can't cross the beck here: the gully's too steep and in any case the beck's too deep and the ground's too boggy. The only bridge I can see is the one we came across earlier and that'd take too long – you'd have to be one of the best horseman in the land to take it at speed. Are you?"

Hal shook his head.

"How far can you shoot an arrow? Can you reach their line from here?"

"I'd have the wind behind me a bit but it's long way and even so, what does my arrow tell them?"

"Well if we don't try something we'll just be watching it happen before our eyes. The only ones who'll hear us if we shout are the ones across there in the trees!"

"Alright but where shall I aim for?"

"Does it make any difference? All you're trying to do is put the idea into their mind that there are enemy soldiers to their left – you can't tell them much else by a single arrow. Let's get as close as we can first."

"What if the soldiers in the wood see us?"

"Well, like us, they can't get across the beck so the worst they can do is shoot at us…"

They dismounted on the edge of the steep slope which fell away down to the swollen beck and Hal strung his bow. He took some time preparing himself before he pronounced himself ready.

"Why don't you try one arrow to get your range and see where it strikes?"

Felix watched him take aim nervously. His hands would be cold, but sweating with both the tension and the effort of pulling the string back far enough. Hal let fly.

Both watched the arc of his arrow as it flew through the sleet and plummeted into the slope well below where the mass of men at arms were fighting. Hal shook his head but made another attempt and Felix could see the effort he put into it but still the arrow fell too short.

"I can't do it, Felix. I just can't get it there!" He hung his head.

"It's too far, Hal but I'm not sure I can just stand here and watch it happen."

"No, no, but what can we do?"

Felix paused for a moment, collecting his thoughts.

"Whatever happens in the field, you must find the Hall - for Amelie's sake. So, you must carry on up the hill. Find the Hall then keep out of sight. Watch and wait – oh, and pray a little while you're waiting."

"What about you?"

"I'm going to ride over there," replied Felix calmly, pointing to Towton Dale.

"Are you mad? What happened to staying out of trouble? Anyway, you said it couldn't be done!"

"I didn't quite say that."

"You said you'd need to be one of the best horsemen in the land!"

Felix forced a grim smile. "Well, now we'll find out if I am. Now you go and do your task and I'll try to do mine. With much help from the Lord we may meet again later."

Without another word Felix wheeled his horse and raced back at breakneck speed along the ravine they had slowly climbed earlier, urging his mount to negotiate the track as it wound back down to the beck.

55

Towton Dale, Mid Afternoon, Palm Sunday 1461

Ned was giving ground and there was nothing he could do about it. A clutch of opponents hammered him back and all he could do was try to block each blow as it came. He knew he couldn't last long like that but all around him it was the same. Many times he had blessed Holton's skill when a blow had struck his plate and it held firm but even with his armour and gambeson beneath he could feel the bruises down to the bone. Both shoulder plates were hanging in pieces and his helm had been dented by a fearsome mace blow. Now he was barely surviving.

But just when he thought there could be no relief, he felt his opponents draw back – only a foot or so, but it was enough. Then he realised why, as a great sword swung forward and cut down one of his assailants with a single stunning strike. He saw the gilt armour cracked and bloodied beside him and the coronet atop the helm. King Edward had come to his aid and to the enemy he must have seemed like a giant wrought from steel.

"Courage, Ned!" the King shouted, "Norfolk's men have arrived! But we must hold this left flank and then we may yet turn them with our right. I'll hold here! Take your men to Fauconberg's aid for if he falls the flank is lost!"

Ned rallied what remained of his own company and moved

behind the ragged heaving line to support Fauconberg on the far left of the Yorkist battle line. To do so he was forced to clamber over a mound of dead just to reach the beleaguered earl but Fauconberg seemed much relieved to see him. Ned's men brought a fresh impetus to the line, but in the throng of opposing men at arms he spotted Trollope's colours. Of course he should have expected that the Queen's foremost warrior would be in the very meat of the battle.

Ned recognised Trollope by his plate armour when he was only a few yards away. He had unfinished business with the Lancastrian knight and worked his way towards him but before he could get within striking range another stepped into his path and began battering Trollope with a heavy falchion.

"I have him, lord!" roared Bagot and at first Trollope, focused on Ned, was taken unawares. But he swiftly recovered and forced Bagot back striking him heavily on head, shoulder and arm. Bagot fell backwards but, before Trollope could finish him, Ned intervened spurred on by the fear that Bagot must either be killed or crushed underfoot.

"Get Bagot out!" he yelled behind him as he threw himself at Trollope. Ned's sword was a good deal heavier and longer than Bagot's and his first blow knocked the great Lancastrian captain staggering back into the rank behind. But Trollope sprang forward again, thrusting and hacking at Ned with a succession of weighty blows. Ned expected nothing less for he had felt the man's power before. Concentrate, he told himself – or this man will kill you!

He landed a blow on Trollope's breastplate which did enough to knock him off balance and then punched the point of his sword into his visor as he had with many others before. Trollope momentarily stepped back, blood trickling from his chin but he was not beaten and swung up his heavy battle sword to bring it down on Ned's head. As he had done countless times already Ned quickly adjusted his grip to block the strike, feeling the force of it shudder through his upper body. Yet delivering the blow had taken much out of his adversary too and Ned took a chance and rammed his sword point up under his opponent's armpit. Trollope grunted with pain and his left arm fell limp. Ned seized the moment and brought the full force of his blade down on Trollope's body hacking through his neck armour and deep into the neck.

Blood poured from the wound and Trollope looked in disbelief at it ran freely down his breastplate. He sank down onto his haunches and then slid to the ground on his back. There was a groan from his comrades nearby as they registered the fall of their leader and talisman. Several bent to drag back his broken body but Ned and Bear pressed forward and others advanced with them. Ned drove on, wrestling forward over a yard of turf and clambering over Trollope's still form to pulverise those who stood behind. Now the shouts of encouragement came from the men of York as they sensed a welcome shift in fortunes.

§§§

"At last!" exclaimed Edmund, "at long last! I knew he'd make a mess of it!"

"But my lord? It looks as if our men at arms are being pushed back down the slope," said Henry.

"Exactly! And now we throw our weight onto the scales." His satisfaction was almost tangible.

As his Lancastrian comrades gave way down the slope, their Yorkist assailants had their backs to Edmund's position at Castle Hill Wood. Now he could bring his horsemen down onto York's foot soldiers and crush them - a manoeuvre which would give the field to King Henry and earn not only a place of glory for him but genuine power. He smiled in anticipation.

"Now you see, Henry, we'll destroy Edward's flank utterly and perhaps even rout his centre. And we'll make sure that Ned Elder is among the very many dead!"

His knights were mounted and waited on the edge of the wood for his command to advance.

§§§

Felix rode hard although he knew it might all be for nothing. Several times he apologised to his horse and pleaded with her not to slip on the treacherously icy track. At the bridge over the beck the animal almost slithered into the freezing water as Felix turned her sharply. He followed the path for another fifty yards until he reached the summit of the ravine and then cut across the field behind the Lancastrian lines – what they would make of him? He hoped they'd ignore him and he was more concerned he'd be taken out by some keen Yorkist archer before he could deliver his warning.

He reached down to untie his quarter staff which he carried slung along the mare's right flank. It was still snowing lightly though the wind had relented a little, he thought. He almost stopped in his tracks when he passed the first corpses and then, as he neared the battle lines, he had to ride around pile after pile of cracked and broken bodies. A brutal clamour assaulted his ears as he rode up the slope where the ground became a grisly patchwork of snow, grey steel and blood. How the devil was he going to get through? Lord! I hope you're paying attention because this poor sinner's going to need your help today!

He aimed for the far end of the line, almost on the edge of the steep drop down to the beck for there the crowd of men was thinner. Several Lancastrian men at arms saw him coming and looked puzzled – they won't be puzzled for long, he thought. Well, here it goes. He filled his lungs, gave a great shout of "Long live King Edward!" and punched his staff into the heads of the men in his path as he tried to penetrate the mass of heaving bodies. Many wore tabards or jacks bearing badges but he still couldn't tell one man from another. He prayed fervently that Ned was somewhere nearby in the Yorkist ranks. A few startled Lancastrian soldiers turned to face him and his terrified mare reared up and clubbed her hooves onto them, scattering them from his path.

This was his chance and he wouldn't get another. Above the din he shouted: "Ned Elder! It's me Felix!"

§§§

Ned was in fact very close by, but reeled with disbelief as the heavily cloaked figure used his staff to knock another man out of the way. "Let me through!" the rider yelled again. For Ned, the quarterstaff told him all.

"Give that horse room!" he ordered. With difficulty, the Yorkist line parted and allowed Felix to dash through. Ned and Will rushed after him, leaving Bear and Stephen to hold the line.

"Felix what in God's name brings you here?" called Ned.

Felix fell off his horse with relief and Ned could see that he was shaking all over.

"Ned! Thank God! I never want to do that again!" he said breathlessly.

"Where on earth have you come from?" demanded Ned.

Felix could only wave vaguely to the west, but when he had gulped in a little more air he explained.

"There are horsemen in the woods yonder and they're set to fall on your flank!"

"How many?" asked Ned, peering towards the wooded ridge to the west.

"Several hundred I'd say, at least."

Ned took a moment to absorb the news and then he moved fast.

"We must meet them mounted or they'll murder us. We're beholden to you Felix - you'd better get yourself back to Saxton now."

"Well Ned, seeing you're so short-handed, I thought I might lend you my staff for a while."

"Nonsense, you're not even harnessed! You've done well enough just to reach us."

"Don't worry on my account: I intend to keep a staff's

length away from the enemy. Anyway, you haven't time to argue – just get going."

Ned quickly searched the line for Fauconberg and went to warn him but before he knew it King Edward was by his side – the man seemed to be everywhere at once!

"They've men in the wood, sire!" Ned announced.

"I've had an eye on that wood all day but I thought if there were any there they'd have joined the fray by now. Take as few as you can, Ned or we'll be giving ground here again! Remember, you don't have to kill them all - just stop their charge. And God speed!"

He clapped Ned hard with his gauntlet on the exposed shoulder wound. Ned winced and then bellowed to the pages in the rear: "Horses! Bring up the horses!"

They scurried away in haste to carry out his orders whilst he quickly reorganised his men.

"Will! Go with Felix and mount up the men! Oh, and get Felix a jack and sallet."

"Horsemen! Horsemen on the ridge!" The cry went up as the enemy riders massed in the west. The Yorkist shouts of alarm were answered by a roar of approval from their opponents.

Ned was still hastily giving instructions: "Stephen, keep Bear with you - the archers can rejoin you once they've used up their arrows!"

He went back to the line, stumbling over discarded pieces of armour and weapons, and knelt by the wounded Bagot.

"I'm riding with you, lord," said Bagot, trying to get up.

"Not this time," replied Ned, putting a gentle restraining hand on the older man's shoulder. Bagot looked up at the tall youth with sorrow in eyes and nodded.

"God and St Stephen go with you, Ned."

Ned heard the young King and Fauconberg rallying their men at arms and he barked more orders to his own men: "Archers, form a line and then stand fast!" He saw with regret that he had barely two dozen archers. He took the archers' captain by the arm.

"I remember you at St Albans: Thomas, isn't it?"

"Yes, lord."

"One last throw, Thomas: bring down those lead riders for me and don't stop shooting until my horsemen hit them."

"We'll do our best. God save you, lord!"

"And you, Thomas."

He mounted the sturdy war horse brought up for him and looked at his men, freshly armed by their pages and squires with mace, axe and lance. There were barely three score of them as far as he could judge and it wouldn't be enough. They were putting a brave face on it, but he knew they were already exhausted. Without a word Will thrust a poleaxe in his hand and one of the pages quickly exchanged his long sword for an arming sword.

"Look after that with your life!" he told the boy and spurred his mount off to the rear of their lines, tracked by the others. The horsemen of Lancaster were already sweeping down the sloping ground from the wood. If he was to stop them he must outflank them and he could only do that by gaining the higher ground to the rear so that he might fall on their right flank... but by then they would be hurtling towards the Yorkist lines. He prayed to God that his archers could slow the attack.

He crested the rise and turned back towards the field. Now for the first time the enemy riders were in sight and almost halfway towards their target.

"Jesus!" said Will, "we're too few!"

"Have faith, Will," said Felix alongside him.

Ned faced his men. "Spread out!" he shouted. "We must take out as many as we can. Remember: if we stop the leaders, we can stop the charge! God be with us all!"

He held his poleaxe aloft and turned down the slope.

"Come on then!!" he cried, "for King Edward!" His words were snatched from his lips as he rode off but his eyes were fixed firmly on the horses leading the Lancastrian charge. His archers worked their sorcery well and he watched as their first arrows struck the oncoming horses. Several crashed down on their chests as they ran, hurling their riders onto the freezing ground. Others, maddened by their wounds, darted across the rest and the charge faltered but it had not stopped.

His men fanned out to make an impact on as wide a front as possible aiming to force the Lancastrians to sheer away down the slope or, better still, press them down the steep ravine into the beck below.

He quickly picked out for himself one of the leading riders but then he saw pennant, the bright crimson pennant and he knew that Edmund, at last, would be amongst them. The archers timed their final volley to perfection striking the enemy riders just before Ned's wave of horsemen slammed into them and the brutal carnage began. Brave horses fell with dreadful injuries, screaming the last breath from their lungs. Some men too were crushed fatally on impact and the air was rent by the cries of wounded men and beasts.

Ned only had eyes for Edmund but had to leap his horse over several fallen riders to reach him. He hacked at Edmund's head with his poleaxe but Edmund swerved aside at the last moment. They both turned at speed and landed heavy blows, unhorsing each other. Ned had lost his poleaxe in the fall but rolled swiftly to his feet and drew his sword to parry a rapid hail of blows from Edmund. Ned went at him hard, chopping at his thigh and cracking the steel plate without drawing blood. He saw at once that the arming sword was almost useless against Edmund's armour and all he could do was try to defend himself as Edmund came at him again and again. His shoulder was hit once more and the gambeson under his armour there was shredded and red with blood.

All around them was mayhem as the vanguard of Edmund's horsemen were stopped in their tracks and those following pulled up, unable to thread their way through the tangle of bloodied bodies. Some looked in vain for Edmund's pennant and when they didn't see it fear took some of them in its grip.

Everywhere the fighting was fierce and bloody: many were now on foot, but others, like Will, reacquainted with his fine blades, delivered savage punishment from the saddle.

"Drive them from the field! Hurl them into the beck!" shouted Ned, determined that his small force shouldn't lose the initiative. But soon he could barely speak, for he'd fought Edmund to a standstill and neither could land a killing blow. They sat back on their haunches barely two paces apart, their energy spent. They would have hurled insults at each other but they didn't have the breath to do so. Instead both cast about the battleground seeking cause for hope but the rolling green pasture was littered with the dead and dying of both sides. Nevertheless, Ned had good cause for optimism for Edmund's men were in disarray, their resolve shattered: the charge had been halted.

Ned tried to get to his feet but swayed down on to one knee. The din around them was terrifying but in the midst of it all a bewildered mare walked gamely across the slope towards them, hampered by the lance point in her neck. She made no sound but the blood pumped rhythmically down her chest until she stumbled and went down on her knees.

"Mordeur!" roared Edmund, "a horse, damn you!" and from the heart of the fighting the Frenchman somehow brought him a mount He snatched up the reins and at the same time Ned clambered onto a horse brought up for him by Felix.

Edmund and Mordeur fled north across the slope towards the rear of the Lancastrian battle line.

Ned looked at Felix. "Thank God! How did we do that?" he exclaimed.

"Timing," replied Felix calmly, "the archers clipped their wings a little - and you took Edmund down... the rest just lost their nerve."

"Well, where are they all?"

Felix pointed back up towards the ridge. "Scattered! We've accounted for some, the beck has claimed a few more, but a lot fell back to the wood."

Will rode up, his mail coat and breastplate bloodied. "What now?" he asked, breathing hard.

Ned looked down on the main field of battle: the left flank was now holding firm and far on the right flank he could just make out Norfolk's reinforcements flooding into the line. But when he looked around at his own men, he was appalled to find that half his command had gone. He shook his head: so many of his best men gone.

"Should we go back to the field?" asked Will.

For once, Ned hesitated. "The battle's all but won … yet Edmund's still alive and he has men – so let's finish him now!"

§§§

Edmund headed for Mawfield with the remnants of his force for there were still matters to settle there. To get there he had to skirt the battlefield at Towton Dale but when he saw the field before him he pulled up sharply: it was a bleak and bitter scene, with King Henry's army streaming from the field in panic.

"My lord, the battle's lost," urged Mordeur, "we must hurry!"

"Yes, I can see that! Lost… it doesn't seem possible," he said, paralysed by the scale of the catastrophe. Mordeur seized his bridle and leaned in close.

"Listen, lord, the whole army is in retreat! They'll be carving us up all night!"

Edmund slowly recovered himself. He was tempted to cut off the insolent hand that held his rein but when he looked at some of his men at arms he could see the defeat in their eyes. These men might fight for their own lives but they had no interest in doing anything more. Mordeur was right. He shook off the Frenchman's hand and turned his horse to the north east. Defeat had already cost him dearly: he'd be attainted, his lands and titles would be lost and, at best, he'd face exile. But if he tried to get to Mawfield now he'd be surrendering his life too.

"It's a butcher's paradise down there!" he said grimly. "We can't go that way now so we must play for time in the woods till the light's almost gone. Then we'll make our way to the bridge when the butchers are well on their way to York."

"My lord," said Henry, "why not simply to ride west now and avoid the beck - leave Mawfield to its fate?"

Edmund turned to him stiffly. "When I want your counsel Henry, I'll tell you." He wheeled round angrily and rode back towards the woods.

§§§

"Sun's going down," said Felix.

"Aye, too soon," replied Ned looking to the western sky. He hadn't seen the sun all day but daylight was fading and time was running out. He led them cautiously through the wood where the birch grew densely and the alder crept up the slope from the beck below. In the late afternoon with flurries of sleet still swirling through the trees he thought it would be hard to see an adversary until they came at him out of the gloom. He reached the far side of the wood where the ravine stretched steeply down to the beck and his eyes were drawn along the gully. The beck flowed swiftly and the desperate cries of the routed enemy soldiers drifted up to them from the distant bridge.

"Defeated, hunted down and hacked to death," said Ned, "that could so easily have been us - we've you to thank for that, Felix."

Felix gave a thin smile. "I'd sooner not have put any man closer to death but sometimes you take sides."

They continued at walking pace, turning back on a different woodland track.

"Keep your eyes open to the flanks," said Ned, though he didn't need to, for all were peering intently into the shadows and most had raised their visors or even taken off their helmets to give them a better field of vision.

Suddenly, there was a rush of movement through the dry bracken to their left and a dozen riders came at them like wraiths. Felix raised his staff to defend himself and found it snapped like a twig by the blade of a poleaxe. Ned glimpsed Mordeur amongst the small group of riders and gave chase, only to lose them almost at once in the trees. Moments later more horsemen attacked them and then swept back into the woods to disappear from sight again.

"Edmund was with those," said Ned, "he's playing us for fools!"

Felix shook his head. "It's not just a game, Ned. He's using up time and I think I know why: he wants to get to Mawfield."

"But he can't get there can he, because there's an army crossing the bridge across the beck," said Ned.

"Exactly!" said Felix.

"Is there any other path he can take?" asked Ned.

"I doubt it. There's just the one bridge and sooner or later he has to make a dash for that bridge. Hal is at a manor house across the other side of the beck that we think could be Mawfield. I told Hal to wait and keep watch."

"If he gets away, Hal will be up there on his own," said Will.

"If it is Mawfield it won't just be Hal up there. It might be Amelie too…" said Felix.

"So let's make sure Edmund doesn't get there," declared Ned, "come on, we don't need to chase him around these woods. We already know which way he's going to run! We'll wait for him as he goes down to the beck."

All the same, Ned could see that his men were restless. They had been fighting hard all day and now, whilst their comrades were pursuing their beaten enemies from the field, they found themselves chasing shadows in the twilight. He knew they wanted him to let them off the leash but he dare not as long as Edmund had numbers with him.

It sounded simple just to wait for Edmund to make his move but, as the remaining light failed, the weather delivered another untimely twist: a fine, icy mist rolled gently onto the bloody meadow of Towton Dale. It drifted on past Ned and his men towards the wood and slowly filled the gully below. Within a few minutes, they were struggling to make out each other, let alone their enemies.

§§§

Henry of Shrewsbury was utterly distraught for all the hopes and dreams he had nurtured over the past months had been destroyed along with Queen Margaret's army. Now he could see no way forward.

"The light's gone, now's the time," announced Edmund, "Mordeur, take your men and make for the Hall."

"There are the prisoners to deal with..."

"Yes, yes, we'll do that when I get there!"

"Take care, my lord," warned the Frenchman, "Ned Elder is here somewhere and he still has men enough with him."

"Just get to the Hall and secure it. I don't want any more surprises today!"

Mordeur nodded curtly and traced a route out of the trees and through the light mist down towards the beck.

For a while longer Edmund remained in the wood but when the thick mist descended he brought his men to a halt and drew Henry close.

"This mist is perfect. Take your men and cause a bit of panic amongst our friends. Then when you can do no more join me at the Hall – if necessary you can leave the men..."

Henry nodded absently, but Edmund was already galloping away into the mist without a backward look.

Henry had perhaps a score of riders left with him and he suspected that Ned Elder probably had a similar number but he could win nothing here. What did he care now whether Ned Elder or Edmund Radcliffe triumphed since he coveted the inheritance of both? Edmund was finished; it was more sensible to run now for there would be better times to come. It could have been much worse for he could have been caught in the bloodbath on Towton field.

He tore off the Radcliffe badge he wore.

"I'm not going to Mawfield," he declared to his men at arms, "I'm riding west and if you've any sense you'll join me - unless you've a mind to go and die in that beck."

Then he turned around and rode south west, away from Edmund, Ned, Mawfield and all the chaos of the bloody meadow. His men at arms wasted little time in following him.

§§§

"This is getting us nowhere!" said Will, "Edmund could be anywhere on this field – that is, if he's still on the field!"

But Ned had already reached a decision.

"We'll make for the Hall – it's all we can do now. Lead on Felix!"

They picked their way through the bloody debris of battle that littered the lower slopes of the field and walked their horses down into the beck gully where more bodies were strewn down the steep muddy slope. A few had died fighting but many looked to have been cut down as they ran, coldly despatched and then stripped of their plate armour and weapons. The further they descended into the gully the thicker the mist was until they could see nothing and the damp air was ripe with the smell of blood.

Ned's straggling column of men became so strung out that soon he, Will and Felix lost touch with the rest of the men. They shouted their names but it was futile as the marshy land by the beck was haunted by the anguished cries of many.

"The bridge can't be far now," said Felix.

"Sweet Jesus!" cried Ned.

His horse had slipped and fallen but he managed to claw his way clear as one by one the other horses either lost their footing or sank deeply into the lethal quagmire churned up by the frantic passage of hundreds of men. They helped each other gingerly to their feet; the horses were frightened and skittish.

"Leave them," ordered Ned.

Out of the mist several shadowy figures appeared but only when they were almost upon them did they recognise the Radcliffe badges and livery.

Will drew his swords with a flourish only to slip in the mud and land heavily on his back.

"Shit!" he yelled and Felix bent to help him up but in the meantime the Radcliffe men melted away into the mist.

"This is madness: we can't tell friend from foe!" said Ned.

They plodded on across the sodden, blood soaked

desolation beside the beck, passing score upon score of broken bodies. The marshy ground was dark with blood and Ned could well imagine the fleeing Lancastrians weighed down by plate and heavy weapons, utterly exhausted and hastily beginning to discard their helmets then their armour, piece by piece, and finally their weapons – but all to no avail.

Somewhere close by a man cried out and then screamed and they heard him thrashing in the water. Ned skidded towards the edge of the beck but could not find where the unfortunate had slipped in. He continued along the icy margins of the water, but the sounds of struggle soon petered out. He stood still, staring into the water below him where the dead lay packed one upon the other in grey soulless ranks.

"Let's hope our men escape this and get back to camp," he said. There was no reply from Will or Felix. He looked behind him but neither was there.

"Will! Felix?" he shouted.

A voice called out: "Ned! Over here!" He could see no-one but he moved towards the voice. Then another, deeper voice called him. Was that Felix? Several were calling him now but it didn't help much. Then, out of the mist a figure appeared ahead of him, slithering away awkwardly through the mud. He almost laughed out loud.

"Your colours betray you, Radcliffe!" he called out.

"You're very popular by the sound of it," Edmund replied, without either stopping or turning round. "I hear your name wherever I go!"

Ned felt he was probably beyond combat but he couldn't help himself. He drew his sword and tried to quicken his pace but his aching limbs did not want to respond. He slipped again, falling into the mire and by the time he got to his feet Edmund had vanished. He continued along the beck and the mist was even thicker but at last he could see the outline of the narrow bridge. The track up to it was a killing ground - a bottleneck where the fleeing soldiers had been at the mercy of their Yorkist pursuers and, judging by the pile of bloody corpses on the bridge, no mercy had been shown.

Merely to cross it Ned had to heave fallen men at arms to one side. As he was doing so he saw, too late, a movement on the ground. A poleaxe punched into his thigh finding a joint in his armour. He gasped and lurched back against the low wall of the bridge. Edmund followed up his swift strike with a body charge which lifted Ned over the wall and threw him into the beck below. He sank like a millstone into the mass of bodies that lay across Cock Beck from one side to the other. As he slipped under the water he saw Edmund standing on the bridge above him.

§§§

Edmund stood for a moment and then leant on the wall, watching Ned flounder in the water and disappear from sight. He waited a little longer to be sure and then, satisfied, he continued across the bridge. His King may have suffered a calamitous defeat that day but he, Edmund Radcliffe, had won the battle that mattered most to him: the last male of the Elder line had finally been extinguished.

How simple the end had been after all that had passed between them. He was almost disappointed it had happened so quickly – almost. Now, though elated, he suddenly felt wearier and made his way slowly up the slope that led to Mawfield Hall. Perhaps he might not lose his lands today after all. With Ned Elder dead there was a chance of brokering a peace with the new king. He had no doubt Edward of York would now be accepted as king.

When he was out of sight of the beck he removed his leg armour to make the uphill walk easier. Despite the climb he began to feel stronger. Then an arrow struck him in the left calf and sent him rolling back several yards down the slope. He cursed angrily as he snapped off the flight and wrenched the shaft from his leg; he rose unsteadily to his feet and looked around for the weapon he had been carrying. The leg was sore and would slow him down a little but it was a trifling wound and he cared little now that Ned Elder was at the bottom of the beck. More of a concern was where the arrow had come from.

Cautiously he moved forward again keeping low and then dived to the ground as another arrow thudded into the turf just ahead of him. He zigzagged across the remaining open ground to a small stand of trees and stumbled on to the front entrance of the Hall, relieved to see a guard in place. Thank God for Mordeur, he thought, everything was as it should be.

Mordeur was in the Great Hall awaiting him with impatience.

"You took your time," he said, not bothering to pay his lord the slightest courtesy.

Edmund suppressed his annoyance at the gross slight and replied: "Yes, and while I was taking my time I killed Ned Elder!"

"Then the delay was truly worthwhile," conceded Mordeur more respectfully, "yet, we should still make haste for there will soon be other men of York about."

"I don't need telling! There's an archer outside somewhere – probably looking for a quick kill and some booty. Take some of the men, flush him out and join me at the stables. I'll fetch my 'dear' lady and finish the others."

Mordeur nodded, grinning.

"And Mordeur, a quick despatch – this is no time to indulge your more ... subtle pleasures. We have a long night ride ahead of us!"

"I pray you do the same!" muttered Mordeur.

56

Cock Beck, near Towton Dale, Sunset on Palm Sunday 1461

Ned couldn't breathe. His helm was filling with water tainted with the blood of a thousand dead. He tried to reach out his arms and kick his legs but he could barely move. Somehow he clawed his way to the surface and tore off his helmet to take a breath, only to sink back down even further below the ranks of the steel shrouded warriors. He choked back the water, a yard below the surface.

In a moment his enemy had undone him. He had a thousand regrets but only one that mattered: he called up a memory of Amelie, a nervous smile on her lips. He would never reach her now, never see her again and never tell her he loved her. The water pressed against his chest, forcing out what little air remained. He closed his eyes and the beck took him.

Something hard struck his face and his eyes flew open in shock: it was the blade of a poleaxe. He stared at it, fascinated. An arm reached towards it – his arm - moving so slowly that the axe seemed to drift further away. But his hand grasped it and pulled on it. Then he moved his grip up the shaft onto the gauntlet that held the axe and raised himself through the water. When he broke the surface he gulped in a great draught of freezing air which all but turned his lungs to ice. He turned to identify his saviour but the arm belonged to a knight who lay stiff and grey on top of the mass of corpses in the beck. He had been reprieved by the frozen arm of a dead man, but he was not out of the beck yet.

The icy water had numbed his body but from the depths of his pounding heart he found a little more strength to heave himself up out of the stream. He rested there for a moment on a raft of the dead, breathing in ice crystals, and then he inched his way across the steel, flesh and blood. He crawled onto the bank and stood up. He was chilled to the bone and every sinew of his body ached with cold. He swayed and dropped to his knees once more. He knew he must warm up or the cold alone would kill him.

He took a few deep painful breaths then forced himself upright and began to shed his plate armour for he knew he couldn't bear it up the slope ahead of him. Holton would be heartbroken, but the smith's artistry had served him well all day. He removed the greaves and cuisses from his legs, leaving only his breastplate. Abandoning the armour would be a risk but it was the only way he might just overtake Edmund. He had lost his weapon in the beck but there were weapons aplenty abandoned near the bridge. He picked up a sword, nothing too heavy, and set off, pumping his legs and swinging his arms to warm his body.

He couldn't see Edmund in the gloom ahead of him, nor did he expect to for his adversary was probably at Mawfield by now. Perhaps he would be too late but he just had to hope he wasn't. He paced himself up the hill moving more freely but when he crested the brow of the hill he trod on a broken arrow shaft. He stopped, picked it up and smiled. The blood on it was still wet and it spurred him on. He saw the outline of the house for the first time when he reached the tree line: this then must be Mawfield Hall. He scanned along the outer wall in both directions but there was no sign of Edmund.

"My lord?"

Ned spun round at the whispered call from behind him. Standing in the trees was young Hal grinning at the look of surprise on his face.

"You're a welcome sight," said Ned.

"You look awful!" replied Hal.

"You've seen Radcliffe?"

"Put an arrow into him!"

"Aye, I thought so, well done. Where did he go?"

Hal pointed to the great door in the courtyard at the front of the building. "He went in there. There's been some comings and goings since."

Ned assessed the young lad's readiness at a glance: he wore only a padded leather jerkin and breeches under his cloak. He had no protection against any weapon of substance.

"Stay here. I'm going into the house and I want to know that you're watching my back when I come out."

"Wait, lord! There's a lot of men in that house - and the tall Frenchie too."

"Did you see Amelie?"

Hal shook his head in disappointment.

"From now on if you see any man at that door that isn't me, take him out," said Ned.

Hal peered doubtfully at the distant door in the murky light but nodded.

Ned stumbled over to the door and paused outside. It would doubtless lead into the Great Hall but he wasn't going to just walk in the front door. He moved on and followed the stone wall around to the side until he came to a smaller gate which gave access to a brew house. He could work his way through the servant areas to the cellars or storerooms where a prisoner might be held.

Inside the buttery he found some household servants cowering amongst the barrels. When they saw him, caked in dried mud from the beck and sword in hand, they fled in panic. He clambered up a short spiral stair, sapping what little strength remained in his legs. Then he passed through the door at the top of the steps and suddenly he was in the midst of a crowd of men at arms in the Great Hall – so much for taking them unawares. There was no sign of Edmund but Mordeur was there and he looked as surprised as Ned.

"On him!" the Frenchman shouted and the men at arms charged at Ned. Weak though he was, Ned still tested their resolve. He carved his blade through one and stabbed at the thigh of another but Mordeur came at him like a raw wind across the barren hills above Yoredale. Ned knew he must get out for he couldn't kill them all: they were better armed and he was moving too slowly. Soon enough they'd work out how weak he really was.

He had the wall at his back but they were all around him. He swivelled and turned, parrying in hope rather than certainty. Some sword blades got through and slid off his breastplate to cut through his gambeson. He bludgeoned his way towards the main door but he was almost spent.

"We have him! We have the devil!" shouted Mordeur.

Ned struck home several more times against his attackers but his blade found nothing but plate or mail. Mordeur got a clear stab at Ned and sliced inside his breastplate through his ribs. He fell back hard against the bare wall clutching at the wound and his sword felt heavy in his hand. The men at arms closed in for the kill but as they did so there was a thunderous banging on the door.

For an instant everyone stopped.

"Look to the door," snapped Mordeur to several of his men, "the rest of us can finish him – but be careful."

The first man threw the door open and took an arrow in the throat. It knocked him back into the room and his blood gurgled briefly as it spilled out.

"Goddam archer!" spat out Mordeur, "shut it then, you fools!"

But it was too late for now, in the doorway, stood Will with his two swords drawn.

Ned stared at him in disbelief then he just nodded and smiled. "Well done, my friend, well done."

The soldiers at the door stood uncertainly and Will launched himself from the threshold, cutting into them with alarming energy. Ned made the most of the distraction and found another ounce of strength to lurch forward at Mordeur once more. Will was in a killing mood and his swords were a blur as he hacked his way through the men at arms. His opponents were backing nervously away despite Mordeur's constant exhortations but then a piercing scream halted them all.

Ned and Will exchanged a glance but Ned knew he couldn't get there in time.

"Go!" he shouted.

Will didn't hesitate and darted out of the hall in the direction of the scream leaving Ned to hold Mordeur and the two remaining men at arms. There was a strange impasse as both Mordeur and Ned kept half an eye on the door out of the Hall. Then Mordeur came at him again and he was relentless. Only Ned's gut strength was keeping him alive but in desperation he fell back towards the main door which still lay open and the two knights pursued him outside.

"Wait!" cried Mordeur, realising the danger, but his cry was in vain as Hal's next arrow pinned one of the men to the door post. God, but he's good, thought Ned, as another arrow took the final man in the leg, blood spurting crazily from the wound. He would bleed to death all too quickly but Ned clubbed him down with his sword hilt anyway.

Mordeur, however, was not to be so easily drawn out.

"You're not going to stay out there for long, Ned Elder," he called out, "for you have to come in, don't you, to find your precious little girl!"

57

Mawfield Hall, Sunset on Palm Sunday 1461

Emma heard the bolt on the door being drawn back.

"Take a deep breath, sisters," Eleanor said softly, "and stay strong - no matter what happens."

One of the usual guards came in bearing a torch and Emma blinked briefly, her eyes adjusting to the sudden burst of light. Edmund entered the makeshift cell and looked at each of his prisoners in turn. Emma knew him well enough to sense that something had changed and he looked like death. He moved to check the chains around the Welshman but was satisfied they were secure.

"Well, my 'lady'?" he addressed her with heavy irony. "We're going now but I trust you've enjoyed your sister's company - however brief it was."

Emma did not move; instead she leaned back against the cold wall with her arms folded above her unborn child and stared at him with what she hoped was a look of cool detachment.

"Delay is pointless," he said, "your brother Ned is, at long last, dead and all those crows that flocked with him. They're all finished so there'll be no last minute rescue, no lucky escape for you all."

Still Emma remained where she was.

"I'm not going anywhere, my 'lord'," she said, "and you won't kill me because I'm carrying your son and heir."

"Well, let's see if I can change your mind," he said and, drawing his dagger, he plunged it hard at Gruffydd's chest. The big man managed to twist so that it caught him in the side but he grunted with pain none the less and slumped down on his chains.

Edmund had taken but a moment to use the dagger but in that moment Eleanor had swept out the knife that she still wore on her back and buried it into the guard's neck. As he fell clutching helplessly at the wound, Emma seized the flaming torch from his grasp and Eleanor drew out his sword and passed her own knife to Amelie.

Edmund was stunned but then he just laughed and shook his head. He stared thoughtfully at Eleanor.

"Ah," he acknowledged, "they didn't search you, did they?"

He left his dagger in Gruffydd and kicked the prostrate soldier. Then he drew his sword with an extravagant flourish.

Emma felt the sweat in the hand that gripped the torch tightly. The women had planned exactly what they would do – certainly they had had enough hours to do so but now she was beginning to doubt they could carry it through. She knew Edmund would be cursing himself for underestimating them but he would still be utterly confident. He was no longer harnessed for war or even wearing a breast plate but he still had a thick leather jerkin to withstand all but the firmest knife or sword stroke. He was grinning again – yes, she thought, he was still very confident, but he had badly misjudged them if he thought they were trying to escape.

"Search the women," Edmund continued, "I've always said this for they dissemble so well. Very well, ladies, it's been a bloody, bloody day but if I must finish this in blood, I will. Try your hardest."

"Oh, we will," replied Eleanor grimly.

Edmund grinned again and made a half-hearted lunge at her but he stopped grinning when she expertly parried his stroke. Emma smiled at her sister with fierce pride: earlier she had ripped off the lower half of her skirt in readiness for the part she would play. She had told them she would give a good account of herself before the end, yet they all knew the end would come soon enough.

Eleanor held the sword aloft, her feet planted firmly apart to give her balance as she awaited his next move. At once Edmund launched a fierce assault and everyone in the room knew that his power would overwhelm her. He drove her back, stabbing at her midriff. She did just enough to deflect his blade onto the top of her hip and screamed at the top of her voice.

Emma almost screamed with her but her sister seemed to shut out the pain. She moved sideways so that Edmund would have his back to the door and Amelie. He glanced behind him briefly and then attacked again, forcing her back to the wall with a slash across her breasts which cut her deeply and left her sliding down on to her haunches.

"Sorry, my dear," he said, "but it was entertaining while it lasted."

But as he held his sword point at her throat, Amelie lunged forward with the knife aiming at the inside of his upper leg – stab him there, Eleanor had said, and he'll bleed to death.

She was right, but the thrust was not hard enough. He turned in anger at Amelie who was almost at his feet and struck her a blow on the head that cracked her skull and sliced open her face. He kicked her angrily away and then took a moment to examine his thigh wound.

"French Bitch!" he said. "Well, not so brave now!"

At that moment Will suddenly stepped into the cell. In the light of the flaming torch she still held, Emma witnessed the look of amazement on his face when he saw Eleanor, cut and bleeding but alive, still alive. He could not drag his eyes from her and opened his mouth to speak her name. Then Eleanor screamed again for Edmund had punched his sword under Will's breastplate, twisting it as he wrenched it out again. Will dropped silently to his knees, his stomach ripped open but his dying heart relentlessly pumping out his blood. Emma shook as she wept and almost dropped the torch.

Eleanor stared down at Will blankly then she turned to

Edmund.

"I haven't finished yet," she said through gritted teeth. She rose unsteadily to her feet, her chest running with blood. She held her sword once more in front of her, arms trembling with the effort. She edged towards the door, putting Edmund between her and Emma who stood by Gruffydd.

Tears streamed down the Welshman's cheeks as he watched Eleanor being bloodied and overcome. Emma touched his shoulder lightly and caught his eye, looking down at the dagger still lodged deep in his side. He nodded grim faced and whilst Edmund's attention was on her sister, Emma gently drew it out allowing blood to ooze from the wound. She held it behind her back, studying Edmund carefully for a vulnerable spot: his leather jerkin was quite long but at the bottom it was only loosely fastened.

Eleanor took a step towards Edmund and he laughed at her audacity.

"I'm getting to like you," he said, smiling through tight lips, "who knows? We might have become lovers!"

"I doubt it," replied Eleanor coldly, "my sister said you were a terrible fuck."

All his rage and power went into the thrust at her unprotected neck. She swayed, not entirely by design, and the blade went straight through her between right breast and shoulder, embedding itself in the timber upright of the door frame. She cried out as much in anger as pain as she was pinned to the wood: if she fell forward now her bodyweight would slice the sword through shoulder and neck. Edmund tried in vain to pull out the sword then shrugged and left the weapon in place.

He turned to Emma. "Now," he said, "perhaps you'll come with me."

Emma looked into her sister's eyes and her own clouded again. She felt the hilt of the dagger in her hand, slippery with Gruffydd's blood.

"Courage sister," murmured Eleanor.

"It seems there's but one course left to me, husband," said

Emma. She placed the torch carefully into the bracket on the wall. Edmund was about to finish Gruffydd when he realised, a fraction too late, that his dagger was no longer in the wound. He was already turning towards Emma when she struck with one swift movement, putting all her bitter hatred into the knife thrust under his jerkin and up to its hilt above his groin.

He did not cry out as she expected and she wondered if somehow she had missed the vital area. Instead he grunted and pushed her to the floor. Then he walked very slowly and deliberately towards Eleanor to retrieve his sword. Eleanor still held her own weapon out before her but her legs shook with the effort of staying on her feet.

Emma watched from the floor with the bloody dagger still gripped tightly in her hand. They had failed. They had done all they could but it was over. She pressed the point against her own breast, then she saw a taut smile on Eleanor's face and Gruffydd, pain contorting his face, swung himself on his chains and launched himself with a howl of Welsh expletives driving his feet into Edmund's back. He propelled him forward onto the point of Eleanor's outstretched sword with a force she could never have achieved alone. The blade cut through his leather jerkin into his chest and Eleanor screamed as her shoulder muscles tore. She let go of the sword and Edmund dropped to one knee.

"Bitches, you murdering bitches!" he cursed them, choking on blood as he pulled out the sword. He gasped for breath as blood welled from the wound. Soon it was dripping down his chest and from his mouth as a ruptured lung collapsed. He fell forward again.

Emma cast about at the others: Amelie lay still, her face in a pool of blood, Gruffydd's lunge had opened up his wound and it was now bleeding profusely and Eleanor, brave Eleanor, her face grey from loss of blood, couldn't stay on her feet and was slipping further down onto Edmund's blade still stubbornly held by the door post.

Then Edmund began moving again, crawling slowly towards

the door on a floor already spattered with blood. Emma watched in horrified disbelief as he got to his feet and staggered out of the cell leaving a bloody trail behind him. She got up and rushed to hold up Eleanor's body to stop it falling further.

"Leave me," breathed Eleanor, "you can't save me, Emma. You must get help for the others."

"But, I can't," she cried as Eleanor passed out. "I can't!"

She clung doggedly to Eleanor's blood soaked body, knowing she mustn't let her slip. If she wasn't holding her she could pull out the sword but if she let her go, the sword would kill her anyway.

On the other side of the doorway Amelie stirred and lifted her head sticky with blood from the ugly tear across her face. Emma flinched to see her so disfigured but tried to shut it from her mind.

"Amelie! I'm sorry but you'll have to take out the sword. You must pull it out!"

Amelie touched her cheek and almost passed out with pain but she got unsteadily to her feet. She managed the two paces to the door frame but could not muster the strength to remove the blade. She swooned dizzily to her knees.

"I cannot move it!" she cried, but after a while she dragged herself up again beside Emma and tried to take some of the burden of Eleanor's weight.

Footsteps sounded in the passage outside. Emma rested her forehead gently against Amelie's and their eyes met for a moment.

"It'll be Mordeur," said Emma, "after all this, to have come so close…"

The footsteps paused. Emma realised she was holding her breath. The steps resumed and both weary women closed their eyes to accept the inevitable.

§§§

Ned was too tired for words and simply came back into the Hall with all he had left. Even so Mordeur was stronger and knocked him to the floor but as he fell Ned lashed out and was fortunate to cut the Frenchman's leg, drawing blood. The wound, though slight, seemed to make up Mordeur's mind and he ran straight out of the doorway where he was narrowly missed by another arrow from Hal.

Ned could not lift himself up and sat bleeding on the floor of the Hall. He had to let the Frenchman go. He tried to imagine getting up off the floor but it didn't help. His body was weak, so weak. It was the second scream that revived him and set him thinking but all his thoughts were dark. Will had gone to stop the screams yet the screaming hadn't stopped – and where was Edmund? A third scream demanded that he get up and find out.

"Come on, Ned," he told himself, "you're not dead yet." Though he had a few doubts about that, he crawled to the wall and rested his back against it. Had he been stabbed in the back? He couldn't remember.

He put his back to the wall and tried to lever himself up. "Christ, that hurt!" he said.

At least now he was standing but when he took a step he almost fell over. He paused and tried to steel himself to move, using his sword as a crutch. He worked his way around the Hall and went into the passage, lurching from side to side. Halfway along the passage he found a trail of blood and followed it. Whatever he expected to find when he entered the torch lit chamber it was not the bloody carnage before him. His gaze fell first on the body hanging from the beam, then on the floor in front of him he saw Will. He bent over his friend but Will's body was still - a look of shock etched onto his white face.

"Ned?"

Even the anguish in Emma's voice didn't prepare him for the sight of the three women locked in an unnatural embrace. It hit him like a blow from a war hammer and he felt weak at the knees. He dropped his sword and stared wild-eyed at each in turn for all those he loved most were there in the cell, huddled together in a tangle of blood.

"Ned, help us..." sobbed Emma.

"Yes, of course, yes!" His head cleared and he saw their predicament. With some effort he removed the sword from the wooden door frame then took Eleanor and laid her down gently on the floor beside Will. He hugged both Emma and Amelie to him and sat them both down, almost unable to look at Amelie's beautiful butchered face.

He took a deep breath and coughed painfully. "I knew I'd be too late," he said bitterly.

Hal ran in. "Oh, shit!" he said and stood in confusion.

"Hal! Pull yourself together," ordered Ned, "and go find me an axe to free that poor fellow."

When Hal returned he still looked dazed. Between them Ned and Hal hacked through Gruffydd's chains with a poleaxe and sat him on the floor. They didn't know where to start in tending so many wounds. But Emma took Ned's hand and drew him to the door.

"It's not over, Ned," she said, "we tried. We fought but we couldn't do enough..."

She stared into her brother's eyes. "He's still alive Ned... and we can't face this again."

He nodded and bent down awkwardly to pick up his discarded sword.

"Hal, stay here and help Emma," he said hoarsely.

Then he stumbled out of the cell, knowing that since Edmund had not passed him in the Hall he must have gone out through the kitchens. He was feeling his own wounds badly but if he flagged now he had only to conjure up the scene he had just discovered.

§§§

Edmund had stripped off his shirt and bound his wounds with lengths of it, though he knew it wouldn't be enough. He should rest but if he did he might be overtaken. If he could rejoin Mordeur or get to the stables, he had a chance. He found Mordeur saddling a fresh horse and stopped, buoyed up with relief.

"Mordeur, thank God! Bring me a horse, quickly."

Mordeur carefully finished saddling his mare and then looked at Edmund long and hard.

"Well? Come on!" said Edmund.

Mordeur shrugged. "I'm tired of getting you out of the troubles you get yourself into," he said, "you know, you don't look too good. I think I'll ride quicker without you."

"So, you desert me as you deserted my father!" said Edmund.

"I serve only lords with power! And, like your father, you have none left."

He mounted swiftly and rode straight past Edmund, saluting him ironically with a wave of his arm and thundering out of the courtyard through the postern gate. Edmund tried to seize his rein but was left clutching air. He was shocked but merely stored the memory away for later retribution and limped to the stables. There were several other horses saddled, so he chose one and leant against it for a moment, gathering enough strength to mount up.

§§§

"I killed your brother in a stable," said Ned.

Edmund blinked and slowly turned, doubting for a moment the evidence of his own ears.

"You're dead…"

"I'm not."

"Well you bloody well should be!" Edmund choked out the words.

"Still, I'm not." Ned took a step forward, using his sword again to bear his weight.

"I saw you go under…"

"You should've stayed a bit longer…"

Ned leaned hard on his sword and knew he wouldn't be

able to lift it more than once. He watched Edmund stumble out with the horse and put it between himself and Ned.

"We've been here before," said Edmund, looking faint from the effort of movement.

"Don't waste your strength climbing onto that horse for if I have to I'll cut it down with you on it," said Ned.

Edmund ignored his advice and swung himself painfully up on to the horse. His breathing was shallow, wheezing as he walked the horse on into the courtyard towards Ned.

"With your Ralph, I was too hot and I'll always be sorry for that."

"He didn't deserve to die," said Edmund.

"No, he didn't. But you, on the other hand, do."

Edmund smiled and urged his mount forward with his knees, but then the smile froze. Ned saw a trickle of blood run down his leg.

"Bloody bitches," mumbled Edmund, pressing his hand to his thigh to stop the bleeding. Ned watched Edmund's face turn paler and took from under his gambeson a small piece of silk.

"This little rag," he said, holding out the embroidered silk in a trembling hand, "is what you sought."

Edmund could not stop himself sliding from the horse for the wound in his thigh was bleeding faster. He attempted to get up, his face clouded by disbelief.

"You had it?" he said, on his knees and trying to press his hand harder against the wound.

"It might have given you some power with the Queen, but now of course it's worthless for the old Queen no longer holds sway. All your butchery in there was for nothing!"

Edmund reached out to touch the cloth but Ned let it flutter to the ground.

"Do what you will," said Edmund."

"I shall and may God forgive me," said Ned. He summoned all his remaining strength and raised his sword bringing it down so hard on Edmund's neck and shoulder that he almost cut him in two. Edmund fell once more and this time he did not rise.

Ned let his sword fall to the ground and picked up the fallen silk. He leant for a moment against Edmund's nervous mount and then he returned slowly to the cell.

Stephen and Felix had made their way up from the beck. The latter was crouched over Will's body. He laid his hand on the youth's bloodied chest and bowed his head.

Stephen was binding up some of Eleanor's wounds. "She has so many wounds, Ned. I fear she'll bleed to death."

"There are others coming," said Felix, "more help will soon be here."

Ned nodded in response to a look from Emma. She hugged him to her and would not let him go.

"We decided to die, you know, and at the end we thought you were dead too."

"So did I," he said. "Ellie?"

"She was so brave, Ned."

He tried to bend down to Eleanor but Felix gently took his arm.

"We'll tend to her," he said, "there's another needs you more."

Ned sat down on the floor next to Amelie but she turned her cut face away from him. He took her blood stained hand and was pleased when she did not pull it away.

"There's something I've been meaning to tell you," he said.

She smiled and rested her pounding head on his shoulder.

"I know, but let's just sit for a while, shall we?"

Author's Note

Thank you for reading Feud and I hope you enjoyed it. As you may know, Feud is the first of a series of books entitled **Rebels & Brothers**. The series charts the struggles of the Elder family through the period of the Wars of the Roses. Their experiences are fictional but not so very far from the real events that faced many such families in England during the period.

Some of you may feel the ending leaves some "loose ends" but that is deliberate, for the story of the Elders, and those around them, continues in the next book, **A Traitor's Fate**, which picks up the story three years later in 1464.

Feud is a story set against almost continuous civil war from 1459-1461 and after Towton England holds its breath. Is the war over? Will the new young king, Edward IV, bring peace?

What about the Elders? Is the Feud really over? What will happen to Ned, Amelie and all the others?

To find out more about the series and future developments as they occur, or to contact me, you can go to my website at www.derekbirks.com

As an independent author, I must market my own work and one thing that helps me enormously is the response from readers. Please feel free to get in touch by using the contact form on my website.

If you have enjoyed my work then you might like to give it a favourable mention, either in the shape of an Amazon or Goodreads review, or on another site of your choice.

Either way, many thanks for reading.

Derek Birks
2015

Historical Note

My purpose is to tell the story of the Elder family as the Wars of the Roses unfolds and the best I could achieve with the history is that the reader will feel that they have been given some insight into the momentous events of 1459-1461. I have always attempted to weave the story around documented events and if I am guilty of any fault it is most likely the sin of omission, for which I apologise unreservedly.

The Wars of the Roses

Everyone knows about the Wars of the Roses – or do they? The range of historical opinion is so broad and varied on this whole period that I could not hope to do more than follow a consistent thread of narrative through it. Besides adhering to an accurate chronology of the events, I have also tried to set the feud between Elders and Radcliffes within a recognisable late fifteenth century context where local rivalries over land ownership were allowed to boil over into riot and retaliation during the long, weak rule of Henry VI. In a very real sense the Elder/Radcliffe feud mimics the rivalry of York and Lancaster or Neville and Percy.

Whenever the story encounters an actual person I have attempted to create a character which would at least be recognisable to students of the period. Since the story is not centred on these characters there is a risk that they might seem like caricatures. Admirers of Margaret of Anjou and Richard Neville, Earl of Warwick, might feel that this is the case.

Major Battles

The major battles of Blore Heath, Mortimer's Cross and

Towton all present some problems of interpretation as none of the three battles is consistently recorded by contemporaries. Towton in particular has been the subject of much recent discussion in the light of new archaeological work. Each battlefield had its complications for those taking part, let alone the student of history!

Where I have taken any licence it has been in offering explanation or embellishment, for example, at Blore Heath there is still some mystery as to why Lord Audley's Lancastrians attacked Salisbury's strongly defended Yorkist camp thus giving themselves a difficult assault across a narrow, but deep brook and up an increasingly slippery slope. The decision to do so seems likely to have determined the outcome of the battle. I have explained this in the narrative by suggesting that the attack was impromptu and brought about by the arrival in the Lancastrian lines of Ned, Will and Sir Roger, though this is pure invention.

The scene where Margaret watches the battle from the tower of Mucklestone church is rooted in local rumour but is unlikely to be true. The church is still there though its tower has been reduced in height since the 1400s.

Mortimer's Cross is such a key battle in Edward, Earl of March's dramatic rise to power yet it remains quite obscure. What we do know is that before the battle, as Edward drew up his forces at dawn in battle array, there was a parhelion or a vision of three suns caused by the effect of the early morning sun on ice crystals in the air. I have described it much as it must have appeared - a wondrous and literally awesome sight to those present. It is typical of the opportunist Edward that he took full advantage of the phenomenon to rally his men. The words I have attributed to him are pretty much what he is supposed to have said.

As for the detail of the battle itself, I have of course given Ned and his companions a prominent role but the structure of the battle as I have described it seems to ring true. Lack of detailed, reliable evidence for the battle manoeuvres means that I have had to use some invention to put the pieces together. My Lord Radcliffe was not at the actual battle but the Tudors were there, as was the elusive Earl of Wiltshire. Wiltshire's ferocious Irish kern was thrown back as described, Edward's centre was hard pressed for a time and Owen Tudor probably did make a late charge before Edward eventually triumphed.

Owen Tudor was indeed captured and later executed with others in Hereford market place and the scene describing how a woman bathed his face and set candles about him is well documented.

With Towton, there have been some radical challenges to the traditional version of the battle and it is really a case of picking an interpretation. I have relied on the traditional view to a great extent though fortunately there are several things that most contemporary observers agree on. I have dismissed some very recent suggestions that the whole Ferrybridge, Dintingdale and Towton sequence is part of one long battle.

I have used some licence in suggesting Castle Hill Wood as the site for the Lancastrian reserve force under the command of the fictional Edmund Radcliffe. Some historians have suggested that the Lancastrians used it and others that, if the Lancastrians did not use it, they were remiss in not doing so. In almost all respects I have followed the long accepted chronology of the battle whilst shaping the telling of it to facilitate the denouement of Feud's story.

Places

Yoredale is the old name for the valley of the river Ure, now called Wensleydale, an area once much more heavily forested than it is now. Ned's home, Elder Hall, if it existed would lie near the river Ure and the Radcliffes' Yoredale Castle would be further east and higher up the northern slope of Wensleydale. Nearby is the giant Neville stronghold at Middleham; it is a ruin now but it is still possible to get a measure of the majesty of this palatial residence.

The imaginary abandoned village of Penholme is on the south side of Yoredale where the ancient forest gives way to more open higher ground. Such deserted villages are not unusual in Yorkshire for the reasons explained in the book.

Even today there is a great sense of history about Ludlow and it remains one of my favourite places to visit. In 1459 the town was sacked when the King's army crossed Ludford Bridge and the town never forgot it. Nor did Edward, for when he became king he saw that Ludlow was well looked after and awarded extra privileges.

The Carmelite Friary in Corve Street did exist and survived the assault of 1459 though it suffered heavy losses of its valuables and other goods. The chapel of St. Thomas the martyr where Ned and his companions took shelter also existed much as described.

The river Corve was more navigable in late medieval times than it is now and it was probably in flood at the time, so it is reasonable to suppose that a small craft could be rowed some distance along it. Corve Manor is an invention of mine though it is modelled on numerous other fortified houses of the period. Stokesay Castle is one such place north of Ludlow.

London in February 1461 was a desperate place as it faced the very real threat of Margaret's northern army. I did not need to exaggerate this fear in particular on the part of the merchant community and the aldermen who controlled the City. They had made serious financial commitments to the Yorkist cause and they now feared the worst. The Queen's army did forage as far as Westminster and the Strand, where Will and Sarah encountered it, but with the City gates closed against them the northerners eventually dispersed northwards.

Derek Birks

2015

ABOUT THE AUTHOR

Derek was born in Hampshire in England but spent his teenage years in Auckland, New Zealand where he still has strong family ties.

He returned to England and studied History at Reading University. For many years he taught history at a secondary school in Berkshire but took early retirement several years ago to concentrate on his writing.

Apart from writing, he spends his time gardening, travelling, walking and taking part in archaeological digs at a Roman villa.

Derek is interested in a wide range of historical themes but his particular favourite is the later Medieval period. He aims to write action packed fiction which is rooted in accurate history.

His debut historical novel, Feud, is set in the period of the Wars of the Roses and is the first of a series of stories following the fortunes of the fictional Elder family. The remaining books in the series are: A Traitor's Fate, Kingdom of Rebels and The Last Shroud.

Lightning Source UK Ltd.
Milton Keynes UK
UKOW06f1209160516

274337UK00001B/2/P